An Unwanted Inheritance

'Brimful of emotion – a wonderful plot and characters that you are rooting for, even when you know you shouldn't. *An Unwanted Inheritance* is that gem of a thing: a story to truly lose yourself in. I LOVED IT!'
—Faith Hogan, bestselling author of *The Ladies' Midnight Swimming Club*

'What happens when you drop a bag of cash right in the middle of three siblings and their families? A whole lot of good fun and drama. *An Unwanted Inheritance* delightfully explores the flaws that come with being human as Clark plunges us into a story about what is right and wrong and what it means to be a family. She ratchets up the tension as the story races to its surprising and oh-so-satisfying conclusion.'
—Boo Walker, bestselling author of *The Singing Trees*

'A gripping tale about money, greed, and what really matters.'
—Anstey Harris, bestselling author of *The Truths and Triumphs of Grace Atherton*

'Imogen Clark deftly peels back the layers of loyalty, family secrets and moral dilemma to examine a family that must make a choice between need, greed and integrity. Pacey, thought provoking, and with characters that test the ties of blood, marriage and friendship to the limit, *An Unwanted Inheritance* will have you wondering how far you'd go to uphold your own principles – and how much, or how little, it would take to betray them.'

'*The Last Piece* is a beautifully crafted, insightful tale about family and the cracks below the surface of seemingly perfect lives. Clark's characters, with their various secrets and flaws, leap off the page. A most enjoyable and riveting read.'

—S.D. Robertson, author of *My Sister's Lies* and *Time to Say Goodbye*

'I couldn't resist going on this journey with the Nightingale family. With emotion on every page and mystery swirling around each character, *The Last Piece* explores how the past can be as unpredictable as the future. I raced through this life-affirming book, which left me buoyed with the promise of second chances.'

—Jo Furniss, author of *The Last to Know*

Where the Story Starts

'Once again . . . Imogen Clark urges readers to turn the pages as the delightfully pleasant facade of her characters' lives begins to crack when the mysteries of the past come to call. Both soothing and riveting, *Where the Story Starts* asks: what if your greatest secret is the one you don't even know exists?'

—Amber Cowie, author of *Rapid Falls* and *Raven Lane*

The Thing About Clare

'Warm and emotionally complex . . . A family drama that's hard to disentangle yourself from.'

—Nick Alexander, bestselling author of *Things We Never Said*

A
Borrowed
Path

ALSO BY IMOGEN CLARK

Writing as Izzy Bromley

A
Borrowed
Path

IMOGEN
CLARK

LAKE UNION
PUBLISHING

Published by Lake Union Publishing, Seattle

www.apub.com

Amazon, the Amazon logo, and Lake Union Publishing are trademarks of Amazon.com, Inc., or its affiliates.

ISBN-13: 9781662525599
eISBN: 9781662518041

Cover design by The Brewster Project
Image credits: © afry_harvy © vikky_arts / Shutterstock;
© Ekaterina Puchkova / Getty Images

Printed in the United States of America

A
Borrowed
Path

1

'Mummy?'

'Mmm?' replied Lyra absently without looking up from the book she was reading.

Skye, her five-year-old daughter, wriggled herself out from their little nest of cushions and throws and stood in front of her, tapping her knee to get her attention.

'Mummy!' she said a little more urgently. 'There's water coming through the ceiling.'

Lyra looked up and her eyes followed Skye's pointing finger to where a stream was cascading down the Anaglypta-covered wall.

'Oh dear. So there is,' she said, but she didn't move.

'Mummy!' Skye's eyes opened wide. 'You must have left the bath running. Maybe you should stop it?'

The ceiling was two-tone now, an ominous dark patch blooming in the place below the first-floor bathroom. It shouldn't be much longer before it gave up the ghost entirely.

'Mummy!!' squeaked Skye.

Lyra brought herself to.

'Yes,' she said briskly. 'Good idea. I'll go and turn the taps off.'

'It's going to be a very deep bath,' said Skye with a knowing nod.

Lyra wanted to explain that the bath couldn't actually get any deeper no matter how much water flowed through their scruffy little flat, but this probably wasn't the moment for a physics lesson. Moving without the urgency that the situation might merit, Lyra made her way up the threadbare stairs to the landing above with Skye trailing behind her.

'Did you forget about the bath?' Skye asked in her little voice.

'I think I must have,' agreed Lyra. 'We made that hot chocolate and it just went out of my head.'

'Silly Mummy.' Skye's tone was affectionate and fond, as if the stupidity of adults were rather charming.

The bathroom door was closed, as Lyra had intended, and she stopped for a second on the landing. She could hear the water hitting the floor and splashing back, like the sound of a particularly wet day. She put her hand on the handle and opened it wide.

The bath was indeed full, and water poured over the edges and on to the nasty patterned lino flooring that Lyra had always hated. It was maybe a few centimetres deep and seemed to be pooling in one corner – how typical of this horrible flat that the floor was on a slant. That must be where it was coming through to the ceiling below.

She hadn't thought to move their dirty laundry, and now it was strewn through the water like so much jetsam and flotsam. That was annoying, Lyra thought. How would she dry it all out?

Skye at her side was stripping off her socks and rolling up her leggings. You had to admire the child's resourcefulness, and Lyra's heart expanded a little as she watched her splash her way through the deluge to the bath. She reached over and turned off first one tap and then the other before looking to Lyra for approval.

Lyra beamed at her. 'Well done!' she said. 'Crisis averted.' She bit her lip to stop herself laughing. That really wouldn't be appropriate parental behaviour. None of this was really, but there was no need to let Skye see how much she was enjoying herself.

Skye put her fingers in the bathwater, tentatively at first and then with disappointment on her face. 'It's a very cold bath, Mummy. Do I still have to get in?'

Lyra grinned at her, pleased to have an excuse to stop covering up her inconvenient emotional response.

'No,' she said. 'We can skip your bath tonight.'

'But what about school?'

'I don't think anyone will notice,' said Lyra. 'But listen. Skye.'

Skye looked up at her, the picture of attention.

'It's probably going to be best if we don't tell anyone about this.'

Skye's face fell. Obviously, the day Mummy flooded the bathroom would be a great story to recount to her little classmates and her teacher.

'I'm sorry, sweetie,' Lyra continued, 'but we don't want anyone to know how silly Mummy is, do we? Mummy might get into trouble.' Lyra's guts twisted. The disaster that was her life was bad enough without getting her five-year-old to lie for her, but needs must.

Skye nodded solemnly. 'Okay,' she said. 'I won't tell anyone, cross my heart and hope to die.'

'Thank you.'

Lyra kissed her daughter on the crown of her head, pulling her close for a quick hug.

'Right then,' she said decisively. 'I think we're going to have to go and stay with Granny for a bit.'

Skye's face lit up. 'At Fox House?'

'Yes. At Fox House. Let's get all your things together. We might not be coming back for a bit' – or at all, she thought – 'so we'd better pack everything. Here are some bin bags for your clothes.' Lyra pulled a handful from the roll and tore down the perforations to separate them. 'And we can put your toys in that box on your bed.'

Skye didn't question why her mother seemed to have the wherewithal for moving out ready and in such close proximity. She turned, splashing back through the puddles on the bathroom floor, and headed for her room.

It was a good job they didn't have much stuff, Lyra thought. She still lived very much as a student, acquiring nothing of any value and not accumulating the stuff that other people seemed to require for their happiness. One day the pair of them would have a home that merited some proper love and attention, but that was a while off yet.

She would strip the flat of anything she wanted to keep and then, when she was far away from Manchester, she would text the landlord and tell him there'd been a flood. No need to explain how it had happened, although that would be obvious as soon as he set foot in there. The main thing was to make the place uninhabitable so she had to flee to Fox House, which would put Rafe off their scent for a bit. Of course, he'd track them down eventually, but by then Lyra would have worked out what she should be doing for the best.

She stepped into the dripping bathroom, pulled the plug on the bath and started to pick their sopping wet clothes off the floor, wringing them out over the lino and then dropping them into an open bin bag. The floor made an ominous creaking sound and then there was a crash and the sound of water gushing.

That'll be the ceiling collapsing downstairs, she thought. Good.

2

Eve peered at the crumpled shopping list.

Pink chips.

That couldn't be right but stare as hard as she might, she couldn't get the cramped letters to reform themselves into any other words. Interpreting her mother's spidery handwriting had always been a challenge for her, but these days the strokes, some broad and confident, others barely there at all, were little more than a jumble of scribbles.

Eve looked up and down the aisle, searching for inspiration, but found nothing. Were pink chips a new kind of snack that her mother enjoyed but which she had yet to discover? It seemed unlikely. Her mother's diet hadn't kept pace with food fashion, had barely wandered far from the 1970s in fact. If pink chips were a new food, it was highly improbable that they would have made it on to her octogenarian mother's shopping list.

She stuffed the list into her jacket pocket and moved back into the throngs of shoppers, allowing herself to be dragged along with the tide. She dropped more familiar items into the trolley as she passed them. Her mother's diet might be limited, but Eve was damned if she was going to give up her own favourite meals just because they were unpopular with her housemate. Into the trolley went ingredients to make chicken fajitas (which her mother insisted were basically chicken sandwiches with too much gubbins), gnocchi with creamed greens (where's the protein?), hoisin salmon noodles (too dry). She must remember to pick up some wine too, as if she'd forget that.

But the pink chips?

She fished the list back out and smoothed it against her thigh. Then balancing it on the trolley handle she took a photo of the mysterious item and sent it to Justin.

Any clue what this says?

She watched the three dots as they danced on her screen.

Pork chops? came the reply.

Of course! Now he'd said it, it was obvious. In fact, she couldn't understand why she hadn't seen it before. It was typical that Justin had grasped it straight away, as if her mother had even designed her handwriting so Justin could maintain his position as golden boy whilst she languished somewhere just up from the woman who came to clean.

Smart arse! she typed back. And then, as the idea occurred to her, Fancy coming over for supper tonight?

No can do. If you'd wanted me at your beck and call you shouldn't have divorced me!

Eve could feel the smile in his words.

Tomorrow then? I'm going out of my mind.

We'll see. Message you in the morning.

What are you doing tonight? She typed as fast as she could, desperate to hold his attention whilst she had it. But she knew he wouldn't reply. She and Justin had been through the most adult of all break-ups and were still the best of friends, but there were some things about his new life that he wasn't prepared to share with her. It was infuriating but she couldn't change it.

She spun the trolley round, almost taking out an elderly man in the process. Apologising to him frantically, she headed back to the meat aisle.

It was a thirty-minute drive from York to Fox House and Eve still hadn't got used to it. For most of her life, she had lived in the city centre, first with Justin and recently by herself. She was used to having shops, restaurants and the cinema all within walking distance and she liked having everything she could need within easy reach, even if she didn't avail herself of their bounty very often. The thing was that she could have if she'd wanted to. Spontaneity wasn't a quality people necessarily attributed to her, but Eve liked to think that it was there somewhere, deep in the heart of her.

Very little could be spontaneous at Fox House. It was too remote for all that. You needed a car for a start and the time it took to get anywhere meant that just turning up on the off-chance of a table or a seat being available was foolhardy and very often disappointing.

Of course, when she had lived in Fox House as a girl its rural location hadn't bothered her one iota. She'd been kept busy at boarding school all term and so she didn't mind the isolation in the holidays. As an only child she was used to having to keep herself entertained, and the ramshackle house had been perfect for letting her imagination run riot. She could lose herself in its nooks and crannies, never minding that she was so far from civilisation. And there had been the woods to play in. And the cottage.

Second time around, however, living in Fox House was starting to feel like a prison sentence to Eve. It was a daily struggle not to let the walls close in around her and she'd taken to going on long walks through the surrounding woodland and sitting in the dilapidated cottage just so she could continue to breathe. She was fitter than she'd been in years – a bonus of sorts, she supposed.

But it wasn't forever. That was what she kept telling herself. Her mother, Agatha, had fallen, tripping herself up on one of the many threadbare rugs that lay scattered and curling around the sitting room. She had broken her hip and it had been immediately apparent, to Eve if not to Agatha, that her former independent existence was now compromised.

When she was discharged from the hospital, Agatha had refused any kind of paid care and so the only remaining solution was for Eve to move in. Temporarily.

That had been a year ago. Agatha was now mobile again, up to a point, but she could no longer drive (or was refusing to try, Eve wasn't sure which) which was a huge disadvantage given where Fox House was situated, and whilst money wasn't tight, it certainly wouldn't stretch to a chauffeur at her beck and call. So that had left Eve.

Eve had tried hard to hang on to her apartment in town, but with fewer clients on her books matching her reduced availability, it didn't take long for the numbers to stop adding up. She would rent somewhere new when she finally left her mother's. This was what she told herself. But she had stopped scanning the estate agents' windows and Rightmove because she could no longer bear to see potentially perfect homes slipping through her fingers.

There were worse places to be stuck for a while, was what she told herself. Fox House, her mother's own childhood home, was a rambling Georgian farmhouse with huge sash windows and a portico over the door. Ivy and neglected wisteria scrambled up the front of the house and into the guttering. 'It's like the M1 for mice,' Justin said, but Agatha had always kept cats so vermin didn't seem to be an issue, so long as you didn't look too closely in the corners of the draughty rooms.

The house sat in an equally neglected garden which ran down to a pond on one side and a wood on the other, hazards for a growing child, but Eve had always kept herself out of trouble in both.

And then there was the cottage. Rundown to the point of dilapidation, the tiny cottage that sat in the wood alongside the house was Eve's favourite part of the whole place. If that little house could have talked then who knew what tales it would have told? On the whole, however, it was probably best that it hung on to its secrets. Eve had discovered some of the most magical, intimate parts of herself there, and for all she knew, so had Agatha.

Eve turned off the lane and on to the driveway. When she was a child, the drive had been covered in a thick layer of crunching gravel which gave the occupants of the house forewarning of any visitors. Now, though, the gravel had long since disappeared, pressed into the earth to return from whence it came, and her approach was as good as silent.

Pulling up in front of the house, Eve saw a scruffy-looking car parked where she usually put hers. They weren't expecting guests as far as she knew, although Agatha was a law unto herself and could have invited anyone. As she pulled up next to it, however, she thought she recognised it, and the child seat sitting proud in the back confirmed things. It was Lyra's car. A rush of love mixed with impatient excitement rushed through her as she slammed the car into neutral and burst out of the door, leaving the groceries lying in the boot, forgotten.

Lyra and Skye had come to visit and her day had just improved immeasurably.

3

Eve could tell that all was not as she had expected as soon as she opened the door. In fact, she could barely open it wide enough to get into the house because of the enormous pile of bin bags that sat in the hallway. Her excitement was overtaken first by curiosity and then by a dull sense of foreboding.

Something was afoot. Had Lyra been helping Agatha to sort through her over-stuffed wardrobes in the short time that Eve had been away at the shops? It seemed highly unlikely.

As Eve shoved at the door, some of the bags slid across the creaking floorboards, allowing her in.

'Lyra?' she called as she went. 'Is everything okay?'

It wasn't. That much was obvious.

Lyra appeared moments later and Eve's heart skipped in her chest at the sight of her child. She was, as ever, dressed in layers of clothing that no sane person would ever put together. Scant consideration had been given to colour, fabric or type of garment. The only unifying factor was that they were designed to be worn. Her hair hung in its beautiful corkscrew curls around her face, a throwback from some part of her family tree that no one had ever identified.

'Oh, hi Mum,' Lyra said breezily, as if she'd been there for days and her sudden and unexpected arrival at Fox House was nothing remarkable. Then she held her arms above her head in a character-istically expansive gesture. 'Catastrophe!'

Lyra, much like her father Justin, was prone to exaggeration. There was rarely anything in her life, she believed, that couldn't be improved by a healthy sprinkle of hyperbole, and Eve had learned to apply a pinch of salt to most of what she said. This time how-ever, if the musty smell emanating from the numerous bin bags was anything to go by, there did appear to be an element of truth to her statement.

'What on earth's happened?' Eve asked. 'Are you all right? And where's Skye?'

Lyra waved a bangled arm in the direction of the sitting room.

'Oh, she's fine. She's with Granny,' she said, and Eve smarted involuntarily. It didn't matter how many times she heard it. That her daughter was permitted to call Agatha by this affectionate sobri-quet when she had been forced since childhood to call her mother by her Christian name still hurt. 'But listen, Mum. There's been a disaster at my place so we're moving in with you for a while. Granny says it's fine.'

Eve was not to be consulted, it seemed, and the fact that Fox House was also her home and had been for over a year was to be overlooked. As ever, her voice counted for nothing.

But this was no matter. Of course she wouldn't object to Lyra and Skye being there. It would be delightful to see them without the sense of time ticking away that usually accompanied their flying visits. Having them around would also take the strain of dealing with Agatha off her shoulders. The thought crept into her head disloyally and she shooed it away before it had the chance to sit down and take its coat off.

Eve threw open her arms to hug her daughter and Lyra fell into them.

'Of course that's fine,' she said into Lyra's chestnut curls. 'It'll be lovely to have you here. But what's happened?'

Lyra pulled away and slipped seamlessly back into full disaster mode.

'A flood,' she said, hazel eyes open wide. 'Total nightmare. Something went wrong with the plumbing at the top of the house and the water just cascaded all the way down. It was like an actual waterfall. Then the ceiling collapsed. God, Mum, it's such a mess, you wouldn't believe.'

The tip of her nose had turned pink, a tell she'd had since being small that all was not quite as she was explaining it, but Eve let it go. If there was more to the story then no doubt it would come out in its own sweet time.

'So I just stuffed everything into bin bags and left. Some of our clothes are dripping wet. It's all going to need a wash.'

Eve was certain it would all have needed a wash before it got drenched in flood water but she wasn't going to say so.

'And was anything ruined beyond rescue?' she asked, thinking of her own treasured possessions – books, pictures, photographs, her sketchbooks – all of which would be destroyed by water.

Lyra looked genuinely confused. 'No. It'll all be fine once it's been through the wash.'

There were no ephemera in Lyra's world. Nothing whimsical, nor sentimental. Her life was contained on her phone, digitally stored as a series of ones and zeros (was that how they still did digital things?) and then sitting on a cloud somewhere way above their heads, safe from fire and flood.

'That's good,' said Eve, and let it drop.

Little footsteps signalled the arrival into the scene of Skye, Lyra's unplanned but very much loved daughter. Skye was the result of a tumultuous and, as it turned out, relatively short-lived love affair when Lyra had been in her second year at university. Rafe,

Skye's father, had stayed with them for the first year or so of his daughter's life, but after graduating with a first (contrasting sharply with Lyra's third-class degree) it had only been a matter of time until the lure of success had tempted him away from the confines of his domestic situation. He was still on the scene though, making sure that he had a strong relationship with his daughter if not with Eve's. Whereas Eve and Justin had remained close friends after their marriage broke down, Lyra and Rafe now only seemed to have the best interests of Skye in common. It was a shame, but Eve had to accept it was normal. It was she and Justin who were the exception.

Even though, given the choice, such early motherhood wouldn't have been what she'd have wished for Lyra, Eve could no longer imagine life without Skye. Once the shock of being thrust into pre-menopause grandparenthood had worn off, Eve found that she relished the opportunity to have another go at parenting, albeit one place removed. All the things she knew she had messed up with Lyra she could try to straighten out with Skye. Wasn't that how it was supposed to work? Eve hoped so at least.

'VeeVee,' sang Skye as she barrelled into the room. 'Me and Mummy have come to stay with you and GeeGee.'

'You have!' Eve agreed, dropping to her knees so that she was at eye level with her granddaughter. 'Isn't that lovely?'

'Everything at home got very wet because Mummy left the bath running,' continued Skye earnestly.

Eve shot a glance at Lyra, who shrugged.

'And we think Mr Patel will say we have to leave because we've made such a mess of his house.'

Out of the mouths of babes, thought Eve. There they had it – the truth of it. Lyra was actually homeless but too proud to say so.

Skye's hand shot to her mouth and she stared, wide-eyed, at Lyra.

'That was secret,' she whispered. 'I wasn't supposed to say it out loud.'

I bet you weren't, thought Eve. Lyra never had been very good at admitting her mistakes. She was too self-reliant for that. Instead she said, 'Well, that doesn't matter. The main thing is that you and Mummy are safe and sound. You can stay here with me and Great-granny as long as you want.'

Skye rushed over and hugged Eve's legs as if she were a stumpy tree and then she scampered back out of the room. Eve turned to Lyra and raised an enquiring eyebrow, gratified to see that her daughter did at least look a little sheepish.

'It was an accident,' she confessed. 'We were making hot chocolate for bath time and then we got distracted. I totally forgot I'd left the bath running. By the time we woke up the ceilings had started to fall in. Not going to lie, they must have been pretty flimsy in the first place.'

Eve watched with wonder as her daughter justified her own mistake. It was remarkable to her how easily Lyra did that. Where was the guilt that would have haunted Eve night and day? There was no trace of it in Lyra. Her inner conviction that life was weighted in her favour must have come from her father's side. Eve certainly hadn't been blessed with it. It could join the long, long list of parenting matters that Eve suspected she could have done better.

But parenting was hard, especially when your own parents hadn't laid a clear path for you to follow. And Eve didn't think she'd done that bad a job with Lyra, really, all things considered.

4

'Where are we sleeping, Granny?' called Lyra from the hallway.

Again. Apparently, Eve didn't merit consultation on this either, even though she was the one who handled the domestic arrangements at Fox House these days. She stifled her resentment. It was only natural that Lyra would see Fox House as Agatha's domain. It was her house, after all. Eve might have been here a while but she was still very much a guest in her family's eyes, and anyway, wasn't that precisely how she saw matters herself? She couldn't have things both ways.

She followed the sound of her daughter's voice and arrived in the capacious hall at the same time as her mother.

Agatha had walked with a cane since the accident. None of your grey, standard-issue NHS walking sticks for her. Her cane was exquisite. Fashioned in beech from Fox House's own wood, it had a beautifully carved fox's head as a handle and its length was as smooth as silk, the knots and grain of the branch it came from polished to a rich conker-brown shine.

Eve had forgotten all about the cane until Agatha had emerged from her bedroom with it after her accident. When she saw it again, hazy memories flitted in and out of her head, none of them stable enough to grasp hold of. A man sitting in the garden carving it, perhaps. Not her father. He would never have had the patience for such a task. Another man. Eve couldn't place him, but the splinters of memory left her feeling warm and safe, which was peculiar.

'Good Lord, I haven't seen that cane for decades,' she'd said. 'Where's it been hiding?'

'It hasn't been hiding anywhere,' Agatha had replied archly. 'It's been in its proper place waiting for a time when it was required. Which is now.'

'I always loved it,' Eve mused. 'Do you remember how you'd never let me play with it?'

An expression Eve couldn't interpret crossed Agatha's face. Maybe she was simply admonishing herself for denying her child such a simple pleasure. After all, what possible reason could there be for withholding the cane? Then Agatha's expression had softened a little, a fleeting wistfulness creeping over it. Did she have fond memories of the cane too? Or maybe the shadowy man who had made it?

And then the wistfulness was gone, whisked away as quickly as it had appeared.

'It's hardly a toy,' Agatha had snapped. 'I'm going to sit in the sun trap. Can you help me with some cushions?' And then she had shuffled off in the direction of the dining room, which had a south-facing bay window and was a perfect spot to read.

The cane was slightly too long for her these days and it made her list to the right.

'Wouldn't you be better with the walking stick the hospital gave you?' Eve called after her. 'That one can be adjusted to the proper height.'

'I'm perfectly all right with this one,' Agatha had called back as she shuffled with steely determination towards her destination.

Fox House had five bedrooms. Agatha had what estate agents would deem the 'master', but it wasn't a suite, just the largest room with the best views over the garden and the wood beyond. When

Eve had first moved back in she had stalked around the remaining four, determined to take her pick.

But she had gravitated back to her old childhood room. It wasn't the biggest of the remaining bedrooms, nor did it have the best view, but there was something about the energy in there that drew her in and that she couldn't really explain.

She had got Justin to help her rearrange the beds, taking the old brass double out of what had been the guest room and repositioning it under the window in hers. There wasn't really room for it and they'd had to squeeze it in with two sides against walls, but as she very much doubted she would be sharing it with anyone, what did it matter?

Agatha must have heard what they were doing and called out from her sick bed.

'What on earth is going on out there?'

Eve had peered round her bedroom door.

'Justin and I are just moving a bed,' she'd said, using what she had learned was the magic word when dealing with her mother. Justin could do no wrong in Agatha's eyes. When Agatha had become mobile again and had seen what they'd done for herself, she had tutted noisily, but there had been no suggestion of them having to put the bed back.

So that left three rooms for Lyra and Skye to choose from – the guest room, which now contained Eve's single bed, the box room and the room with the locked door. Well, that really made only two.

'You can have the spare room, the one next to Granny's,' Eve said, pointedly disregarding the fact that Lyra had asked the question of Agatha, 'and Skye can have the little one. That'll be fine for you both, won't it?'

'Yeah. Whatever. I might put the mattress on the floor though. That old single bed is knackered.'

It wasn't that bad, just a little quirky in places. Eve found herself wanting to defend her poor little childhood bed frame. It hadn't done anything wrong.

'Oh, we can get you a new bed,' said Agatha, as if this were as simple as buying a pint of milk. 'That old one of your mother's should have gone to the tip years ago.'

'Oh, cool. Thanks, Granny.' Lyra beamed at Agatha and then at Skye. 'Race you upstairs,' she said to her daughter, eyes sparkling.

Skye squealed and then pelted up the stairs, barely able to keep her balance as her momentum gathered, with Lyra thundering behind but intentionally not quite catching up.

Eve watched them go. A new bed? There had been no suggestion of her having a new bed when she had given up her life to come and care for Agatha. But then, she supposed, she had created her own solution by taking the newer guest bed for herself, so it wasn't so unfair. She pushed down the sense of injustice that tended to loiter just under the surface. The important thing was that Lyra had somewhere comfortable to sleep for the duration of her stay. Exactly how long that would be Eve had no idea, but with Lyra and Skye being effectively homeless, it would take some time to unpick.

The bed in the little box room was more of a day bed, piled high with patchwork quilts and ancient horsehair cushions. Would that work for Skye? Eve had her doubts but she followed her daughter and granddaughter up the stairs and into the room.

Skye had already fashioned herself a little burrow amongst the quilts and was pretending to be sound asleep.

Lyra put her fingers to her lips and made an exaggerated shushing sound.

'I think Skye likes her new room,' she said with a wink at Eve. 'She's sound asleep already.'

The strain of dissembling was too much for Skye. She managed another few seconds and then her eyes sprang open and she sat up.

'I'm not really asleep, VeeVee. I was just pretending.'

Eve opened her eyes wide in mock surprise. 'Well, you're very good at it,' she said.

Skye beamed at her and then leapt off the day bed and ran off for further investigating.

'Are you sure she'll be okay in here?' Eve asked. 'It's not really a bed.'

Lyra shrugged. 'She'll be fine. It's an adventure!' And then she followed Skye out, calling as she went, 'Have you found the secret tunnel yet?'

Eve stood where she was and wondered how being a mother seemed to come so naturally to her daughter when it had been such a struggle for her. She must have done something right after all.

'What's in here, Mummy?'

Eve could hear Skye trying the door of the locked room. She could go and explain. They could do it in a way that a five-year-old could understand, she was sure. She could even get the key from where it was hidden in the vase on the landing and show Skye inside. But did she have the energy for that? She wasn't sure she did.

Then Lyra stepped up. 'It's Great-granny's room where she keeps things that are super-precious. That's why we don't go in.'

'To keep the things safe?' Skye's curious little voice asked.

'Exactly that.'

Eve was relieved when she heard Skye running down the stairs to find something else to explore.

5

Lyra was sitting on the hall floor sorting her belongings into piles of wet and dry items when Eve judged it appropriate to mention something that was troubling her. She didn't want to spark an argument, not when Lyra was so newly arrived, but she did want to know what her daughter planned to do about Skye's ongoing education, given that she appeared to have relocated them a two-hour drive away.

'What will you do about school?' she asked. It came out more baldly than she had intended, almost an accusation.

Lyra didn't look up.

'I'll sort something out,' she replied in a tone that suggested she wanted to close the subject down.

Eve pressed on. 'But surely she should have been there today, and tomorrow.'

Lyra shrugged. 'Two days off won't do any harm. She's only five. And then it's the Easter holidays so that's two weeks off. I'll work something out then.'

Eve knew she was being dismissed but she persisted, searching for something that she and Lyra could work on together.

'We could chat it through,' she suggested tentatively. 'If you like. Go through the options.'

Lyra grunted, neither accepting nor quite rejecting the offer of help.

'I don't even know where the nearest school is,' said Eve. 'Obviously the village school where I went closed down years ago, and then Agatha sent me into York. Skye's too young to board . . .'

Lyra's head snapped round. 'She's not going to boarding school, no matter how old she is. She's my child and she stays with me.'

'Of course,' floundered Eve. The implication that a real mother wouldn't send their child away to school, as Agatha had done to her, was clear. 'I just meant that I don't know where the local schools are.'

'I'll work it out,' snapped Lyra. Subject closed.

'Well, I'm here if you need me,' Eve couldn't help but add.

'Mummy. Can we go to the cottage?'

Skye ran into the hallway. Did she run everywhere? It was just the excitement of exploring somewhere new, Eve supposed. Maybe Lyra had been the same; maybe *she* had, and Agatha for that matter. Eve couldn't remember, couldn't imagine running for the sheer joy of it.

Lyra looked up and smiled broadly, and when she spoke, the coolness of the tone she'd used with Eve was gone.

'Of course we can. In fact, let's go right now. Is the key still in the same place, Mum?' She stood up, immediately abandoning the piles of clothes to some other moment.

'I think so,' replied Eve vaguely. 'I've not been out there for a while so I'm not sure.'

That wasn't true. Eve took herself out to the cottage at any opportunity she had. It provided a welcome sanctuary from the pressures of being with her mother twenty-four/seven. She had even contemplated living out there herself rather than in Fox House, but it had no heating and years of standing empty had made the place feel damp and unwelcoming. She wasn't sure why she'd just lied about going in, except that she felt the need to protect her little shelter from invaders, wanted to keep it all to herself.

But already Lyra had arrived at the ancient brass hooks where Agatha kept all the keys and had the one for the cottage in her hand.

'I'll come with you,' Eve said weakly, feeling her tiny snippets of freedom slipping away from her.

Outside the day was bright and crisp with the scent of spring in the air. The winter had felt longer than usual, and the cheerful yellows of the newly flowering daffodils still felt shocking, an assault on eyes unused to anything other than drab browns and greys. Eve found she could no longer imagine the garden and the woods lush and green, even though the change came every year. When summer rolled round, she could never picture the branches of the trees bare either. Maybe she simply lacked imagination.

Lyra and Skye skipped on ahead, their exuberance matching the brightness of the flowers. Seeing them so carefree made something catch inside Eve. A darkness had crept up on her over the winter, throwing a caul over her so that she saw everything in a kind of half-light. How long had she been feeling like this? she wondered. Since she moved into Fox House? Since before then?

Choosing to ignore the question, she pushed her lips up into a smile and found that once her face was there it didn't take much effort to keep it that way.

The garden at Fox House must once have been rather grand, although Eve only remembered it as chaotic. There was a walkway of arches over which dog roses scrambled, leading to a sunken lawn and a box knot garden, all of it now leggy and grown out of shape. (Agatha employed an elderly gardener who did his best, but more than keeping the lawns cut with the ancient sit-on mower was beyond him.) An enormous rhododendron hedge ran down one side, a wall of pink when spring tipped over into summer.

And then there was the wood. It was probably more of a spinney than a wood as it only measured an acre or so, and was surrounded on three sides by farmland. When Eve was a child it had felt like the deepest, darkest of forests and she wondered if it seemed that way now to Skye. She hoped so. There was something magical about being a little bit frightened when you were young, although the feeling lost its appeal later on.

The cottage, which must have been built to house a farmhand and his family, was visible from the garden of the main house, and the path that cut through the trees to its front door was still serviceable as long as you kept an eye out for the brambles.

Skye skipped on ahead, although she kept turning to check that the grown-ups were still behind her. She reached the peeling door first.

'Shall I knock, Mummy?' she asked.

'You can, but no one will answer.'

'Does no one live here?'

Skye already knew the answer to that. Apart from herself and Justin for a brief interlude, no one had lived in the cottage for as long as Eve could remember.

'No,' replied Lyra. 'This cottage is just for us. Here.' She handed her the key. 'Open the door and let us in.'

6

The cottage door hinges gave the kind of blood-curdling creak added as a sound effect to television comedy sketches, and Skye turned back to look at Lyra, her expression a mixture of terror and thrilled eagerness.

'I keep meaning to oil that,' said Eve, and then blushed as she realised she had just exposed herself in a lie. Not been out here for a while, my eye. Lyra pulled a knowing face but didn't pass comment. Like daughter like mother, at least in the honesty stakes: Eve with the cottage and Lyra with the flood.

'Pooey!' said Skye as she stepped over the threshold, wrinkling her little nose and squeezing her nostrils tightly between finger and thumb. 'It pongs.'

She was right, but it was the odour of neglect rather than anything less palatable; certainly nothing that some circulating air wouldn't fix. The front door opened straight into the living room and there was a kitchen behind. Those two rooms made up the whole of the ground floor. Upstairs there were two bedrooms and a tiny bathroom that had been carved out of the room at the back.

'Can I go upstairs?' asked Skye, racing in the direction of the stairs without waiting for an answer.

'I can't believe you used to live here,' said Lyra. 'Was this really all you had?'

Eve took in the sagging sofa, a pale green Dralon with its tired cushions, and the threadbare Persian rug that Agatha had donated to the cause when they'd moved in.

'We didn't need much back then,' Eve replied. 'We were just grateful to have somewhere to stay that wasn't our parents' houses. And it wasn't for long, just straight after we got married when we had nothing. Maybe a year or so.'

Lyra shook her head. 'A year! On that sofa?'

'Things were different in the nineties. People didn't have such high expectations. And we were newly-weds. What kind of sofa we had wasn't high on our priorities back then.'

Lyra's expression was sceptical, and now Eve looked at the state of the place she could understand why. It was pretty basic and the nineties weren't that long ago. They could have bought some decent furniture cheaply enough, but it had been more of a mindset. She and Justin had been brought up by parents who remembered rationing. That left its mark.

'I think you might even have been conceived on that sofa,' she added, more for the effect the statement would have than anything else. She doubted it was true. She and Justin might have been in the first flush of marital bliss but even they would have drawn the line at the lumpy, too-short second-hand sofa when there was a perfectly comfortable bed upstairs.

Lyra's face twisted in disgust.

'God, Mother. Too much information,' she said.

'You Generation Zedders are such prudes,' laughed Eve.

'Pardon me for not wanting to picture my parents having actual sex!' Lyra's expression changed to something more impish. 'Actually I brought Max here a few times as it goes, although that was strictly snogging only.'

'I'm very glad to hear it,' Eve replied, although hadn't she always used the cottage for activities she would rather the world didn't see, too? That hadn't started with Justin. It went much further back. She didn't know who this Max was but if he was a boy from the village then there was a good chance his father had been there before him. There were so few youngsters around that everyone had kissed everyone eventually.

Eve crossed the room and went into the kitchen. The stand-alone electric oven was still there, its white enamel chipped in places and tarnished silver foil still lining the grill pan. She could almost smell the bacon sizzling, part of Justin's trademark full English breakfasts, and picture him standing there in just his boxers, wincing as the hot fat spat on to his bare skin. And there were the free-standing cupboards with their pale milky-blue doors, all the rage in the 1940s she was sure, but which now belonged in a museum. On the floor, the chequered lino was lifting in the corners. Dead bluebottles littered every surface.

The place could certainly do with some TLC. Eve ran her fingertips across the top of the pine dining table, feeling the smooth grain of the wood. She remembered the day Justin brought it home, pleased as punch with himself. It had come from a school art room and primitive graffiti, the sort you made with a pair of compasses and a biro, trailed along the edges and down the legs.

'No more eating from trays on the floor,' he'd said with an air of triumph. 'We can pretend we're grown-ups. We could even throw a dinner party if we wanted.'

Eve didn't want. She liked eating from trays. Agatha would never have permitted it and so it had an air of the forbidden about it that made it particularly appealing. But Justin was so obviously delighted that she didn't have it in her heart to say so.

'It's perfect,' she said instead. 'I shall dust off that Delia Smith book your mum gave me for Christmas and get cooking. Although if we're having a dinner party we'll need some more plates. And cutlery. And glasses.'

26

They had laughed together then and he had kissed her on the tip of her nose, and then on her lips, and then he had chased her up the narrow staircase, making her squeal just as Skye had done earlier.

Lyra called out to Skye then, cutting through Eve's reminiscences.

'What's it like up there?'

'There's a picture on the wall of a pond with some flowers growing out of it. And there's a fairy.'

Lyra smiled at Eve. 'One of yours?'

Eve nodded.

'There are two fairies,' she shouted back to Skye. 'If you look really carefully.'

Silence and then, 'Oh yes. There's another one in that daisy.'

'Well spotted,' called Eve as she made for the stairs. 'They're actually water sprites.'

'They look like fairies,' called Skye, and Eve decided to let it go because her granddaughter was only five and had a lot to learn.

'Are you still painting?' Lyra asked.

Eve shook her head. 'My stuff is all boxed up with the rest of my things in storage,' she said. 'I suppose I could get it out and bring it here but there never seems to be time.'

Lyra tipped her head to one side and gave her an uncomprehending look. Of course there's time, it said. Just be better organised.

In fact, this was the first thought Eve had given to her painting since she'd moved in, possibly for longer than that. Had she done anything since the divorce from Justin? She wouldn't like to swear she hadn't, but she was fairly certain.

'I might do that,' she added. 'It would be nice to do some painting again.' She knew she was mainly talking to herself.

Eve followed Lyra and Skye upstairs where the rooms were as sparse as downstairs. One had a double bed, the striped mattress bowing towards its centre, a dark wood wardrobe in a heavy between-the-wars design and a chest of drawers made from flimsy plywood.

'We couldn't afford Ikea,' said Eve, 'so we just had to make do.'

'It's quite romantic really,' replied Lyra. 'Although I can't picture Dad living here. Didn't Granny drive him mad?'

'Your dad has always been rather fond of Granny,' said Eve. 'Do you not remember how they used to gang up on me?' She sounded like a victim and Lyra gave her a look that suggested she thought so too. 'But as I said, we didn't live here long,' she continued. 'A year maybe, eighteen months.'

Lyra walked over to the wardrobe and yanked at the sticking door, which resisted at first and then flew back with such violence that the empty coat hangers inside clattered together noisily.

'Do you think Granny would let me and Skye move in? Just for a few weeks while I get something else sorted out. It would be pretty cool to do this place up. New furniture. Some artwork on the walls, plants.'

Eve could tell from the look on Lyra's face that her imagination was running wild, visualising the unpromising cottage as something entirely different.

'But it's so grim in here,' she said. 'And cold. There's no central heating.'

'It was cold in the flat,' replied Lyra, 'and anyway it's nearly spring.'

'You'd be much cosier in the house with me and Granny,' Eve persisted, but Lyra had caught hold of the idea and was running with it as fast as her dreams would carry her.

'I'm not sure Agatha will agree to it,' Eve added with an air of desperation. This was her secret place, her bolthole. She didn't want to share it with anyone, not even her daughter and granddaughter.

'Well, I'm going to ask her anyway,' said Lyra. 'What do you reckon, Skye? Would you like to move in here?'

Skye looked around the shabby room and let her eyes settle on Eve's painting of the mystical pool with its water sprites.

'Yes!' she said, her little head nodding rapidly. 'I really, really would.'

7

Come for dinner. Please. Lyra wants to move into our cottage. I think I need backup.

Eve pressed send and then watched the screen. Justin was typing.

We'll see.

Eve smiled to herself. Justin liked to paint himself as a man of mystery but she knew he'd come. He wouldn't be able to resist the draw of all four women at the same table.

She would make a simple family-style meal – a big bowl of pasta drenched in sauce, salad, good bread, a decent bottle of Chianti to wash it down. Or two. Agatha could still drink when she had a mind to.

Eve wondered if she should discuss the question of the cottage with Agatha beforehand but decided there would be little point. Her mother would do as she pleased and anyway Lyra would no doubt have mentioned the idea already. Her daughter wasn't one to let the grass grow.

Thinking of her table, Eve headed to the back door to go and pick some daffodils. Agatha would complain about the smell, but they were so cheerful. She would dig out a tablecloth too, make a bit of an effort.

As she crossed the kitchen she thought she could hear Lyra talking to someone but couldn't locate the sound. She stood still and listened. Lyra was in the sitting room and whilst the door was pulled to, it no longer sat neatly in its frame and the sound of her voice drifted out into the hallway.

'But you can't do that.'

There was no response. Lyra must be on the phone. Eve shouldn't listen but something about the desperation in her daughter's tone made her strain to hear.

'That was an accident! Like I'd flood us out of our home on purpose.'

'No. She's fine here with me.'

'It's almost the holidays. And it will be sorted out by then.'

'No. Don't.'

'For fuck's sake, Rafe. Just leave it, will you. I'm hanging up now. I'll let you know if anything changes.'

'I don't care. I'm not doing that.'

Then there was a thud, as if Lyra had hit out at something. And then a muffled scream of frustration.

Eve stood frozen to the spot, unwilling to move in case she gave away that she had been there listening. A string of muffled swear words crossed the space and then a sound that suggested Lyra was moving, so Eve set off across the hallway. The door opened and Lyra appeared. Eve tried to act surprised.

'Oh, hi. I've invited your dad over for dinner. I hope that's okay,' she said casually.

Lyra kept moving with purpose towards the stairs without meeting Eve's eye.

'Yeah. That'll be nice,' she said in a flat monotone before bounding upwards to her room.

31

Eve puffed her cheeks out. Whatever was going on there, she assumed Lyra would tell her in due course.

Or not.

◆ ◆ ◆

Justin arrived just after six. He didn't knock or announce himself in any way and Eve stumbled across him in the kitchen lifting lids on saucepans and inspecting their contents.

'You came then,' she said wryly.

'Couldn't keep away from you. Plus I had no food in the house. Bit of a no-brainer. This smells good,' he added, nodding at the pasta sauce. Eve ignored him, finally immune to his flattery after so many years of craving it.

'Lyra's upstairs with Skye. Something's going on with Rafe but she's not told me what it is yet so tread carefully. Agatha is in the sitting room. You'd better go and announce yourself there first.'

'Ah yes. My adoring public.' He grinned and executed a generous bow.

Eve rolled her eyes at him. 'I'll open the wine. You can take her in a glass.'

The cork came out of the bottle with a satisfying pop and she poured three generous glasses and then added a dash to the sauce. Justin grabbed two and headed off, taking a slurp as he walked.

'Dinner in twenty,' she called after him.

Justin and she hadn't so much fallen out of love as fallen into friendship. It had been a gradual process but eventually it became apparent that that was all that was left of their once-burning passion. They could just have drifted along together into old age, but Eve wanted more. At forty-six, she hadn't felt ready to give up on love, had hoped that there would be someone else out there for her. It turned out that once the idea was put to him, Justin could see the sense in her thought process and so they had agreed to end the marriage amicably and with very little fuss.

But now, almost seven years later, she was still very much single. She believed Justin had had a string of new lovers but she tried hard not to ask and he didn't volunteer that kind of information about his new life. There was no one serious, though. Eve was pretty sure of that. A new permanent partner surely wouldn't tolerate his ongoing relationship with her or the way he dropped in and out of Fox House as the mood took him.

She had set the table in the dining room. The kitchen table wasn't quite big enough to seat five comfortably and in any event, she preferred the dining room with its air of shabby formality. It was a light room darkened by heavy chintz curtains and even heavier furniture. The table, a mahogany antique dating from some time in Queen Victoria's reign, sat grandly in the centre, its top generally covered by a heavy felt mat on to which Agatha had taken to piling books. The removal and replacement of these piles had been an ongoing but silent battle between the two of them.

Today, Eve had brightened the space considerably with a white damask tablecloth and the daffodils from the garden. She wondered now, though, as she thought about the red wine and the tomato-based sauce, whether the cloth might have been a mistake. Could she add an extra layer around Skye's place, and Justin's too for that matter, without causing offence? She decided she probably could and spread a red napkin under both placemats, and then did the same to the others in case it did.

The sound of Agatha's laugh rang out from the sitting room. Justin must be working his customary magic on her. Eve both marvelled at and resented her ex-husband's easy rapport with her mother. It showed that Agatha wasn't as icy as she sometimes liked to project, but also that Eve must be lacking in some way because she struggled to find that kind of connection with her. But whose fault was that? she wondered. Hers or Agatha's?

Skye appeared at the door. She was wearing a pretty princess dress with puffed organza sleeves that looked like it might be intended for dressing up.

'You look lovely,' said Eve.

Skye gave a little twirl and the dress stuck out like an upside-down tulip as she spun.

'It's my best one for Grandpa,' she said proudly.

Hearing Justin described as Grandpa still made Eve want to laugh out loud. She had come to terms with her own role as a grandmother, but in her head Justin was still stuck somewhere in his thirties and she just couldn't get the idea to latch on.

'When we move into the cottage, can I have the picture with the fairies in my room?'

If you move into the cottage, Eve thought. It wasn't yet settled, not by a long chalk, but where was the harm in playing along?

'Of course you can,' she said.

8

Dinner was a success with everyone except Agatha.

'You know the Italians eat pasta as a little extra course between starter and main course. I don't know where this habit of serving huge bowlfuls of the stuff on its own started up. A very British phenomenon, I suspect,' she said.

Despite this objection, Eve noticed that Agatha had cleared her plate and was wiping up the last of the sauce with a hunk of bread. She might be eighty but there was nothing wrong with her appetite.

'I remember when I was in Rome,' she continued in a tone that suggested that she should be listened to. 'It was before I was married, in the mid-sixties maybe. Anyway, a girlfriend and I were travelling around to see the sights. The sixties weren't as liberated as everyone says, you know, and especially not in Italy. Two young women travelling without a chaperone raised some eyebrows, I can tell you.'

She leaned back in her chair and let her eyes drift upwards as if she were trying to recall the trip in her head. Eve waited. She enjoyed it when Agatha shared parts of her past with them. Such moments had occurred so rarely when she was a girl that now, when she was granted glimpses into Agatha's life beyond her, she was captivated.

'Anyway,' Agatha pressed on. 'We'd been warned that Rome had gangs of gypsy children that marauded around the city capturing unsuspecting tourists and holding them hostage until they gave up all their worldly goods. So we were on our guard. If a child so much as looked at us we would grasp our knapsacks to our bosoms ready for the fight.'

Skye looked aghast.

'How old were the children, GeeGee?' she asked.

'Ooh, not much older than you,' replied Agatha, although Skye was barely five and that couldn't possibly be true. Even Skye looked sceptical, her eyes shooting over to Lyra for confirmation. Lyra shrugged, choosing to neither confirm nor deny her grandmother's claim.

'I actually caught a young woman in Florence with her hand in my bag. Searching round for my purse she was, as my bag was sitting on my shoulder. No shame at all. Well, I soon saw her off. I shouted at her in English and she shouted back at me in Italian. But she left me alone after that.'

'Glad to hear it,' said Justin, reaching for the Chianti and pouring himself another glass. He was gently mocking her but Agatha appeared oblivious, either not registering the nuance or more likely not giving him the chance to steal her spotlight.

'But then we went to Naples . . .' She paused for dramatic effect and they all waited obligingly. 'Have you been to Naples, Justin?' She didn't give him time to reply and Justin, who had opened his mouth to speak, closed it again and stifled a smirk. 'Amazing place. We went off from there to Pompeii. Quite unspoiled back then. None of this visitor centre and Perspex over the mosaics business like it is now. We were free to roam in and out of all the villas, just like the Romans themselves.'

'I think it's important that the visitors are more controlled now,' said Eve. 'We need to preserve our history for the generations to come.'

'What airy-fairy *Guardian*-reading nonsense,' scoffed Agatha. 'Pompeii has been standing for thousands of years, despite what Mount Vesuvius threw at it. I very much doubt it's going to be damaged by a few tourists.'

'It's hardly a few,' Eve said under her breath, but Agatha continued as if she hadn't spoken.

'They have the remains of a couple who were at it when the lava hit. Imagine that. You go to bed for a bit of afternoon delight and end up preserved in flagrante delicto and fated to be laughed at by schoolboys until the end of time. The ignominy.'

Skye was tapping at Lyra's elbow, requesting a translation, but Lyra shook her head and whispered something.

'Anyway, no one had told my friend and I that Naples was a Mafia hotbed and that just looking at someone the wrong way could result in a knife in the guts.'

Eve flinched and Skye nudged her mother again.

'So, having been scared witless in Rome, we just wandered around the backstreets of Naples without a care in the world. And no one bothered us. I supposed we were giving off different signals when we didn't believe we were at risk. It's all in the body language, you know, Justin.'

'Is it?' asked Justin studiously and Eve could barely keep her face straight. She squeezed her lips together tightly to make sure they didn't misbehave. Whilst part of her was fascinated by Agatha's story, she also enjoyed Justin's mischief-making.

'It is. If you're going to do something then do it with confidence, that's what I've always said, haven't I, Eve?'

Eve had no doubt that this was the kind of thing her mother would have said, although she couldn't bring an actual incident to mind. She nodded her agreement in any event.

Agatha paused for a moment.

'Now, how did we get on to that?' she asked no one in particular.

'The pasta?' suggested Lyra.

'Yes. Indeed. The pasta.' Agatha sat back in her chair and the veil drew back around her.

'Speaking of which,' said Eve, 'would anyone like any more? There's plenty.'

'Portion control,' said Agatha. 'Never one of your strengths, if I may say so, Eve. If you'd been brought up with rationing like I was then you would understand the horrors of food waste.'

There you go. It was never far away, that need to ensure that everyone knew how hard Agatha's life had been. Eve drew a breath in through her nostrils as she mentally waited for the desire to snap back at her mother to pass.

'It's the same now really, Granny,' chipped in Lyra. 'The amount of perfectly good food that goes to landfill when people are starving. It's deplorable. There's a scheme near me where you pay a fixed amount and you can choose a bag full of food that the supermarkets would have thrown away. There's nothing wrong with it. I have stuff in my fridge that's older than the things you buy there. And anyone can go but most people don't bother. They keep buying more from the supermarkets and then throwing it away. People need to understand what's going on with the planet and make the effort to rethink how they do things.'

'What an interesting idea,' said Agatha and the conversation tripped off in a new direction, following after Lyra and her food waste.

So, saving food is interesting, but saving Pompeii is airy-fairy *Guardian*-reading nonsense, noticed Eve, but rather than make the point, she stood up and went to get another bottle.

9

Lyra lay on the rickety single bed and stared up at the ceiling as she tried to work out what to do next. She'd never been any good at strategy. She couldn't even play chess that well, despite the hours her dad had spent trying to get her to see three moves ahead. Or even one move. Her head just didn't work like that. She was an instinctive thinker, always responding to the situation before her on impulse rather than through considered thought.

Coming here had definitely been an impulsive move, but had it been the right one? She wished she could talk to someone about what was happening but her mother . . . Lyra thought for a moment about why she didn't want to talk it through with her and couldn't put her finger on the reason. There wasn't anything specific, just more of a feeling that Eve wouldn't have anything helpful to say. Lyra loved her mother deeply but she was a bit . . . she tried to think of the word. Ineffectual. Maybe that was it.

Perhaps she could speak to her dad. His advice was generally practical and robust. Or even her grandmother. Lyra had always been able to talk to her.

But Lyra was supposed to be an adult and this was her mess. She would sort it out on her own.

Her phone buzzed on the counterpane next to her. She left it where it was. The message might be from a friend, someone who was wondering why she had disappeared without warning and was concerned for her wellbeing. But it was more likely to be from her landlord or Rafe, and whatever either of them had to say it wouldn't be good and she didn't want to know.

She really hadn't meant for things to go this far but it was all Rafe's fault. He had backed her into a corner and she had done the only thing she could think of to get herself out which, looking at it now, hadn't been that smart.

Anyway, what was done was done. There was no undoing it and she didn't have the wherewithal to fix it, so that was that. She had to live with the consequences. And it wasn't a total disaster, as long as no one found out what she had done. At least she had Fox House to hide in. And the cottage.

The phone started to buzz again and this time she picked it up and looked at the caller ID. 'School'. She could ignore it, but they would only ring back, and she was supposed to be an adult with responsibilities that she had to deal with.

She took a deep breath and answered. 'Hi. Lyra Sterling speaking.'

'Hello, Ms Sterling. It's Debbie Harding here, from Skye's school.'

Lyra squeezed her eyes tightly shut. 'Oh hi. I was just about to ring you,' she lied. 'I'm sorry but Skye won't be in school for a couple of days.'

'Oh? Is she ill?'

'No. Not exactly. Well, not at all, actually.'

'So why isn't she in school?'

Lyra swallowed. 'Erm. We had . . .' She paused as she tried to think of an explanation.

'You do know, Ms Sterling, that we look very unfavourably on holidays taken in term time. That kind of unauthorised absence—'

'Oh, no. That's not it,' Lyra interrupted. 'We've had a family emergency, with Skye's great-grandmother. We had to leave Manchester in a bit of a hurry.'

'I'm sorry to hear that,' said Debbie Harding, sounding anything but. 'Is she seriously unwell?'

The clear implication was that Agatha must be about to die and that only this would justify Skye's absence.

'No. Well, yes.'

'Which is it?' asked Ms Harding.

God, this was like a police interview. Lyra wanted to scream that it was none of her business.

'She has been unwell,' she said vaguely. 'So, Skye won't be back in school this week.'

'I see,' said Ms Harding brusquely. 'As I say, we take a dim view of unauthorised absences. We have the right to fine the parents if the student is out of school for longer than five days.'

'She won't be,' replied Lyra quickly. 'It's just this week. She'll be back after the holidays.'

Lyra had no idea if this was true but she said it anyway. The silence at the other end of the phone reverberated with judgemental overtones. She thinks I'm trying to add a couple of days on to the holiday, Lyra realised.

'We're not going away, or anything,' she blurted. 'We're just at my grandmother's in Yorkshire.'

'I thought you said it was Skye's grandmother.'

'Well, she's here too.' Lyra could feel her temper beginning to fray. 'Look, I'm not doing anything wrong here,' she snapped. 'I'm sorry I forgot to ring but we are genuinely with my family in Yorkshire. We'll be back after Easter.'

And then she killed the call.

Lyra flopped back against the headboard. Why had she run away from Manchester? What had she been thinking? And she'd

41

trashed the flat. She'd made them homeless with her ridiculous impetuosity. None of it was the behaviour of a responsible parent.

She knelt up and looked out across the garden towards the wood. You could see the cottage from here, well, part of it at least. That place would be perfect for them. A little tingle of excitement fizzed in the pit of her stomach. She could do it up so it was super-cute. Mum and Dad would help her, she was sure. And then she and Skye could live there, just the two of them on their own, but with Mum and Granny on the doorstep. That would get rid of her babysitting issues too. There would always be someone around to keep an eye on Skye, which would make her life considerably easier.

And she could work there as easily as anywhere once she got wi-fi installed. She pictured herself at the kitchen table with a steaming cup of coffee and her laptop. The walls would be freshly painted, the sparkling windows letting golden sunbeams trail across the newly laid floor. She could probably tart up those ancient cupboards too, brighten the whole room. She pictured lush green plants trailing and open shelving with hand-painted mugs and those glass storage jars with the cork stoppers. The cottage was so tiny that it wouldn't take her long to lick it all into shape. Dad would probably lend her some cash. He was always so relaxed about money. And Granny had said she would get her a new bed to replace the one she was currently kneeling on. Surely she wouldn't mind if the bed ended up in the cottage rather than in the main house.

Suddenly the fractious call with the school felt unimportant. Lyra would ask Granny about moving in today. She had meant to do it the day before, but then her dad had arrived for dinner and the opportunity had slipped away. They might even be able to start on the decorating that weekend. How hard was it to throw some paint at the walls? They could whitewash the whole place, a perfect backdrop for her vision. Half an hour in B&Q and she'd be set up with everything she needed.

She was aware that the idea was running away with her, but she let her excitement take hold rather than reining herself back in. After all, it was pretty much a given that it would happen. What reason could Granny possibly have to say no to her proposal?

Skye appeared in view then. She was turning cartwheels on the lawn, or trying to. She hadn't quite got her body position right so whilst her arms were straight, she was bent at the waist making the move look comical, like a little spider in a ball. Lyra knocked on the window and Skye looked up, scanned the windows to locate where the sound was coming from and then grinned at her.

'Watch, Mummy!' she shouted, her voice sounding thin because of the glass between them. She performed a few more of her funny little cartwheels, ending up in a heap on the grass. She fell backwards with her legs in the air, laughing at herself, which made Lyra laugh too. Whatever she'd messed up in her life, Skye was one thing she had definitely got right, so far at least.

Maybe she could home school her daughter and then they would never need to leave the sanctuary of Fox House. The idea appealed to Lyra more in concept than reality, but she could give it some thought. Skye was only five. How hard could it be at that age? A bit of reading and maths and some crafting. That would surely cover it.

The cottage. That was the key to the whole thing. If they could live there then it wouldn't feel like Lyra had simply moved back in with her mother (and her grandmother) when the going got tough. There would be more of a purpose to being there, even if that purpose hadn't been in her mind when she'd fled from her destroyed flat. This way, she could make it seem to anyone who asked that moving here had been the idea all along.

Yes, it would be great to move in with the sense of a grand plan supporting her. Lyra was tired of making excuses for herself. She'd started when she fell pregnant with Skye in the second year of her graphic design course at university and she'd been doing it ever since.

'It doesn't matter that I got pregnant accidentally, because I still managed to finish my course and look! Now I have a degree *and* a perfect daughter.'

'It doesn't matter that I couldn't follow my dreams of going to London. I can work anywhere with just my laptop. Just look at the freedom that gives me.'

'It doesn't matter that I have had to turn my back on pretty much everything a twenty-five-year-old enjoys doing because I have more important priorities than them.'

But all that was about to change. The cottage was her future. It was going to be the start of something new, something fresh and irresistible.

She bounced down from the bed, which creaked beneath her weight ominously, and went off in search of Agatha.

10

Before Lyra could locate Agatha, Skye was at her side and tugging urgently at her sleeve.

'Mummy, there's a man in the garden.'

Immediately Lyra's panicked mind raced to her landlord or Rafe – but no. If it were either of those two lurking in the garden, Skye would have referred to them by name. Rafe was her father, after all.

'What kind of man?' asked Lyra.

Skye shrugged. 'Just a man.'

'It's probably the gardener,' said Lyra, but Skye shook her head emphatically.

'It's not the gardener. It's a stranger.'

Lyra took Skye's soft little hand in hers and gave it a reassuring squeeze.

'Well, let's go and find out what he wants, shall we?' she said. 'We can't have randomers wandering around, can we? Show me where he is.'

As Skye led her out through the back door, it occurred to Lyra that perhaps Skye should stay safely in the house, but she dismissed the idea at once. Whoever he was, the man was unlikely to be dangerous. He was probably a hiker who had taken a wrong turn and ended up on private property by accident.

When they got outside, however, it appeared he had wandered off of his own accord. The garden was refreshingly free of strange men.

'There,' she said to Skye, running a hand across her tousled hair. 'Whoever it was, he's not here now.'

But Skye was pointing through the trees towards the cottage.

'He's there,' she said, cowering behind Lyra's legs and pointing with a wavering finger.

And she was right. There was a man there and he wasn't lost. He had the air of someone who knew exactly where he was, and why. Well, Lyra would find out what that was. She bent down and put her arm around Skye's shoulder.

'You go back inside, sweetie, and I'll see what he wants,' she said.

Skye seemed to hesitate, so Lyra gave her a gentle push in the direction of the house.

'Go on. I won't be long.'

Reluctantly, Skye did as she was told.

Lyra stood for a moment watching the stranger, who was clearly oblivious to her presence. He was peering in through the cottage windows, his forehead on the glass and one hand making a shield to block the light from his eyes.

What the hell was he doing? Righteous indignation flooded through Lyra and propelled her towards him.

'Excuse me,' she called out, but she was still quite a long way away and he didn't appear to hear her. She strode across the grass towards him, arms folded across her chest. 'Excuse me,' she tried again as she got closer, 'but what do you think you're doing? This is private property. You need to leave.'

The man heard her then and turned in her direction. She was still on the lawn and there was a fence and several trees between them. If she needed to, Lyra reckoned she could make it back to the house before he could catch her.

He didn't look like he was a threat, however. His body language suggested curiosity towards her rather than aggression and his face was gentle, quite attractive in fact, for an older man. He must have been about the same age as her dad, maybe a little older. It was hard to tell. He certainly looked more careworn than Justin. His clothes were clean but shabby, and his hair needed a cut.

But it didn't matter how benign he looked. He was in their garden where he had no right to be and was peering through the windows of what was about to be her home.

Lyra got up to the fence, instinctively feeling like she wanted to keep a barrier between them.

'Did you hear me?' she said in as forthright a tone as she could muster. 'You need to leave.'

He nodded and pulled away from the window, but he didn't make any moves to go.

'Are you the granddaughter?' he asked.

The question threw her off balance. How did he know that? She replied with one of her own.

'Who are you?' she asked.

'Dylan,' he said. 'I'm Dylan,' as if that was all the explanation required.

'And you know my grandmother?'

'Kind of. More know *of* her.'

His obtuseness was irritating, and was there an element of menace creeping into his voice or was Lyra imagining that?

'Well, that still doesn't give you the right to go wandering around private property without permission,' she said spikily.

'Well, you see, that's where you've not got your facts quite straight,' he replied.

47

There was something about his attitude that Lyra found unsettling. Where was this confidence coming from? He was in the wrong here so why did she feel that he thought otherwise?

He took a couple of steps over to the cottage's front door and tried the handle. It was locked, but his audacity was breathtaking.

'What are you doing?! You can't go in there. You need to leave. Now.'

Lyra's voice sounded higher than usual, part outrage, part fear. The man was bigger than her and no doubt stronger. How fast could he move? she wondered. Not as fast as she could, she reckoned, but she had no way of knowing for sure. She could feel her heartbeat starting to speed up, ready for fight or flight.

The man turned so that he was facing her, a stand-off of sorts. Everything about him was casual and relaxed and in total contrast to the jitteriness that had taken hold of Lyra.

'This is my cottage now. Or it will be soon,' he said. His tone was defiant and he stared straight at her, challenging her to deny the truth of what he'd said. 'Which is no more than I deserve.'

'Don't be ridiculous,' snapped Lyra. She was feeling less sure of her ground with every passing moment but she knew that this had to be wrong. 'That cottage has been in my family for generations. It's not for sale. It never has been. You have got your wires crossed somewhere along the line.'

The man raised a shoulder insouciantly, as if he had no interest whatsoever in what Lyra thought.

'You ask her,' he said. 'See what she says.'

Was he talking about her grandmother? If so, what gave him the right to be so disrespectful? Anyone who knew Agatha would refer to her by her name. Her natural authority commanded it. Why was this stranger any different and what gave him the right to talk about Agatha with such familiarity?

'I will!'

Lyra knew she sounded petulant and very young but what was she supposed to do? The man was clearly deluded. Was he actually dangerous? She'd hoped that Skye would have fetched her mother or even Agatha herself, but no one appeared. Lyra was on her own with him.

She was about to ask him to leave for a fourth time when he broke eye contact and began to saunter towards the gate that led from the wood to the garden.

'I'll go now,' he said. 'This can wait for another day. But you give the old woman a message from me. Just tell her Dylan called by.'

He was on the lawn now, strolling towards the drive without a care in the world.

'See you again,' he called over his shoulder, raising an arm in salute.

Lyra watched him go, her head a torrent of questions.

11

Lyra turned on her heel and ran back towards the house, almost colliding with Skye by the back door.

'Who was that, Mummy?' she asked. 'Has he gone now?'

Lyra needed to speak to Agatha at once, but she made herself slow down to reassure her daughter.

'I don't know who he was, sweetie, but he's left.'

'Will he come back?'

Wasn't that the sixty-million-dollar question?

'I don't think so,' replied Lyra, the lie tripping off her tongue before her head had caught up. 'He was just lost.'

Skye accepted this and headed back to the lawn as Lyra sped off in the opposite direction.

Her grandmother was in the sitting room with her mother. Eve had a reporter's notebook in one hand and a stubby pencil in the other, intent on making a shopping list. Lyra noticed that there were little sketches of each item to be bought down the side of the page. They both looked up when she burst in.

'Lyra, what's the matter?' Eve asked, sounding concerned. 'Has something happened? Are you all right?'

Lyra steadied herself. Her grandmother didn't tolerate hysteria of any kind.

'There was a man in the garden just now,' she said as calmly as she could. 'He was trying to get into the cottage.'

Eve stood up and took the few short steps to the window, although you couldn't see the cottage from there.

'Is he still there? Was it a peeping Tom, maybe? Shall I call the police?'

'Like a stalker? No. That wasn't it. He's gone now anyway, but he seemed to know you, Granny. He said his name was Dylan.' Lyra scanned Agatha's face, hoping to see something that would suggest the stranger was a lunatic and that nothing he said should be taken seriously. But Agatha's expression was inscrutable. She barely even blinked. It didn't look as if the information had come as a surprise, however.

'Is he a local?' asked Eve. 'Someone from the village?'

Agatha ignored her questions.

Lyra pressed on. 'He said the cottage is his, or soon would be. He said I should ask you about it. But that's crap, isn't it, Granny? Actually, I was going to ask you today if Skye and I could move in . . .'

Her sentence drifted to a stop. She had prepared her request about the cottage so thoughtfully, carefully judging each word so that her grandmother would see the sense in her plan and be guided towards the correct response. But now she had just blurted it out without addressing any of the clever arguments that made the plan a winner. She had no choice, though. In the light of this new and incomprehensible information, it was suddenly vital that Agatha knew of her proposal before the situation slipped any further from her grasp. After all, why would she give the cottage to a total stranger when her own granddaughter and great-granddaughter wanted to live there?

Agatha focused her attention on the over-stacked bookcase. Her eyes were perfectly still and her face gave nothing away. Lyra's chest tightened. The cottage plan was barely twenty-four hours old, yet in her head it had already become the perfect solution to all her problems. She couldn't have it snatched from her before it barely had time to breathe on its own. And by a stranger.

Experience told her, however, that if she tried to push her grandmother faster than she wanted to move then it wouldn't end well. Agatha had a habit of swinging from one extreme to the other if matters didn't appear to be going the way she wanted. Eve called it the 'Cancelling Christmas' effect, where one minor mishap could result in the collapse of an entire plan. So Lyra bit her tongue and waited.

Eve spoke next. 'He said what, Lyra? That the cottage is his? Well, he's clearly a sandwich short of a picnic.'

Lyra winced at her mother's old-fashioned expression but she had to agree with the sentiment. The man was clearly mentally unstable in some way, or at the very least mistaken.

'Yes,' she confirmed. 'He said his name was Dylan, that he knew you, Granny, and that you'd given him the cottage.'

Agatha pushed herself to her feet and, grasping the fox head walking cane, moved slowly towards the window.

When she reached it she stared out, not seeming to focus on any one point.

'Yes,' she said eventually.

'Yes what?' asked Eve, her exasperation plain.

'Yes. That's all true.'

There was a brief hiatus, a moment's silence as Lyra and Eve took this in, and then they both spoke at once.

'But you can't?' said Lyra.

'What do you mean, you promised our cottage to a total stranger?' said Eve.

Agatha ran her fingers over the fox head carving, stroking it as if it could respond to her touch.

'He's not a total stranger,' she said. 'Not to you, at least, Eve.'

Lyra's gaze shot to her mother's face. Was her mother part of this terrible conspiracy which was about to rob her and Skye of their perfect home? But Eve looked as confused as she was.

'I don't know anyone called Dylan,' she said. 'And definitely no one we know well enough to just give a huge part of the estate to.'

Agatha threw her a chilling stare.

'Estate is it, now?' she said coldly. 'You'd do well to remember that Fox House and its estate, as you call it, is mine. It belonged to my mother, and her mother before her and now it belongs to me. I can do with it exactly as I choose.'

Lyra watched her mother retreat from the fight and change tack. Lyra's instinct was to go back in fighting but she made herself hold back and let Eve take the lead. Eve had decades more experience of dealing with Agatha than Lyra had.

'Of course you can,' Eve replied in a remarkably conciliatory tone, given what Agatha had just proposed. 'But I'm just wondering why you would want to. I'm afraid I have no memory of this man Dylan, so you're going to have to help me out on who he is and where he fits.'

'I will have to do no such thing,' snapped Agatha. 'This is my business. It's nothing to do with you.'

Lyra opened her mouth to object, but Eve waved a hand at her to close her down.

'But you must see,' Eve continued, her tone calm, 'that whatever you decide to do with the cottage will affect all of us. Of course it's up to you what you do with your own property, but think about the consequences. You've always said that Fox House is special because it's been passed down the female line. Why would you want to break that tradition when there are three generations of women below you?'

Agatha seemed to be struggling to meet anyone's eyes. Her gaze made its way around the room and then landed once again on the garden.

The silence was stifling, filling the room with its malignancy. Lyra could hardly breathe. This couldn't be happening. She had only just created the solution to all her problems and it had been brilliant. And now it appeared to be gone, just like that.

And on an inexplicable whim of her grandmother's.

'That's as may be,' said Agatha without turning from the window. 'But I have decided. Dylan will have the cottage and that's an end to it.'

And then Agatha brought her walking cane down on the uneven wooden floorboards hard. The crack, sharp and loud like gunfire, made Lyra jump, and the shock brought hot tears to her eyes.

'But Granny . . .' she began.

Her mother placed a hand on her arm firmly and gave a single shake of her head.

They let Agatha stalk away.

12

Lyra stared at her mother open-mouthed. The tears, kickstarted by the crack of her grandmother's cane on the floor, now trickled down her cheeks. She wiped them away aggressively with the back of her hand.

'What the fuck just happened?' she asked, ignoring her mother's grimace at the expletive. 'Has she lost her mind? Is it dementia or something? She can't just give away the cottage to a total stranger. It's ludicrous. Do you think we need to get her checked out by a doctor? Could she be ill? Or maybe he's forcing her to do it? You hear about that, old people getting ripped off by conmen.'

Her mind was racing, searching for a solution, but she could tell from the expression on her mother's face that she needed to slow down and take stock. She made a gargantuan effort to stop talking, adding one last and rather feeble, 'What do you think?' to the end of her diatribe.

Eve shook her head slowly.

'I have no idea,' she said. 'But whatever's going on, we will get to the bottom of it. I know your grandmother can be capricious if the mood takes her, but this is different. She loves Fox House. She's never lived anywhere else. She was born in the bedroom she sleeps in now, you know. So if she really is giving part of it away to this Dylan character then there's going to be a bloody good reason for it.'

'Yes, but what?'

They were going round in circles.

'Who is he anyway?' Lyra asked. 'Granny said you know him.'

Eve shook her head, frowning in her confusion. 'I know, but I can't think how. It's not ringing any bells with me. How old was he, would you say?'

'Around your age, maybe? Definitely not any younger and I don't think he'd be much older. I'm not great at guessing old people's ages though.'

Her mother pulled a face at the implication of her comment, but let it go.

'I've no idea who he could be,' she said. 'What was he like? Did you speak to him?'

Lyra tried to remember their conversation exactly but already the details were slipping away. It must be the shock. She did remember his attitude, however.

'He was very relaxed when I told him he should leave,' she said. 'Said he knew Granny and that she'd given him the cottage. He seemed pretty sure of his ground. I didn't like him.'

'What did he look like?'

'Nothing special. Brown hair. Thinning a bit. About Dad's height, maybe a bit taller. He looked scruffy, like he didn't have much money.'

Lyra looked at her own choice of outfit that day, which might also suggest an impoverished life to a stranger. But hers was a style decision, not something she did from necessity, and somehow she could always tell the difference. The man she'd met had been trying to do his best with not much.

'And there was something else as well,' she added as the idea came into her mind. 'It's a bit vague, more like a feeling than anything I could put my finger on. But he seemed bitter, you know, like he had a right to the cottage or something and it had been taken away from him. I don't know. He didn't actually say anything like that. It was just the impression I got. And I don't think he likes Granny that much.'

'That's a bit rich if she's giving him a house.'

'I know, right.'

Eve walked over to the sofa and slumped down in it. Dust puffed up into the air as she hit the cushions. She blew out her lips in a long sigh.

'What on earth is she up to?' she said, more to herself than to Lyra.

They sat in silence for a few moments whilst the shrapnel from the recent explosion settled around them.

'We'll never get it out of her if she doesn't want to tell us,' Eve added. 'She can be as stubborn as a mule. And the house is in her name. She's right when she says she can do as she pleases with it.'

'Unless we can prove . . .'

'That she's got a screw loose? There's no hope of that. She's as sharp as a razor. No. We'll just have to let things play out and see what happens. I'll try and talk to her, see if I can't get her to be a little bit more forthcoming.'

Lyra didn't have time for that. She needed a new life plan NOW. Her phone was full of increasingly irate messages from Rafe and Mr Patel, and far more concerned ones from her friends. She couldn't ignore them all indefinitely. The cottage and the freedom it represented for her would have been perfect. It was perfect.

'What if I spoke to her?' she said. 'No offence, Mum, but Granny seems to like me and Skye more than you. She might listen to me.'

'Ouch!' replied her mother, but she was smiling.

'You know what I mean,' continued Lyra. 'Things can be a bit' – she paused, searching for the right word – 'intense between the two of you. But there's none of that with her and me. I could see if she'd tell me a bit more, something that might help it make sense. I'd be careful.'

Eve seemed to be considering this. Lyra wanted her to trust her. But she knew that the relationship between her mother and grandmother was balanced on such a fine knife edge that the wrong word from either of them could easily make the situation a whole lot worse. Although what any worse might look like, Lyra couldn't imagine.

And then suddenly she could. What if Agatha wanted them all to move out? Where would that leave her? Right up shit creek, that was where.

Her mother was shaking her head.

'Thanks, Lyra, but I think it would be best if I handle this. I'll talk to Agatha when things have calmed down a bit. She owes us an explanation and I think she'll see that. I'll just have to pick my moment carefully. But don't worry.' She gave Lyra a warm smile that made the tiny lines around her eyes crinkle. 'We'll sort it out.'

Lyra tried her best to match her mother's smile, but she was aware that something about her own was lacking. It was all very well promising to fix this but when would that be? And would it be soon enough?

13

February 1952

There was always someone crying in Fox House. Usually it was her mother, whose gentle sobs seemed to seep out of the walls no matter where Agatha went to escape them. Or sometimes it was the hot angry tears of the housemaid who often caught the sharp end of her father's tongue and occasionally the sharper end of whatever he had in his hand as well. And sometimes it was Agatha herself, although no one ever took much notice and so Agatha had decided a long time ago that her crying served very little purpose and consequently tried to refrain.

Today, however, the daily tears seemed to be different from usual because no one was attempting to hide them. Her mother, the housemaid Elsie and the cook Mrs Banners were all standing in a circle in the hall and crying together.

Agatha shuffled a little closer to the banister and peered through the gap to get a better look, but apart from the three crying women she could see no other clue to tell her what had happened.

Perhaps her father had died. She suppressed a little smile. Agatha knew that the glee that passed through her at that thought was very wrong, but she still let the fantasy dance around in her head for a moment or two. Who would know, after all? They couldn't read her thoughts. Thank goodness.

She strained to hear what the women below her were saying. It did appear that *someone* had died, although it was unlikely to be her father. Surely they would have come and told her of that happy event.

'It's just such a shock,' Mrs Banners was saying. 'To just up and go in your sleep like that.'

'Yes.' This was her mother now. 'We knew he hadn't been well for a while but I never expected this.'

'That's how my gran passed,' sniffed Elsie. 'We just woke up one morning and she was dead as a dodo and stiff as a board.'

Agatha stifled a giggle. She pictured Elsie's gran, ironing-board rigid in curlers and a housecoat, and stuffed her fist in her mouth so no squeaks could escape. She didn't want them to discover she was here, just a few feet above them. Not until she had worked out what had happened.

'Me mam said it were a blessing, though. To pass in your sleep,' Elsie added and the other two murmured their agreement.

'And now that poor girl. All that responsibility thrust upon her and her so young too.'

'Isn't she abroad with Prince Philip? They'll have to come back now, I suppose,' Mrs Banners said.

'Yes. She's Queen. Just like that.'

Oh. The light dawned for Agatha. The King must have died and so Princess Elizabeth was going to be Queen. Was that all?

Agatha would like to be a queen, or a princess at the very least. She would live in a grand palace and wear beautiful silk dresses even for playing out, and have servants at her beck and call, and anything she wanted to eat. She would bet princesses didn't have rationing. She would make sure she had lots of brothers and sisters too, mainly sisters of course, so there would always be plenty of other children to play with. Like in Queen Victoria's household. Didn't she have nine? That would do very nicely.

Sometimes she wondered how different her life might have been if her brothers were still at home. Of course, they would be much, much older than her. They had gone to fight in the war so she knew they were grown-ups. Her mother didn't like to talk about the twins, but Agatha had pieced together various clues and worked out that they were born in 1923 so they would have been twenty-nine by now; twenty years older than her. Not really playmate material but at least them being at Fox House would have given her someone to talk to, and her mother would have been less sad.

Agatha turned her attention back to the conversation in the hall beneath her but it seemed to be coming to an end. Her mother blew her nose delicately and then pushed her lace-trimmed hand-kerchief back into the sleeve of her dress. Mrs Banners dutifully took her lead.

'Now then, Elsie my girl, those rugs aren't going to beat them-selves. Did you get the chance to check the menus for next week, Mrs Ferrier?'

Her mother waved a hand airily. 'I'm sure they'll be fine. Just do as you think fit, Mrs Banners.'

Agatha's frustration rose. Why couldn't her mother just look at the menus? Left to her own devices, Mrs Banners served them liver and onions at least once a week and often twice. Agatha hated liver and her mother knew that. She also knew that her father would stand over Agatha until she had forced down every last mouthful. Her mother could put an end to it all just by reading the menus beforehand and refusing the liver.

But she wouldn't. Agatha's mother didn't do anything that would make Agatha's life better. It was almost as if she were against it on principle.

Agatha touched her forehead to check her temperature. This was her second day off school but in truth there was nothing wrong with her. She had made herself look flushed by standing on her head for ten minutes and then told her mother she felt peculiar. It had worked. It always worked. She could paint chickenpox on to her skin with her art set and her mother wouldn't question it. But it would be better if they didn't catch her out of bed.

She shuffled herself so that her back was against the wall and then stood up slowly. The women hadn't noticed anything. Her mother was heading back to the drawing room and Mrs Banners and Elsie to the kitchen. No one had thought to come upstairs and check on her, although Mrs Banners would bring her a cup of Bovril in a while, she didn't doubt.

Agatha crept back along the corridor. She would be snuggled under the blankets long before anyone bothered her. She had a new Enid Blyton book to lose herself in and the hours would fly by.

Hers was the second door on the left. The first door was the twins' bedroom. Agatha went in there from time to time, but only when her mother was out. There wasn't much to play with – some model aeroplanes which she didn't dare touch and a set of Arthur Ransome books that she'd read cover to cover several times over. There was also a little toy train set but that was in a box under one of the beds and something told Agatha that she wasn't supposed to touch that either.

Agatha liked her bedroom better in any event. It had a view over the garden and part of the wood. She could see Mr Wilson's cottage, too, and she liked to watch the smoke curling out of the chimney pot. The cottage looked like something out of a fairy tale, so much homelier than Fox House. Mr Wilson was kind and he always seemed to have time for her, something that was in short supply elsewhere. He would make her honey sandwiches and tell her adventures from his time in the merchant navy, long before he became their gardener. She loved his stories of faraway lands even if she didn't quite believe them.

She took off her dressing gown and slippers and climbed back into the bed, rearranging the blankets on top of her. Maybe she could go and see Mr Wilson later. She was getting a little tired of being ill anyway. Then she opened *The Ship of Adventure* and began to read. No doubt she would get to the end before anyone thought to disturb her.

14

The trouble with taking time off school, Agatha found, was that all the days just ran into one another. Now it was Saturday but there was very little to distinguish it from the days that had gone before, except that her father would be in the house instead of out of it.

Saturdays began with a leisurely breakfast, her father reading his newspaper held out in front of him, a wall of tiny words. Her mother would flick through a magazine, barely lingering on each page long enough to take in the pictures, let alone the articles. Agatha had looked at her mother's magazines before – *Vogue* and *Harper's Bazaar* – and found them to be impenetrably dull. The glossy pictures were the only part Agatha bothered with because there was no story, nothing to get lost in. She couldn't understand why her mother wasted her time on them when there were so many books to be read.

Given her parents' penchant for bringing reading material to the dining table, Agatha had tried it herself. She had sat in her place at the far end and balanced her copy of *The Lion, the Witch and the Wardrobe* against the marmalade pot, with her knife carefully positioned to prevent it from sliding down.

Even though she could sit at the table in her underwear and her parents wouldn't notice, the appearance of a book gained their attention in record time. Her father lowered his newspaper and glowered at her.

'We do not read at the dining table, Agatha,' he said, and Agatha had stared at him wide-eyed as he raised his newspaper and continued to do whatever it was he did with it if he was not reading.

'But Daddy . . .' she began in protest.

Her mother had raised a finger at her without lifting her eyes from her magazine, and waggled it slowly from side to side. And so Agatha had let the matter drop and sat there, meal after meal, in silence.

This was why she liked Mr Wilson so much. In contrast to her parents, who seemed to see her as an inconvenience, she was sure Mr Wilson loved her. When he saw her approaching as he was weeding a flower bed or cutting back a climbing rose, he would stop what he was doing and smile his crinkly smile.

'And who do we have here?' he would say, which made Agatha laugh because of course he knew exactly who she was.

'It's me, silly. Agatha,' she always replied.

'So it is. And how are we today?'

'Shipshape and Bristol fashion!' she would trill back, which meant that everything was in good order. Mr Wilson had taught her that. He was always teaching her things, from how to tie a knot that you could unfasten in a jiffy to the names of the birds that came to wash in the stone birdbath in the middle of the lawn.

Today, though, she was very far from being shipshape. She had done what she thought was some very pretty embroidery on a piece of red binca. She had taught herself some new stitches from a book borrowed from the library and was particularly proud of the lazy daisy stitch. It had been tricky to get the tension of the thread just right so that the petals formed the right loopy shape, and she had had to unpick her work several times before she'd been happy with it.

Then she had taken it to show her mother, who had been sitting at her writing desk in the drawing room. She wasn't doing anything, just staring out of the window. It seemed to Agatha as if she wasn't even looking at anything in particular.

'Mummy, look what I made,' Agatha said as she went in, holding her embroidery out for her mother to examine. She was hoping for appreciative 'Ooh's and possibly the odd, 'Aren't you clever?' but her mother only turned her head briefly, gave the work a cursory glance and then returned to her staring at nothing.

Agatha was disappointed with this initial reaction but determined to improve it.

'Look at the daisies, Mummy. I learned those myself. And the leaves are satin stitch.'

The leaves weren't her best work. She had had trouble getting the stitches just the right length to make the gentle curving shape, but that didn't matter. The main thing was to get her mother to see them.

'Very nice,' said her mother absently.

'But you haven't even looked,' snapped Agatha petulantly. 'You never look.'

'Don't be silly, Agatha. What can you mean? Of course I do.'

Her mother took the binca from Agatha's hand, let her eyes fly across it and then handed it back. 'There. I've looked. Now run along, and don't get into any trouble.'

Agatha wouldn't cry – not crying was a new challenge that she had set herself – but she could feel her bottom lip tremble and her eyes sting. She snatched the embroidery out of her mother's hand.

'You don't care about me,' she spat.

Answering back was most definitely not allowed, but Agatha knew that her mother wouldn't reprimand her for it unless she did it in front of someone else.

'Don't be such a goose. Of course I do,' said her mother, her brow lined in something that might have been concern, and Agatha thought she might even think she meant it. But it was obvious that she didn't. Not really.

She'd thrown the embroidery to the floor and rushed from the room. Slamming the door had been tempting, but her father and his belt were in earshot, so she resisted that urge and instead ran out into the garden where she found Mr Wilson pushing his wheelbarrow through to the compost heap in the wood.

He lowered the wheelbarrow as he saw her approaching.

'And who do we have here?' he asked in his customary fashion, but then his smile slipped. 'Is everything all right, Miss Agatha?'

'My mummy hates me,' she replied. She didn't really believe this, but she liked how dramatic it sounded.

'Now then, I'm sure that's not true,' he said kindly.

'It is! She never takes any notice of me. She doesn't care whether I'm here or not.' This part was most definitely true, Agatha was certain.

Mr Wilson sat himself down on a tree stump and removed his cap, resting it over his knee.

'Come and sit next to me,' he said and Agatha sat at his feet, twigs snapping and brown leaves rustling as she did. The ground was damp and cold but she didn't care. She hoped it left muddy marks on her dress. That would serve her mother right.

'Your mother does care. I'm sure of it. All mothers love their children. But your poor mother is sometimes a little sad and so she forgets herself.'

'She's sad about the twins dying,' sniffed Agatha. 'I know that. But that was ages ago, before I was born even. They're not here any more but it's like they are. And I AM here and it's like I'm invisible.'

'It's very hard for you. I know,' said Mr Wilson. 'But your mother is grieving. And your father too.'

'Well, I wish they'd stop. It's stupid. And it won't change anything. The twins aren't ever coming back.'

'No, that's true enough.'

They sat in silence for a moment. Agatha kicked at a fir cone with the toe of her shoe.

'I'll tell you what,' said Mr Wilson. 'How about we go inside and I'll make you a nice cup of tea. I'm due a break around now. And I might even be able to rustle up a slice of seed cake.'

He stood up from his stump, groaning a little and stretching his back. Then he held out a hand and Agatha took it. She didn't like seed cake much, but she liked being in the cosy cottage with its warm fire and all the strange and interesting things that Mr Wilson had brought back from his travels. She smiled up at him and then she began to tell him how to do lazy daisy stitch.

15

NOW

What on earth was her mother up to? Agatha had always been a mystery to most people, and particularly Eve, but giving the cottage to a stranger was pretty left-field, even for her.

Eve couldn't think of a single reason why she might want to do that. And Lord knew she'd tried. She'd thought of little else since her mother had dropped this particular bombshell, but she couldn't make any sense of it. And she still had no idea who this Dylan was. Despite Agatha insisting that she knew him, Eve couldn't remember ever having met anyone with that name.

The whole thing was a puzzle.

They needed to talk about it. However, conversations between them that went deeper than the quotidian mundanities of life had always been scarce and were now as rare as wasps at Christmas. Eve had always felt that somehow her relationship with her mother had got stuck when she was a girl and had never segued into her adulthood. Partly this was because she was wary of showing any vulnerability to Agatha for fear of it being dismissed as childish or weak. On top of that, any such conversations would have been too one-sided for Eve's taste. Whilst she didn't know much about sharing confidences, the clue had to be in the word 'share'. Agatha never shared anything about herself and so this had always discouraged Eve.

But this was a conversation they needed to have.

The first time she tried to raise it, her mother was in the kitchen making herself a cup of tea.

'Agatha,' Eve began tentatively, but her mother put up her hand, palm showing, and placed it squarely between them, a clear barrier to any discussion. One word was all she was to be permitted, it seemed, and Eve knew her mother well enough to not bother trying further at that moment.

On the second occasion, Agatha was in her favourite chair in the sun trap, a book of Florentine art on her lap and her face raised towards the light, like a sunflower. She opened her eyes as she heard Eve approach and then snapped them closed again, like shutters on a shop window. We are not open for business. Please try again later.

But when was later to be? Eve knew she would have to wait until her mother was ready, if she ever was.

Lyra was less patient. She prowled round the house, tutting and sighing loudly.

'Let me talk to her, Mum,' she offered. 'She might open up a bit more with me.'

Eve shook her head. She felt instinctively that this, whatever this would turn out to be, was a conversation that she needed to have with her mother herself. The proposal about the cottage was so out of character that Eve was almost fearful as to Agatha's reasoning. She didn't want Lyra stumbling into whatever it was.

And still Agatha put up barriers. No matter how many opportunities for her to explain that Eve tried to orchestrate, her mother simply refused to cooperate.

Unsettled by the atmosphere at Fox House, Eve drove herself to York under the pretence of picking up some groceries, but really she simply wanted to get out of the way. And, just as she had done for most of her adult life, she sought out Justin as her sounding board of choice.

The city centre was busy with tourists, the narrow streets bustling and the quirky little shops all full of people searching for something a little out of the ordinary to take home with them. She cut a purposeful path through the throngs, snaking her way over the River Foss to where Justin's design agency was situated. She assumed he would be there, and she wandered in as if she worked there herself.

The reception was a cavernous space clad in industrial-looking wood panelling and with huge glass baubles hanging from the ceiling. A marble chessboard, the pieces based on Greek mythology, sat on one of those eighties coffee tables that had a computer game installed into it. As ever, a chess game was in progress and it looked to Eve's untrained eye as if black (or in this case verdigris) was beating white (here gold) hands down.

Not touching the chessboard was a rule. There was always a game ongoing between Justin and his business partner, Rob, each taking their next move as they came in and out of the office. Sometimes they would sit at the table together to play and work through a decision that needed making about the business, maybe with a bottle or two and long into the night.

Each time Eve was in the agency she longed to switch the pieces around just because she knew it would annoy Justin and the naughtiness of it made her giggle, but part of the receptionist Jody's job was to ensure that no one went close enough to the board to sabotage the game.

'Is he in?' asked Eve.

Jody looked up from her screen and then, when she saw who it was, gave Eve a wide smile.

'Yeah. Just go through. He's got toothache again, though, so tread carefully.'

Justin was sitting at his desk and fumbling with a packet of painkillers. He looked up when he heard someone approach, irritation etched on his face, but he softened when he saw it was her.

'Is it bad?' she asked, not unsympathetically.

Justin grunted.

'You could just get it taken out.'

'But it's part of me,' he whined. 'And I'm not ready to say goodbye to it just yet.' He massaged his lower jaw gingerly.

'Well, you're not going to miraculously grow another. You should just get rid and be done with it.'

'Who asked you?' Justin's tone was spiky, but Eve let it bounce off her. Anyhow, he was right. If the state of Justin's teeth had ever been her problem it most definitely wasn't any longer.

'Listen, have you got ten minutes?' she said. 'Agatha's gone truly bonkers this time and I could do with someone to chat it through with.'

'I'm all ears,' Justin said, as he poked at the inside of his cheek with his tongue and then winced. 'It'll take my mind off how much my tooth hurts.'

So Eve explained what had happened so far and Justin listened, his expression growing more incredulous as she went on.

'And when she says "give him the cottage",' he asked, 'does she mean let him live there or actually transfer the title?'

Eve shrugged and raised her hands, palms upwards. 'Haven't got a clue. That's what she said and since then she's refused to talk about it so we're no wiser. From what Lyra gleaned when she spoke to him it sounds like he's expecting to own it outright.'

Justin leaned back in his chair and ran a hand through his hair, still thick and curly but now more grey than chestnut.

'Transferring the title would be complicated,' he said thoughtfully. 'I imagine there'll be no right of access to the cottage. She'd have to create one across the garden or build a new road through the wood, which would need planning permission, you'd assume. And then would he use the Fox House driveway? That might be a nuisance if he had a car, or a lot of people coming and going to the cottage.'

Justin drove her mad when he did this, homed in on the minutiae when it was the bigger picture that was the problem.

'I've no idea. I don't care,' she said. 'The important thing is *why* does she want to do any of it? I'm not being entitled or anything, Justin, but Agatha has always said how the house gets handed down from mother to daughter like it did for her. So I've always assumed I'll get it when she dies and then I'll pass it on to Lyra. But if she's giving chunks of it away . . .'

Justin pulled a sceptical face.

'You're making a lot of assumptions there,' he said. 'As Agatha has just shown us, she doesn't always do what's expected. And where does it say that you'll inherit Fox House?'

Irritating though it was of him to point this out, he was right. She'd never seen a will and even if she had, wills could be changed.

'That's just the way it's been in the past. And anyway, who else is there?'

'Well, there appears to be this Dylan character for a start.'

Eve sighed. Justin was being particularly unhelpful and she was almost regretting coming to talk to him about it. But then again, Justin never told her what she wanted to hear. It was annoying sometimes, but he refused to polish anything for her. He told her what he thought with all the ugly, knobbly parts on full display, which was part of why she asked him about things in the first place.

'What should I do?' she asked.

Justin rubbed his hand over his lower jaw as he thought about his response.

'Well, if Agatha won't tell you, maybe you need to ask Dylan,' he said.

16

There was only one problem with Justin's proposal. Eve had no idea who Dylan was or where she might find him. She rolled her eyes at him and shook her head slowly.

'Brilliant!' she said. 'Pure genius. And how am I going to find this stranger when I know nothing about him except that his name is Dylan?'

'Fair point,' replied Justin. He steepled his fingers and tapped them against his lips, something he always did when he was thinking. 'Maybe you'll just have to lie in wait until he returns to claim his cottage, and then you can pounce.'

Ridiculous though it sounded, this wasn't a bad idea. Dylan had appeared once. It was likely that he'd be back. Next time he might even knock on the door of Fox House instead of sneaking around unannounced. It wasn't his cottage yet, and there were rules about these things. Laws, in fact. That was what really grated for Eve, his audacity, the fact that he thought he could just come and go as he pleased. It crossed her mind that this was exactly what Justin did as well, but that was wholly different.

'It's the not knowing,' she said. 'It's so infuriating. If Agatha wasn't being so bloody' – she searched for the right adjective – 'so bloody Agatha-ish then she could just explain. But you know what she's like. She's enjoying being enigmatic. I know she is. She's got me on a hook and is watching me squirm.'

'So don't squirm,' replied Justin. 'You're playing straight into her hands by being so curious. Stop trying so hard to get it out of her and maybe she'll tell you of her own accord. It's such a habit with her, playing her cards close to her chest. Perhaps she's secretly dying to offload.'

This might be true, although history didn't suggest it. Her mother wasn't known for her tendency to share. But there was always a first time.

'Okay.'

Justin grinned at her, eyes mischievous.

'How about a little flutter on what the secret might be? Just between us. What do you reckon? Could he be blackmailing her for some past misdemeanour?'

Eve tightened her lips into a thin line and glared at him. 'Oh stop it! This is serious.'

He turned the corners of his mouth down and pulled a sombre face. 'Just a bit of harmless fun,' he said.

'Hmm.'

She wasn't really cross with him, but it suited her to pretend she was from time to time. People who saw them together couldn't always understand why they had divorced when they appeared to get along so well. But then they hadn't been in the marriage.

She changed the subject.

'Did you get a chance to talk to Lyra at all when you came round the other night?' she asked.

'Not especially. Just the usual chatter. Why?'

Eve screwed her nose up. 'I'm not sure. It's probably nothing but I think there's something she isn't telling us about why she left the flat.'

'There was a flood,' replied Justin. 'That's enough, isn't it?'

'I don't know. Something feels a bit off. Call it mother's intuition.'

Justin wrinkled his nose. He never liked it when she suggested that her parenting had something that his lacked.

'Well, my father's intuition is telling me that everything's fine,' he said pointedly. 'And now, if you've finished sharing your domestic hiccups with me, I have work to do.'

He was diminishing her problems on purpose now to wind her up and so she resisted the temptation to bite, even though the potential loss of the cottage was hardly a hiccup.

'Hope your tooth gets better,' she said instead, glossing her words with a fine coat of insincerity, but she grinned at him to show that she wasn't really being mean, and then she left.

As she crossed reception Jody's desk was empty and so, taking a quick look around her to make sure no one was watching, she bent over the chessboard and moved the verdigris bishop up and along a bit and then a gold pawn to somewhere nearer its queen. Ha!

She wandered slowly around town, stretching out the few errands she had to do. Justin was right. Agatha did like mystery and rarely gave anything away, but maybe that was because Eve had let that happen by never asking much – a self-fulfilling prophecy. It was like a game they played with one another, with Eve always trying to second-guess her mother's next move and then countering to take the heat out of it. In fact, it was very much like a game of chess. Or at least it was for Eve, always trying to stay on top of the board, never wanting to lose a strategic advantage. Perhaps Agatha was desperate to share.

Was Lyra behaving in the same way as her grandmother, closing down and not sharing what had really brought her to Fox House? Eve really hoped not. She had tried so hard to make sure that their mother/daughter relationship was richer, deeper, more meaningful than her own experience so that Lyra could tell her anything and not hold things inside. She supposed she would never know how successful she'd been in that.

Philip Larkin's poem 'This Be The Verse' came into her head, as it so often did. She could recite its three short stanzas off by heart and had been carrying a copy of it, a small square of paper now creased almost beyond legibility, around in her purse since Lyra was a baby. She had no idea what she might have got wrong with Lyra, she was just certain that there must be something. It was inevitable. But she hoped that she hadn't made as many mistakes as Agatha had done with her.

She didn't think Agatha had fucked her up as the poem suggested, not really, but she had always kept herself at a distance, as if someone had slipped a pane of glass between mother and daughter. Eve had often wondered if she did it on purpose, if there was something about Eve herself that Agatha found loathsome. As she aged, however, she had decided that was unnecessarily melodramatic, thoughts born of the inherent self-absorption of a teenager. Agatha did love her in her own way. Eve had to hold on to that.

It hadn't helped, she now supposed, that her father had died when she was eight. Her memories of him were sketchy at best, as if her brain had blotted him out. Had that been to protect her against the pain of grief? Eve had no idea, and she didn't really go in for cod psychology, but whatever the reason, she didn't remember much about him at all. Nor could she recall whether the distance between herself and Agatha had come after her father's death or whether it had always been there.

Not that it mattered. They were where they were with their relationship, but Eve really hoped that she had done a better job with Lyra. She mused on her daughter on the drive back to Fox House. Perhaps Justin was right and there was nothing untoward going on. After all, it wouldn't be the first time in her life that Eve had over-thought something.

Yet there had been the tears when Lyra thought she was alone, and then her vehement reaction to the news about the cottage. That had been odd as well, Eve thought. Lyra had only just come up with the idea of moving in. Agatha hadn't even agreed, so having to abandon the plan so quickly shouldn't have been an issue. But somehow Eve felt that it had been.

As she pulled her car into the driveway she resolved to speak more to Lyra and less to Agatha and see where that took her.

17

Lyra's head felt like it was going to explode. Her genius plan to move into the cottage had been sideswiped by her grandmother and now she didn't seem to be able to move beyond it. No matter how hard she thought, she couldn't come up with a solution to her problem that was half as neat as that.

The messages from Mr Patel were becoming increasingly irate. Apparently, flooding caused by the accidental leaving-on of a tap wasn't covered by his insurance. It was a good job he didn't know she'd done it on purpose, then.

Her erstwhile landlord was a small round man whose forehead was forever dotted with glistening beads of sweat. Lyra could picture him screaming his increasingly incandescent voice notes into his phone, his face growing puce from the effort. He would give up soon. It must be obvious he was flogging a dead horse. Even if he did get hold of Lyra, where did he think she would get the money to pay for the repairs? He had enough money. He would patch up the damage and then re-let the place to someone else at an increased rent. He might even be better off in the long run.

The messages from Rafe were more difficult to ignore. He was the reason for the flood, for her secret flight to Fox House. And she had to keep ghosting him until she had a plan in place, a watertight plan that he couldn't get his fancy lawyers to blow apart.

Anyway, that was all for another day. Today she had promised Skye that they would go to the zoo. Lyra wasn't sure what she was supposed to think about zoos. Cruel incarceration of animals or vital conservation and research work? It could fall either way, but the zoo would be there whether Lyra visited it or not. And it was the only way she and Skye would get to see a giraffe. On balance she thought she was in favour. For now, at least.

The school holidays were hard to cover by herself. Keeping Skye entertained during the day required some serious burning of candles from both ends as Lyra worked into the small hours to meet her deadlines, but it was a small price to pay. And given what Rafe was proposing, what choice did she have? She had to demonstrate that she could support them both in reasonable comfort. Another reason why moving into the cottage would have been so perfect.

Should she invite her mother to go to the zoo with them? Lyra tossed the idea back and forth. Eve would be delighted to be asked and would probably drive, which was handy as Lyra wasn't entirely convinced her car would get them there and back. And Eve might pay, too.

Lyra cancelled that last thought. She had money. She could stump up for an outing for her and her child. There was absolutely no need to sponge off her parents and she wouldn't do it. Yes, she was currently staying at Fox House rent-free, but that was only temporary and if she had the cottage she would definitely be offering her grandmother the market rate for the place.

But she wasn't going to get the cottage. She could feel it in her bones.

'Lyra!'

Her mother was calling her from downstairs.

'Rafe is on the phone.'

Lyra froze, pinned to the spot as if Rafe could actually see where she was hiding. She blinked rapidly as her mind raced. What was her mother on about? Her phone was right here in her hand and it hadn't rung.

'Lyra? Are you coming?' came her mother's voice again.

Shit. The landline. Her grandmother must be the only person on the planet to still have a landline with a registered number. Rafe must have guessed she'd be hiding here. It didn't take a genius to work that out. Where else could she have gone? She had counted on him being too busy to make the trip up from his home in London to see her straight away and so if she didn't answer her phone, she could cut off his means of communication for long enough to get a plan together. She hadn't reckoned on a landline.

Lyra was thinking fast as her heart hammered in her chest. She could refuse to speak to him but he would just keep ringing and her mother would want to know why she was avoiding him. And then it would all come out. She wasn't ready to share it with her parents yet. They would go into fixing mode and she didn't want that. This was her problem. She was going to fix it herself.

She sucked in a big breath and headed downstairs.

'Coming,' she called as she went.

The phone, on a very short cord attached to the wall, was in the hall. There was another one in the sitting room and a third in Granny's bedroom. Lyra thought that you could answer a call on any of them, but she had no idea how you did that, so she'd be forced to speak to Rafe in the hall and hope that she wasn't over-heard. How did they have any privacy in the old days?

Her mother was standing at the bottom of the stairs and held the receiver out to her as she approached.

'There you are,' she said. 'It's Rafe.'

'Thanks,' said Lyra, and took the phone from her. When her mother showed no signs of leaving, Lyra raised her eyebrows and cocked her head in the direction of the kitchen door. Eve took the hint and left, but Lyra still felt horribly exposed.

'What do you want?' she half whispered into the handset.

'What do I want? You've got a nerve, Lyra. I want to talk to you about our daughter's future, as well you know.'

'Well, I don't want to talk. I've said everything I have to say. As far as I'm concerned the subject is closed.'

There was a silence. Lyra could picture Rafe composing himself. Maybe Amina was there too, mouthing instructions at him, telling him to be more conciliatory.

'Listen,' he began, his tone gentler. 'I know this is hard, but we're just trying to do the right thing here.'

'So taking our daughter away from everything she knows. That's the right thing, is it?'

'It'll be tricky at first, for all of us. But Skye's a great kid. She'll adapt. And you have to agree that the opportunities are incredible.'

'There's nothing wrong with the opportunities she has here,' snapped Lyra.

'No home, no school, living in a rundown wreck of a house in the middle of nowhere with her grandmother and great-grandmother? Sure. She's tripping up over opportunities.'

'She's with me,' retaliated Lyra. 'I'm her mother. You must see that that's the most important thing.'

'And I'm her father. She has two parents, don't forget. And there's Amina too. She wants to be a mother to Skye. Not like you, obviously, but in her own way.'

Lyra's hackles rose and she pulled her hands into tight fists to stop herself screaming back at him. There was no way that condescending, sanctimonious, vacuous woman was going anywhere near Skye.

'You gave up the chance to call yourself her father when you abandoned us. As soon as we graduated, I didn't see you for dust.'

Lyra knew she wasn't being entirely fair, but she was being backed up against a wall here and being fair didn't feature in her thinking.

'We've talked about this, Ly.' Rafe's voice had slipped over into that patient tone he sometimes used with people he thought were being particularly obtuse. It made Lyra want to punch the wall. 'I had to go to London. That's where all the best jobs were.'

'Easy for you with your shiny first-class honours degree. Funny how my A levels were so much better than yours but I only scraped a third. I wonder why that might have been, Rafe. Possibly something to do with me doing most of the caring, maybe?'

'You can't hold the fact that I got a decent degree over me forever.'

'Can't I though,' muttered Lyra under her breath.

'Anyway, the point is that now I have the opportunity to take Skye with me, give her the best education, the best experiences. Surely you can see that that would be great for her right now, before she gets too deep in the British education system.'

'But I'm her mother!' repeated Lyra, spitting the words into the phone. 'It doesn't matter how amazing you try to make it sound. I will not agree to you taking my daughter halfway round the world to live with total strangers and away from everything she knows.'

'Amina and I are hardly strangers.'

Lyra scoffed down the phone but her palm was so slippery that she had to switch the receiver to her other hand.

'I could go to the courts, Lyra,' Rafe continued. 'I don't want to, but my barrister says we could persuade a judge that Skye should go with me.'

A vein started to pulse in Lyra's temple and she felt her jaw tighten.

'"Persuade a judge",' she repeated, hissing down the phone so that no one else could overhear her. 'Can't you see that that means it isn't the obvious thing to do? Taking a child from her mother for no reason. No judge is going to do that. I haven't done anything wrong. True, I don't have as much money as you – although whose fault is that? I couldn't get a fancy job when I had to spend most of my time at uni looking after our daughter. But not being rich doesn't make me a bad mother. And just because you can give her all these "opportunities" doesn't make that the right thing to do.'

Lyra slammed the phone down. Then she closed her eyes and tried to slow her breathing. She wasn't going to let him take Skye no matter how hard he tried.

When she opened her eyes Skye was tripping down the stairs, dressed and ready to go out.

'Are we going to the zoo now, Mummy?'

18

Lyra looked at her daughter standing on the stairs in her favourite dress, which was far too thin for March, a sequinned bolero jacket and a pair of pink sparkly tights. She had clearly had trouble with the tights and they bunched around her calves. She had attempted a ponytail in her hair. It sat slightly skew-whiff to one side of her head and the bits she'd missed hung in straggles around her face.

To Amina, Skye would no doubt look neglected, allowed to dress in such inappropriate clothing and without anyone to even brush her hair. But to Lyra this was her fiercely independent five-year-old who was radiating pride at getting herself ready for her outing without help.

Lyra's heart felt like it might burst with love for her.

'Wait!' Skye said and thundered back up the stairs to get whichever finishing touch to her outfit she'd forgotten.

Who the hell did Rafe think he was, Lyra thought, assuming that what he could give Skye was better than anything she could manage? He wasn't a terrible dad, though. Despite the anger and fear she was feeling at what he was proposing, Lyra had to admit that. Even though he'd moved to London, he had worked hard at keeping in touch with them and came to take Skye out on well-prepared and thoughtful trips most months. But California? It was unthinkable. America might be the land of opportunity but Skye had everything she needed right here.

A voice cut through her thoughts.

'What did Rafe want?'

Her mother was standing behind her, having crept up on her in that way mothers seemed able to do (despite not having yet mastered it herself).

Lyra wiped away any stray tears of frustration with the heel of her hand before she turned around.

'Nothing of any importance,' she said. 'He and Amina are going to work in California for a while. Some fancy job he's landed in Silicon Valley. I don't know much about it. Not interested. Anyway, he wants to see Skye before he goes.'

'That's nice,' replied Eve. 'It's good that he makes time for Skye, isn't it?'

Lyra curled her lip up.

'He's her dad,' she spat back.

'I know,' Eve replied quickly, flustered, and Lyra felt bad for taking her own feelings out on her mother but not bad enough to apologise.

Eve blundered on. 'It's just some fathers don't show any interest . . .' The sentence tailed off.

'How long is he going for?'

Lyra shrugged. 'Six months? A year? I don't know. I haven't taken much notice. But he can't just expect us to drop everything just because he has a timescale to work to.'

Eve tipped her head to one side and gave her *that* look, the one she deployed when she had something to say that she knew Lyra wouldn't want to hear.

'Well, it's not as if you're particularly busy,' she said. 'It can't be that difficult to make an arrangement. Not if he's leaving the country soon.'

Over my dead body, thought Lyra. What if he took Skye out and didn't bring her back, had a little case packed for her, went straight from Fox House to the airport? The thought made panic flood through her. To be fair, it wasn't the kind of stunt she'd expect from him, but could she take the risk? Who knew what he might do to get his own way? He was Skye's dad, after all. He had rights, although she wasn't sure what they were. He might have got Skye her first passport. He could have been planning this for months for all Lyra knew.

She checked herself. Rafe wouldn't just take Skye. That was the stuff of soap operas. But she'd rather not think about California or Rafe or any of it because at the very back of her mind was a tiny little nagging thought that he might actually be right.

Skye reappeared at the top of the stairs wearing her favourite bobble hat with the party dress, and Lyra's hand went instinctively to her pocket to find her phone and take a picture and capture the moment. Skye posed obligingly.

'Now then, my little munchkin,' she said, stuffing the phone back into the layers of clothing and turning her enthusiasm up to full. 'Don't you look gorgeous? I think the lions and tigers will think you're the prettiest little girl to ever visit them.'

'And the iguanas, Mummy. Don't forget them.'

Iguanas! Where on earth had she come across iguanas? Her daughter truly was the most amazing human on the planet.

'Yes. And the iguanas. Although I've heard that iguanas actually prefer stripes to sequins.'

Skye screwed her face up in a caricature of anger. 'Then they're very silly, aren't they, VeeVee?'

'Very silly indeed,' replied Eve with an indulgent smile. 'Do you think you might get a bit cold outside in that beautiful dress? Maybe your jeans would be warmer. And your boots. Shall we go and see what else we can find for you to wear? Something all the animals will like.' And then to Lyra, 'You're going to the zoo, right?'

Lyra nodded and in that split second made a decision. 'Do you want to come?'

Eve's face lit up, just as Lyra had known it would. 'Oh, I'd love to. If you don't mind me tagging along.'

'Not at all. That would be great, wouldn't it, Skye, if VeeVee came with us?'

Skye grinned and punched the air gratifyingly. 'Yes!'

Eve took Skye back upstairs to rethink her outfit leaving Lyra standing alone with her thoughts. They were the kind of thoughts that chilled her to her marrow, the sort that crept over you in the night, their long spiny fingers finding a pathway direct to the centre of your heart. Could Rafe really take Skye, lawfully? He was her father, after all. Lyra believed that mothers' rights were stronger, but she'd only seen that in films. She had no idea if it was actually true. Maybe she needed to get some advice, proper legal advice. How did you go about getting yourself a lawyer? Lyra had no idea about that either. All this adulting was exhausting.

The sitting-room door opened and Agatha appeared. She was leaning heavily on her walking cane but other than that she looked amazing. Her porcelain skin was still tight across her cheekbones, translucent with just a hint of blush. And she always dressed so strikingly, today in a vibrant purple trouser suit with a flame-orange scarf at her neck.

This was the first time Lyra had seen her grandmother on her own since she had made her cottage announcement, and now they were face to face all Lyra's well-rehearsed arguments deserted her.

As she tried to gather her thoughts, her grandmother filled the silence.

'Is Rafe being tiresome?'

How much had her grandmother heard? How much did Lyra need to confess to? She tried to rerun the conversation in her head to see what she had given away, but it was too difficult to do in the moment.

'Yes,' she replied simply.

'Hmm,' said Agatha. 'I do sometimes wonder if that is what men do best. I'm told some women do find good ones. Your mother, for example. Although she didn't manage to hold on to him. Well, don't let Rafe do whatever it is unless you think it's the right thing to do. That would be my advice.'

Without waiting for a reply she set off towards the staircase, her cane tapping on the wooden floor.

'Actually, Granny . . .' Lyra called after her.

Agatha stopped and turned slowly on the spot.

'I was hoping to have a word with you about the cottage.'

Agatha's pale grey eyes were impassive, her expression giving nothing away, and Lyra felt colour coming into her cheeks.

Was this her moment? She wasn't sure. She would feel much happier having this conversation sitting down, preferably over a cup of tea. But Agatha was showing no signs of wanting to do that. Lyra decided to press on.

'I was hoping to ask you if Skye and I could move into the cottage. We'd pay rent, of course. And I could decorate the place for you. I was thinking we could relocate here permanently. I could get Skye into a school nearby. I can work from anywhere and it would be lovely for her to be near you and Mum. And for me too, of course . . .'

She was rambling, but the longer Agatha's silence ran on the more she felt the need to fill it.

'And I just thought, seeing as it's sitting there empty . . .'

Lyra finally ran out of steam and the sentence drifted to a stop.

Agatha was still giving nothing away. She seemed to be contemplating what Lyra had said. Lyra had to take that as a good sign. Maybe this plan to give the cottage to someone else wasn't as fixed as she'd suggested. Perhaps all was not lost.

'That's a lovely idea,' Agatha said, and Lyra's heart caught a little in excitement. She was going to agree. Thank God she'd asked. 'I can just picture the two of you in there. I'm sure you'd make it so very cosy.'

Lyra was grinning now. She couldn't help it. She would show Rafe. He might be moving to a fancy apartment in California, but she and Skye would have a cute cottage in a wood.

'However,' said Agatha, and Lyra's heart plummeted. 'As I said, I've promised the cottage to Dylan. So if you want to move in, you'll have to clear it with him. Although I do believe he intends to live there himself. I'm not sure he has any alternative.'

Lyra's frustration got the better of her. 'But why, Granny? Why are you giving it to a total stranger? It makes no sense. Fox House has been in your family forever. I don't understand why you'd split it up and portion it off like this.'

She sounded petulant and Agatha didn't respond well to petulance. But she couldn't help it. It just slipped out of her.

Agatha shifted her position, taking the weight off one hip and moving it across to the other.

'I am giving the cottage to Dylan because I owe him an enormous debt. I can never repay him fully, but giving him the cottage will go some way to fixing what needs to be fixed.'

And then she turned and tapped her way to the staircase.

The conversation was clearly over.

19

Eve thought that the trip to the zoo had been a great success. Skye had been delightful, racing from enclosure to enclosure with wide-eyed wonder. She had asked questions about the animals endlessly and Lyra had fielded with remarkable ease, although she'd had to resort to the information boards from time to time. Eve noticed how she always seemed to have time to answer Skye's questions, no matter how trivial or repetitive. Her patience appeared to be bottomless.

Eve reflected how Agatha had been so very different with her as a child. Her questions had so often been batted away as unimportant that eventually she had given up asking them. Sometimes she had seen an expression skitter across Agatha's face. It wasn't irritation exactly, more a kind of curiosity as to why Eve thought that Agatha might be the one to ask.

There was none of that with Lyra. She was Skye's one-woman encyclopaedia for whatever her daughter wanted to know. Justin had been much the same with Lyra. That would be where she had learned to do it, Eve thought now. Lyra surely hadn't picked it up from her.

'Which was your favourite animal?' she asked a tired Skye as they made their way back to the car park.

Skye, who was sandwiched between them with each of them holding a small hand, turned her face up to Eve and crinkled her forehead.

'I think . . .' she began. There was a pause as she considered the question. 'The bats.'

'The bats?' repeated Eve. 'Really?'

Eve didn't mind bats, but she would never have chosen them over the big-ticket animals.

'Yes!' replied Skye emphatically. 'I like their ears. And the way their bodies are kind of furry. And it's cool to live in the dark.'

Was it? Eve didn't agree, but that wasn't relevant. 'I always like the giraffes,' she said, although no one had asked her. 'They always look as if someone had fun putting them together.'

Just too late she realised that a comment like this might prompt a discussion about God which she wasn't really up for. She didn't know what Lyra had said to Skye about religion and she didn't want to upset any apple carts. However, Skye turned to her mother and started to chat to her instead.

As the car pulled out of the car park Eve thought about when Lyra had been small like Skye was now. Her memories were hazy. High days and holidays she had fixed in her mind, but the day-to-day reality of living with the five-year-old Lyra had all but gone.

How could that be? Lyra was her only child and had been the centre of her world for over two decades. And yet there were huge holes in her recollections. Where did that leave the memories she thought were secure? Were they genuine or just what her mind had concocted to fit the facts? She wanted to tell Lyra to try to preserve days like this, fix snapshots in her mind to anchor them there. Eve knew she had made many mistakes as a mother, not least taking things like memories for granted. She didn't want Lyra to do that too.

'Hold on to these precious days,' she said, as if she had voiced all her thoughts out loud. 'They'll be gone before you know it.'

Lyra turned in her seat, frowning. Her face said, 'Well, of course,' but she didn't speak.

Skye had fallen asleep, her ceaseless chatter silenced for a while, giving Eve the opportunity to talk to Lyra that she had been hoping for.

'When you were a baby,' Eve began, 'I thought that I had to do everything myself. I'd never had the kind of relationship with Agatha where I thought I could ask her for help. There was your dad, of course, but sometimes what I really wanted was an alternative point of view. Or even just someone to listen to me—'

Lyra cut across her, mid-flow. 'I'm fine, Mum,' she said.

The dismissal stung Eve like a slap across the face but she pressed on. 'I'm just saying that I'm here if you need me.'

Lyra said nothing.

The silence filled the car, heavy, accusatory. Lyra had spurned her offer of help. Eve could see what she was aiming for as a mother but had fallen short. That was the difference between herself and Agatha. She wasn't convinced that Agatha had ever seen the target.

Day trips like this one hadn't been a feature of her life with Agatha. They had argued about it once. It had been one of those rows that bubbled up out of nothing and then became a tsunami of held-back guilt and resentment. Eve had done well in some end-of-year exams and had come home to Fox House for the holidays delighted, clutching her results and ready to have praise heaped on her.

Agatha's response had been typically lukewarm.

'What do you want me to say?' she'd asked, when Eve's response had made it clear that she hadn't said enough.

'How about, "Well done, Eve"? Or "I'm so proud of you"?'

Agatha had appeared mystified.

'You're a bright girl, Eve,' she said. 'Am I supposed to praise you for your inherent abilities?'

'Yes!' Eve countered. 'That's exactly what you're supposed to do. But you never do. It's like you're not interested.'

'Of course I'm interested, but I don't see why you need me to shower you with approval for something that you should have done in any event. You're not a child, Eve.'

'But I am a child!' Eve had objected. 'I'm fourteen. And telling me how well I've done is exactly what you, as my mother, are supposed to do.'

Agatha looked flummoxed.

'Never mind. It can join the long list of mothery things you're no good at,' Eve had continued, her anger and frustration carrying her beyond where she should have gone. 'Like, why don't we ever go on holiday? Everyone else goes on holiday. We don't even go on weekend breaks. In fact, I can't remember you ever taking me anywhere.'

'That's just not true,' Agatha had countered. 'We went to Robin Hood's Bay.'

'Once, Agatha. We went once. Normal families do stuff together all the time. We just rattle round this house entertaining ourselves. It's weird. And there are no rules. All my friends have stuff they can't do or wear or say. With you there's nothing. No boundaries.'

'There are boundaries,' Agatha replied. 'But you never push up against them.'

'Oh, so you want me to behave badly. Is that what you're saying? That I'm not bad enough?'

'Now you're being ridiculous,' Agatha had said as she walked away from her. 'I'm not prepared to discuss this until you can put together a reasoned argument.'

And then she had left the room, leaving Eve frustrated and angry and confused as to why her mother was so different to everybody else's.

Eve had thought about encounters like this when Lyra was little and she'd tried hard not to let history repeat itself. Justin, whose family life had been something closer to 'normal', provided checks and balances. Each time she made a parenting decision that he considered odd he would tell her. Her 'Agatha moments', he called them, and they'd laughed about it most of the time, or argued if Eve was feeling vulnerable. Those moments had happened rarely, but often enough for Eve to wonder if she, like Agatha, was not a natural mother.

And now here she was, years later, being shut out by Lyra for reasons that she didn't understand. Maybe she, like Agatha, didn't have what it took to be the kind of mother she longed to be.

When they got back to Fox House it was dark and well beyond Skye's bedtime. Lyra scooped her up in her arms and took her upstairs. There was no sign of Agatha either and so Eve found herself on her own in the sitting room. She messaged Justin.

Hi. Been to the zoo today. No sign of the wolves.

Whenever they had taken Lyra to the zoo they had never seen the wolves. They were always inside their shelter out of sight. They had joked that there weren't actually any wolves at all, the enclosure put there simply to trick the visitors.

A message came straight back. Justin must be on his own as well.

You know those wolves are imaginary, right? Had fun?
Yes. Skye is gorgeous. Lyra's a bit quiet.
Is it still the cottage?

No idea.

Want me to talk to her?

A prickle of resentment spiked Eve but she tried to ignore it. It was a thing, wasn't it? Dads and daughters. Mothers and sons, that was the other cliché, but she didn't have a son, so it didn't seem fair.

Maybe. She won't talk to me.

Was that you on my chessboard?

????

I know it was.

You're ridiculous.

It pleased me.

I'll bet. Got to go.

Hot date?

Mind your own. I'll speak to Lyra.

OK. Thanks.

Justin disappeared, leaving Eve feeling more bereft than she had done before she started the conversation. It made it worse, knowing that he was off having fun and she was in on her own with only her immediate family for company. And even they were elsewhere.

She felt cross with herself for messaging him. When she was in this kind of mood, speaking to Justin never made her feel better and often made things worse. If she hadn't messaged him, for example, she wouldn't have known that he had a life whilst she was stuck caring for a mother who refused to be cared for. But it was too late now. The damage had been done.

She contemplated having a glass of wine, decided against it, changed her mind again. For God's sake, what was wrong with her? All of a sudden everything seemed to be coming untethered.

Wandering into the empty sitting room, she dropped onto the sofa and realised at once that she was sitting on something. A sharp corner dug into her thigh. She tipped herself over to one side and retrieved the book. But it wasn't a book. It was a photo album. Agatha must have been looking at it earlier and then forgot to put it away.

Eve smiled to herself. She loved looking at these old pictures. Lyra seemed to have thousands of photos of Skye but things had been very different when she was growing up. Film had been expensive and processing even more so. There were relatively few photos of her as a girl and so she remembered them all, even remembered many of them being taken, although that might have been her brain filling in gaps again.

She settled back on the sofa and opened the album on the first page, ready to be transported back in time. The album seemed to start in summer 1977, when she was seven. A holiday in Cornwall before her dad had died, back when they'd gone on holidays. A new bike. A fancy dress party. Not her party, of course. Agatha had always been too busy to arrange more than a birthday cake for her, and that would have been picked up in a hurry from a shop with only the outside chance of there being any accompanying candles.

This must have been another child from the village. Eve smiled at the homemade costumes, so unsophisticated by today's standards. She was dressed as a dice, the dots painted on a huge cardboard box in orange poster paint. She had made the whole thing herself. It hadn't been the most practical of costumes as it severely limited her movement, but she still remembered how proud she'd felt in it.

Her eyes scanned across the other outfits. A Womble, a bed-sheet ghost, Dennis the Menace. She had a vague recollection of the children who were wearing them, but they weren't people she had stayed in touch with. Here they all were though, grinning at the photographer, filled with the promise of lives yet unlived. Eve wondered idly how a copy of the picture had ended up in their album. The birthday child's mother must have made prints and distributed them with the thank you letters. A thoughtful gesture.

Agatha would never have done that. She wasn't that kind of mother. Eve would have been lucky to get a party at all.

There were barely any pictures of her father, which probably accounted in part for her sketchy memories of him. He must have been behind the camera most of the time. Maybe he had even been dead by then. Eve did a quick calculation and decided that he must still have been alive but not by long. His death had been so sudden. Heart attacks were so cruel. One day he had been there and the next she had no father and Agatha was a widow. And shortly after that she had been sent away to school, which would account for the dearth of photographs of her as a teenager.

She turned the page. There she was again, smiling through a wonky fringe in bell-bottomed jeans and a striped jumper that she'd worn to rags. In the next one she was with a boy of a similar age to her. He was taller, his limbs long and somehow out of proportion, as if the rest of him had to catch up. She was holding a fishing net and a bucket and they were both laughing, as if the camera had caught them in the middle of saying something funny.

Eve stared at the picture. She looked so young that it was almost impossible to find the woman she had become in the child's face. And who was the boy? They had obviously been close when the photo had been taken but somehow the intervening years had stolen him from her.

Agatha had always been methodical about her photos, recording who was in each one and the date it was taken. Eve teased the photo out of the sticky corners that held it in place and flipped it over to look at the writing on the reverse. There was a date. February 1979. It must have been taken days before her father's death, so not long before she went away to school. Then she looked at the names written in pencil in her mother's distinctive handwriting and her heartbeat seemed to falter.

Eve and Dylan – Fox House.

20

Eve stared at the words on the back of the photograph.

Eve and Dylan – Fox House.

She flipped the picture back over and studied the image again. It was just her and the boy, no other clues. There was nothing remarkable about him. Taller than her. Dark hair. More than that she couldn't say. The photo was small, his face barely bigger than her thumbnail. She found her reading glasses, looked again. It was no clearer. This was just a snap, not a portrait. Its lines were blurred and the colour faded, as if a vintage filter had been applied over the top.

Squinting at the tiny image, she tried to mine her memory to find something, anything, to build on. She recognised what she was wearing so at least it was certainly her in the picture and not a labelling mistake. And was there something about the boy flickering in the darkness of her recollection? Perhaps, but the flame was so very dim that it wasn't strong enough to see more by.

Frustrated by her own failings, Eve flicked forward through the pages of the album, searching for another photograph, one that could provide her with more clues, but this was the only one of the boy. Dylan. The man, Eve assumed, that her mother had gifted the cottage to.

She scooped the album up and almost ran up the stairs to her mother's room, bursting in without knocking.

The room had barely changed since her childhood, the same heavy between-the-wars furniture, the same swirling Persian rug on the floor. The curtains, a heavy ruby damask that the sun had faded to pink in patches, were drawn against the dark evening.

Agatha was sitting at the dressing table brushing her hair. She wore it in a chignon during the day but now it hung around her shoulders, silky and white. She didn't turn as Eve went in, watching her approach in the age-spotted mirror instead. She didn't seem surprised by Eve's intrusion and it crossed Eve's mind that she might have left the album out on purpose for her to stumble over: an aide memoire.

'Good evening,' Agatha said. 'Pleasant trip?'

For a moment Eve was thrown by the question. Her mind was entirely focused on her discovery and it took a moment for her to make the leap.

'The zoo? Yes. Lovely, thanks. Listen, I've just seen this photo. Is this Dylan? The one you're giving the cottage to?'

Eve opened the album at the page and thrust it towards Agatha, stabbing at the unfamiliar boy with her finger, but her mother gave it only a cursory glance.

'I should imagine so,' she replied vaguely.

'Is that why you said I knew him? Because I once saw him as a child?'

'Oh, it was more than once. You were great friends. I'm very surprised you can't remember him.' Agatha continued to pull the silver-backed hairbrush through her hair. It was as if they were talking about nothing more significant than the trip to the zoo.

'But I was eight,' replied Eve. 'I can barely remember anything from when I was eight.'

Agatha shrugged. 'Well, that's hardly my concern,' she said, but there was something about her posture that belied her words. Even from where she was standing, Eve could see how tensely Agatha was holding herself.

Eve wanted to say that of course it was her concern, that rarely had there been anything that was more her concern than the future of Fox House, but arguing with Agatha never got her anywhere. Agatha loved confrontation, thrived on it, and it was never a good idea to feed the fire.

That said, looking at her mother now Eve would have said that the last thing Agatha wanted was a fight. She looked frail and vulnerable and every one of her eighty years.

'Who is he, Mum?' Eve asked gently.

Agatha flinched slightly at the use of the forbidden word, but didn't object and continued to stare at her reflection, moving the silver brush through her hair like an automaton. She didn't speak.

Eve waited.

The silence ran on, filling every corner of the room.

Eve knew they were balancing on a precipice. Agatha could change direction without warning if she felt cornered, so she shouldn't try to rush her mother into an answer. She squeezed her lips together to stop herself asking her question again.

The silence was punctured only by the ticking of Agatha's alarm clock. It seemed astonishingly loud. Eve had never noticed how loud before, but then she almost never came into her mother's bedroom. She had not been allowed to enter as a girl, the room an inner sanctum. And those childhood rules still left her feeling adrift in here, as if even as an adult she didn't belong.

Still she waited. Maybe Agatha wasn't going to reply. Or not now, at least. Currently, her mother had all the power and she was usually reluctant to concede that without a bit of a game. She didn't seem powerful in that moment, though, or as if this were a game to her. For once, Agatha appeared to be lost. Eve almost felt sorry for her.

Then she remembered what Agatha was proposing and her determination to get to the truth redoubled inside her. Now she had something concrete to go on it could only be a matter of time. Her mother would weaken; the temptation to show her hand and bask in the reaction was often greater than the fun of keeping a secret. Eve just had to be patient.

But then Agatha replied and Eve, so busy with her internal strategy, almost missed it.

'Dylan is the son of a very good friend of mine,' she said.

Such a good friend that Eve had never heard her mother mention her before, let alone actually met her. Something about this didn't add up, and Eve was about to say so when Agatha continued.

'He helped me at a time when I very much needed help and for that I owe him greatly.'

The friend was a man? This was surprising and bore some exploring, but Eve knew this was not the moment to become distracted from the main issue.

'What did he do?' she pushed.

'That's not important. He helped me. That's all you need to know. Dylan will be coming to the house soon, to go through the details of the transfer. You can meet him again then. I'm sure he'll remember you better than you seem to recall him.'

Eve wanted details of this arrangement, when it would happen being chief amongst them, but there was no point asking. Agatha wouldn't tell her. For now, she would just have to accept what little she had been told.

'I'm tired,' Agatha said as she put down her brush. 'I think I'll go to bed. Close the door on your way out, would you.'

21

Agatha heard the bedroom door click shut and she slumped down over her dressing table, her spine losing all its strength as soon as she was no longer on parade. She had known that she wouldn't be able to just give the cottage away without eyebrows being raised, but she hadn't been quite prepared for the storm that was billowing on the horizon.

It didn't help that she had made the decision so quickly without giving herself time to think everything through. Dylan turning up on her doorstep had been a surprise, a shock even. He had come, ostensibly, with news of the death of his mother Mary, her erstwhile friend, although as Agatha had not seen Mary since the events of 1979 they could no longer have been described as close.

There had been a second, unspoken agenda to their meeting. Dylan had been too well mannered to express what he was looking for directly, but Agatha was astute enough to read his meaning loud and clear despite the lack of actual words.

A wrong had been done. It couldn't be undone, but moves could be made towards ameliorating the damage and she had caught his drift before he had needed to spell it out. What if she hadn't? she had wondered since. Would there have been accusations made, or even threats? She hoped not, and anyway the question was immaterial as she had offered him the cottage before things had reached that pitch. The gesture obviously wasn't enough to make up for what had happened, but it at least showed regret on her part.

The silver hairbrush shone in the dim light. Her mother had told her to give her hair one hundred strokes before bed to make it shine and here she was, decades later, still following her advice. It was the only thing she remembered her mother ever telling her to do. There had been no other guiding wisdoms for her to absorb, no maternal direction to help her life run its course more smoothly.

Henry had bought her the dressing table set on their first Christmas together. She believed, but did not know for sure, that he had also asked for her hand in marriage that holiday too. There had been no other explanation for the time spent behind closed doors with her father. She remembered the bolt of excitement she had felt, trying to guess what was being said, and then picturing her parents' joy when Henry proposed.

She ran her fingers over the horsehair bristles, feeling them soft against her skin, and despite it all she smiled. They had been so in love, she and Henry. Everything had felt possible in those early days. Neil Armstrong walked on the moon and Lulu won the Eurovision Song Contest. Even Henry's football team had won the league, an unheard-of achievement. There was the scent of opportunity in the air, as if anything were possible in this new age.

Agatha certainly felt this. With her parents having moved abroad after her marriage, there was nothing to remind her of the shortcomings of her childhood. All that lay ahead was the chance to do things differently, and when she fell pregnant with their first child it felt as if nothing could get in her way of creating her much-dreamed-of family.

They had lain in bed, Henry's heavy hand resting on her stomach to feel the baby kick beneath her nightdress, and talked about the future. Or she had talked, she realised now, and he had listened, often bemused by her plans but already knowing better than to object or question.

'This will just be the first of lots of babies,' she said, placing her hand over Henry's and giving it a little squeeze. 'There must always be children at Fox House. And not just ours but all their little friends too. This will be a place where children want to be, always something going on, lots of games and little plays being staged, music. Maybe we can build a swimming pool. Do you think that would be fun? Or they could swim in the pond if we clear the edges back a bit. We can have swings and a slide at the very least. We could build a little playground. Or a tree house! Wouldn't a tree house be wonderful?'

Henry had smiled at her indulgently, never contradicting her but never contributing to her vision, she had realised later.

'And cake. Children love cake, don't they? There was never enough cake when I was a girl. The war, I suppose. Rationing. And my mother . . . well, she never seemed to think I might like it. But there will be cake here now.'

'Can you bake?' Henry asked her doubtfully.

Agatha pulled a face. 'Not as such, but how hard can it be? All mothers can bake, can't they? It goes with the job. I expect I'll just pick it up once the baby is born. But the main thing is, Henry, that Fox House will be a proper family home and you and I will be at the heart of all of it.'

She had been so sure. First would come babies and then the rest of her dreams would just fall into place around them. It would be as natural as night follows day. She knew what it felt like to be left unloved, made to believe that you shouldn't be there, that you were superfluous. So she knew exactly what not to do when this baby was born. She would just do the exact opposite of what her own mother had done with her and that would make her the perfect mother.

It hadn't turned out to be quite as easy as that, though.

Not in the end.

22

When Agatha awoke the next day, none of it felt any easier. Giving the cottage away was proving to be harder than she had anticipated. Of course she had known that there would be some resistance to her proposal. It was only natural that Eve would be concerned, angry even. After all, it was part of her inheritance that Agatha was disposing of, and Lord knows, there wasn't much to give – only the house and what would be left of her savings.

She had half expected Eve to insist on a visit to a doctor to get her mental capacity checked out, and she wouldn't have blamed her daughter. Gifting property to a stranger without warning was exactly the kind of thing that an old lady losing her connection with reality might have done. At least Eve couldn't accuse Dylan of inveigling his way into her affections. She couldn't even remember him, and he had only been to the house twice in recent times. It was hardly the behaviour of a con artist.

Lyra's reaction she hadn't seen coming. Agatha wasn't quite sure what Lyra was doing at Fox House in the first place. There had been talk of a flood but anyone could see that that was just an excuse. Lyra was clearly running from something, or someone, which was entirely her own business. The timing, however, was unfortunate. How could Agatha have guessed that Lyra would want to settle with Skye in the cottage, something that hadn't ever been considered a few days before? Agatha's heart sank. She would have loved that. Her granddaughter and great-granddaughter both at Fox House – light and laughter, and something so much closer to the life she had hoped for than the one she'd managed to achieve.

But the request had come too late. By the time Lyra arrived seeking shelter, Agatha had already promised the cottage to Dylan. She couldn't go back on her word now. She owed Dylan so much. It was unthinkable to change her mind. And she daren't. She barely knew him and had no idea how he might react to such a betrayal.

No. There was nothing else for it. Agatha had to press ahead with the plan and hope that Eve and Lyra would come to accept her decision, and maybe even understand it, in time.

She fetched the key to the cottage down from its hook and, cane in hand, opened the back door. She would go over there. Who knew how many more opportunities there might be to go inside? She and Dylan hadn't talked about timings. She had no idea what his plans were but perhaps he would want to move in straight away.

She set off at a steady pace. Her hip was a blessed nuisance but she could get about as long as she didn't try to do things too quickly. As she walked down the path and towards the wood, she hoped that no one looked out at that moment and saw her. Eve would admonish her for going out alone, and both daughter and granddaughter would subject her to yet more questions. Agatha didn't want to answer any questions. And it really wasn't safe to answer them anyway, in case she gave herself away.

But no one did spot her and she completed her snail-paced passage through the garden alone. At the cottage she stopped and looked up, taking in its sorry state of repair. It was looking more than a little woebegone, the paint on the window frames cracked and flaking, a couple of roof tiles slipping, ivy running rampant up one wall. Agatha had rarely so much as cast a glance in this direction, let alone visited the cottage, for more than twenty years.

She had paid for some basic maintenance to be carried out, hadn't let the place go entirely to wrack and ruin. But it had lacked any affection, any genuine care. That wasn't surprising, she supposed. Who was there to do that but her?

Agatha put the key in the lock and turned it. The front door opened with a ghastly creak that had her anxiously looking over her shoulder, her heart beating hard in her chest.

But there was nothing to be scared of. Agatha didn't believe in ghosts, vindictive or otherwise. She might get Eve to apply a little oil to the hinges, though, just for her peace of mind.

She shuffled inside. The air was heavy with a musty, stale odour, slightly damp, although whether that was just the chill she couldn't say. She moved straight through the sitting room and into the kitchen at the back and then stood in the doorway. The table confused her. That wasn't the same. Then she remembered that Eve and Justin had lived here for a while when they first got married. This was their table, acquired from a school somewhere. And their chairs too. The furniture that had been here when the cottage was lived in by her parents' gardener had been gone for many years.

Agatha turned and made her way back to the front door. She had seen enough. She could let the cottage go. The nostalgia for the place that she'd feared she would feel hadn't materialised. It was just an old cottage in need of human habitation. And what was wrong with passing it on? Eve didn't want to live in it. She had been at Fox House for over a year and had never once suggested moving in. And Lyra only thought she did. It was a temporary solution to whatever had happened in her life. Soon enough she would want to be back in the thick of things and leave them behind.

No. It was right that Dylan had it.

Right and just.

It was, in fact, the very least that she could do.

23

They were all in the kitchen together and it felt busy, bustling even. Agatha was at the table waiting for dinner to be served, although she wasn't holding her breath. Despite all the activity, she couldn't sense any urgency about its preparation, even though the time at which she preferred to eat had been and gone.

Eve and Lyra were cooking, supposedly as a team, but there was a degree of discord over the best way to approach each task which added to the time required considerably. Skye was on the floor playing with a pair of plastic horses. The horses were talking to one another, with Skye as interpreter, but Agatha's hearing wasn't keen enough to pick up what was being said. Maybe they were complaining about the slow progress of the meal too.

Her daughter, her granddaughter and her great-granddaughter all here in her house. Agatha watched each of them in turn and wondered how many other families could boast women from four generations all living under one roof. Not many, she suspected.

To be fair, it had only happened at Fox House as a result of a series of unfortunate incidents. There had been her breaking her hip that had brought Eve to her door, and whatever was going on with Lyra and that young man of hers that accounted for generations three and four being here.

If Lyra hadn't had Skye by accident when she was only twenty then who knew if it would even have been possible? Agatha might have been dead long before Lyra had had a child otherwise. Did that make Skye an 'unfortunate incident'? That would depend on how you looked at things, she supposed. She most definitely didn't see it that way. Children should always be a blessing, no matter how or when they arrived.

'If you chop the onions first then you'll only need one board,' Eve said patiently.

'But the recipe says to chop the chicken first and fry that, and then add the onions,' replied Lyra, her nose almost touching the iPad screen. Agatha had dozens of cookery books on her shelves but they had remained undisturbed. None of them contained quite the right recipe, evidently.

'Well, you could do it that way. But then you have issues of cross-contamination. Whereas if you chop all the veg first you only need one board.'

'But then it's ready in the wrong order.'

Agatha watched as Eve swallowed before replying. There hadn't been time for her to count to ten but she was clearly working on some kind of similar yet truncated system.

'I'm not sure it really matters which order it goes in the pan,' she said. 'It's only a curry.'

Lyra looked at the recipe again and then started to chop the chicken breasts first. Eve closed her eyes and turned on the hot tap ready for the washing-up.

Had she and Eve been like this, working side by side, tensions rising and falling as easily as heart rates? She couldn't remember the two of them cooking. She couldn't remember them doing much together at all. Did that mean it hadn't happened or had the memory of it just got lost in the passing years? Agatha didn't know.

But they must have cooked together. Surely. Henry had died when Eve was eight. That meant a great number of meals when it could only have been the two of them in this kitchen. Yet she couldn't bring a single occasion to mind.

She must just have forgotten. The alternative scenario was unthinkable.

One of Skye's horses gave a little whinny and then Skye galloped out of the kitchen.

This was her moment. She should tell them now, get it out of the way. She didn't really have the stomach for the fallout but better to get everything out in the open. She took a deep breath.

'Just so you know, Dylan will be calling round tomorrow,' she said.

Lyra kept chopping and Eve didn't appear to hear her over the sound of the running water. Agatha took her cane and banged the steel tip on the floorboards.

'I said, Dylan will be calling round. Tomorrow.'

That did it. Lyra's knife paused in mid-air and Eve turned off the tap. They exchanged glances but neither of them spoke for a moment. Agatha filled the gap with the answer they no doubt wanted.

'He's coming to chat through the final arrangements about the cottage. I just thought I'd mention it in case you want to come and say hello. You've already met him, I think, Lyra.'

'Yeah, but it wasn't that friendly,' she said. 'I basically accused him of trespassing.'

'I'm sure he'll have forgiven you for that.'

Eve seemed to bristle although Agatha wasn't sure why. She really was going to have to get over these petty objections to Dylan. They were where they were and being annoyed about it really wasn't going to help.

'What time is he coming?' Eve asked.

'Sometime tomorrow,' replied Agatha. 'It's not like the dentist's. We didn't fix an appointment.'

'It's just that it would be easier for Lyra and me if we knew exactly when, then we can work round it.'

'Well, he's coming to see me. And I don't have a schedule to work round.'

What did they want? She had told them he was coming to save all the drama of him just turning up, but it seemed that wasn't good enough.

Agatha saw Eve employ the same self-calming tactics she'd used with Lyra moments before. Did Eve find her as frustrating as she seemed to find her daughter? Surely the issue was Eve's, then?

'Do you have any idea if it will be morning or afternoon?' Eve asked in a tone that might be described as patient, but bordered on patronising.

How could that matter? He would just come when he could. But she didn't want to start a row.

'No. And I'm not sure I can get hold of him. He doesn't have a telephone.'

'What?!'

That expression really was most unflattering on a woman of Eve's age. She should maybe mention that to her. Maybe not now.

'He doesn't have a telephone,' Agatha repeated. 'We made the arrangement by letter.'

Eve's jaw dropped. 'Letter!'

'Yes. Letters have worked perfectly well as a method of communication for centuries.'

'Of course. It's just quite unusual these days.'

Agatha shrugged. 'Well, there you have it. Dylan is coming tomorrow. And if you're here you can meet him.'

Skye ran back into the kitchen, the horses galloping through the air above her head.

'When's dinner, VeeVee? We're starving.'

Lyra had finally finished chopping the chicken. She scraped it from the board into the pan, where it sizzled. She looked at the state of the chopping board, put it down on the side and got a fresh one out of the cupboard. Then she placed an onion down on it and began to peel away the brown outer skin.

'It won't be long now, sweetie pie,' replied Eve.

24

Eve looked around the kitchen and sighed internally. How had her life got to this? She was living in her childhood home with her mother as if all the intervening decades had been scrubbed from the records and she had been forced back to the start, like a life-sized game of snakes and ladders. Four generations of women all jammed together into the same space. The concept could probably be used as a form of mental torture without too many tweaks.

On top of that, her mother was being even more exasperating than normal, clearly delighted about knowing something that Eve did not. Would it kill her to be transparent for once and tell her only daughter what was going on instead of being so bloody enigmatic?

Not that living with Lyra was much easier. No parent should be made to share quarters with their adult child. It was too confusing. All the rules you thought were well established seemed to be brushed aside once your child grew up. Life became a kind of free-for-all, with everybody's individual rights battling for supremacy. It was hardest for the mother though, Eve reflected. The mother was the one who had to compromise the most. As Eve thought this, she realised that that statement must apply to Agatha as much as it did to her and immediately changed her mind. Agatha never compromised about anything.

Each of the four generations was living by a different set of rules anyway. Since being small, Lyra had insisted that respect was not gained simply by virtue of age, whereas Eve had always been taught the exact opposite. Show respect to your elders no matter what because they have earned it, even if you can't see how. That was what Eve had always thought and Lyra turning it on its head confused and irritated her.

Where had Lyra got her mutinous attitudes towards authority from? Certainly not from her and probably not from Justin, although he could be a subversive sod when he put his mind to it. It must have been school. Or just from living. The messages that society pushed out now were so different from the ones that Eve's young radar had picked up.

That also begged a question: where was Skye, at just five, getting her strongest influences from? And what about her children, Eve's great-grandchildren? Would there be any of Agatha's values left by the time Skye was a mother?

She watched Lyra use twenty utensils where three would do and concluded that she shouldn't be so controlling. Hadn't she followed recipes to the letter when she was Lyra's age? That was how you learned – trial and error, working out which corners you could cut and still get safely to your destination. Still, it was common sense not to make more work for yourself than necessary. Celebrity chefs probably had someone to do the washing-up for them. Come to think of it, so did Lyra. Eve plunged the chickeny board into the hot soapy water.

'I don't see what's wrong with not owning a telephone anyway,' said Agatha. 'Why should we be at the constant beck and call of the world?'

'You can always turn it off, Granny,' replied Lyra without looking up from the onion that she was laboriously chopping. 'Then you have options. Phone or no phone, depending.'

'And how often do you turn yours off, Lyra?'

'Well, never. But I put it on silent at night.'

'My point exactly.' Agatha sounded triumphant. 'You place yourself in a constant state of alert, always waiting for the next person or thing to demand your attention. You have ceded control of your life to your device.'

'I haven't. It's my choice.'

'And it's Dylan's choice to not have a telephone.'

'All we're saying is that it's not very convenient,' Eve chipped in, trying to appease.

'For you, you mean. It's perfectly convenient for Dylan.'

There was no arguing with her mother when she was in this kind of mood.

Skye had taken her horses under the table and now her little voice floated out like an apparition.

'I can't wait to have my own mobile,' she said. 'Only six years to wait.'

'See. You've brainwashed the child already.'

'I have done no such thing,' replied Lyra indignantly, but even Eve felt a little queasy about her granddaughter counting down the years like that.

'You. Society. It makes no odds. This little girl has been tainted by the world around her.'

A tut slipped out of Eve before she could stop it. 'Oh, Agatha, you're being ridiculous. We're all products of the world we grew up in. You had the war. I had a ridiculous supposedly progressive seventies education. Lyra had the breaking down of arbitrary class and authoritative barriers. And now Skye is growing up in the age of the internet.'

Eve felt quite pleased with this little speech. She'd never thought of things quite like that before and now she wanted to explore her hypothesis more thoroughly, ruminate over a glass of wine or two.

But for that she needed Justin. Agatha rarely gave consideration to any idea that hadn't originated, for the purpose of that discussion at least, from her own mouth.

'You can't compare the war and the internet,' was Agatha's response, and Eve knew there was no point even trying to unpick that.

The doorbell rang and then, as if summoned by the power of her thoughts, in walked Justin.

'Oh, thank God you're here,' Eve said. She was only half joking. 'But *why* are you here?'

She loved the way that Justin felt at ease enough to saunter in and out of their home. There was something so very modern and liberal about it. When she told her friends that she and her ex still had this easy relationship she enjoyed watching their faces as they failed to process it.

She would have liked a little bit of privacy sometimes, however. She had nothing to hide (the more was the pity) but it was the principle of the thing.

'I was at a loose end so I thought I'd pop over and see how my four favourite ladies are doing.'

Skye wriggled out from under the table and launched herself at Justin, who staggered at the impact. He whisked her up and put her over his shoulder in a fireman's lift. She was getting too big for that, even with the high ceilings of Fox House.

'Careful, Justin!' she said, before remembering that Skye was Lyra's responsibility, not hers. More minefields.

'Something smells good,' he added.

'It's a curry,' said Lyra as proudly as if she were cooking for the King. 'You can have some if you want. There'll be plenty.'

'Not tonight, thanks, sweetheart. But it's you I wanted a word with. I thought you'd have eaten by now.'

'So did I,' said Agatha pointedly.

'Oh?' Lyra didn't stop stirring, moving the veg purposefully around the pan. Eve saw her swallow, her face tighten.

'Nothing urgent,' said Justin. 'It can wait.' He turned his head to Eve and gave the most minute raise of an eyebrow. You're right, it seemed to say. There is something up.

'Dylan is coming back tomorrow, Dad,' said Lyra in a classic diversionary move. 'So we'll get to meet him properly. Hopefully.'

'Ah. The mysterious Dylan.'

'There's nothing mysterious about him.' Agatha's tone was crisp, which was unusual when she was speaking to Justin. He rarely felt the sharp end of her tongue.

'He doesn't have a phone, Grandad,' said Skye from her prone position on Justin's shoulder.

'Well, that's mysterious in itself,' he said.

Eve pulled a face at him as if to say, just don't go there, and for once Justin followed her lead.

'What time is he coming?'

Eve sighed again.

25

The curry had been really good, Lyra decided, despite the snarky comments from both her mother and grandmother, and now Lyra was in the kitchen finishing the washing-up with her father, who despite not eating anything seemed keen to help.

'Your mother is worried about you,' he began as he wiped the plates with a York Minster tea towel.

Lyra should have seen this coming.

'Oh yes? Well, there's no need. I'm fine,' she said, hoping she sounded convincing.

'She's worried that there's more to you leaving the flat than meets the eye. And is there something going on with Rafe?'

This was it, surely. Her father had provided her with the perfect opening to explain all and seek guidance. But instead of doing that Lyra felt herself swerve away from the issue.

'Why didn't she just ask me herself?' she heard herself say.

'I think she tried, but you're not always entirely open to her questions,' Justin replied. His expression suggested that she ought to know exactly what he was talking about and Lyra gave a defensive little shrug.

'It's just that I never find her advice that helpful. She's so . . .' Lyra searched for the right word and failed to find it. 'She never seems to help that much,' she settled on.

'I don't think you're giving her enough credit,' said Justin. 'Your mother can be very astute. Her antennae are usually spot on.' He paused, seeming to consider what he had just said. 'Actually, she might be a bit off it at the moment. Since she moved back here she's got a bit lost. But generally.'

'Hmm,' said Lyra. She balanced the last plate on the draining rack and picked up the dirty frying pan. Keen to deflect attention away from herself, she said, 'What's the vibe between Mum and Granny? It's always been a bit odd but now that I'm here with both of them . . . well, it's like they don't really talk. I mean, they talk. Of course they do, but it's all "What do you want for lunch?" and "Shall I pay the gas bill?" They don't actually *talk* to one another. Don't you think that's weird?'

Her father plucked another plate from the rack.

'Maybe. A little.'

'I mean, they get on okay, and they must love each other. Mother-daughter. That goes with the territory . . .'

Lyra paused to let her father agree.

'Of course,' he said, nodding forcefully.

'But it's like there's something getting in the way. Me and Mum talk, about most stuff at least.' Lyra felt the heat rising up her chest as she considered what she wasn't talking about to her mother. She pressed on. 'And I know Skye's only little but I can't imagine a time when we won't talk about the important stuff. So why don't they?'

'I'm not sure Agatha's the opening-up sort,' said Justin ironically.

'You reckon?' laughed Lyra. 'It's just that, then? A personality thing?'

Her father shook his head. 'I gave up trying to work out what was going on there years ago. And anyway, stop changing the subject. Your mum is worried about you, not Agatha. What's going on? Can I help?'

She could just tell him, shift all the worry from her shoulders on to his. She considered this as she scrubbed at a particularly stubborn patch of baked-on curry sauce.

'It's Rafe,' she began. 'He—'

The kitchen door burst open. It was Skye, ready for bed, skin pink and glowing from the bath, the tips of her hair damp.

'Grandad. Can you come and read my story. VeeVee said I could come downstairs and find you as long as I went straight back upstairs.'

Her father's gaze flicked between her and her daughter as if he wasn't sure where to place his attention.

'It's fine, Dad. You go and read the story. We can catch up later.'

Justin looked unsure. 'Well, if you're sure whatever it is can wait.'

Skye pulled at his trouser leg. 'Come on, Grandad. You can choose the story. Can you do all your best voices?'

'Go on,' said Lyra, smiling at Skye. 'I'll finish off here.'

Justin placed a hand on her shoulder and gave it a little squeeze.

'Hold that thought,' he said as he hung the tea towel up and then followed Skye out of the room.

'Right,' Lyra heard him say. 'Where's this book?'

It was probably better that she sorted Rafe out on her own anyway.

26

Dylan finally turned up around three the next day. It was unseasonably warm for the end of March and they had all gravitated towards the garden, even Agatha, who would generally complain it was cold on the hottest of days. It was like a compulsion, as if they all had to be where they could see the cottage whilst they waited for its new occupier to appear. The fine weather simply gave them the excuse.

Eve had made a jug of fresh lemonade with Skye's able assistance. Skye had been disappointed that the drink wasn't fizzy, as all lemonade should be in her world.

'Maybe if we shake it up really hard,' she suggested, and Eve made a note to buy sparkling water next time she was at the supermarket. Agatha wouldn't like the break from tradition, but then Agatha didn't have to have any if she didn't want.

Agatha, Eve and Lyra sat at the warped teak table on the patio outside the dining room. The patio was made of the same brick as the house and thyme grew up through the cracks between each one, in places creeping so far that you could barely see the terracotta red beneath the carpet of green. In the summer it could get too hot to sit here comfortably, but the rest of the year it was sheltered from the wind and in full sun for most of the day. It also had the added advantage that you could partially see the cottage.

They had each turned their chairs for the best view, so they sat in an awkward line as if they were waiting at the doctor's. Eve wanted to make a joke about this but it really wasn't a laughing matter, so she held her tongue.

A host of golden daffodils, as the poem went, were swaying in the gentle breeze, although there seemed to be fewer flowers each year. Eve remembered there being a vast sea of yellow trumpets when she was a girl, but now there was no more than a sprinkling of colour. The bluebells would emerge next but happily their number grew year on year, undisturbed as they were in the ancient wood-land. Might that change now? Whatever this Dylan had planned for the cottage it surely wouldn't involve disturbing the bluebells. Eve's stomach knotted at the realisation that if Agatha gave him the cottage outright then he could do as he pleased. Would she give him part of the woodland too, the part surrounding the cottage, or just the right to be in it? There were so many wrinkles to be ironed out that yet again Eve wondered what could possibly justify her mother's actions.

Skye was turning her squat little cartwheels and insisting that they give her a score for each one. It had been fun to start with, but the game was becoming tiresome and the three adults took turns to call out a random number that bore no correlation to the quality of the move. Skye must have known that but she seemed content to go along with the fiction.

Conversation was stilted. Eve kept starting fresh topics that lasted for a sentence or two and then died away. No one seemed to want to talk, except perhaps to speculate yet again about Dylan and his circumstances, but Agatha quickly put paid to that.

Eve wasn't sure why they were watching the cottage so intently. Surely he would come to the front door this time? She pushed at the French doors with her foot, opening the gap up a little wider so she could hear the bell if it rang.

In the end it didn't ring. Just as before, Dylan sauntered round the side of the house and materialised before them without warning. He was remarkably untroubled by social norms, it seemed.

'Oh!' said Eve in surprise when he was almost on top of them. 'Hello.'

'Good afternoon,' he replied with a little dip of his head at Agatha, who gave him a hesitant nod in return.

There was, as Lyra had suggested, nothing remarkable about him. He was around her age. Tallish, leanish. His straight brown hair was thinning at the front yet with quite a thatch at the back. It needed a cut. His face was lined with its fair share of wrinkles, maybe a few more than she carried herself. The areas around his eyes were smoother. Did he never smile? Eve had always told herself that her own crow's feet were a result of her sunny disposition.

His eyes were interesting, though. Grey in the late afternoon, but they might also be blue in brighter light. It was hard to tell without staring, which was what Eve suddenly realised she was doing. He didn't seem disconcerted by this. He watched her impassively, allowing her to examine his features without response until Eve felt her cheeks start to flare and she looked away.

'Good afternoon, Dylan,' Agatha said. 'How nice to see you. Sit down and sample some of my great-granddaughter's lemonade. That's her doing gymnastics. Skye. Say hello to Dylan.'

Skye tried to look over mid-cartwheel and consequently landed in a small heap.

'Hello,' she called but then she carried on with her practising.

'I'm Lyra. We've met already.'

Eve sensed Lyra's wariness. She was giving nothing to this stranger, her expression and body language closed, challenging almost. So it was unsettling to realise that she herself didn't feel like that at all. Eve had assumed that, faced with the man who was stealing her birthright out from under her nose, she would respond in the same way as her daughter. But if anything, something inside her seemed to warm to him, wanted to smile and make him feel welcome, which totally contradicted what her head was telling her.

'We have,' he replied to Lyra. 'Thank you, Agatha. Lemonade would be nice.'

He pulled up a chair and sat next to Agatha, continuing the line they had created to look out for him. Now it looked like they were there to watch a cricket match. At least it made it more difficult for Eve to stare. For this she was grateful.

Agatha reached for the glass jug, barely half full, and poured some into the glass that had been awaiting his arrival all afternoon.

'The ice has melted, I'm afraid,' she said as she handed him the drink.

He acknowledged this with a slight twist of his mouth, tipped the glass and drained it one go.

'Very good,' he said as he placed it back down on the table.

The cuff of his shirt was frayed. He seemed to notice it but made no attempt to cover it up as Eve would have done. There was no shame attached to his modest means, which interested Eve, sitting as they were in the garden of the rather grand, albeit slightly shabby, Fox House.

'So,' he said, turning to Agatha. 'To business.'

27

To business?

Was that it?!

No pleasantries? No gentle getting to know each other before the bomb fell?

The unaccountable warmth that Eve had been feeling towards this man moments before evaporated. Well, if that was how he wanted to play things, then she was up for it. She could be as cold and aloof as the next woman. Who did he think he was anyway, strolling into their lives and then just blowing them apart? Well, she supposed that might be a bit of an exaggeration, but still. He surely owed them a little bit of common courtesy.

Agatha spoke next.

'All in good time,' she said. 'I see no rush.'

Dylan pursed his lips as if he were considering whether to contradict her, but apparently decided against it and nodded instead.

'All right,' he said.

A howl rang out to their left and they all turned to see Skye in a little pile on the grass. This was how she had been for much of the afternoon but now she was shaking and seemed to be crying rather than laughing. Lyra was out of her chair and at her side before Eve had really registered what was going on.

'What's the matter, sweetie? What happened?' she asked the anguished Skye, brushing her hand across Skye's forehead to move her hair out of the way so she could see her face.

'My ankle,' sobbed Skye. 'It hurts.'

'Let's have a look,' said Lyra. 'Can you move it at all?'

Skye stretched her leg out and tried some tentative wiggling, with an added howl for good measure. It was clear from the range of movement that nothing was broken, and Eve relaxed.

'Do you know what you need?' Dylan said.

He was on his feet and approaching Lyra and Skye, stopping just far enough away so as not to be threatening.

Skye stopped sobbing and looked at him, instantly interested in anything that she might need.

'Rice,' said Dylan.

'Rice?' Skye's voice took on the tone she used when she thought she was having her leg pulled but wanted to brazen it out until she understood what was going on.

'Rest. Ice. Compression. Elevation,' he said. 'That's what all the top gymnasts do when they're injured.'

Skye looked at Lyra for confirmation and Lyra nodded, but without looking at Dylan.

'That's right,' she said. 'Let's go inside and get some ice from the freezer, and I'm sure GeeGee must have a bandage somewhere.'

'There are some of those tube things in the bathroom. They're for sprained wrists but your ankle is so tiny, Skye. I'm sure it'll be perfect.'

Skye beamed at all the attention and Lyra scooped her up and carried her across the lawn towards the open French doors, Skye making an ambulance siren sound as they went.

Dylan sat back down.

'We did know that,' said Eve crisply.

'I'm sure,' replied Dylan, his tone even and completely unaltered by her aggression.

His eyes met hers and then held her gaze until Eve had to look away. She could feel that he was still watching her even though she could no longer see it for herself.

'You don't remember me, do you?' he said.

Eve felt totally wrong-footed. It wasn't fair that her memory had let her down so that he had the advantage. Not keen to reveal any weakness when she didn't know what was at stake, she tightened her face.

'Should I?' she asked. Her tone was barely civil and she sounded so unlike herself that she felt like an actress playing a part.

Dylan just shrugged as if it were nothing to him one way or the other. 'I suppose not.'

Agatha evidently could bear it no longer. 'Dylan is the son of a friend of your father and mine. You played together as children,' she said, as if this simple statement explained the entire mystery.

'Hence the photo?' Eve asked her mother, bypassing Dylan.

'Photo?' he asked.

'I found a photo,' she said, trying but failing to maintain her briskness. 'Of me and a boy. You, it appears. It said Dylan on the back.'

'Outside the cottage?' he asked.

Eve nodded. 'I'm holding a fishing net,' she added reluctantly.

There was a pause as Dylan contemplated something. The photograph? The memory? Her? Eve had no idea. She shuffled in her seat and played with a thread on her cuff, and then stopped in case he thought she was drawing attention to the state of his.

'But you don't remember?' he said eventually.

Eve shrugged, but she thought she might now, maybe a little. She tipped her head to one side and studied him again. It was less awkward this time as he had, in effect, invited her to stare. There

129

was something familiar about him, but the memories danced just out of reach.

'Maybe,' she conceded. 'But it's all so vague.'

Scenes at the cottage dipped in and out of her mind's eye, perhaps, but mainly it was the wood she could see. In the few splinters she could grab hold of she and Dylan were always outside. There were no rooms, no cosy kitchens or televisions. Just her and a boy and trees and water and . . .

Eve shook her head dismissively. 'I don't know. Perhaps it'll come back to me.'

'Shall we go and look inside?' asked Agatha, pushing herself to her feet. Her fox head cane slipped from its resting place against her chair and clattered on the bricks below. Agatha and Dylan both stared at it for a heartbeat, and then at one another, something passing between the two of them that Eve saw but couldn't follow. Then Dylan bent down and picked the stick up, passing it, fox head first, to Agatha. She took it without meeting his eye.

They set off across the lawn, Agatha's head erect and doing a passable impression of a woman in control, although Eve noticed how her hand had been shaking when she took hold of the cane. Dylan followed just behind her, but whether this was in deference to her status as grande dame or as a way of avoiding conversation, Eve couldn't decide.

'The place is in a bit of a state,' Agatha said without apology. 'It's been empty for so long now. Structurally sound, or so I believe, and the water and electricity are still connected. But other than that . . .' Her sentence drifted off, leaving Dylan to fit the rest together for himself.

'I lived there for a while,' chipped in Eve. 'With my husband. Ex-husband,' she added, although why this detail was any of his concern she had no idea. 'And my daughter Lyra had intended moving in with Skye. Well, until my mother told us of her plans for the place.'

'I imagine that was a bit of a shock,' he said. 'Hearing that she was passing the place to a stranger.'

He had done it again. Taken the wind out of her sails with his empathetic comments. It was disconcerting. And inconvenient. It made him more beguiling than he had any business being.

'Yes. It was actually. My mother announcing that . . .' Eve paused, not wanting to suggest that the cottage was to go to him outright in case that wasn't the agreement. 'That she had plans for the cottage outside the family. Well. You must know how unsettling that has been.'

'Not really,' said Dylan. 'My family has never had a pot to piss in.'

He didn't say it as if it were a complaint, just a statement of fact. What had Lyra said about him seeming bitter? There was nothing like that on display today.

'Where do you live?' asked Eve, boldly chancing a personal question.

'A way away,' he replied vaguely.

'And are you planning to move in here?'

He shrugged. 'Maybe. We'll see.'

For God's sake. He was worse than Agatha. Eve squeezed her mouth shut and followed her mother across the grass.

28

It took ten minutes for Lyra to sort out Skye's ankle to Skye's satisfaction. As Lyra carried her inside, Skye kept muttering RICE under her breath until they got to the kitchen. Lyra placed her down on a chair carefully and then pulled out another for her to rest her ankle on.

'Cushion please, Mummy,' said Skye, sending Lyra scampering off to the sitting room to find one. 'Is this the' – she paused, trying to get her mouth around the complicated word – '"elevation" part?'

'That's right,' confirmed Lyra. 'And we need ice.'

She found a tea towel and tipped the contents of an ice tray into it, gathering it up into a little bundle and tying a knot in the top. She placed it gently on Skye's ankle. There was no swelling. The ankle was fine, but making a fuss of her daughter would do no harm. The poor child had had plenty to deal with over the last week.

'And rest,' said Skye. 'That's not sleep though, is it?' she added doubtfully.

'No. Just no more cartwheeling for a bit.'

Skye nodded as if that would be all right.

'I can't remember the last part,' she said, her face suggesting that she was disappointed in herself.

Lyra had to think. What did the 'c' stand for? She couldn't bring it to mind but there was no way she was going back out to ask that man. Then it came to her.

'Compression,' she said, relieved that she had dredged it up. 'That means a bandage. GeeGee said she had some in the bathroom. You stay here and I'll go and find one.'

The tubular bandage was easy to locate. There was a small pile of them, all used but clean and neatly folded in the corner of the cabinet, making Lyra wonder how often her grandmother had cause to wear one. Agatha wasn't as robust as she had been. That much had become obvious over the last few days. Why Eve hadn't left Fox House after Agatha was able to walk again had been unclear to her when she was still in Manchester, but now she was here she understood.

Her grandmother had always been a tour de force. It made Lyra's heart hurt to think that she was becoming less so. And being compelled to hand the cottage over to that man now, when she was at her most vulnerable. It was unthinkable. Lyra had no doubt that there must be an element of coercion somewhere. It made no sense otherwise. But she was here now. She, Lyra, would stop it from happening.

'Mummy!'

Skye's voice cut through her thoughts and she grabbed a bandage from the top of the pile and ran back downstairs with it. Skye obligingly pointed her toes, another indication that there was nothing broken, so that Lyra could feed the bandage over the delicate ankle and up her little leg.

'There,' she said. 'Now, you should sit still with your foot up with ice on it for a while. Shall I put the television on for you, or I could get you a book?'

She should have thought of the book first, Lyra realised immediately, because Skye obviously opted for the television. As she carried her through to the sitting room, Skye pressed the ice pack against her ankle as though her life depended on contact being maintained at all times.

Lyra lowered her gently on to the sofa and switched the television on, passing Skye the remote. There wasn't much choice on Agatha's set but there was enough for a five-year-old.

'Right, I'm going to go back outside to talk to the others. Will you be okay?'

Skye nodded, but her attention was already absorbed by the screen.

Lyra set off back across the garden with purpose, concerned about what might have happened in her absence. She didn't trust her mother not to cave under pressure. She was always too eager to please, never wanting to cause offence. Her grandmother was quite the reverse, but her grandmother, as architect of this lunatic scheme, was on the wrong side of the argument.

Lyra was going to fight for the cottage even if her mother wasn't. It was meant to be her future home and she had caught a flicker of dismay on her grandmother's face when she'd asked if she could move in. It was only a tiny chink in the defences, but that was all Lyra needed. She could work away on it until it was large enough to crawl into and then she could topple the whole ridiculous suggestion over on its back.

She broke into a run.

The others were nowhere to be seen, but the front door of the cottage was standing open. Lyra raced through the gate that separated the garden from the wood and then, just as she reached the door, slowed her pace. There was no need to show her hand by rushing in, all anxious. This situation needed careful handling. The man needed to think she wasn't that fussed so that he dropped his guard.

As she approached, she could see they had only got as far as the front room and were standing scattered about the space, not speaking. She might have expected the man to be behaving like a prospective buyer but he didn't seem interested in how well appointed, or otherwise, the cottage was. He stood at the window and was staring out at the wood beyond. Maybe he was disappointed in what he saw and wouldn't be taking up her grandmother's offer after all. Lyra's heart did a little skip at the idea. She might not have to push very hard to get what she wanted.

Yet now that she was in the same space with them all, Lyra wasn't quite sure what to say. It wasn't easy to simply walk into a room and object to a state of affairs when there was no conversation ongoing. That said, needs must.

She stood with her back to the open door.

'I don't know what is going on here,' she began, trying to make her voice as authoritative as she could. 'But I can't see a single reason why my grandmother would choose, of her own free will, to let you have this cottage. It makes no sense. I can only conclude that you are forcing her in some way and that we should be ringing the police to get them to sort it out.'

She folded her arms and glared at the man. She was ready for a fight and to give as good as she got.

But she was getting nothing in return. Dylan eyed her impassively and then turned his gaze to fall on her grandmother.

'Over to you to explain, I think,' he said to Agatha.

29

'You can't just pass the buck like that,' said Lyra. 'You're the one making all these demands of us. The very least you can do is explain yourself.'

She narrowed her eyes and thrust her hands on her hips, hoping to make herself look like a force to be reckoned with. By contrast, her mother's expression was the appeasing one she wore when she wanted to avoid a row.

'Lyra's right,' Eve said. 'This whole situation is quite hard for us to get our heads round. It would really help if we understood what was behind the decision.'

Irritated, Lyra shot her mother a frustrated look. Why couldn't she be more assertive rather than making out that for him to explain would be doing them a favour? She always did this, became placatory, accommodating, rather than getting to the nub of an issue.

Lyra rephrased. 'It's not about getting our heads round whatever it is. It's our *right* to know,' she said defiantly.

The man looked across at her grandmother again, his face questioning. It looked as if he were asking Agatha's permission to speak.

Agatha drew herself up tall, barely leaning on her cane at all. 'I appreciate how frustrating this must be for you, Lyra, for both of you. But you must accept the situation as it is. The cottage is mine to do with as I please. I choose to give it to Dylan, the son of a good friend of your father and grandfather. That is my right. And whilst this decision may be difficult for you to understand, I really don't have to explain myself.'

'I thought you said he was *your* friend,' snapped back Eve accusingly.

There was some fire in her, then, Lyra thought.

Agatha flinched. Was it Eve's tone that she didn't like or had she revealed something she hadn't meant to? Lyra searched her grandmother's face for more clues, but whatever it had been had gone.

'He was a friend to both of us. Jack was my friend first,' her grandmother said. 'I introduced him to Henry after we were married. And now Dylan finds himself in need of help and I am happy to offer it to him.'

Eve opened her mouth, looked over at Dylan, closed it again. Whatever she had to say, she was clearly uncomfortable voicing it in front of the stranger. But he held his ground and showed no signs of allowing them to discuss him in his absence.

'But do you have to give him the cottage?' Eve asked in a half whisper, as if Dylan wasn't there to hear her. 'Couldn't you just rent it to him? Or give him a life interest over it if you like, so that it reverts back to the family after he dies?'

This solution hadn't occurred to Lyra and she quickly thought it through. It wouldn't help her immediate situation but it would at least mean that the cottage would stay part of the estate for Skye to inherit.

But Agatha jutted her chin. Lyra recognised the gesture. It was one they saw when Agatha wasn't getting her own way and was about to dig her heels in.

'I could do that,' she said. 'But I don't want to. I am giving the cottage to Dylan and that is that. So, it would be much better all round if you two stopped challenging me at every turn and just came to terms with the idea.'

And in that moment, Lyra knew that they had lost. The cottage would go to Dylan and she and her mother were just going to have to deal with it.

A final scheme occurred to her. It was worth a try.

'You said he might rent the cottage to me and Skye,' she said, her tone suddenly far less aggressive than it had been.

'I did,' conceded Agatha, and turned to face Dylan. 'Dylan. What would you think of that idea?'

Dylan shuffled from one foot to the other but he didn't break eye contact with Agatha.

'I am going to be living here myself,' he said.

'So there you are, Lyra. It was a reasonable suggestion but it doesn't accord with Dylan's plans.'

Lyra felt her life crumble. The cottage as a solution to her problems had appeared like an oasis in front of her, shimmering with possibilities. Now, the mirage had vanished, leaving her future looking arid, desolate.

And as it became clear that she would have to think of an alternative solution, her problems suddenly felt insurmountable. How could she fix everything on her own? If she couldn't show that she could provide a stable home for Skye then the court would surely let Rafe, with all his money and plans, take her away to America.

And what was worse, his proposal was almost starting to make sense, even to her. Of course the life Rafe could offer Skye in California would be better than anything she could scrape together. Given the choice, who wouldn't take his side?

Lyra could hear the line of cross-examination playing in her head.

'And where are you living, Miss Sterling?'

'In the spare room at my grandmother's house. Skye doesn't even have a proper bed.'

'What happened to the flat you were living in?'

'I flooded it.'

'And why would you do such a thing?'

'I was angry, and then I thought I could run away so no one could find us.'

'You mean you wanted to deprive Skye's father of access to his daughter?'

'Yes.'

'And how exactly did you think flooding your flat so that it was uninhabitable would achieve that?'

'I don't know. It just seemed like a good idea at the time.'

But she could see now that it had been a stupid thing to do. Stupid and petulant, the act of a spoiled child rather than a responsible adult and mother. There was no way it was ever going to improve matters and was obviously likely to make things worse. In fact, given how she had behaved, Rafe almost deserved to take Skye with him. She had played straight into his hands, shown herself to be reckless and immature – a questionable mother.

And now, her parachute plan was gone, the cords cut, and she was plummeting to the ground. She gulped and blinked hard as she fought to keep herself in control. She wouldn't cry in front of them, but not doing so required more resources than she had to spare just then.

Lyra turned and ran from the cottage.

30

May 1975

Marry in haste. Repent at leisure.

Wasn't that what they said? And was that what Agatha was doing? She and Henry had certainly married in haste, there was no denying that. They had only known each other for six months, introduced at a hunt ball and then falling headlong into a torrid love affair that carried them downstream and up the aisle before either of them really knew what had happened.

If Agatha was being truly honest, her hurtle into matrimony had been as much about Fox House as it was about her love for Henry. She had known from childhood that the house would be hers when she married. Her mother, who had grown up in Fox House herself, had always insisted so.

'It's a family home,' she said. 'We have a responsibility to pass it on, not to let it rot and fester with half its rooms closed up.'

Even as a girl, Agatha had been able to see the irony in this statement. Fox House didn't even come close to the definition of a family home as far as she could see, primarily because the Ferriers weren't much of a family. Agatha had been in effect an only child since her twin brothers were killed in the war, before she was even born. As an adult, it had become clear to her that she had been conceived at the eleventh hour of her mother's fertility, presumably in a misguided attempt to fill the gap left by her brothers. It hadn't worked. On top of that, her parents didn't seem to like each other very much, nor were they so very fond of her. The Ferriers were far from being a picture-perfect family, if such a thing even existed.

Knowing that Fox House would come to her, Agatha had resolved to make a better job of the task of 'family' so that she could do justice to the place. She would marry well, she decided, and then fill Fox House with children, lots of children who would never be bored or lonely. There would be music and laughter ringing out from morning to night. She would make their childhoods everything that hers had not been.

When Henry came along, he seemed to slot neatly into her vision. He was the second son of a local landowning family. There wasn't enough money in the land to support both him and his brother, but he had a good job in a bank and as Agatha would bring Fox House to the marriage, he seemed like a good enough prospect financially.

And he was handsome. Henry always turned heads as he walked into a room, and she was proud to be on his arm. People buzzed around him, vying for his attention, which he bestowed on them each in turn so that no one felt excluded. He was gracious and funny and he had a way of making even the darkest corners of a room if not light up, then at least glow. Agatha could see how he would play his part in making their home all that she longed for. She pictured parties that their guests would talk about for years, laughter, merriment, a house echoing with joy. Henry would be the kind of father who hoisted his offspring on to his shoulders and raced through the house, ducking at the last minute to avoid overhead obstacles to uproarious squeals of delight. He would never read the newspaper at the dinner table or be too tired to respond to curious questions about why the sky wasn't always blue or exactly how the pictures got inside a television. In short, Henry would be everything Agatha needed to bring her dreams to reality.

Her mother said he was 'charming', which Agatha had thought wasn't meant to be entirely complimentary. In fact, she herself had noticed in him a slight tendency towards pomposity, no doubt brought about by all the favourable attention that he garnered. Agatha chalked this as a mark against him, but it was almost alone in the 'disadvantages' column of her checklist and so she decided to overlook it. She could handle a little self-importance, given that it seemed he had the other qualities necessary to be a family man. There were whisperings in the village that they would make a striking bride and groom almost from the start and these pleased her.

And so they were married one Friday in May 1968 and by the time they returned from honeymoon on the Isle of Wight, her parents had moved out of Fox House so that she and Henry could move in. Her parents left most of the furniture so that made logistics simple. Her mother only had one request: that Agatha leave the twins' bedroom as it was.

'Not forever, of course. I don't mean that,' she added with an expression that told Agatha that this was precisely what she meant. 'I'm sure you'll need it soon enough. But just until then . . .'

Then had followed the familiar glazing over of her mother's eyes, and Agatha had nodded solemnly and said that of course she would respect the memory of the brothers she had never known but whose ghosts had destroyed her childhood, whilst fully intending to take the contents of the bedroom to the tip at the first opportunity.

But then the years passed and, sadly, the room never became needed. Each time she thought about clearing the space, she remembered the sound of her mother's sobbing as it echoed along the landing, and she just couldn't quite bring herself to throw the things away.

As for her hasty marriage, it had gained her early access to Fox House and one child, Eve, but there was little else that was positive that she could find to say about it. Agatha should have focused harder on her checklist of disadvantages. She tried hard not to repent, however. All was not lost yet. Eve was only four and she was a sprightly thirty-two, her childbearing days certainly not yet behind her. There was still time for the gaggle of children she had dreamed of.

31

Henry and his friend Jack were at the kitchen table, a bottle of whisky open in front of them. Jack had been Agatha's friend first – her closest, in fact. He had been brought up in the village, too, and Agatha had known him since before they went to school. She had introduced him to Henry before they were married and had been delighted that the two most important men in her life had quickly become fast friends, not realising then just how much of a lifeline that would become for her as the years ticked by.

The men had had a successful day's fishing and were now sharing tales of expeditions past. Agatha glanced at the whisky bottle as she walked by, judging their condition by how much remained, but they were both on good form thus far.

'Come and join us, Agatha,' Henry called over to her. 'You're making me dizzy with all that buzzing around.'

Agatha had been hoping for a snatched hour curled up with a book, but Jack brought the best out in Henry and it could be fun when the three of them were together, with echoes of the rumbustious life she'd originally pictured for them.

'All right,' she said as she sat down. 'But I'm not drinking whisky.'

'If I say you're drinking whisky then that's what you'll do,' said Henry, wagging a jocular finger at her. He was slurring slightly.

Maybe there had been more in the bottle than Agatha realised. 'It'll make a change for me to wear the trousers round here,' he added with a mirthless laugh. 'You have no idea the pressure I'm under here, Jack, my man.'

'Aggie's always been a force to be reckoned with,' replied Jack, throwing her a conspiratorial grin, and Agatha rolled her eyes as if never a truer word had been spoken.

'The thing is,' continued Henry, 'the thing is, and I mean nothing hurtful by this, you understand.' He took a drink and placed the glass back down carefully as if he didn't quite trust himself not to spill it. 'The thing is,' he said for a third time, 'I've never been quite enough for our Agatha.'

Agatha sucked in her breath, not sure where this was going but certain that it needed to be closed down.

'Oh, don't be silly, Henry,' she countered quickly. 'Of course you are.'

'But am I though?' he continued ponderously. 'She had this plan, you know, Jack. This grand plan. Babies. It was all about babies. A big family. Lots of noise and what have you. And a tree house. There was a tree house involved.'

Agatha closed her eyes and hoped that Henry would move on. It was a familiar path, one that they had been down many, many times before.

'Oh, that was all just newly-wed silliness,' she said lightly.

'But I didn't quite make the grade, you see, Jack, my old friend. I fell short.'

'I don't think that's right,' said Jack. 'Aggie's lucky to have found you.'

Agatha nodded enthusiastically. She knew where this was going. Henry would become maudlin about what he saw as his failings and in many ways he would be right. Their life wasn't working out the way she'd pictured it.

'There's only Eve, though,' slurred Henry. 'She' – he pointed a wavering finger at Agatha – 'wanted legions of children and I've only managed to fire out one.'

'There's nothing wrong with that,' replied Jack. 'Me and Mary only have Dylan and that suits us just fine.'

'Not part of the grand plan, though,' said Henry, shaking his head slowly. 'Not part of the plan.'

He was quite drunk, Agatha realised now. She wished he would shut up. This was private and not to be shared with Jack. She didn't want to have to explain about how she felt, what was missing in their lives, which hole she had been trying to fill.

'You've had too much to drink, Henry,' she chided gently. 'You're not making any sense.'

But Henry was warming to his theme. 'A man is supposed to be in charge of his household, don't you agree, Jack?'

Jack threw a surreptitious glance at Agatha as if to ask how he was supposed to react. She shrugged by way of response. But Henry's question was apparently rhetorical and he pressed on without a reply.

'I'm not in charge here. It's not even my house. It's her bloody house. And I've failed her on pretty much every score, haven't I?'

'No!' objected Agatha. 'Of course not.'

But he had. His early promise had failed to materialise. His career was stalling, so he spent more and more time away from Fox House as he tried to appease his bosses at the bank. And where was their longed-for big family? Agatha knew that it took two to make a baby, but had she not proved that all her parts were in working order? So their failure to conceive a second time must be his fault. The alcohol, perhaps. Or maybe the pressure he felt he was under.

As if to prove her point, Henry reached for the bottle and refilled his glass with a shaking hand.

'It's emasc . . .' he began. 'Emasci . . .' He failed to find the word and slumped back into his chair, head drooping.

She and Jack shared a look over the top of him.

'You're a fantastic fisherman, though,' said Jack with unnatural enthusiasm. 'An amazing hunter.'

Henry sprang back up in his seat.

'I am,' he agreed. 'I am. And men are supposed to hunt, aren't they? That's in the job description.'

Relief made Agatha smile.

'They are,' she said, running her hand over the crown of his head affectionately.

'Therefore, I'm doing something right,' Henry added, nodding at himself.

'You're doing everything right,' agreed Agatha.

But he wasn't. The rooms of Fox House rarely rang with longed-for laughter. In fact, the place was starting to look tired. The three of them only occupied a handful of rooms and with no money for staff, Agatha had simply closed the doors on the rest. The twins' room remained locked. It was easy to keep her promise to her mother when they had no call for the extra space. And without the gaggles of children that she had imagined were the prerequisites of motherhood, Agatha didn't seem to be very good at the job. She and Eve had a functioning relationship, but it wasn't what she'd dreamed of all those years ago when her own mother had barely noticed her existence.

Agatha tried hard not to blame Henry for all this, but she rarely succeeded.

32

NOW

The removal van pulled up outside Fox House on Saturday, a scruffy white affair with rust patches over the wheel arches and traces of the previous owner's signage still showing through the poorly executed paint job. Eve, standing at the window, could just make out the word 'Bottom', which she imagined had once said Bottomley, and an image that might have been of a plunger. As she reflected on how unfortunate this was and how she might have been a bit more liberal with the paint, Lyra arrived at her side.

'He didn't waste much time,' she said.

'No,' agreed Eve. 'It makes me wonder whether your grandmother hasn't been cooking this plan up for months. No one can move house that quickly.'

Lyra dropped her chin and raised an eyebrow, and it dawned on Eve that this was precisely what her daughter had done the week before, albeit with no furniture in tow.

'Well, most people take a little longer,' added Eve. 'It's quite a trek from there to the cottage. Do you think we should offer to go and help?'

'No way!' replied Lyra. 'I'm not helping him, the Judas. He can carry his own shit.'

Then she left Eve to continue watching on her own.

Dylan jumped down from the passenger seat of the van. He was wearing jeans today and an old sweatshirt and looked much more comfortable than when he'd been with them a few days before. He had dressed up for the meeting, Eve realised now, had wanted to make a good impression on them. If you ignored the fact that he was stealing part of Fox House out from under her nose, his apparent effort was quite sweet.

He didn't seem to have noticed her watching him, or didn't care, so she stayed where she was, spying. He walked to the back of the van and opened the doors. She couldn't see what was inside. The driver of the van went round to look too and they stood there for a moment in that way men do when they're sizing up a task.

From her vantage spot, Eve examined him for something familiar. There was something; it was more nebulous than a memory, little more than an impression, a feeling. But it was definitely there and trying to get out.

She had been as angry about the situation surrounding the cottage as Lyra, all fired up and ready for a fight to defend what was hers. But when she met Dylan something held her back. Some deeply held instinctive belief that he was friend, not foe, made it hard for her to generate any fury towards him. That had to be coming from a childhood memory she couldn't access, but which still held her tightly in its thrall nonetheless.

Apparently finally becoming conscious of being watched, Dylan looked round and caught her staring. He raised a tentative hand and before she knew what she was doing she was smiling and returning his wave. She drew back immediately. It was one thing wondering if they had some shared happy memories. It was quite another actually fraternising with the enemy.

She was curious, though. Maybe something he took to the cottage would unlock her memories. She left that window and moved to the one directly above, in the bedroom that Skye was using, and from there she continued her vigil. She still couldn't see inside the van but she watched as Dylan and the driver moved a few sticks of furniture and a couple of boxes out and across the drive towards the cottage. There was very little, certainly not much to show for over fifty years of life. But then couldn't you say the same about her? All her worldly goods were currently in quite a small storage unit on the outskirts of York. She had always thought that gathering no moss showed a discipline of sorts, but maybe it was simply that her life thus far hadn't amounted to much.

That needed attention, she decided. If all this disruption was showing her anything it was that things needed to be thrown up in the air from time to time. If she was going to be stuck at Fox House for the foreseeable future then she needed something other than work and looking after Agatha to occupy her. In the absence of any distractions, Eve would inevitably rely on Justin to keep her entertained and she couldn't do that forever.

Maybe she could dig out her painting things from the storage unit. She had forgotten all about painting. It had become lost in the sound and fury of life. Yet seeing the picture of the water sprites at the cottage had reminded her how much she used to enjoy losing herself for a few hours in her work.

Her resolve strengthened. That was what she would do. And maybe she could interest Skye in painting too. It might be a lovely thing to do with one's granddaughter. Somehow she had never made the time for art with Lyra other than the obligatory finger painting and collage. There just never seemed to be the time. Lyra was creative, though. She and Justin had argued over which of them was responsible for that particular gene. Justin had won as he ran a design agency and she was an accountant. Eve had never been sure that things were as cut and dried as that, not that it mattered, except it fuelled the doubts she harboured about not being quite enough.

She could put that right with Skye, though, especially whilst they were all under the same roof. Yes, she would go to the storage unit today and retrieve her paints and brushes.

As she reached this pleasing decision, the bedroom door opened behind her and Skye bounded up.

'What are you doing, VeeVee?' she asked.

Eve, embarrassed to have been caught snooping, drew away from the window.

'I was just watching what was going on,' she replied vaguely.

Skye sidled up next to her and looked down.

'Is that that man?' she asked. 'The one who's stealing our cottage?'

What had Lyra been saying to her?

'That's Dylan,' Eve confirmed. 'But he's not stealing the cottage. GeeGee has given it to him.'

'Whatever,' Skye replied before skipping off and out of the room.

She should really have a word with Lyra about being careful what she said to Skye. Was Lyra bad-mouthing Rafe too? For all that she and Rafe seemed to have had a falling out, she really shouldn't be influencing his daughter against him. Not that Eve had heard Skye say anything bad about her father, but still.

Eve hadn't yet managed to get to the bottom of what it was about Dylan that had upset Lyra so viscerally. She suspected it had very little to do with the cottage and much more to do with whatever had brought her to Fox House in the first place. It was so hard to know what to do. Lyra was an adult and she didn't want to pry, but still.

Justin said she would tell them whatever was going on when she was good and ready, and he was probably right, but the waiting was killing her. She had considered using the last number redial option after Rafe had called, but she had dithered for too long and then the phone had rung for Agatha and she'd lost her chance. It would have been the wrong thing to do anyway, Eve knew that. She was a little bit ashamed that she'd had the idea in the first place, but only a little bit.

The sound of a van door slamming broke her train of thought.

'Thanks, mate,' came a cheerful voice and then the van pulled away, smoke billowing from its exhaust pipe.

Dylan was standing in front of the house with one remaining packing case and a wistful expression on his face, and Eve found that she could barely muster any animosity towards him at all.

33

'I think we should invite Dylan for dinner,' said Eve at lunchtime. 'I can ask your dad, too, so it's not as awkward.'

'For God's sake, Mum,' snapped Lyra angrily. 'You can't.'

'I don't see why not,' replied Eve, realising as she spoke that she felt quite strongly on the subject. 'We need to face facts. He's moved into the cottage in our garden. Things will be a whole lot easier if we can all get along. I'm not saying we should be best friends but I don't want to be living in a war zone either.'

Eve looked over at Agatha for confirmation but Agatha's expression suggested that her position lay closer to Lyra's than her own. This simply made Eve more determined, and before Agatha could formulate her objection, Eve had decided that dinner with Dylan was precisely what would happen.

'It can be something simple. More of a gesture than anything. But I for one don't want to be looking over my shoulder every time I go outside in case I accidentally bump into him. That's no way to live. I'll pop over now and invite him.'

Her words fell into a stony silence which Eve resolutely ignored.

'Why not bake him a cake as well?' muttered Lyra as Eve slipped on her shoes and left the kitchen.

The early spring warmth of the week before had vanished and there was a nippy breeze and droplets of rain in the air. Ordinarily she would have gone back for a coat but she didn't want to face the naysayers again, so she folded her arms tightly to her chest and pressed on across the lawn.

How would this work now? she wondered as she walked. Would Dylan use this little gate too or would he open up the old pathway through the wood? When Agatha had lived in Fox House as a child they'd had staff living in the cottage, a thought that made Eve queasy. They must have accessed the cottage without going through the garden. Would Dylan do the same? That would be better for everyone's privacy, she supposed. And if they couldn't see him coming and going it might be easier to forget that he was there at all.

When she reached the cottage, the door was standing open despite the chill of the day. Eve hovered on the threshold. There was no doorbell and she wasn't sure he would hear a knock, so she called out.

'Dylan. It's Eve.'

Nothing.

Eve assumed he was in. The front door was wide open. And the cottage was only small; it was unlikely that he wouldn't have heard her. Did that mean he was hiding upstairs and hoping she would go away?

She stood where she was, not wanting to shout again in case she sounded impatient, but not quite ready to give up on her plan. Perhaps he was thinking along similar lines to her mother and Lyra – that they could all live in close proximity but without any relationship.

Okay. If that was how he wanted to play it then no one could say that she hadn't tried. Disgruntled, Eve turned to leave and just as she did she heard the toilet flush. That this was awkward popped into her head before she had time to tell herself that she was fifty-two years old and well beyond being embarrassed by bodily functions. Still . . .

She called out again so she could pretend she had only just arrived.

'Hello.'

Dylan came down the stairs drying his hands on his jeans. 'Yes, I heard you. Sorry, I was otherwise engaged. What can I do for you?'

Eve couldn't tell from his tone whether he was being friendly or resenting her visit. It threw her and she started pulling at her bottom lip, something she only did when she was nervous. She made a conscious effort to stop.

'It was nothing, really,' she began. 'I just wondered if you'd like to come over for supper tonight. Nothing special. Just the four of us, Skye will be in bed of course, and possibly my husband, well ex-husband actually, might come so that would be five, if you don't count Skye.'

She was rambling. What on earth was wrong with her? She stopped talking.

Dylan, who had watched her as she prattled, appeared to be considering her proposal.

'How's the ankle?' he asked.

Eve was confused. There was nothing wrong with her ankle as far as she knew. Was this a reference to something that had happened when they were children, another memory that he possessed and she did not?

'The little girl,' Dylan added. 'Skye?'

Oh, Skye's ankle! She felt like an idiot.

'It's fine, thank you,' she replied. 'I'm not sure there was much wrong with it in the first place.'

'We all like a bit of attention from time to time,' he said.

There was a pause. Her invitation hung in the air waiting to be addressed, but who should do that? Was asking about Skye a deflection? Should she just leave as if she had never mentioned it? Why was she overthinking this so badly?

'Supper sounds good,' he said. 'Thanks.'

Eve was struggling to keep up with the voices in her head and it took a split second for her to register what he had said. He had agreed, hadn't he? Okay. She focused back on the matter in hand.

'Great! Shall we say seven o'clock?'

'I'll be there,' he replied.

There was another pause. He didn't speak, just stood watching her. Eve could feel a blush building.

'Right. Good. See you then,' she said briskly. 'Bye then.'

No small talk. No chat about how the move was going. Just the bare minimum that a conversation required. So why was she blushing like a schoolgirl?

She turned and strode back to the gate into the garden, conscious that he might be watching her but not wanting to turn and see. There was definitely a very odd dynamic between the pair of them but Eve had no idea what it was or why it was there. In the only photo she could find of them she was eight, so he couldn't have been her childhood sweetheart. If he had, she would surely have remembered. First love wasn't the kind of thing you forgot easily.

But something was sending her off kilter. There was absolutely no doubt about that.

She fished her phone out of her pocket and dialled Justin.

'Can you come round tonight?' she asked when he answered. 'For supper. Nothing fancy. I've invited Dylan so I need some reinforcements.'

'Was that wise?' Justin asked.

'Possibly not. But I think we need to make a bit of an effort with him, at least at the start. I can see his house from my bedroom window, for God's sake.'

'I can see a lot of houses from my bedroom window,' countered Justin, 'but that doesn't mean I feel compelled to invite the occupants round for dinner.'

Eve tutted in frustration. 'Don't be difficult. That's not the same and you know it. I don't want there to be an atmosphere. It's weird enough that he's living there. We don't need things to be awkward on top of that.'

'I'm sure you know best,' replied Justin.

Eve hated it when he did that, replied in a way that suggested she was making a mistake but without actually saying so.

'I do,' she said shortly. 'So will you come?'

'What time do you want me?'

34

September 1978

'Can we go and see *Grease*?' Eve asked Agatha.

Agatha didn't understand the question.

'What is *Grease*?' she asked, and Eve's forehead crinkled as if she was now struggling in turn to comprehend.

'*Grease*,' she said, as if this was all that was required to make things clear. And then, when Agatha showed no recognition, she added, 'The film? With John Travolta and Olivia Newton-John?'

Agatha was still none the wiser. She thought she might have heard of John Travolta. He wore a white suit and danced on a floor that lit up. She knew nothing about the film.

However, going to the cinema was one of those things that real families did, the kind of family she'd had in mind when she married Henry. The family she had ended up with had no such entertainments.

But she was still holding out hope for change.

'Yes!' she said. 'I don't see why not.'

Eve looked delighted and then almost immediately concerned.

'What about Daddy?' she asked.

Another excellent question. What about Daddy? Henry would have no interest in going to the cinema with them and would express that in a way that left neither of them in any doubt about how he felt, which would hurt Eve's feelings and so was to be avoided. Agatha's life was made up, in the main part, of shielding Eve from Henry's disappointments, which seemed to colour the rest of him more and more.

'What about Daddy?'

Henry's voice boomed out behind them and Agatha jumped. Eve took a step behind Agatha and Agatha placed a hand on her daughter's head – an involuntary response, she realised, as her palm made contact with her hair.

'Eve was just asking if we could go to the pictures,' Agatha said brightly. 'We were wondering if you'd like to come too.'

It must have been clear from the tone in which Eve had asked the question that this wasn't what she had been asking. Her question had been more along the lines of, how will we square a trip to the cinema with Daddy, rather than would Daddy like to come too.

But Henry didn't appear to have picked up on the nuance. Nuance really wasn't his forte.

'Great idea,' he said, rubbing his hands together enthusiastically, which threw Agatha even further off balance. 'What are they showing? We've not been to the pictures for ages, Aggie.'

A tiny shoot of hope began to unfurl in Agatha. Henry had been in the doldrums for a while, his moods black and his temper inexplicably short, hence Eve's trepidation about his response to her request. Maybe a family trip was what they needed to bring him out of himself a little. Agatha hoped so. The atmosphere at Fox House could be very dark on his really bad days.

'*Grease?*' replied Eve, the upward inflection in her voice making it apparent that she was expecting to have to explain this to Henry too.

'About the American high school,' he said, surprising them both.

'Yes!'

'I saw it reviewed on *Film 78*,' he replied. 'It's got that blonde Australian woman in it.'

'Olivia Newton-John,' supplied Eve.

Henry nodded to himself. 'That's the one.'

'So can we go?' asked Eve. 'Everyone at school has seen it. They said it's brilliant. And I know some of the songs already.'

'Ah yes,' said Henry, his momentary enthusiasm waning. 'It's a musical. I'd forgotten that.'

Eve's face fell, but Agatha stepped in. 'Well, I'm sure it will be fun. Shall we ask Jack and Mary if they want to come, bring Dylan along too? We could make it a little outing, maybe go to the Wimpy for tea afterwards.'

Eve beamed and bounced up and down on her toes.

'Please Daddy. Please!'

Henry's eyes tracked from one of them to the other, his face unreadable. Then he broke into a smile.

'Yes, let's,' he said, and Agatha relaxed.

Agatha rang Mary who said that Dylan was away with the Cubs for the weekend, but she and Jack would love to come. They decided on the matinee showing and Henry drove with Jack in the front and Agatha, Mary and Eve all bunched up on the back seat.

Standing in the queue to buy tickets, Agatha realised with a sickening feeling that she hadn't really done her research. Wasn't she supposed to check that the film was suitable for her daughter? That was what she believed a responsible mother would do, but it hadn't crossed her mind until they were already there. Yet again Agatha had fallen short.

But this time her maternal failings didn't matter. The film looked innocuous enough, the poster featuring the two stars all dressed up for a party. It gave nothing away about the content, but Eve had said that her school friends had seen it. Agatha had to admit that Eve looked quite young by comparison with the other children in the queue, although she wasn't quite the youngest.

A thought occurred to her. Weren't films categorised so parents knew what was suitable? Agatha looked around for the film's rating and found it on a board above the door. It was rated 'A', but this meant nothing. She and Henry didn't go to the cinema often enough to be au fait with all the classifications. 'U' meant suitable for everyone, she knew that. But 'A'?

Making sure that Henry was deep in conversation with Jack, Agatha turned herself sideways so he wouldn't hear and half whispered her question to Mary.

'What does an "A" rating mean?' she asked. She was going to be in so much trouble if they'd come all this way only to find that Eve couldn't go in.

'I think children need to go in with an adult,' replied Mary, and Agatha relaxed. That was all right then. She hadn't done anything wrong.

They got to the front of the queue and Henry pushed himself forward to buy the tickets.

'Four adults and one child,' he said to the girl in the kiosk.

'No, Henry. I'll pay for our seats,' said Jack.

Agatha held her breath, bracing herself silently.

'I'll get them,' said Henry pleasantly.

'But there's no need. I can . . .' Jack stepped forward, wallet in hand, and spoke to the girl.

'I'll pay for two,' he said to her.

Sometimes that was all it took for matters to take a dark turn. A simple enough thing, innocuous in its own right but at which Henry, inexplicably, took offence. Jack knew that, so why didn't he just let Henry have his grand gesture?

Henry's eyes went dark. His face was calm, affable even, but Agatha could hear the undertone of menace in his voice.

'I said I'll pay,' he said slowly.

Jack, to give him his due, knew which battles to fight and this, at the head of a long queue and in front of a busy foyer, was not one of them.

'Well, thank you,' he said graciously. 'Let me buy the popcorn.'

Instantly Henry's expression lightened. He smiled broadly, the girl handed over the tickets and balance was restored. Agatha saw Mary glance wide-eyed at Jack and Jack gave her a little 'I told you so' expression back.

So, Jack and Mary talked about her and Henry behind their backs. It wasn't surprising, she supposed, but Agatha could feel the shine start to rub off her afternoon.

They settled down in their seats, the women and Eve together at one end and Henry and Jack at the other. The auditorium smelled of popcorn and chocolate, and was almost full. An expectant hush descended as the adverts finished. Eve beamed up at Agatha, and gave a little shiver of excitement. 'Thank you,' she mouthed, and Agatha smiled back at her conspiratorially.

The film began with a couple kissing on a beach but then ran into a cartoon and finally opened up into a school scene. The tightness in Agatha's chest lifted. The actors looked far too old to be playing schoolchildren but the film seemed harmless enough and Eve was sitting forward in her seat, totally entranced.

They were half an hour or so in when Agatha first heard Henry make a disapproving sound. John Travolta and his friends were doing up an old car. It all seemed innocent enough to her, but

Henry tutted and then spoke to Jack without bothering to lower his voice.

'Did you hear what he just said?'

Agatha turned to see Jack shaking his head, smiling appeasingly. She hadn't heard anything untoward in the lyrics but then she'd been more caught up by the spectacle of the scene. Eve clearly hadn't noticed a thing.

Not long after that Agatha realised that the character on screen was talking about becoming pregnant accidentally. Her stomach clenched, but when she looked at Eve it was clear that that whole part of the storyline had gone right over her head. Eve would only be seeing what was appropriate for an eight-year-old because she didn't have the understanding to see any more.

Then she became aware of a kerfuffle to her right. Henry was standing up.

'Out!' he said at normal volume, no concessions made. 'Eve. Agatha. We're leaving now.'

Agatha was frozen in her seat, not sure what to do. She could hear Jack whispering at Henry, trying to placate him, but Henry was having none of it.

'No, Jack. This is appalling. Totally unsuitable for my wife and daughter.'

Henry leant across and grabbed for Agatha's arm, yanking at her sleeve to make her stand up. Eve, now aware that something wasn't right, started to object and Agatha shushed her to stay quiet.

There was a loud tutting behind them and other people were starting to mutter. Someone called out, 'Hey, mate. Sit down.' Henry took no notice but continued to complain loudly about the content of the film whilst trying to drag Agatha to her feet.

The usherette came over, aiming her torch directly at Henry.

'Please can you sit down, sir, or leave. You're causing a disturbance.'

'Oh, don't you worry,' replied Henry. 'We're leaving. I'm not sitting through another moment of this filth.'

Agatha could see that she had no choice.

'We have to go, Eve,' she said, but Eve sat firm in her chair and refused to budge. Agatha was mortified. Not only was Mary witnessing her husband's appalling behaviour and her daughter's insubordination, but the entire cinema was being treated to it as well.

'Eve, please,' she begged.

Eve crossed her arms and scowled.

'Eve. Stand up this instant,' bellowed Henry.

Eve didn't move and kept her eyes trained on the screen, watching intently despite the chaos that was unfolding around her.

Henry wouldn't hit Eve. Agatha was almost certain of that. Almost certain, but she didn't know what might happen if Henry got angry enough, because she had never let that happen. She always stepped in, took the heat out of whatever was upsetting him.

Henry was trying to push her out of the way so that he could reach Eve. Agatha stood her ground. Jack was attempting to talk Henry down, the usherette was telling them to leave and the other cinema-goers were booing and shouting at them to move out of the way. Everything was building to a massive crescendo around her.

Agatha didn't know what to do. She couldn't get Eve to cooperate and there wasn't room to pick her up and carry her bodily from the cinema. So instead she squared up to Henry.

'Stop it,' she hissed. 'Just sit down and we can talk about it afterwards.'

She tried to sit down herself, but Henry had hold of her sleeve and wouldn't let her.

'You will not tell me what to do,' he said. 'I have decided we are leaving and so we will leave. NOW!'

And then, with his spare hand, he lashed out as if to hit her on the side of the head. Agatha squeezed her eyes tight shut, preparing herself for the blow, but it didn't come. She opened her eyes and saw that Jack had grabbed Henry's arm. There wasn't enough room for Henry to push Jack away, but he thrashed about, trying to free himself. Jack held on tight.

'Let's go,' Jack said in a low voice. Agatha had never known Jack to be so authoritative, and Henry bowed to his will at once as if he were a small boy being reprimanded. His anger seemed to dissipate and his arms dropped to his sides, letting Agatha's sleeve go. He allowed himself to be manoeuvred out of the seat and down the aisle. Agatha fell back into her seat and immediately felt Mary find her hand and squeeze gently. Her skin felt soft and slightly moist against her own.

'Are you all right?' Mary whispered, and Agatha gave her a tight nod, tears of shock pricking her eyes. 'Do you want to leave?' she heard Mary ask. She didn't know. She couldn't think what would be for the best.

Mary answered her own question.

'Let's leave Jack to calm him down,' she whispered. 'And we'll stay here.'

She didn't add 'where it's safe', but Agatha heard the words loud and clear. Agatha nodded again. That would be the best thing to do. She was sure.

She looked over at Eve. She was watching the screen intently, laughing at a pyjama party scene as if nothing had happened.

35

NOW

Why had her infuriating mother invited that man for dinner? Lyra was so angry it was making her temples throb. In what world could bringing him into their lives improve matters? Even her grandmother, the one who had started all this off, was keeping her distance from him. Although, now she came to think about it, that was weird. Surely the two of them should be bosom buddies or else why would she have given him the cottage destined for her?

She blew her lips out in a huge expulsion of breath. She had to move on from this cottage business. She was going round and round in circles, and none of it was helping her solve the more immediate problem of where she was going to live so that she could convince a court that her life was safe and stable and preferable to anything that Rafe could offer.

Maybe she needed a lawyer. Wasn't that the grown-up thing to do? The thought made Lyra want to cry. She didn't know any lawyers. Why would she? She hadn't even needed a divorce because she and Rafe hadn't bothered getting married. She'd had other things on her mind – having Skye and then getting her degree with a baby to look after.

She googled 'How to find a lawyer'. The government's website was top of the list, something called The Law Society after that. But she didn't have the headspace to plough through those dry pages with their endless words. She just wanted the solution placed in front of her so she could pick it up and run with it. She killed the screen and put her phone back in her pocket.

She steadied her screaming mind and tried thinking clearly and logically instead of letting the anxiety take over. There were three simple steps to resolving her own issues, assuming she ignored Rafe's bombshell. First, decide where to move to, then find somewhere to live there and finally find a school for Skye.

Or should those be the other way round? Find a school first and then somewhere near that to live? Lyra didn't know. All primary schools were much of a muchness, weren't they? For the hundredth time, she cursed herself for the out-of-proportion panic that had made her run from their old flat. She had made everything a thousand times worse. Maybe she should just go home. She could find a new flat near the old one. At least that would mean Skye wouldn't have to change schools. But that felt like going backwards, and how would any of it help with the Rafe situation?

God, what a mess.

Well, she could at least decide on one thing. She wouldn't go to her mother's stupid dinner party. She'd put Skye to bed early and eat in her bedroom. Yeah, she thought, great plan, because that was a really grown-up thing to do.

Actually, what she needed to do was talk the situation through with someone. That would help her get some perspective.

She got her phone out and FaceTimed Heather. It rang twice before Heather picked up. She must have been getting ready to go out. Her hair was hidden beneath a towelling turban and she only had mascara on one eye which gave her an unbalanced, unhinged look.

'Oh my God. Where've you been? I thought you'd fallen off the face of the planet. A whole week and no word. I've been super-worried about you. Is everything okay? Is Skye okay?'

Lyra tried a 'what can you do' smile and rolled her eyes.

'It's been a bit busy,' she said vaguely.

'No shit. I mean, a week and no contact. Nothing. A whole week! I nearly rang the police!' Heather's voice rose to a squeak.

Heather had sent messages every day, each increasingly concerned, but Lyra had read and ignored them, not feeling able to confess to what she'd done.

'Yeah. I'm sorry about that,' she said. 'I had some stuff. But I'm here now.'

'Okay, hun. But it's all okay now, yeah?'

Lyra felt her eyes starting to prick. She blinked hard and twisted her hair up into a bun as a distraction. She so wanted to tell Heather everything but it felt too big, too overwhelming. She just didn't know where to start. She let her hair fall.

'Yeah,' she replied. 'All good.'

'Cool,' said Heather, apparently appeased. 'So, we're going out tonight. Can you get a sitter? It'll be great to see you. A few drinks. A bit of a boogie . . .' She waved her arms over her head, grinning. 'And you can tell me what could possibly be so fabulous that it's distracted you for a whole week. I'm hoping it's sex.'

Sex. That was a joke. Lyra envied Heather her easy, carefree existence. Her life was so simple with no worries beyond eking her wage out so she could have a new outfit to go out in each Saturday. Lyra hadn't felt carefree since she'd peed on the pregnancy test stick. In the years since then she'd been in a perpetual state of nervous anxiety. People who didn't have children just had no idea how scary life could be.

She pulled a disappointed face. 'I can't, babe. Sorry. I'm not at home at the mo. I'm at my granny's for a bit.'

Heather's expression slipped into concern at once. 'God, is she all right, your granny?'

That was a joke, although of course Heather hadn't intended it as such. Of course Agatha was all right. She would probably outlive all of them. But Lyra could see that pretending otherwise would at least explain her radio silence.

'Yes, she's okay now, thanks. But she wasn't great so we've come to stay just until she's better.'

'Aw, that's nice. Your mum lives there too, right?'

Lyra nodded.

'Aw,' said Heather again, her head tipped to one side as if this arrangement was actually quite sweet. 'And Skye's all good?'

'Yeah. Being spoiled rotten,' said Lyra, realising as she spoke that in the middle of all this turmoil Skye was fine, happy as Larry, in fact. Lyra was keeping her safe from the storm that was raging all around her. That was good, at least.

'Well, I'm glad you're not dead!' laughed Heather. 'Shame about tonight though. It would have been fun. Need to fly now, hun. Can't go out looking like this.' She gestured to her towel turban. 'Speak tomorrow, yeah?'

Lyra nodded. 'Definitely,' she said. 'Have a great night. Say hello to everyone from me.'

'Will do. Love you. And no more ghosting, OK?' Heather blew her a kiss and then she was gone.

Lyra stared at the black screen and at her own reflection in it.

'Well played, Lyra,' she said out loud. 'That really helped sort everything out. It's all totally crystal clear now.'

There was nothing for it. She was going to have to chat it through with one of the real grown-ups. It was a pity Skye had interrupted the conversation with her dad the other evening. She had almost told him then. Maybe she could catch a few minutes on her own with him when he came over for the dinner thing later. It wasn't that likely, though. Not when they had a 'guest'.

Her mum was here, just downstairs in fact. But she would be busy cooking and anyway, she had a tendency to the over-emotional and was likely to panic. Lyra needed a cool head to offset her own hot one.

What about Agatha?

Lyra paused. How would her grandmother react if she told her everything? Lyra had no idea. Agatha was a mystery to her. She played her cards so close to her chest. Yes, she could be confrontational and she loved a good debate, but Lyra had the impression that she was playing devil's advocate a lot of the time rather than arguing from the heart. What did she actually think about anything? Lyra wasn't sure, which made it hard to appraise her as a potential confidante.

Still, Lyra was reaching desperation point. Agatha it might have to be.

36

But when Lyra made her way downstairs there was no sign of Agatha. *He* was there. The usurper. She could hear his voice. And her dad had arrived. Lyra sometimes wondered why her parents had bothered getting divorced given that they seemed to enjoy each other's company so much.

'Shall I get Granny?' she asked her mother.

'She's not coming down,' replied Eve, and Lyra detected a trace of irritation in her voice. 'A headache, apparently, although she was perfectly all right an hour ago.'

Granny's rebelling, thought Lyra gleefully. She's refusing to buy into Mum's little happy families charade. Well, good for her. In fact, Lyra wished she'd done the same, but it was too late now. Her mother was holding out a glass of wine and ushering her towards the lounge. Lyra accepted the glass and stepped into the room.

Her father was sitting on one sofa and the man on the other. Justin was wearing his customary slim-fitting trousers and a roll-neck merino jumper. He was pretty cool for an older man. Lyra had always been proud of him when he showed up at stuff. So much more stylish than her friends' dads in their sloppy athleisure wear.

The man – she supposed she should start calling him Dylan – wasn't wearing athleisure either. His jeans had seen better days and he was wearing a sweater that might have come from a charity shop.

It had that vintage look about it, but not in a cool way. He looked clean but poor. Lyra winced as she thought that. Was 'poor' still a term you could use to describe someone? She decided not. It was true though. That was how he looked.

No, Lyra corrected herself. That was how he was dressed. His demeanour was no different to her father's. He looked quietly confident in his skin, like he knew who he was and he was happy with that. Not cocky though, or as if he had something to prove. Lyra hated herself for thinking it, but Dylan looked interesting.

Well, she wasn't interested in him. He was still there illegitimately, a cuckoo in their nest. She wanted no part of it. She pursed her lips, sat down next to her father and glared at Dylan.

'Hi there, darling,' said Justin. 'You've met Dylan, I take it.'

Lyra nodded tightly.

'A couple of times, in fact,' said Dylan. 'First when she caught me looking at the cottage and accused me of being a trespasser, and then again when her little girl turned her ankle. Oh, and she ran from my cottage in tears. So that's three.'

There was no agenda in his tone, no judgement. He was simply delivering information. Lyra noticed the possessive pronoun and her lips tightened still further. His cottage. He'd only moved in there that morning. Was he trying to rub her nose in it?

But no. Reluctantly Lyra had to admit that he wasn't. That didn't seem to be part of his agenda at all.

Her dad looked as if he might be about to question the tears thing but then remembered where they were and seemed to think better of it.

'And are you settling in okay?' he asked instead, and Lyra winced again. Was there nothing to talk about except the bloody cottage? 'Eve and I lived there for a while back in the day. It's a bit on the basic side.'

'It's fine for my needs,' replied Dylan. 'And I'm grateful to Agatha.'

I'll bet you are, thought Lyra.

172

'So, what's your story?' Justin asked. 'Where were you living before?'

That was just like her dad. Straight in with the difficult questions. Although, Lyra thought, it shouldn't really have been difficult to ask for such basic details. It was Agatha who was making that hard.

Dylan crossed his legs, scratched at his scalp and eyed Justin. And then Eve, with her impeccable sense of timing, called to tell them that dinner was ready.

As there were only four of them Eve had chosen to eat in the kitchen, but Lyra noticed that the counter tops were clear of pans and other cooking detritus. She had obviously made an effort to tidy up before she'd invited them to join her. Lyra searched for something concerning this that she could be irritated about but came up short.

They settled themselves around the rectangular table, her parents at either end and she and Dylan sitting opposite one another on the longer sides. Eve put the serving dishes in the middle and handed around steaming plates of a beef casserole that Lyra knew would be rich and delicious.

'I'm sorry Agatha isn't here,' she said. 'She sends her apologies.'

'I hope she feels better soon,' replied Dylan, and then, 'This looks fabulous.'

Eve gave him a bashful smile, which Lyra clocked and then saw that her dad had too.

'So,' Justin said, serving himself some broccoli spears, 'Dylan was just about to tell us his life story.'

'Really? How interesting. Do go on,' said Eve unnaturally, like they were characters in a novel.

'There's not much to tell,' said Dylan. He speared a chunk of beef with his fork and they all waited to see if he would elaborate.

He put the food into his mouth, chewed, swallowed, and then gave Eve an appreciative nod which she accepted as if she was a lowly housemaid. Lyra was surprised she didn't go for a full-on curtsy.

'I was brought up round here, as you know.' He glanced at Eve again and Lyra made a mental note to quiz her mother on exactly what she did know. She'd given the impression of being as much in the dark as Lyra, but that comment and her subsequent look suggested otherwise. In spite of herself, Lyra was starting to find the mystery more intriguing than irritating.

'Then we moved away when I was nine. My dad went away and my mum took it badly so I looked after her. We moved around a bit, caravan parks mostly, some houses. We lived in an old windmill for a bit. Not as cosy as it sounds. Then my mum died quite recently—'

'Oh, I'm sorry,' interrupted Eve and Lyra resisted an eye roll. Her mother had never met this woman and she barely knew Dylan. How could her death be of the slightest concern?

'Thank you,' replied Dylan. He glanced at Eve and again something passed between them, although Lyra couldn't identify what it was. She looked sidelong at her dad. He'd spotted it too. She saw his eyes narrowing.

'That all sounds a bit grim,' he said, and Dylan shrugged.

'It is what it is. She was old.'

'And what do you do? As a job?' her dad asked. His tone wasn't quite as open and friendly as it had been, Lyra noticed.

'This and that,' replied Dylan. 'I can turn my hand to most things.' He took another mouthful of food. 'This really is delicious, Eve. Thanks.'

That was to be the end of the little trot through his life, it seemed, but Justin wasn't ready to let it go.

'And the cottage?' he asked, his eyes not leaving Dylan's face. 'How come you've landed up there?'

Dylan chewed slowly and then took a drink.

'Well,' he said. 'I suppose you'd have to ask Agatha about that.'

37

'Actually,' Eve said. 'She said we would have to ask you.'

She gave him a funny little half smile and a shrug as if this were one of life's odd conundrums, but then she held his gaze, waiting for a reply. Lyra was impressed. It really wasn't like her mother to be so direct.

'Did she now?' replied Dylan. 'I see.'

'It's all a bit cloak and dagger for me,' said Justin. 'Not sure why we need this secrecy, but then Agatha has always been one for games.'

'She said she owed you something,' Eve continued. 'That she had a big debt to you that she needed to repay.'

They were all staring at Dylan now. They might as well have been training a spotlight into his eyes. Lyra would have cracked under the pressure, but he was so calm. He didn't meet anyone's gaze, though, as he chased a piece of potato around his plate.

'Well,' he said. 'Yes. I suppose she might see it like that.'

They were just too polite to go in for the kill, although Lyra could see that her dad was dying to. There was a pause as her parents seemed to be deciding if they could push him further.

Then Eve said, 'And do you have plans to live in the cottage for a while? We'd hate for it to be sold off to a stranger, what with it being so close to the main house.'

'Someone stranger than me, you mean?' Dylan asked. He winked at her mother. Actually winked.

Lyra felt her dad bristle next to her. He cleared his throat and sniffed.

'I think Eve is genuinely concerned that Agatha has opened up a can of worms by parcelling the estate up as she has done. You can understand that, I'm sure.'

Gone was the gentle bonhomie of earlier. Dylan had her dad rattled, although Lyra wasn't sure why. What her grandmother did and how that might affect her mother was definitely none of his business any more, although it might be hers, she supposed, so maybe that gave her dad a legitimate interest.

'Let me put your mind at rest on that score at least,' Dylan said, but he was looking at her mother and not her dad. 'I've spent most of my life so far moving on from one place to another. It's time to put down some roots. I've always liked it round here. We used to have so much fun in those woods, didn't we, Eve?' He smiled at her mother fondly.

But as Lyra turned to see how her mother had responded to this comment, all there was on Eve's face was confused embarrassment. It was apparent that she didn't have a clue what he was talking about.

'So, when I contacted Agatha to tell her about my mum dying, she suggested that if I needed somewhere to live I might want to come here, back to Fox House. I thought about it and decided that I did. Finding you here again, Eve, has just been an added bonus.'

Lyra's eyes flicked over to her mother again. She was blushing! Actually blushing like a schoolgirl. Dear God. She didn't fancy him, did she? That would be the absolute pits.

'How very convenient it all is,' said her dad spikily.

'Indeed,' replied Dylan. Either he couldn't sense that he'd annoyed Justin or, and Lyra thought this was more likely, he just didn't care. Dylan didn't seem like the kind of bloke who worried much about what anyone else thought.

'It's a bit of a shit-hole, though,' added her dad.

'Justin!' Eve remonstrated.

'Well, it is. It was barely habitable when we lived there and that was nearly thirty years ago. It's going to need some serious work to bring it up to scratch.'

'I don't mind hard work,' replied Dylan levelly. 'Like I said, I can turn my hand to pretty much anything.'

Involuntarily, Lyra found herself looking at Dylan's hands. They were working hands, some of the joints swollen and with silvery scars in several places. Her dad's hands were soft, the hands of a man who created with his mind rather than with tools.

'It's expensive these days, doing a place up. Materials get pricier by the day. Where will you get the cash?'

Lyra's jaw dropped. This was definitely a question too far. She doubted even her grandmother would have got that personal. Dylan would be well within his rights to refuse to share that kind of detail. But Dylan wasn't thrown in the slightest. He stared straight at Justin to reply.

'That's part of the arrangement with Agatha,' he replied. 'She'll pay for the materials. I'll provide the labour and then when the work is done, she'll transfer the cottage into my name, together with a ring of the surrounding woodland and a right of way across the drive.'

So that was it. Finally they had the details of the deal. A silence fell across the table as they each contemplated it.

Lyra could see how it made sense, kind of. But then, she reasoned, the cottage would go to Dylan at the end of it. So actually, he was getting the cottage *and* the money to make it lovely. Without understanding exactly what debt Agatha owed to Dylan, it was impossible to make proper sense of any of it.

The silence continued to spike around them until her mother stood up, an unnaturally bright smile on her flushed face.

'Who's for banoffee cheesecake?'

38

October 1978

It was hot for October. The autumnal sun still had the power to warm them through to their bones as they sat on the sunny patio outside the dining room and looked out across the garden. On the table before them sat three empty wine bottles and half a bottle of whisky. Also on the table was Henry.

To be fair, Henry wasn't on the table as such, but having consumed the greater part of the alcohol himself over a late breakfast, lazy lunch and afternoon tea he now slept, his head heavy on his forearms. He was snoring, the sound like a pig snuffling through mud, and it grated on Agatha. She wanted to give him a shove to make him stop, but that might wake him and on the whole she preferred the irritating noise to her husband conscious.

Agatha wasn't one for daytime drinking. It felt like a waste of time that could be spent doing something useful, and anyway one of them had to be together enough to look after Eve. She would never trust that to Henry. Even if he were sober, there was no telling what he might do. She nursed her cup of tea, now cold in its china cup, and tried to ignore the snoring.

Jack sat close by. He was carving a long branch that he'd found in the wood. Beech, apparently. It just looked like a stick to Agatha, who could only identify timber if it still had leaves growing from it, but Jack had said it was beech and she had no reason to disbelieve him. Over their many years of friendship Agatha had come to know that there was very little that Jack wasn't right about.

He seemed to be doing something interesting with his chisel to a large knot at one end of the stick.

'What's that going to be?' she asked him.

Jack stopped whittling and held the stick out for her to see. It looked like a misshapen rugby ball.

'I can't tell what it is,' she said, squinting slightly in case that helped. It didn't.

Jack looked at his work appraisingly, twisting the stick in his hand so he could see the shape from all angles.

'Not much so far,' he replied. 'But I'm aiming for a fox. Well, its head at least.'

Agatha looked again. She could just make out the shape of an animal's head starting to emerge. Two ears and a long thin snout. Maybe.

'Good,' she said, although she remained unconvinced. 'Does it need to be on the end of such a long stick?'

Jack stared at her, shaking his head and laughing.

'It'd make a pretty rubbish walking stick if it was only six inches long.'

'Oh! I see!'

Agatha felt a little stupid. It was obvious now he had said that that was what it would be.

'What will you do with it when it's finished? Sell it?'

Jack looked at the carving again. 'As it's a fox, I thought I might give it to you. A fox head for Fox House.'

'Clever,' laughed Agatha. 'Although what am I going to do with a walking stick? I'm only thirty-six!'

'You never know when it might come in handy,' said Jack.

'Oh, you're a bundle of fun,' replied Agatha, but she was smiling. No one ever gave her presents, especially not thoughtful ones like this. It felt nice.

They settled back into quietness, the only sound the birdsong from the wood, Jack's chisel against the grain and Henry's rasping snores.

'Where's Mary?' Agatha asked vaguely. 'She's not still washing up?'

'No, she's taken Dylan home. You must have been in the loo. She said to say thank you and she'll see you soon.'

Agatha nodded, taking the fact that she had left without saying goodbye in and wondering if it had anything to do with Henry.

'She's lovely, Mary,' she said. 'I don't know how you ever persuaded her to marry a reprobate like you.'

'She is lovely, and that she agreed is one of life's greatest mysteries,' replied Jack.

He fell silent again and Agatha watched as he worked on the fox's snout.

'You can't carry on like this,' he said then, in a low voice.

Agatha knew exactly what he meant but pretended that she didn't.

'Like what?'

Jack cocked his head at the sleeping Henry. Agatha looked at him too. He was drooling, a thin silvery string of spittle running from the corner of his mouth. She wrinkled her nose in disgust and looked away.

'You know what I mean. The way he treats you and Eve. The drinking. All of it.'

Agatha shifted in her seat so she could no longer see Henry.

180

'Oh, it's not that bad,' she said brightly. 'You make it sound like he's a monster.'

'And isn't he?'

Agatha rested her cheek on her hand and stared out over the garden, now much less well kept than it had been in her parents' day. She sighed deeply.

'I keep thinking things will improve,' she said. 'He's been having a hard time at the bank. He thinks they might let him go. It's a lot of stress for him.'

'Lots of people have stress in their lives but they don't all treat their wives like dirt and then drink themselves into oblivion.'

Agatha opened her mouth to protest, but what was the point? Her false loyalty to Henry would be ignored. This was Jack. He knew her inside and out. She could never hide anything from him so there was little point in trying.

'I know,' she confessed. 'And I do worry about Eve. What is it doing to her, growing up like this? If only we'd had more children, then at least she wouldn't be on her own so much of the time. She hears everything, I'm sure.' She sniffed and her shoulders drooped. 'It wasn't meant to be like this,' she added.

'What wasn't?' asked Jack without looking up from his whittling.

'This!' Agatha waved her hands to indicate her entire world. 'I had such plans, to make everything so different from the way I was brought up, but history seems to be repeating itself. We were supposed to be the perfect parents. I wanted our children to grow up in a house full of laughter, to know they were loved. But no one ever laughs here . . .' There was a pause. She didn't dare comment on the second part of that sentence. She pressed on. 'I used to hear my mother sobbing every day, you know. I knew she was crying for the twins. I'd wonder what she must have been like when they were small, when she had nothing to be sad about. I longed to be enough for her, but it was like I didn't exist. Nothing I did would ever ease her pain. If I'd had siblings maybe I wouldn't have been so aware of how inadequate I was.'

Jack stopped what he was doing and looked directly at her. 'Nothing about you is inadequate, Agatha. You are amazing. You're strong and curious and funny and quite good at cooking. If I hadn't married Mary, I'd have married you myself,' he added, lightening the tone.

'You wouldn't have had the chance!' laughed Agatha. 'You were never the man for me, Jack Brooker, more's the pity. Life would have been so much simpler if I'd just fallen for you instead of him.'

Jack grinned and went back to his carving.

'How did you and Mary learn how to be parents?' Agatha said thoughtfully.

'What do you mean?' Jack replied. 'You don't learn how to do it. You just are.'

This wasn't what Agatha meant and she tutted in frustration. 'No. Or at least, that's not how it is for me. I don't know what I'm doing most of the time,' she said.

'No parent does,' replied Jack. 'You just do what you think is best and hope to blazes it works.'

'That's the trouble,' she replied wistfully. 'I have no idea what is best. It's like someone tore that chapter out of the manual.'

Henry uttered a huge reverberating grunt as his contribution to the conversation. They waited to be sure he was still asleep and then the conversation started up again.

'What are you going to do about him?' asked Jack quietly, cocking his head towards Henry.

Eve looked at her husband.

'What do you mean?' she asked disingenuously.

'He's getting worse all the time,' said Jack. 'He's turning into a drunk, Aggie. I'm not sure he's good for you. Or Eve either, for that matter.'

Agatha sighed. A tiny part deep in her heart knew he was right. But without Henry she had no chance of ever making her plans work out the way she had always hoped, and she was nothing if not determined.

'You could always get him to leave,' Jack continued. 'Just tell him it's over and that you want a divorce. This is your house and I assume you still have enough money to live without his.'

This was true. Her parents had left her very well provided for. She didn't need Henry. But she was married to him. She had made her bed and all that.

'I'm not sure things are so bad,' she said. The unspoken 'yet' hung silently in the air.

'Aren't they?' Jack paused, and when Agatha didn't reply he continued, 'Mary was horrified by that scene he made at the cinema. It was all I could do to get her to bring Dylan today. She doesn't think it's safe for him here.'

Agatha's head shot up. 'No! Really? Not safe? She hasn't said anything to me.'

'Well, she's not likely to, is she?'

'No. I suppose not. God, that's terrible. I'm so sorry.'

'Don't be ridiculous, Aggie. None of this is your fault.'

Jack threw a look of pure venom at Henry. It took Agatha by surprise. Weren't the two men supposed to be friends? But then maybe Henry had burned his boats there too. There was only so much abuse one friendship could bear before the cracks began to threaten its strength.

'I'll think about it,' said Agatha. 'I promise.'

Jack nodded. 'Good,' he said, and then refocused his attention on the fox's head as Henry snored on.

39

NOW

'Shall we have a little run out?'

The idea had just popped into Eve's head but as soon as she said it she knew it was exactly what they all needed. Agatha looked more doubtful.

'A run out? You make me sound like an old lady,' she said grumpily.

Eve resisted the obvious response.

'A change of scene,' she said. 'It would do us good, don't you think? Just the four of us,' she added.

'Well, I suppose some fresh air might be nice. Where were you thinking?'

'Oh, I don't know. We could make a day of it and go to the coast. How about Filey? You always say you love the sea and I'm sure Skye would have a ball playing on the beach. We could have a go at the pitch and putt. She'd like that.'

A deep crease appeared between Agatha's eyebrows.

'I have never pitched and putted in my life,' she said wryly. 'And I don't intend to start now.'

'You can sit and watch,' replied Eve. 'I assume they have clubs for children so Skye can play. It's a family game, after all.'

For a second, Eve thought she saw an unusual expression on her mother's face: regret. Agatha wasn't one for regrets as a rule. She was far too pragmatic for that. Never having played pitch and putt, though? Now that spoke volumes. Eve had never played either, not until she had met Justin. He had introduced her to all the delights of the English seaside resort – slot machines, fortune tellers, candyfloss, fun fairs, those stripy sticks of rock that stuck to everything.

'What do you mean, you've never been on a waltzer?' he'd asked her, mystified by the concept. 'How have you got to twenty-five and never been on a waltzer?'

Eve had shrugged. 'We didn't really go to the seaside when I was a girl.'

'But what about fun fairs not at the sea?' he'd pressed. 'You must have been to those.'

Eve grinned and shook her head. 'I had a terribly deprived childhood,' she'd laughed, and he had made a joke about ringing Childline for her.

She had never thought about why they hadn't been to the coast when she was a girl, but perhaps this was the answer. If Agatha had herself not been taken to the seaside then maybe that was why she had never thought to take Eve.

'So,' she said brightly. 'Shall we go?'

Agatha crossed the kitchen and peered out at the sky, which was a pretty blue and dotted with candyfloss clouds that looked as if a child had painted them on.

'Yes,' she said. 'I think we shall.'

It took a while to get them ready as clothing was selected and rejected as being not warm enough for the east coast in April. A pile of outer garments for every eventuality was collected and then dumped in the boot of Eve's car. She wanted to take a picnic, but the contents of the fridge meant that a trip to the shops would be needed first by which time it would hardly be worth going.

'We'll have fish and chips on the prom for lunch,' she trilled. 'What do you say to that, Skye?'

'I say yes!' said Skye. 'We always have fish and chips at the seaside, don't we, Mummy?' she added, and Lyra confirmed that they always did.

As it was a sunny day in the Easter holidays, Skye wanted to go straight on to the sand so Lyra and Agatha went to secure deckchairs in a good place. Eve watched as the little band of three, her family, moved further away. Agatha was still gripping her fox head cane tightly as she walked, but she definitely seemed to be relying on it less and less. Eve had heard such sad stories of elderly people who lost their mobility due to an accident and then seemed to give up and fade away. Agatha certainly didn't appear to be ready to fade just yet.

Eve found a beach shop and bought a bucket shaped like a castle and a spade that didn't look as though it would snap on first use. She scoured the shelves for the little paper flags that Justin had bought her on their first trip but found nothing similar. They would probably be considered litter these days.

Happy with her purchases, she went to locate the others. They had chosen a place on the edge of the block of deckchairs so that Skye had a vast stretch of sand to play on to their right. Eve handed over the bucket and spade and Skye's face lit up.

'Thanks, VeeVee,' she said without being prompted.

Well done, Lyra, Eve thought. Despite the obvious challenges, Lyra was doing an excellent job of bringing up her daughter alone. Skye's manners were impeccable.

The sea was a long way away.

'Is it going out or coming in?' she asked, squinting at the horizon and shading her eyes with her hand. Lyra looked the tide tables up on her phone and declared that the tide had just turned and the water was on its way back.

'It won't get all the way here though,' she added. 'The deckchair people won't have set up where they'd have to move everything twice a day.'

The promising blue skies had been deceptive and there was a distinctly chilly nip in the air. Eve zipped her coat up and instinctively gave Agatha a quick up and down to make sure she was warm enough. When had she stopped checking on her child's well-being and started checking on her mother's? she wondered briefly.

'Actually, I do remember coming here just once as a girl,' she said. 'Well, I was more of a teenager, really. Just the two of us, Agatha. Do you remember?'

'Of course I remember. I'm not going senile.'

'I'm not sure you can use that word any more, Granny,' chipped in Lyra. 'It's called dementia now.'

'Whatever it's called, I don't have it,' huffed Agatha. 'So yes, Eve. I remember.'

'It's funny,' mused Eve, as much to herself as to the others. 'I've been thinking about memories a lot since this cottage business, and I've realised it's all a blank until I'm about ten. I remember next to nothing. And I've totally forgotten Dylan, yet he clearly remembers me.'

Damn! She hadn't intended to mention Dylan all day, and yet here he was already.

'I don't think that's so strange,' replied Agatha. 'It is over forty years ago now, after all.'

'Yes. Thanks for that, Agatha. And there was me thinking these grey hairs were an illusion.'

'Do you think you can forget things on purpose?' mused Lyra.

Agatha seemed to consider this. 'I suppose you can choose not to bring things to mind. I'm not sure that's quite the same thing.'

'Your mind blocks bad things out, if they're too difficult to deal with,' said Eve. 'I saw a programme about it once. It's a coping strategy. Soldiers often forget what they see in wartime if it's too psychologically traumatic. And people in a serious car crash. Their brain might not be injured at all, but it still won't let them remember what happened.'

'But what about PTSD?' asked Lyra doubtfully. 'How does that fit with that theory?'

Eve thought about it. 'I don't know,' she concluded. 'It doesn't, I suppose. If it did then no one would get PTSD because they'd have forgotten all the traumatic parts of their life.'

'Maybe there are degrees of trauma,' said Lyra lightly. 'On a sliding scale. See a body being blown up in Afghanistan – no memory. Witness the severing of a hand in a car accident. Details all fully captured.' She was laughing at the absurdity of it, but Eve saw that Agatha wasn't even smiling.

'You shouldn't joke like that, Lyra,' she snapped. 'Skye might hear you.'

'Might hear what?' asked Skye.

'Don't be so nosy,' laughed Lyra. 'Can I borrow that spade to dig a moat?'

Skye handed the spade over and continued to fill the bucket with sand by hand. I should have bought two spades, thought Eve.

They watched as the number of sandcastles grew and the moat became more and more complex. Bucket and spade. Water and sand. Such simple pleasures at any age.

Skye wanted water in the moat. Lyra explained what would happen if they tried to fill the trench but Skye didn't believe her, and so the two of them took the bucket and traipsed off to where the waves were lapping to collect some water.

'Do you really not remember?' asked Agatha when they were out of earshot.

'What? Dylan? No. I really don't. Well, maybe a vague shadow or two, but nothing concrete. He says he's going to do the cottage up,' she added.

'Yes. He's handy like that. A bit like his father. Jack could turn his hand to most things too.'

'What happened to Jack?' Eve asked. 'You said you were friends?'

Agatha went very still.

'He died,' she said.

Hadn't Dylan said his father had left and implied that it had broken his mother's heart? That didn't accord with what her mother was saying now, although he could have left and then died, she supposed.

'It was all such a long time ago,' Agatha added in the tone she used when Eve was to understand that the conversation was over. 'Where have those two got to with that bucket? It's quite a trek for so little water.'

'Not when you're young like they are,' replied Eve, and immediately wished she hadn't. She had to stop this 'I'm getting old' business. She still felt closer in age to her daughter than her mother, even though, in truth, there was very little in it. It was all a question of mindset. Hers just needed a bit of a reset.

'Did you stay in touch with him?' Eve asked. She knew she was fishing and it was a risky strategy, but she really had very little to lose.

'With whom?' asked her mother.

'Dylan's father. Jack.'

'I did.' Agatha cast her eyes out over the faraway ocean as it twinkled in the sunshine. 'He was the best friend I've ever had.'

'And that's why you're giving his son the cottage?'

Agatha's head snapped back to look at Eve.

'That's none your business,' she said sharply.

189

'No, Mum,' she said. Agatha flinched at the name but didn't correct her. 'Don't you see, it is my business. Mine and Lyra's, and Skye's too really. We're not being nosy. We're just trying to understand. Giving the cottage away is such a strange thing for you to do and from where we're sitting it makes no sense. We need to understand at least part of your reasoning so we can be sure that there's nothing untoward going on.'

Agatha rubbed at her hands. The rings she had always worn, chunky and with heavy settings, were starting to dwarf her fingers. She'd never worn a wedding ring, though, not as far as Eve could remember, and the third finger on her left hand was bare.

'I know you need to know,' Agatha said in a tone more gentle than Eve had heard her use in a while. 'I understand that. But I can't tell you. You will just have to trust me. I'm sure you would do the same in my shoes. And believe me, it really is best left in the past.'

'But . . .' Eve began, but Agatha silenced her with a combination of a raised finger and a raised eyebrow.

'Enough,' she said as she pulled her coat more tightly around her. 'It's getting a bit chilly and I'm peckish. Shall we go and find those fish and chips now? Go and tell the others that we're ready to eat.'

The conversation was over.

40

Dylan appeared to be as good as his word when it came to doing the cottage up, and his work ethic was impressive. In fact, he was beginning to make Eve feel guilty. She wasn't sure what she even did with her time when she saw how he carried on.

Each day he traipsed backwards and forwards carrying building materials from the drive of Fox House to the cottage, and then tools could be heard whirring away until dinner time.

After a few days of this, her conscience could bear it no longer. She pulled on a pair of old trainers and went outside to speak to him. Dylan was just shouldering a large paper sack of something heavy. Concrete, maybe, or plaster? Well, she couldn't shift one of those but possibly something smaller.

'Need any help?' she called over to him.

Dylan started and then looked in her direction and smiled, broad and open. The smile, she thought. She remembered that smile, didn't she? That, at least, was familiar.

'Morning,' he said. 'Thanks, but I think I've got it.'

Eve looked at the pile of things that still needed to be moved. There were small cardboard boxes amongst the sacks. Surely those wouldn't be beyond her.

'Don't be daft,' she said. 'You'll be at it all morning. Here. I can take these.'

She picked up a box experimentally and discovered that it was light. The label suggested it contained things for the cottage's electrics. Could he fix that too? Eve had visions of a stray spark sending the whole cottage up in flames, but she dismissed it. Dylan didn't seem like the kind of man who would attempt anything dangerous unless he knew what he was doing. She balanced four of the boxes on top of one another and followed him to the cottage.

The front door was standing wide and Dylan went straight in and dropped the sack on the floor. It landed with a thud and a little puff of dust bloomed in the air. Dylan pressed his hand into the small of his back and arched backwards.

'Not as young as I was,' he said.

'How old are you?' asked Eve. The question caught them both by surprise. 'God, I'm sorry,' she added quickly. 'I don't know where that came from.'

'It's okay. It's not a state secret. I'm fifty-three.'

'I'm fifty-two!' replied Eve as if this was an astounding coincidence.

'Yes, I know. You were in the year below me at school. For a while anyway.'

Of course. She was such an idiot.

'I don't remember much about school here,' she said. 'Actually, it's starting to look like I don't remember much about anything.'

'I wouldn't worry about it. It's a hell of a long time ago and really not that memorable.'

'I suppose not,' she replied. 'So, what are you doing to the old place?'

She looked around her. So far things looked much as they had done before, only dustier. The furniture, such as it was, was pushed to the edge of the room and had been covered with a huge plastic sheet whilst the rest of the space was chock-a-block with building

192

supplies. There was surely enough stock in there for him to open his own shop.

'Rewiring,' he said. 'Central heating. New kitchen and bathroom. The stairs might need replacing but I can't do that on my own so I'm hoping they'll be okay. Then replastering and decorating. At least the roof looks sound.'

Eve blew her lips out. 'Not much then. And you have all those skills?'

Dylan shrugged. 'There's not much I can't turn my hand to,' he said. 'The staircase will need someone else just because of the sheer size. It's not a one-man job. But the rest I can handle. I take things slowly and work them through methodically, one task at a time until it's done.'

'But where did you learn it all?' asked Eve with the incredulity that came from having no practical skills whatsoever.

'Well, not all at once,' he said, making Eve feel suddenly stupid. 'Dad always loved working with wood so when I left school I trained as an apprentice with a master carpenter. Then over the years I picked up the other trades. Working with men on sites you soon learn. I'm not that keen on plumbing and my plastering isn't to City and Guilds standard, but it's all good enough.'

'I'm very impressed,' said Eve. 'I can barely rewire a plug.'

'What do you do? As a job I mean.'

'Accountant,' she said and rolled her eyes. 'Well, book-keeping really. It's very dull but I could fit it in around Lyra when she was at school, and I can pick and choose my clients now so it's pretty easy.'

Dylan gave her one of his disconcertingly direct stares and Eve tried to match it but couldn't. She played with the hair at the nape of her neck.

'I always thought you'd do something creative,' he said. 'An artist or something. Isn't that one of yours upstairs?'

Eve was embarrassed that the picture was still there. It was as if she were proud enough of it to want to display it.

'I forgot about that,' she said. 'You should throw it away.'

'Why would I do that?' he replied. 'It's really good. Not sure it matches my bachelor vibe though.' He grinned again and then the smile fell away. 'You still paint, I assume.'

'Well, no. Not really. Not at all, in fact.'

'That's a shame. You were always drawing or painting something when we were kids. Whenever I picture you it's generally with a sketch pad in your hand.'

He pictured her? This felt more intimate than she was comfortable with, yet at the same time there was something very appealing about being remembered.

'Was I?' she asked. 'I wonder when that changed. I never draw any more. I was only thinking the other day that maybe I should start again.'

'You should.'

Eve felt her cheeks burning. 'Oh, I don't know about that. I did use to enjoy it though. Back in the day.'

Dylan ran his hand through his hair. 'And now you're a book-keeper,' he said.

Was that a hint of disappointment in his tone? Eve bristled, but she wasn't sure if she was irritated with him or herself.

'Actually, maybe you can help me,' he continued. 'I'm crap at paperwork. That said, work's been mainly cash in hand. Nothing steady. Mum's health wasn't great and I needed to be around for her.'

Eve pulled a 'don't I know it' kind of face in an attempt to empathise.

'Yes. I understand what that's like,' she said. 'I pretty much upended my life when Agatha broke her hip.'

Dylan's expression suggested that he didn't think she did understand, but he didn't say anything. Another awkward silence grew up around them until Dylan stepped towards the door.

'Better get the rest of it indoors,' he said. 'The light is changing. Looks like rain.'

He was right. The sky had turned an eerie yellow, heavy and slightly menacing. He set off and Eve trailed after him, suddenly feeling chastened, although she wasn't sure why.

'How long have you been living here?' he asked as they crossed the lawn.

'Too long. It's been nearly eighteen months. I came when Agatha came out of hospital and couldn't do anything for herself. After a while, I let the lease on my flat go and then . . .' Her sentence drifted to a stop, which was pretty much what her life had done. 'And Lyra and Skye turned up just before you did. Their flat was flooded so they had nowhere else to go. I don't really know what Lyra's plans are. She had thought to move into the cottage but I'm not sure that would have worked out, no matter how cross she is about not doing it. She needs to go back to civilisation. There's Skye's schooling for one thing, and something's troubling her but she won't tell me or her dad what it is, or not yet at least. So, we're just biding our time whilst she works it out. She'll have to make a decision soon, though. The Easter holidays won't go on forever.'

'And you and Justin are divorced, right?' Dylan asked.

'Yes. It's been six years now.'

'He doesn't like me being here.' He said it so directly that Eve had to ask him to repeat himself.

'Oh, I don't think that's true,' she replied, but when her mind took her back to Justin's uncharacteristically sharp comments at dinner, she thought Dylan could be right. He didn't argue the point, just left the thought out there. 'And anyway,' Eve added, 'it isn't any of his business.'

Why had she said that? Dylan would think she was making a play for him when she absolutely wasn't. She needed to stop being so unnatural around him. It was sending out all the wrong signals. She dropped her head and just followed him before she could say anything else stupid.

Back at the pile of supplies on the drive, Dylan hefted another sack on to his shoulder and Eve picked up a few more boxes.

'There,' she said, 'many hands make light work. We'll have this done in a jiffy,' and then instantly decided she sounded like Agatha and wished, yet again, that she'd kept her mouth shut.

41

The next day was Easter Sunday. Eve had noticed that people seemed to make far more fuss of celebrating the day than she thought it merited unless you were religious. The television was full of adverts showing huge, happy gatherings of people around tables groaning with food, as if hosting an enormous Sunday lunch complete with fluffy chick decorations were compulsory and if you didn't do it you somehow weren't living your best life.

Maybe that really was what happened in other families. Eve had no idea. She only knew how her Easters had always been and the two scenarios didn't tally.

Nothing special had happened for Easter at Fox House when she'd been growing up. Agatha would buy her one enormous chocolate egg which would be sitting on the kitchen table when she came down for breakfast, but there was never any suggestion that she might have to hunt for it. Eve had once suggested that it might be fun if Agatha hide the egg somewhere in the garden or the woods but Agatha had dismissed the idea out of hand.

'What would be the point? You've already seen it. Just eat it and save yourself the effort.'

When Lyra had been small, Eve and Justin had tried much harder. Eve always bought far too much chocolate for one child and then Justin would write clues for an elaborate treasure hunt that directed Lyra around their house and garden collecting the eggs in a little wicker basket as she went. The clues became more and more esoteric as Lyra grew until she had eventually declared them unsolvable, and the tradition had ground to a halt.

This year, with them all together, Eve had decided that they would do things properly. She had bought a big, boxed egg for each of them and several bags of little foil-wrapped ones for Skye to hunt for. As she retrieved them from their hiding place, she suddenly wondered whether she ought to have bought an egg for Dylan and felt immediately guilty that she hadn't, before scolding herself for being ridiculous. He was a stranger and he most definitely didn't need to be involved in family events.

Eve covered the eggs with a tea towel, a rather feeble attempt at subterfuge, and went upstairs to find Lyra to see if she wanted to help do the hiding. She stood outside Lyra's bedroom door and knocked lightly.

'Can I come in?' she asked, pushing the door ajar and peering into the room.

Lyra was sitting on her bed in her pyjamas, her curls wild and untamed after a night's sleep. She was on her laptop but she shut the lid as soon as Eve appeared and looked up guiltily.

Feeling thrown by this and torn between asking what she'd been doing and not being nosy, Eve said, 'Happy Easter. I've bought some eggs and I wondered if we should do an egg hunt for Skye.'

Lyra leant to one side, fumbled under her bed with a searching hand and retrieved a cotton tote bag with a llama on it. She held it open for Eve to see.

'Snap!'

'There's going to be a lot of chocolate,' laughed Eve.

'I'm sure she won't mind if we eat a few. Give me ten minutes to get dressed and I'll come and help you hide them. Is it dry out?'

Eve walked to the window and pulled back the curtain to reveal a grey but dry morning.

'Just about,' she said.

'Brilliant! We've never had a garden to hide eggs in before,' Lyra said. 'Can we put them all outside?'

'We can do whatever you like. But I haven't written any clues,' Eve added.

Lyra batted the idea away with her hand. 'No worries. Those clues of Dad's were always way too hard. Just hunting for eggs is enough,' she said, and Eve felt gratified. She had always thought that too.

This would be a good moment to ask Lyra what was going on. Keeping her gaze on the garden, Eve said, 'Listen, Lyra. If there's anything you want to talk about, you know I'm here, don't you?' She kicked herself at once. Why had she framed her question like that? It gave Lyra the perfect opportunity to side-swerve away. She tried again before Lyra could reply. 'I mean, turning up here out of the blue like that, not that you aren't welcome. You are, of course. It's just, it's a bit odd. And then there was that phone call with Rafe and, well, I'm here. Whatever it is we can talk it through, if that would help.'

She risked turning round but Lyra was getting dressed, her attention on the pile of clothing on the floor rather than on Eve.

'I know, Mum. Thanks,' she said. 'Shall we go and hide these eggs then?'

Eve's heart sank. What was she doing wrong? Why wouldn't her daughter open up to her? She had thought they could talk about anything. Apparently she was wrong.

They found Skye bouncing round the sitting room. She must have asked Agatha if the Easter bunny had visited Fox House because Agatha was quizzing her about who exactly the Easter bunny might be and where it fitted in ancient folklore or, indeed,

Christianity. The conversation appeared to be unsatisfactory for both of them.

'Mummy and I are going to hide some eggs in the garden,' Eve said. 'Is that okay?'

'No Easter bunny?' asked Skye, looking slightly disappointed.

Eve hoped she wasn't about to ruin Skye's childhood with her honesty. Father Christmas she could buy into and even the tooth fairy, but the Easter bunny was a fictional figure too far. She would stop short of denying his existence though. That was for Lyra.

'No,' she said. 'It's me and Mummy this time.'

Skye nodded, apparently happy with this recalibration of her norms.

Lyra added Eve's eggs to her tote bag and they headed out into the garden to start hiding. When they had found places for about half of them Eve started to worry that they would never be able to relocate them all. She didn't even know how many there were.

'Should we take photos? Of where they are?' she asked.

The look Lyra gave her could have shot birds out of the sky. Well, it was only an idea.

'Your memory is better than mine,' she added quickly, making light of her suggestion. 'I'm sure it'll be fine.' She did a quick scan of the garden anyway, however, to try and fix the positions in her head.

When they let Skye out into the garden to start the hunt it was like releasing a greyhound from the trap. She raced across the grass darting this way and back as glimpses of brightly coloured foil came into view.

Agatha joined them, barely hobbling at all any more.

'Someone's having fun,' she said.

'Isn't she just,' replied Eve.

'Oh, to be able to move as fast as that. Funny, you were never interested in that kind of thing when you were a girl,' Agatha mused.

'That's not true!' The words were out of Eve's mouth before she could stop them. 'I was always asking for an egg hunt but you said it was silly.'

'I'm sure I said no such thing,' replied Agatha.

Eve bit her tongue. There was no point going there. Agatha had never engaged with her in the way that she and Justin had tried to do with Lyra. She just hadn't been that kind of mother.

She felt a nudge at her elbow and turned to see what Lyra wanted. Lyra cocked her head towards the little gate that led to the cottage and when Eve looked over Dylan was standing there. It looked as if he were waiting to be invited into the garden.

'What does he want?' tutted Lyra under her breath.

'I didn't buy him an egg,' said Eve.

'Well of course you didn't. That would have been ludicrous. He must realise that this is a family thing. He's not welcome. Shall I tell him to bugger off?'

'No!' replied Eve. 'You stay here. I'll go and speak to him.'

She headed out across the grass, shouting encouragement to Skye as she went.

'Morning,' she called as she got closer.

'Morning. That looks fun and I don't want to interrupt. I just wanted to give you this. I was thinking the little girl could hunt for it, but it looks like you've got that covered.'

He looked over at Skye whose bag was overflowing with boxes and then he held his hand out to Eve. In his palm there was a wooden egg. It was about the size of a duck egg and covered all over with intricate patterns that had been carved out of its surface. There were daisies set in a circle, with a separate design created from triangles surrounding them. It was exquisite and Eve gasped.

'That's beautiful,' she said, 'You didn't make it, did you?' She glanced up at him, searching his eyes for the truth.

Dylan nodded. 'I thought she might like it. And I enjoy making that kind of thing. I've never really seen the point of television and I'm not a great reader, but I have to pass my evenings somehow.' He smiled bashfully and again a flicker of something crossed Eve's mind, a snapshot of another smile at another time.

'She'll love it. Skye! Come over here and see what Dylan has made for you.'

Skye put her over-stuffed bag down and ran across to them. Dylan held the egg out towards her.

'Happy Easter,' he said.

Skye's eyes grew wide. 'Wow!'

She took the egg, turning it over in her hand and running her finger over the intricacies of the design. 'That's so cool. Did you make it?'

'I did,' replied Dylan.

'Wow!' she said again and then she ran off towards Lyra. 'Mum! Look what Dylan made for me.' Then she stopped, turned. 'Thank you!' she shouted over to Dylan and pelted away again.

Eve watched her go and they stood in silence for a moment.

'Thanks, Dylan,' she said after a moment. 'That was really thoughtful.'

'You're welcome,' he replied.

'Do you want to . . . er.' She gestured at the garden, but he shook his head.

'No. It's a family occasion. I don't want to intrude. I just brought the egg for Skye.'

He turned and headed back to his cottage before she could argue with him, and Eve fought the urge to call after him and invite him to share the leg of lamb that was marinating in the kitchen.

That would most definitely go down badly with the rest of her household.

Lyra joined her a moment later, a half-eaten chocolate egg in her hand.

'Tell me you didn't invite him for lunch,' she said.

'Of course not,' replied Eve, hoping that she hadn't laid the indignant tone on too thickly.

42

It was the egg, Eve thought, that had triggered the memory, the one that Dylan had carved for Skye. It must have released something in her head because when they came, the images were as clear and fresh as something that might have happened five years before rather than more than forty.

It had been summer. She knew that because she had a clear sensation of the heat on her skin. There had been some good summers in the 1970s. They were the stuff of legend even though, what with the planet getting warmer year on year, prolonged periods of hot weather were becoming more and more common. She didn't know which particular summer. There was nothing to pin a date on to.

They were in the woods near the cottage unsupervised by any adult. Eve didn't know for sure, but she was willing to bet that most of her play had been unsupervised. Of course, life was very different in the seventies. Children had far greater freedoms than she had ever allowed Lyra. It wasn't that there were fewer dangers, but children were given greater credit for being able to keep themselves safe.

Agatha hadn't been big on playing with her anyway. Rather, they did similar activities side by side and at the same time. Eve might draw as Agatha did the crossword. Eve might be practising her embroidery whilst Agatha polished the silver cutlery. They did read simultaneously but rarely the same book.

Playing outside was definitely something Eve had done alone. Or with Dylan, it seemed, if this memory was to be relied upon. It hadn't been served to her complete, like an episode from a soap opera. She didn't know what they had been doing immediately before or for long afterwards, but she did remember the nest.

She found nests in the wood most summers, usually after they had been abandoned. Carefully woven bowls made out of twigs and moss, their inside surprisingly smooth to the touch and more robust than seemed possible, given their raw materials. Eve was no naturalist and never discovered a nest complete with eggs. That would have required more patience than she had. This one had had occupants, however, and they had been alerted to it by plaintive and then ever more desperate cries.

They had been playing a complicated game. The details had long since left Eve's head yet she knew instinctively that when she and Dylan played together, the games would have been complex. It was sultry that day. The air was heavy with the scent of roses from the garden on one side and the earthy sweet smell of the wheat ready to be harvested from the fields beyond, and the woods provided welcome dappled shade.

They had long since finished the bottle of Vimto that she'd brought with them and Eve's thirst was starting to be a nuisance.

'We could just drink a bit,' she said. 'If we mixed it with what's left in the bottom of this then it would probably taste fine.'

She held up the plastic squash bottle and waved it at Dylan. Dylan shook his head.

'Mum says we mustn't drink the pond water unless we've boiled it first,' he said. 'She says it's stagnant so it might have bugs in it. We can only drink fast-flowing water without boiling it.'

'Then let's boil some,' said Eve, at first excited by the idea and then immediately deflated. 'But we used all the matches from the cottage when we had the bonfire.'

'I'll restock,' said Dylan with an air of importance. 'We mustn't let our basic supplies run out.'

'That's no good, though,' sighed Eve. 'I need a drink now.'

'We could go on a secret mission to get some water from the house. Or steal the cottage keys so we could get some in there.'

Eve sighed again. 'We're bound to get caught and then she'll remember that it's teatime and you'll have to go home.'

Dylan stared up at the sky, forehead creased in thought. 'I could cut my arm and you could drink my blood.'

Eve curled her nose. 'Blood doesn't quench your thirst,' she objected.

'Does if you're a vampire,' replied Dylan, and bared his teeth at her.

'You're so stupid,' said Eve coolly.

And that was when they'd heard the little cries.

'Shh,' said Dylan, body tensed and eyes wide. He shot a hand out and placed it on Eve's forearm to stop her moving. 'What's that?'

Eve listened. 'Sounds like a bird,' she said. 'A baby one.'

Slowly they turned on the spot, twigs snapping beneath their feet. Everywhere were branches and brambles and saplings and dead leaves and waving green ones. It was hard to see beyond the whole wood to focus on one tiny part of it. They stood still and listened. The pitiful squawking sound had stopped but as they waited it started up again.

Dylan put his fingers to his lips and then pointed towards where the sound was coming from. They tiptoed as stealthily as they could towards the noise.

'Look,' whispered Dylan. 'There. On the ground.'

Eve followed his finger and could see a tiny fluffy shape, not discernible as anything until it opened its beak and she saw the orange lining of its throat.

'A baby bird!' she squeaked.

'A blackbird nestling, last brood of the summer,' Dylan confirmed solemnly. 'It must have fallen out of the nest.'

They looked up to see if they could work out where it had come from but if there was a nest it was camouflaged by the twisted branches of the hawthorn.

Eve took a step closer. The creature barely looked like a bird at all. Its feathers were sparse and random over its pink, wrinkly body and there were grotesque bulges for its eyes and stomach. When Eve thought of baby animals she pictured kittens or puppies or maybe a lamb, all cute and fluffy and appealing. There was absolutely nothing appealing about this baby.

But it was still a baby and Eve knew instinctively that it needed its mother.

'What should we do?' she asked.

'Dad told me,' said Dylan confidently. 'If it looks healthy, we should pick it up and put it back. But if it looks ill then it might have been kicked out of the nest to die so we definitely shouldn't because it might make the others ill too.'

'Maybe there's a cuckoo,' suggested Eve excitedly, proud that she too had some knowledge of the natural world, but Dylan shook his head.

'It'll just have fallen out,' he said, but he didn't make Eve feel stupid or small like she did sometimes. He crept closer and bent down to examine the nestling. 'It doesn't look ill or hurt, just scared. It needs its mother.'

Eve looked up, running her eyes over each branch in turn until she spotted what might be the nest. She pointed.

'Is that it?' she asked him. 'Is that the nest?'

Dylan followed her finger and then a wide smile broke over his face.

'Yes. Well done. Not too high either. If I stand on that root I can reach, I reckon.'

Eve looked at the vulnerable little sack of skin. It seemed far too delicate to survive being picked up by an ordinary human hand.

'How do we do it without hurting it?' she asked. 'Can we scoop it up with something?' She looked around for something suitable but everything looked so hard and rough next to the delicate little bird.

'I'll do it,' said Dylan and Eve felt at once relieved but slightly disappointed in herself. She knew she couldn't bring herself to pick the ugly creature up but she wished that she were brave enough.

Dylan bent down and lifted the bird into the cup of his hand and then stood on the tree root and then his tiptoes to place it carefully in the nest.

'There's another one in here,' he whispered down.

'Is it a cuckoo?' asked Eve, not quite ready to let that theory drop.

'No, just another baby blackbird. There you go, little man. Back with your family.'

Dylan jumped down and grinned broadly at Eve.

'We saved a life there,' he said.

Another thought occurred to Eve. 'What if their mother has abandoned them?' she said. 'What if she's left them to look after themselves?'

Dylan shook his head sternly. 'Mothers never do that,' he said. 'It's not nature's way. She'll have gone to get them some food. She'll be back any minute. Or the father will be. They both look after the chicks together.'

And then the shrill alarm call of a male blackbird filled the air. Without conferring she and Dylan turned and ran from the nest, laughing as they went.

Dylan looked at his watch, a smart new Timex with a blue leather strap that he'd been given for his birthday.

'I have to go,' he said, 'or I'll be late for tea. See you tomorrow though?'

Eve nodded and then Dylan sprinted off through the wood towards the garden. She followed behind, although with not as much urgency.

'Bye, Mrs Ferrier,' she heard him call, and then there was the crunching of the gravel on the drive and he was gone.

Eve slowed her pace, not wanting to lose the excitement of their adventure too quickly. She thought about what Dylan had said. Mothers never left their babies, he'd said. It wasn't nature's way. Eve liked that. It made her feel safe. She wasn't sure she would have trusted her mother not to abandon her before, but if it wasn't nature's way then that was all right.

43

It was almost the end of the school holidays and the deadline was looming over Lyra. She had to make a decision. Go back to Manchester or find somewhere new to live. Somewhere new was tempting – the idea of reinventing their life had a tantalising feel to it. Turning up in a fresh town where no one knew her or anything about her life was incredibly appealing.

But then reality would wash over her like a cold shower. This wasn't a novel or one of those saccharine coming-of-age films, and she wasn't on her own. There was Skye to think of too. She was the important one in all this. Lyra had to put Skye's interests before her own. Lyra might want something new, but should she uproot her daughter from her friends, from everything she had always known and make her start again? Plenty of people did that, Lyra knew, but that didn't make it right.

If they *were* going to set up somewhere different, though, wouldn't it be better to do that whilst Skye was still small when it didn't really matter where she went to school? Kids were resilient and adaptable. Wasn't that what everyone said? Yes, she had good friends at the school she'd been going to but she had been there less than a year. She could make new friends within a few days.

Then Lyra thought of her own friendship group and let out a sigh. That would be harder for her to replicate. When you were five, you just sat next to someone in class and asked them to be your friend. When you were twenty-five, things didn't work like that.

However, where they were going to settle was a secondary concern. More worrying was that she was no closer to solving the problem of Rafe. He knew where she was now, and each day she dreaded a knock at the door, someone standing there with a court order to thrust into her hand like they did on the television. The thought made her stomach clench. No one could accuse him of being a bad father. Yes, he lived in London now but lots of parents lived away from their children. It didn't make them unfit to look after them.

Maybe she was tempting fate by staying at Fox House. Then again, running away made no sense. Her life wasn't a thriller. She didn't need to go off grid to avoid Rafe. No, she needed a lawyer.

Skye was on the lawn in front of her. She had almost perfected her cartwheels now. It was amazing what you could achieve with some time and solid practice. That wouldn't have been a possibility in the flat. There just wasn't the space. The Easter holidays would have looked quite different if they'd still been there. Lyra would have come up with activities to keep her daughter entertained, but the days would have been made up of a string of short bursts of activity rather than long hours focused on one thing.

Maybe they should move somewhere where she could afford to have outdoor space. Like the cottage, for instance. Now, that would have been perfect.

Skye looked up and waved at her.

'Watch, Mummy,' she called, and then turned a pretty passable cartwheel.

'That's great, sweetie. Well done!'

Skye beamed at her. 'Can you do one, Mummy?'

Could she? It had been a while, but she would give it a try.

'You betcha!' she replied with more confidence than she felt, and stepped out on to the lawn. She put her arms over her head and leaned into the starting position. Muscle memory took over as one hand and then the other planted in the cool damp grass. It felt good to be upside down, she thought, as the blood rushed to her head in the brief moment before her momentum carried her back to her feet.

Skye clapped vigorously.

'Well done, Mummy,' she sang out enthusiastically, echoing the praise Lyra uttered to her countless times a day.

More confident now, Lyra turned another cartwheel and then tipped into a second and then a third. She could still hear Skye cheering her on, but the sound was becoming lost as her brain became more and more disorientated. She leant in for a fourth but lost her balance and fell out of it, landing on her bum. She tumbled backwards on to the grass, laughing.

'Get up off that wet grass, Lyra. You'll get mud everywhere,' she imagined her mother shouting at her, but she ignored the voice in her head. Who cared that the grass was wet and muddy? She most certainly didn't.

Skye was now trying to do two cartwheels in a row, her face a study of concentration. Out of the corner of her eye, Lyra noticed something lying in the grass nearby. It was the egg that Dylan had carved for Skye. It really was beautiful, she couldn't deny that. He was an irritating tosser who had stolen her new home from her, but he was a talented irritating tosser.

Skye had barely let the egg out of her sight since he'd given it to her. She had even made a little nest for it out of some pink cotton wool balls that her great-grandmother had given her. Who had pink cotton wool? Lyra had never seen any before. Some relic from the 1970s, no doubt. Fox House was full of stuff like that.

She became aware of someone watching her and knew that it would be Dylan even before she looked up. He was like a malevolent spirit haunting them. There he was, standing on his side of the fence, a faded baseball cap on his head and a power tool of some sort in his hand. When he saw her looking, he raised a hand in greeting.

'She's getting the hang of that,' he said.

'Yep,' replied Lyra grudgingly.

'Good old-fashioned fun,' he added.

Lyra didn't know what he was trying to do but she wasn't up for it. She turned her back on him and told Skye that she was going inside to get some work done. Then she left without speaking to him again. Rude, she knew, but she didn't care. Where was it written that she had to be polite to him? The usurper.

'Lyra! Lyra, are you there?'

It was her mother and she was using her best telephone voice. Lyra had a split second to work out what was going on before her mother added, 'Rafe and Amina are here to see you.'

44

Lyra thought she might be sick right there on the lawn. Why were she and Skye still here at Fox House? She had made it so easy for Rafe. She should have moved on days ago, as soon as he had rung her on the landline. Hanging around had just been asking for trouble. For a split second she considered grabbing Skye and just running, but where would she go? It was pointless.

'Do come through,' her mother was saying to Rafe as Lyra came into the house. 'Can I get you both a drink? Tea, coffee, something cold?'

Why was she being so bloody nice to him? Did she not realise that he was trying to steal her only grandchild out from under her nose? But of course she didn't, because Lyra had failed to tell her, to tell anyone.

'Thanks, Eve,' said Rafe in his mother-pleasing voice. 'Coffee would be great.'

They used to laugh about that voice, how Rafe had a special way of talking to her mother, his charm turned up to max. It had always worked. Her mother had thought the sun shone out of his arse, and still did by the looks of things.

'Daddy!!'

Skye came hurtling into the hall and launched herself at Rafe. He scooped her up and hugged her tightly to him.

'Well, hello there!' he said. 'And how are you?'

'Do you know how many Easter eggs I found?' She didn't give him time to respond. 'Seventeen! Although some of them were tiny little ones.'

Lyra chipped in. 'Most of them were tiny little ones,' she confirmed before anyone could suggest she had been too indulgent with her daughter.

'And Dylan made me this.'

Skye wriggled down and, pulling the carved egg out of her pocket, she thrust it at Rafe. Rafe took it and turned it in his hands, admiring the craftmanship.

'That's lovely, Princess. Who's Dylan?'

He shot a look at Lyra, clearly assuming that he was something to do with her.

'A friend of Granny's,' she replied quickly.

'Cool!' said Rafe. 'Now, me and Mummy have something important to talk about but I'll catch you later, okay?'

'Wait till you see my cartwheels. I'm really good, aren't I, Mummy?'

'You are, baby. Go and practise and we'll come and watch you in a bit when we've finished talking.'

She has no idea that her future is balanced on a knife edge, thought Lyra as Skye ran off, totally trusting them both to be as good as their word.

In the sitting room, Rafe sat not on the sagging sofa but on a hard dining chair that had found its way in there. A power play, Lyra thought, so he could be above her and force her to look up at him. Well, she wasn't playing that game.

She walked over to the fireplace and leaned against it, trying to look nonchalant. Amina sat on the edge of the sofa and crossed her ankles, her hands resting in her lap tidily. Everything about her was tidy, from her shiny black bob to her polished boots. Lyra herself had dressed without a care, as usual, layering clothes until she thought she was wearing enough for the prevailing temperature. Looking at Amina now, with her smart jeans and powder-blue blouse in a fabric that was probably silk, Lyra had to fight hard not to allow a sneaking sense of inadequacy to engulf her. She was not inferior to this woman just because she dressed differently. She straightened her spine, raised her chin and narrowed her eyes.

'What do you want?' she hissed when she was sure that her mother was out of earshot.

Rafe tipped his head to one side and looked at her. His expression was condescending, like he was having to explain something simple to someone stupid.

'Come on, Lyra. You know what we want.'

'But why did you have to come here? You're not welcome, Rafe.'

She pointedly ignored Amina, focusing only on her ex.

'Well, if you'd replied to any of my messages . . .' said Rafe, pulling his 'I am being completely reasonable here' face. It made Lyra want to spit.

'We don't want a row,' Amina chipped in, her saccharine smile fixed. 'We just want to talk.'

'It's none of your fucking business,' said Lyra, not even looking at Amina.

'Don't be stupid,' said Rafe. 'Amina is my partner. She's going to be my wife, stepmother to Skye. Of course it's her business.'

Lyra fought the urge to say that this would happen over her dead body because she knew she was on a hiding to nothing.

'Sit down,' said Rafe, his voice that kind of fake calm that people use when they think they have the moral high ground. 'Let's talk it through. We're not the enemy here, Lyra.'

Lyra remained standing.

Rafe sighed. 'Have it your own way,' he said. 'Would it be help-ful to go through what we're proposing?'

Lyra shrugged. She didn't care what they were proposing. The answer was still and irrefutably no.

'We go to California in September. The contract is for a year and the pay is generous enough that Amina can take a sabbatical if she wants. So, we would like to take Skye with us. They don't start school over there until they turn six but there's the kindergarten. Did you look at that link I sent you?'

Lyra kicked at the rug with her foot, stuck out her bottom lip and shrugged. She hadn't looked at the link. What would be the point? Skye wasn't going there.

'You should look, Lyra,' said Rafe gently. 'It really is amazing, the trips they take them on, camps and so on. And what this kin-dergarten is really known for is languages. They teach eighty per cent of the time in the second language we choose for her. She'll come back bilingual. I thought Spanish might be the most useful but we can discuss that. They offer French and Chinese as well. We can sign her up for whatever you think is best.'

Lyra could feel the knot in her chest working its way up her throat. If she wasn't careful she was going to cry. Rafe was right. It did sound like the most amazing opportunity. Who wouldn't want to live in the Californian sunshine for a year and come back speak-ing another language? Didn't they say the best time to learn was when you were really young?

Lyra sucked in a deep breath. No. Just no. None of that oppor-tunity crap mattered. She wouldn't let him take her daughter. What if he never brought her back?

'What I think is best is that she stays at home with me,' she snapped.

Rafe scanned the room with his eyes and raised an eyebrow.

'You don't appear to have a home currently,' he said, just as Eve bustled in with three cups of coffee and a plate of bourbons on a tray.

'Here we are,' Eve said brightly. 'Does anyone take sugar?'

'Not for us, thanks,' said Amina with an insipid smile.

Us. It was so fucking nauseating.

Eve looked from Rafe to Lyra. She was desperate to ask if everything was all right, Lyra could tell, but didn't want to interfere.

'Well, if you need anything else I'll just be in the kitchen,' she added and then she left, closing the door behind her.

'Look, Lyra,' began Rafe again, his tone gentle. 'I'm not trying to get at you or knock you when you're down. I can see that things are tough for you right now—'

'They're not,' interrupted Lyra.

'Whatever. The thing is, this is a once-in-a-lifetime opportunity for us and Skye. We should leap at the chance while we have it. You must be able to see that.'

All Lyra could see was her child halfway around the world without her.

'And it would only be for three months to start with. Just until Christmas. That's all we're asking, to give it a go,' said Amina.

Rafe threw his girlfriend a look that Lyra recognised from when they'd been together. Annoyance.

'Obviously, if it's all going well we could extend it,' he added.

And there we have it, thought Lyra. You will take her for three months but then you'll never give her back. I will lose my baby forever.

'No,' she said. 'You're not taking her.'

Rafe leant back in his chair and tutted loudly. 'You do know how selfish you're being,' he said. The conciliatory tone was starting to slip. 'It's an amazing opportunity for Skye. Which five-year-old gets the chance to experience living in a different culture for a while?'

'That's the point. She's only five. She won't remember any of it, but she will remember being snatched from her mother and made to live halfway round the world where she can't see me.'

'You can come for visits, and there's video calling,' said Rafe. 'And if you don't let her come then she won't see her father. It's as broad as it's long.'

'No, it isn't,' Lyra spat back. 'You only see her once or twice a month. She lives with me. I am her whole world. It doesn't matter how great an opportunity you think this is for her. She's not going and that's that.'

'You can't deny me access to my own child,' said Rafe.

'I'm not! You are doing that yourself by going to Silicon Valley or wherever. You can see her whenever you like.'

'You know what I mean. How can I see her? I can hardly take her out for tea or nip back for the weekend.'

Lyra folded her arms and stared at him.

'See,' she said triumphantly. 'That's my point entirely. That is what you'd be taking from me and I'm. Her. Mother.' She shouted these last three words, speaking to him as if he were either very dim or very deaf or possibly both.

Amina lifted her coffee cup to her lips, took a sip and then smiled her nauseating smile.

'I think maybe we're forgetting something important here,' she said. 'What does Skye want?'

Adrenaline spiked all Lyra's nerve endings at once. She hadn't mentioned any of this to Skye. Why would she? It was never going to happen anyway and it would only confuse her, make her think she had to choose between her parents. She suddenly became aware of them both staring at her.

'That's a good point,' agreed Rafe. 'What has Skye said about all this?'

'Well, I haven't asked her,' spluttered Lyra. 'Why would I? She's far too young.'

'Too young to have an opinion about where she lives for a while?' asked Rafe.

'Of course!' Her voice had leapt up an octave. 'You can't ask a five-year-old to make a decision like that.'

'We're not asking her to make the decision. Just what she might like to do,' replied Rafe.

'She's too young,' repeated Lyra desperately, but she knew as she spoke that Skye would be delighted by the opportunity. She loved adventures and was always up for new experiences. And she was as bright as a button and would probably fly at this fancy kindergarten.

Rafe stood up. 'I can see this is all getting a bit much for you,' he said. 'We should probably have warned you that we were coming. Why don't you have a proper look at the kindergarten website and the other links I sent, for the apartment and the general area. Then we can speak again once you've taken it all on board a bit more. And we can ask Skye what she would like to do, just to throw her view into the mix.'

Lyra couldn't stand any more. 'Can you go now?' she said.

'But you'll think about it. Properly,' said Rafe.

Lyra pursed her lips, set her jaw.

'For God's sake, Lyra. You're starting to behave like a child yourself. I want to do this amicably but if you're going to stick your head in the sand then I'll just take it to the courts and ask them to decide. I can get my solicitor to draft the papers this afternoon. Is that what you want?'

'What I want,' said Lyra, standing as tall as she could, 'is for you to leave. Now.'

She crossed the room, opened the door and stared at Rafe pointedly. Amina stood up.

'We should go,' she muttered. 'I told you it would be a waste of time coming here.'

'You can't just pretend this isn't happening, Lyra,' said Rafe. 'If you push me I will go to the courts and let them decide.'

'Whatever,' she replied with a shake of her head.

'I'll say goodbye to Skye on my way out,' he said.

She didn't go with them. Instead she stood there, conflicting emotions surging through her. He was right. It was an amazing opportunity. But it was her child, her entire life he was going to steal.

After a while she heard the front door open and then close. The sound brought Eve from the kitchen.

'Oh,' she said, looking round the room. 'Have they gone already? Is everything okay?'

She should do it now, tell her mother what was going on, ask for help. But what if Eve thought that Rafe had a point? Maybe Eve secretly believed that Lyra was an inadequate and emotionally immature parent who couldn't provide for her child. What if they all agreed and she was the only one holding out, the sole voice of reason?

She couldn't risk it. 'Yes. They had to rush off. Some appointment or other.'

And then, before her mother could see through her lie, Lyra ran away.

45

December 1978

It would be Christmas in a week.

Of all the things that reminded Agatha of just how far she was from the life she had envisioned for herself, Christmas was the most stark.

Her own childhood Christmases had been bleak. Her mother rarely made an appearance until the afternoon and when she did arrive downstairs, her face wan and swollen, she had barely taken any notice of Agatha, brooding instead on Christmases past when her sons had been alive. She and Agatha's father would recount endless tales of Christmas mornings to one another, presents thoughtfully wrapped, shining eyes, whoops of excitement as perfect gift after perfect gift was unwrapped.

'Weren't they treasures?' her mother would ask her father. 'My perfect little boys.'

But I'm here, Agatha wanted to scream. Your perfect little girl. Here and not dead.

She didn't though. Instead, she tried to look grateful for her gift, which generally came unwrapped and was something she might have appreciated a year before but which now felt childish.

The Christmases of Agatha's dreams were bright and loud, filled with colour and light and laughter. She imagined a house filled with children. When she'd been younger these children were her imagined siblings, ready-made playmates who shared her excitement and enthusiasms. Then she had assumed they would be her own offspring, but that hadn't worked out as she'd hoped. Over the years, she became less choosy. Any children would do for her Christmas dream. Agatha didn't mind, as long as they came with fun and games and laughter.

Yet, despite how clear her vision, she had never managed to create the magical Christmases of her imagination. There were the three of them, her, Henry and Eve, all rolling around the corners of Fox House like marbles in a jar, never quite managing to come together. Three people weren't enough for the kinds of noise and fun that her mind had created, especially when one of them seemed only interested in how early he could open the port.

Agatha pondered on how she might improve things. The obvious solution would be to invite friends to Fox House for the celebrations, but their social circles had diminished over the years so potential candidates were thin on the ground. Added to this was the worry about Henry. She couldn't trust him to be civil to guests, let alone play the role of welcoming host, and she couldn't face having to cover for him all day. That would probably make for a worse Christmas Day than they managed on their own.

The only serious possibility would be to invite Jack and Mary. Of course, they only had one child as well, but one was better than none and Dylan was a nice boy; a little quiet and serious, but perfectly pleasant.

Once or twice, Agatha had picked up the telephone to issue the invitation only to rest the handset back down in its cradle moments later. She was reluctant to humiliate herself, to have to listen to the hastily devised excuses because, of course, they wouldn't want to come. Why would they? No doubt they had their own Christmas traditions and wouldn't want to spoil their own day just to rescue Agatha from hers.

Since the incident at the cinema, Mary had been different with them, slightly detached from any meeting they had as if she were always poised and ready to take her child and flee at the first sign of trouble. Agatha couldn't blame her for that. Wasn't she the same? The only difference was that Mary was a visitor and could leave. This was Agatha's life.

Agatha had thought about what Jack had said, had thought about it often. She could throw Henry out. It was her house, after all, and she still had money squirrelled away from her parents, money that she'd had the good sense to keep secret from Henry.

But then Agatha would think about her plans, the way she had envisioned her life. With Henry present, there was still a chance that she could achieve it. Yes, the odds were diminishing with every passing year, but having another child wasn't impossible. And if she threw Henry out it would just be her and Eve forever. Would that not be worse?

Agatha had been into York to order the turkey and buy other treats that she imagined the family in her perfect Christmas would require. It was one of those crisp blue winter days and so instead of heading straight home she decided to take a walk through the park. She even bought a bread bun to feed the ducks.

She had left Eve at the house, a decision she thought she might now regret. Surely a good mother would have brought her daughter with her to enjoy the buzz of the town at Christmas time.

But Eve had been happy watching *Belle and Sebastian* on the television and so Agatha had left her there. She could travel so much faster on her own, she'd reasoned, and Eve was a sensible child.

That had been the wrong decision. Agatha could see that now. Why was the right thing to do only ever obvious to her after the event? Nothing about being a mother came instinctively to her. It never had.

She made her way to the kidney-shaped pond in the centre of the park and stood at the edge, searching for the ducks. They were all on the opposite bank, flapping and quacking around a woman with a gaggle of children who all had Sunblest bags full of crusts. The children laughed and pointed and bickered about who had thrown which piece of bread to which duck.

Agatha's hand dropped despondently to her side and she let the bread bun fall to the floor, still in one piece.

'They'll come over here soon enough,' said an elderly male voice. 'They're greedy so-and-sos, ducks.'

Agatha turned and saw a man sitting on a bench behind her. He was wearing a Crombie coat and a trilby and was holding a folded newspaper that he had either already read or was yet to start. It wasn't clear which.

'I've rather lost interest in feeding them now, anyway,' she said. 'And they look to be much better off over there.'

She left the bread bun where she'd dropped it and went to sit on the opposite end of the bench, slumping down against the backrest and pulling her scarf up around her neck.

'Looks like they're having fun,' said the man fondly, 'just like children should.'

'Indeed,' she replied.

They watched the children and the ducks for a while. One boy had paced his bread distribution more slowly than the others and so had plenty of crusts left when the bags of the others were empty. There seemed to be a negotiation of sorts being conducted, the child with the remaining bread bargaining with his siblings. The mother looked on, laughing. It was all in good humour, it seemed.

'It's not fair,' Agatha heard a reedy voice whine, the sound drifting across the water towards them. 'Why does Richard get more bread than the rest of us?'

'He didn't. It's just that Richard doesn't throw his all at once,' their mother replied with a knowing smile.

What was said next was too quiet for Agatha to catch, but she could see that there was a grudging acceptance that Richard's strategy was the better one. The woman dropped to her haunches and the breadless children launched themselves at her so that she almost lost her balance. They hugged. More laughter ensued.

Agatha turned away.

'I am a terrible mother,' she said aloud.

She might have assumed the man would have been made uncomfortable by this statement but he showed no sign.

'I'm sure that's not true,' he replied, all matter-of-fact as if they were discussing what time the sun would set that day.

'No. I assure you that it is,' Agatha continued. 'I'm really not at all clear on how one ought to behave, as a mother, I mean.'

'Are there any oughts?' asked the man.

'Oh yes, I do believe so. I think the trouble is that my own mother was so very terrible at it. I never really picked up the skills, you see. I thought it would come naturally, mothering. Just have the child and the rest would follow. But I seem to be missing some essential part, and without it I can't . . .' She tipped her head in the direction of the family across the pond, who were now gathering themselves into a little band ready to leave.

'Ah,' replied the man.

'I do try,' she continued, her focus on the trees that stood erect and bare beyond the water. 'But somehow I always fall short. Are you a family man?'

'I am. Three strapping lads, all grown now.'

'And do you have any tips?'

The man leant back and looked up at the sky, the blue now diluted with high wisps of cloud.

'Well, let me see. Consistency, that's an important one. And clear barriers so they know where they stand. No always means no, etc.'

Agatha screwed up her nose. 'But that's just discipline,' she said. 'I can do that part. But what about' – she paused, struggling to express what she wanted to say – 'that thing, the special thing that means the child is secure and happy and knows that they are wanted and belong.'

'You mean . . . love?' asked the man.

Now he was starting to feel uncomfortable. Agatha could tell from the way he had shifted to the front of the bench as if he wanted to move on and leave her well alone.

But he had missed her meaning. She did know about love. She loved Eve. She loved Eve with all her heart. And Eve loved her back, or at least Agatha thought she did.

But that wasn't it. Or at least, it didn't appear to be all of it. There was that other thing too. That secret, mysterious thing that made you a real mother.

But he was a man. How could he know what it was?

'Yes,' she replied, suddenly wanting to bring the conversation to an end. 'Yes. That must be it.' She stood up. 'Well, it's been nice chatting. I must be getting along. Merry Christmas.'

'Yes, Merry Christmas,' he replied uncertainly.

Agatha took two steps to where the bread bun lay on the tarmac. And then she swung her foot and kicked it hard. It flew through the air and landed with a plop several yards out.

By the time the ducks had raced over to investigate, the bread bun had sunk without trace.

46

NOW

There seemed to be some kind of kerfuffle going on downstairs. Agatha had heard the front door open and guests be let in. Then not long after that the door had opened again and the guests had, she assumed, left but without any goodbyes. Then she had heard someone, Lyra she assumed, running up the stairs and into her room.

Agatha looked out of the window. Skye was still on the grass but now she had been joined by Eve and the two of them looked to be having an earnest conversation. It was lovely how the two of them got along. It appeared to be effortless – grandmother and granddaughter. A relationship as old as the hills, without the tensions of the mother and daughter one. The pressures were different, Agatha supposed. You were allowed to be more relaxed as a grandparent, were expected to be in fact. The role brought with it far less discipline and the emotional intensity wasn't there, getting in the way. So, with fewer conflicts things could be less fraught.

With this in mind, she picked up her cane and went to knock on Lyra's door.

'Lyra. It's me, Granny. Can I come in?'

Agatha didn't wait for an answer. This was her house, after all. She opened the door and stepped in. Lyra was sitting on the bed, her knees up under her chin with her arms wrapped tightly around herself. She looked up.

'Oh, hi, Granny,' she said, her voice listless.

'Is everything all right, Lyra?' asked Agatha as she closed the door behind her and sat delicately on the edge of the bed, careful that she had control of her balance.

Lyra nodded.

'Well, forgive me for saying, but it doesn't look all right from where I'm sitting. Would you like to talk about whatever it is?'

Lyra shrugged but didn't speak.

'Of course, there's no compulsion to share whatever it is with me, or anyone for that matter,' Agatha continued, making sure that her gaze fell anywhere other than on Lyra. 'But you'll forgive me for noticing that you did arrive here in a bit of a maelstrom. I'm sure there must be something at the root of that.'

Agatha waited. Lyra would either talk to her or she wouldn't. She supposed it didn't really matter which, but something stirred deep inside Agatha. It was a kind of longing that she hadn't felt in forever, the desire to be of use. Lyra was not her child and helping her with whatever this was wouldn't do anything to limit the damage she feared she might have done to Eve, but it was better than nothing.

However, the silence stretched on. It appeared that offering to help was not enough. The offer also had to be accepted and acted upon.

Agatha was on the point of pushing herself to her feet and leaving when Lyra spoke.

'I don't know what to do,' she said, her words so quiet that Agatha had to strain to catch them.

'Ah yes,' replied Agatha. 'I'm familiar with that problem. What specifically is causing the dilemma?'

'It's Rafe. Well, not him exactly, but what he wants. He's got this job. In America. He wants to take Skye with him.'

'Oh,' said Agatha. 'I see.'

'He says it's an amazing opportunity for her. It's in California and he's found this great pre-school place where they teach them to speak a second language and have really cool extra stuff.'

'Languages are best learned young,' agreed Agatha.

Lyra shot her a look, and Agatha realised too late that there was an agenda to this that she was expected to follow.

'Yes, well, the thing is, I don't think she should go. She should be here. With me.'

'I see,' said Agatha again. 'And where is "here" precisely? You seem to be without permanent abode at the moment, not that you aren't very welcome at Fox House, but I imagine it's not what you want long term.'

Lyra sighed and pulled her knees even closer into herself. 'That's the thing. I don't know what I want. And I don't know what to do about Skye. And I don't know where to go. It's all such a mess, Granny.'

Agatha had never been particularly tactile, but she reached out and touched Lyra's back. The gesture felt unnatural to her but Lyra seemed to respond, so she tried a stroke or two, much as one might do with a cat.

'And what does your mother suggest?' Agatha asked.

Lyra pulled a face. 'It's no good talking to her,' she said. 'She'll go into panic mode or just fire solutions at me until I can't think straight.'

'I'm told grandparents can prove useful in situations such as these,' Agatha replied. 'Not that I have any personal experience. My grandparents were all dead by the time I was old enough to remember them. My parents were very old when I was born. I was something of a last-chance saloon for them.'

'Well, I can't talk to Mum and that's for sure,' said Lyra. 'Dad's a bit better, but not by much.'

'Then it appears you will have to resort to me,' Agatha replied.

It was pleasing that Lyra was happy to share her problems with her. She and Eve would never have even admitted that there was anything that needed discussing, let alone actually do so. The intimacy that that required was somehow missing, and maybe the trust as well, although a lack of trustworthiness was definitely down to Agatha and not Eve.

'I find,' she continued, 'that in these tricky situations, your gut response is often the right one. What is yours in this situation?'

Lyra looked up at her, the tumble of her curls framing her face. Her eyes shone unnaturally and Agatha realised that she was holding back tears.

'That she should go?' Lyra replied with a question in her voice. 'I don't want her to. I want her to stay here. But it's not about me, is it?'

Agatha was about to say that of course it was, that this was Lyra's life and ergo it was completely about her. But if that were true then Lyra wouldn't be facing the dilemma. What to do would be entirely clear. It would simply be whatever Lyra wanted to do.

No, this was what being a mother was supposed to look like, Agatha realised. Of course, this wasn't a total revelation. She knew that mothers made sacrifices for their children all the time. Her own mother had made precious few sacrifices for her, yet over the years she had learned that part of being a mother was giving up things you wanted for your child, and she had tried to do that for Eve.

There had always been little things you had to let go. Choosing a fast-food joint rather than a gourmet restaurant, or a blockbuster movie over something arthouse with subtitles. But this was different. This was about the rhythm of Lyra's entire life. What she wanted and what she thought she should do for her child were out of alignment.

'On the one hand,' Lyra continued, 'I can see that Rafe might be right. Going to live in California for a bit is a great opportunity. But at what cost, Granny? She'll be uprooted from everything she knows and dumped in a strange place with strange people and a weird culture. And I know Rafe has been around and she knows him, but she's only ever lived with me. What if she misses me and it makes her sad every day? What if she changes while she's there? What if she comes back and what I can offer her isn't enough any more? What if she forgets all our little jokes? What if she doesn't want to come back at all?'

Lyra took a juddering breath and buried her face in her knees.

'I want to say no,' she muttered through her hair. 'But I think I ought to be agreeing.'

Agatha continued to run her hand down Lyra's back. She liked the way it felt; the gentle rhythm of it was comforting and she felt compassionate without having to speak, which was good because what she wanted to say wouldn't be what Lyra wanted to hear. She decided to press on anyway.

'Is it right to deny Skye the chance to experience something different because she might like it more than what she has with you?' she asked.

She felt Lyra's spine stiffen beneath her hand. Had that been a mistake? The last thing she wanted to do was upset Lyra further, but at the same time her advice had been sought. It was not for her to change her views to match what Lyra might be hoping she would say.

Lyra's back slumped again, the tension ebbing out of it, and Agatha relaxed.

'Another way of looking at it,' she continued, 'might be to ask what would be the point of disrupting her world for something which, at only five, she is very unlikely to remember, but which might leave significant psychological scars for her future.'

Lyra sat up, eyes wide. 'Yes! You see, Granny. It's so hard.'

Agatha wasn't sure that she had helped, but Lyra seemed to be taking some comfort from her words.

'I think, my darling girl, that it is something we need to take our time over. Let's let it ruminate, consider all the pros and cons, including where you are going to live going forward, assuming you don't want to stay here.'

Lyra nodded vigorously and wiped away a stray tear with the heel of her hand.

'Rafe said I should ask Skye what she wanted too,' she said. 'But I daren't.'

Agatha was taken aback. Ask a five-year-old for their view on something as serious as this? What a bizarre and quite frankly foolhardy idea! It was such an outlandish concept to her that Agatha had to work hard not to scoff. However, she managed to maintain her composure.

'Let's just take our time,' she said instead. 'Why don't we talk again tomorrow and see how the land is lying then.'

Lyra smiled weakly. 'Yes. That's a good idea. Thanks, Granny.'

'It's my pleasure,' replied Agatha.

And, she realised, it really was.

47

Lyra felt calmer. A solution still felt a very long way off, but at least she had spoken to someone about it. And Agatha had confirmed that it was indeed a conundrum, so at least she wasn't making a mountain out of a molehill. It was a really difficult decision, even for real adults. She resolved to think about it again later as Agatha had suggested, and then pushed it back into the dark recesses of her mind.

The weather was again unseasonably warm and so Lyra took her laptop to the sunny patio and started to watch YouTube videos on redecoration on a shoestring budget. She was going to have to live somewhere and wherever she ended up, she wanted it to be nice.

A shout shattered both the peace and her concentration.

'Hey. Dad. Are you in there?'

She looked up and then over towards the cottage, which was where the sound had come from. There was someone at the cottage, a guy about her age with shaggy blond hair and something draped across his shoulders. Lyra stared. Was he wearing a fur stole? The rest of his clothing was perfectly ordinary so she assumed not, but there was definitely something around his neck.

'Dad!'

Was he talking to Dylan? She didn't know he had a son, but then she knew next to nothing about him. It was a surprise, though. He'd been so closed off about himself, hadn't given even the slightest hint that he might have a family.

The guy disappeared into the cottage and Lyra stared for a while and then recommenced her search, but her focus was dinted again when he reappeared. This time the fur stole was in his arms and she could see it wasn't an item of clothing but a cat. Random.

The two men stood outside the cottage chatting, but they were too far away for her to hear what they were saying.

Skye was on the lawn by the birdbath, dipping a stick in the water and then using it to write on the paving stones beneath.

Lyra called her over. 'Skye. Come quick and see this. I think Dylan has a son and he's got a cat.'

Skye was instantly enchanted.

'I'm going to see if he'll let me stroke it,' she said, running off towards the cottage before Lyra had time to tell her not to.

Lyra watched as Skye approached the gate, but she didn't go through into the wood, just waited to be invited. Lyra's heart swelled at how polite her daughter was. Then she got up and followed her over, mainly in her capacity as a responsible parent, but also out of sheer nosiness.

As Skye got close, the guy dropped to one knee so he could talk to her at her level. Lyra was close enough to make out his words.

'You must be Skye,' he said. 'I'm Cameron. And this is Flea.'

He held out one of the cat's paws for Skye to shake, which she did, taking it in her hand and moving it very gently.

'Hello, Flea,' said Skye. 'That's a funny name for a cat.'

'Isn't it? My dad' – he pointed to Dylan – 'said I couldn't call her that but I did, and it just stuck. I don't think cats really care what we call them.'

'Like TS Eliot,' said Lyra as she got close enough to be part of the conversation.

Cameron looked up and Lyra wondered if he would get the reference, hoping smugly that it would wash over him.

'Yes,' he said. 'Just like TS Eliot. And you must be Lyra. Good to meet you. I'm Cameron, Dylan's son.'

Lyra nodded, pleased that he'd passed her test.

'I gather he stole the cottage from under your nose,' he added. He was grinning and looked remarkably like his father but with fewer sharp edges, a much more feminine face. Lyra wondered what his mother looked like.

'I did no such thing,' chipped in Dylan. His tone was light, but Lyra saw him glance over at her to make sure that his comment had been taken that way. She decided to respond in kind. She couldn't keep this mini feud up forever, and this was as good a time to lower her defences a little as any, especially as the arrival of the son and his cat changed the dynamic a little.

'He did! The rat. But I suppose I'll get over it if I have a decade or two to do it.'

'So, you're staying with your mum and grandma for a bit,' Cameron continued.

'For a stranger, you know a lot about me,' she laughed.

'News travels fast around here,' he said, apparently unconcerned to admit that they had been gossiping about her.

'So it seems,' replied Lyra. 'Yes. I had a bit of a domestic disaster . . .'

Skye put her hand to shield her mouth and whispered, 'She flooded our whole flat.'

'Yes. Well, thanks for that, Skye. Why not tell the world just what an idiot I am,' Lyra said with a big smile for Skye, who might not understand that she was joking.

'Do you need any help fixing it? I'm sure we could . . .' Cameron glanced at Dylan, who looked more sceptical but nodded his agreement.

'Thanks, but the landlord made it very clear that I wasn't to darken his door again, so we're on the lookout for somewhere else to go.'

She thought Dylan might look a little shamefaced at this, but if he felt even vaguely bad that that place would not be the cottage, it didn't show.

'Interesting,' said Cameron. 'Where do you fancy?'

Lyra shrugged. 'At the moment I haven't a clue, but I'm on it. I'm sure I'll think of something.'

'But you don't want to stay here, with your family?'

He had one of those enquiring faces, open, his eyes wide in expectation of her response, and he continued to hold her gaze as she considered her answer.

'I can't decide whether living here would be moving forwards or backwards,' she said, surprising herself. 'This isn't where I lived when I was a kid so it's not as if I've run home at the first sign of trouble. But living with your family . . . ? Is that the sign of a fully independent adult?' Then Lyra had a sudden thought and her hand shot to her mouth. 'Oh my God. You're not moving in here, with your dad? I didn't mean . . . That's just what I think but . . .'

He held up a hand. 'Stop panicking. No. I'm not moving in. I'm just here to help with the work. Not that I wouldn't want to live with you, Dad.' He threw Dylan a playful smile.

'It's okay,' replied Dylan. 'I get it. No one wants to live with their parents.'

'Well, I wouldn't say that for definite,' Lyra chipped in. 'It's just that I'm not sure, that's all.'

'But it's great in the meantime, right?' said Cameron.

237

'Right. So, what have you been up to in here?' She peered her head around the door to try and get a sneak peek.

'Want to see?' asked Dylan.

She was torn. Part of her didn't want to know what he was doing. Seeing that would just be rubbing salt into her tender wounds. But part of her really wanted to have a look because, objectively, the transformation of a house was a really interesting process. Even this one. Maybe she could share some of her YouTube ideas.

And then there was Cameron.

'Why not?' she asked, and followed him inside.

48

There wasn't much to see inside the cottage. Apart from the sacks of builders' materials and piles of boxes scattered across the floor, it looked unchanged. It smelled different, though – a mixture of plaster dust and cardboard, which gave it an oddly new feel. The familiar stagnant and musty air had all been blown away because of the front door standing permanently open.

'I like what you've done with the place,' she said as she surveyed the chaos.

Dylan threw her a laconic smile. 'It's a work in progress. But it will be nice, when I've finished.'

'Yeah,' replied Lyra, aware of a certain bitterness in her tone. 'I had a vision for it too.'

Dylan didn't respond. He never apologised for his part in her downfall. She'd noticed that. She could have a grudging respect for him for it, she supposed. He had no shame over his actions.

'Right. This work won't do itself,' said Dylan, more to Cameron than her. She was being dismissed.

'I'll leave you to it, then,' said Lyra. 'Come on, Skye. Let's go. Say goodbye to the cat.'

'Flea, Mummy. He . . . she . . . ?' Skye looked up at Cameron for confirmation.

'He,' he confirmed. 'Definitely a he.'

'He's called Flea,' finished Skye.

'Well, say goodbye to Flea, and then come with me. We have important things to talk about.'

She raised an eyebrow at her daughter to indicate just how important. Skye looked reluctant to leave, but she did as she was asked.

'Bye, Flea,' she said, giving the cat a little wave, but he had already turned back to Cameron, no longer interested in Skye. Lyra knew how that felt.

'Can we have a cat, Mummy?' Skye asked as they trooped back across the lawn. 'When we have a flat again, I mean.'

'Absolutely!' replied Lyra, because getting a cat felt a whole lot easier than all the other things she had to get.

'My egg!' Skye stopped in her tracks, panic-stricken. 'I left it . . .'

And at that moment Cameron called over to them.

'Lyra.'

He was leaning over the fence and holding the carved wooden egg above his head. Skye raced towards him to reclaim it, but Cameron started to move in her direction even after he'd handed the egg back to Skye. Lyra stood and watched his insouciant stroll across the grass.

'Do you fancy going for a drink later?' he asked when he reached her. There was no introduction to the idea, no prevarication. Straight to the point. 'It's thirsty work, all this being a builder's mate.' He grinned at the description of himself and Lyra wondered what he actually did for work. 'I passed a pub in the village. Looked okay.'

'The Green Man? Yes, it's all right. I've not been there for years, though. It might have had an existential crisis.'

'Shall we risk it? I'll be finished with Dad around five, I reckon.'

'Okay,' she heard herself say. 'I'll be here.'

And then he turned and headed back to the cottage, leaving Lyra spinning in his wake. This was not a date, was the first thing she told herself, just so she had it clear. She wasn't entirely sure what it was, but it most definitely wasn't a date.

Her mother was at the kitchen table when she got back to the house, a pile of scrappy receipts and her laptop in front of her. Her mother's job was a mystery to Lyra. How could she be bothered to trawl through all the minutiae of someone else's life? It must be terminally boring.

'That looks fun,' she said with a healthy dose of irony. 'Tea?'

'Yes, please. Do you know, I've been living here for eighteen months and I still haven't sorted myself out with a decent work space.' Eve stretched in the seat, arching and rounding her back. 'This chair is not even vaguely ergonomic.'

'You should get a proper chair at least,' said Lyra. 'It's really bad for you to work all hunched over like that.'

'I know. It's just, well, I never expected to be here as long as this.' Eve's shoulders drooped. 'I kept telling myself that there was no point getting one because I'd be gone soon. And yet here I still am. What did Rafe want?'

After the conversation with Agatha, Lyra wasn't ready to go over it all again with her mother. There would be drama and Lyra had enough of that going on in her head. She turned her back on her mother, ostensibly to set the kettle to boil.

'Nothing really,' she lied. 'They were on their way back from somewhere and called in on the off-chance.'

'Oh?' Eve sounded dubious. 'But he didn't want to see Skye for longer?'

'He did, but he didn't have time to stay.' The lie sounded ludicrous, but it was the best she could do in the moment.

'I see,' said Eve slowly. 'So he called in to see you, then?'

This had the potential for getting out of hand. Lyra's mind was racing as her head tried to keep up with her tongue.

'They're going away for a bit. To America for work. He just wanted to make sure I was okay with that,' she said. 'As they won't see Skye for a while.'

There. That sounded plausible, didn't it? Lyra swallowed and held her breath.

'Oh,' said Eve again. 'Well, that was considerate of him.'

She needed to close this down before her mother got any closer to the truth.

'Yeah. Anyway, let's not talk about him,' she said. 'You're more important. What are your plans? Going forward, I mean. Are you planning to stay here until, you know . . . ?' Lyra grimaced and hoped she had expressed Agatha's death without actually having to say the words.

'Well, I wasn't,' replied Eve. 'I definitely wasn't. But now . . . I've been here so long. I don't know what's for the best any more.'

'But Granny doesn't need you, does she?' said Lyra. 'She can walk pretty well again now and she's nothing if not determined.'

Eve played with a strand of her hair, letting a finger twist it round and round until it became a knotty mess.

'I don't know,' she said. 'The longer I stay the more I think that I can't really leave. I know she comes across as all independent, and that she only tolerates me being here because she has to, but actually I think your grandmother relies on me more than she'll admit. I'm not sure she'd eat properly, for example, if I wasn't doing the cooking.' Her mother drew in a big breath. 'But all the time I'm here, it feels like my own life is on hold.'

'Then leave,' said Lyra. She really couldn't see what her mother was deliberating over. 'Granny will be fine and even if she's not, is it really your job to look after her?' It crossed Lyra's mind as she said this that what was so obvious to her was clearly far more complicated for her mother. There were echoes of her own dilemma in what Eve seemed to be going through. She softened her tone.

'It doesn't have to be you, Mum. Granny can pay someone to come in and cook or whatever. Or she can move into an old people's home.'

Eve snorted. 'Can you see your grandmother in an old people's home?'

Lyra thought about it for a moment, imagined her grandmother at the head of a gang of riotous octogenarians. The thought made her smile, which in turn made her mother smile.

'She'd be a tyrant,' continued Eve. 'Even if we got her to go, we'd never find somewhere that would put up with her for long.'

They were both laughing now.

'She'd be like one of those gangster bosses in prison,' said Lyra, 'who get their cell fitted out with the latest gadgets and have all the screws totally under their thumb.'

The mental image this was conjuring made Lyra laugh even more, and quickly the laughter became hysterical. She laughed so hard that her eyes watered. Her mum was the same, tears rolling down her cheeks.

But then she thought maybe the tears weren't the same. Was her mum actually crying?

'Mum? Are you okay?'

Eve swiped at her tears with the heel of her hand. 'Yes, yes. Of course. I'm just being silly.'

'Not if it's making you cry,' Lyra said.

'Don't you worry,' replied Eve, refocusing her attention on her work. 'I'll sort everything out.'

I'll sort everything out. How many times had Lyra said that to herself over the last couple of weeks? And yet she was no further forward with any of it.

And her mother had been at Fox House for over a year now.

Sorting things out didn't seem to be a family strength.

Lyra paused for a moment, waiting to see if her mum said anything else, but when it became apparent that the subject was closed she stood up and saw to the tea. She placed a cup at Eve's elbow.

'It'll be fine, Mum,' she said quietly.

Eve nodded. 'I know. Thank you, darling,' she said. 'Things always work out in the end.'

'And if they haven't worked out . . .' Lyra continued.

Her mother smiled at her weakly. 'Then it's not the end,' she said, finishing the saying that Justin always trotted out at moments like this.

Lyra screwed her nose up as she left the room, out of her mother's sight. Her mother needed to do something, take control. Sitting around waiting for the universe to deliver a solution wasn't the way Lyra liked to do things. Then again, wasn't that kind of what she had been doing over the whole Rafe thing? She had physically run away but in many ways, she was just as stuck as her mother.

Lyra went upstairs and lay on her bed to collect her thoughts. In the space of ten minutes, she'd been invited out on a date by a total stranger, which was pretty cool, and learned that her mother was as lost as she was, which was less so. What was she supposed to do with that information? Her mother was a real grown-up. Wasn't she meant to have all this stuff straight by now? It had never crossed Lyra's mind that Eve might still be working things through. At her age!

She would ask her about it again, gently.

Maybe she could help.

49

Seeing all the renovation going on at the cottage was unsettling Eve. It made her look around Fox House with new eyes and what she saw was shabbier than she'd thought. Where she had previously seen quaintly scruffy, she now saw down-at-heel and ramshackle. She might even call it neglected and uncared for, but that segued uncomfortably into how much she had left her mother to her own devices over recent years and that wasn't a place she wanted to go to.

Something probably needed to be done. She had got herself all aerated about the cottage being detached from the property and, by default, she assumed, her inheritance, but if they weren't careful Fox House itself would have very little value and might even end up being sold for the land alone. The thought of some unsentimental developer tearing the place down was awful and would have Agatha spinning in her grave, not to mention all the women who had been custodians of the house before her.

Maybe the threat of that happening was a way into the conversation that she knew her mother wouldn't want to have. Was there any money to renovate the house, or even decorate? Eve knew very little of her mother's financial position. There had always been enough for their needs when she was growing up. They hadn't lived extravagantly but they hadn't been particularly frugal either, and Agatha had never had a job as far as Eve could remember.

But how much of that money was left now? Maybe there weren't the funds to do much more than keep paying the bills. Then again, if that were the case, how come Agatha had just given away a substantial asset? None of it made much sense to Eve.

It couldn't do any harm to wander around and have a look at how bad things had got. She could apply a critical eye to each room and make a rough estimate of what was required, even if calculating the costs was beyond her. Perhaps if Dylan was as handy as he made out then he could help.

Carrying her trusty shorthand notebook and pen she set off, beginning in the hallway and taking in what she saw. It wasn't very encouraging. The paintwork was discoloured and peeling in places. There was what looked like a small damp patch beneath the sash window where the frame didn't quite meet the casing, and the plaster around the front door was cracked and coming away in lumps. And this was just the hall.

Eve's heart sank, but she noted it all down and then went into the sitting room. There she found Lyra and Skye sitting on the rug.

'Look what Skye found under her bed,' said Lyra. 'I'd totally forgotten about it. I can't get it to go though. Do you know how it works?'

The rush of memories that hit Eve was almost strong enough to knock her over.

'Oh, Stanley!' she exclaimed. 'God, I haven't seen him for decades.'

'Well, it can't be decades, can it?' replied Lyra, quite matter-of-fact. 'I'm only twenty-five and I remember Dad showing him to me again quite recently.'

'Oh, you know what I mean,' tutted Eve. Lyra's being so literal drove her round the bend sometimes. 'I mean it's been ages. I'd totally forgotten him.'

'Looks like you're not the only one. He's covered in dust. I wonder if that's the problem.' She blew on Stanley to remove some of the debris.

'Don't do that. It'll get in his works. There's a cloth in his box. Use that instead.'

Stanley was an automaton, a papier-mâché figure standing about a foot high and dressed in huntsman's scarlet, with white breeches and a top hat. When he was wound up he moved his head, eyelids and arms and – this was what had delighted Eve as a child – he smoked a real cigarette, the smoke billowing out from his mouth in a truly convincing fashion.

Lyra plucked the ancient duster out of the box and wiped Stanley carefully all over. Then she picked him up and held him aloft so she could look underneath the pedestal he stood on.

'Careful,' warned Eve. 'Don't drop him.'

Lyra gave her a 'do you think I'm a moron' look but then lowered him again when she couldn't immediately see anything helpful.

'It's very naughty that he smokes cigarettes, isn't it, VeeVee?' said Skye with that self-righteousness that the young often have.

Eve thought it was just a doll and therefore for fun, but she didn't want to say the wrong thing or be seen condoning something now frowned upon, so she nodded at her granddaughter earnestly.

'Yes. Very naughty indeed. But when he was made people didn't think smoking was bad like they do now,' she said.

'How old is he?' asked Lyra. 'Do you know?'

'Mid-Victorian, I think. Your grandmother always said so. He's Parisian,' she added.

'That explains a lot,' smiled Lyra.

'I don't think he's broken,' said Eve, although she had nothing to base this statement on. 'He probably just needs winding up. The key, if I remember correctly, is . . .'

She stood up and made her way across the room to Agatha's writing bureau, dropped the flap and opened a tiny drawer. Sitting there amongst drawing pins and perished elastic bands was a little brass key.

Eve plucked it out and held it up triumphantly. 'Ta dah!'

Skye clapped her hands together.

'Will it work now, Mummy?' she asked, her eyes focused on Lyra, full of trust.

'Let's hope so,' Lyra replied. 'Is there a cigarette anywhere, Mum? It's more fun if he smokes.'

'There were always some . . .' Eve opened another drawer, this time full of old biros and felt tips. 'Yes. Here. God, they're ancient.' Eve fished out the bent carton of Embassy Extra Mild with its pale blue banner. 'I think we only ever had these for Stanley,' she said. 'Although I'm sure your grandmother smoked. Everyone smoked, didn't they?'

'How would I know?' asked Lyra. 'I wasn't born.'

Eve rolled her eyes at herself. Sometimes she forgot that Lyra was her child and not her peer.

'Here. You'll need these.' She tossed over a box of England's Glory matches, which Lyra caught deftly.

Lyra found the little hole in Stanley's pedestal into which the key fitted and slotted it in. Then she turned. The automaton made the distinct sound of clockwork winding up. She stood Stanley on the floor, tipped a cigarette from the packet and lit it confidently, making it clear to Eve that this wasn't the first time she'd done it. Eve fought her natural instincts to pass comment as Lyra slotted the lit cigarette into the little tube in Stanley's hand and flicked the switch on his back.

Stanley started to move at once. His stiff ventriloquist dummy-like jaw dropped up and down and his eyelids drooped as if he'd taken more than just tobacco. Then the smoke from the cigarette began to billow from his mouth. The sight of it was just as fascinating to her now as it had been when she was a girl.

Skye was entirely captivated, her eyes increasingly wide as she noticed each of his moving parts in turn.

'Look, Mummy, his head turns. And his eyes move. And how does that smoke get inside him to come back out?'

This was a question Eve remembered asking Agatha. Agatha had refused to answer, telling her only about magic rather than mechanics. It was one of the only times Eve remembered where Agatha had got as excited about something as she had herself.

'I think there are some bellows inside him that work by clock-work when you turn the key,' she said to Skye, although it then occurred to her that Skye wouldn't know what bellows were. 'A bit like lungs,' she added, unsure whether this would help.

The smoke from the cigarette wafted around them and the smell of it took Eve right back to when she and Justin had first got together, the smoky pubs and dark nightclubs of her youth. That had been before the smoking ban when cigarette smoke had given pubs a sexy, slightly seedy edginess, rather than smelling of stale beer, bleach and the toilets as they often did now. She missed the smell, although given the dangers of passive smoking she recognised that that was perverse.

'Isn't it funny how we've all loved Stanley so much?' she said. 'Over the years this funny little man has entertained each of us, and now Skye too.'

Skye was focused on trying to see inside Stanley's scarlet jacket for any clue as to how he worked.

'I only remember seeing him a couple of times,' Lyra said. 'I suppose that's because I didn't live here.'

'Maybe. He came out on high days and holidays for me. I remember Agatha telling me once that he was about the only toy she had.'

'He's not really a toy!' said Lyra. And then more thoughtfully, 'Granny had quite a hard time growing up, didn't she?'

'She never talks much about it,' said Eve, 'but, yes, I think so. I'm not sure she ever felt particularly loved or even wanted.'

Lyra pulled a sympathetic face. 'Poor Granny. I suppose it must have been hard, having the brothers who died in the war—'

'She never knew them,' Eve interrupted.

'But still. They must have been here, in the shadows.' Lyra looked thoughtful. 'I suppose that's why she is as she is,' she said.

'How is she?' asked Eve. She thought she knew the answer, but was curious to know how Lyra felt about it.

'You know. A bit kind of aloof, stand-offish. I mean, she's hardly a huge hugger, is she?'

Eve grinned. 'No. No one could ever accuse Agatha of that.'

'This might sound a bit mad,' Lyra said, 'but I sometimes wonder how that must have been for you, growing up, and now really. You've always been there for me, and I'm there for Skye—'

'Agatha was there for me too,' Eve said.

'Yeah, but it's not quite the same. With Granny it's like she's always holding something back. She's so . . .' Lyra searched for the word. 'Undemonstrative. And a kid needs to know they're loved, don't they? Like I do. It's not just something that you can just guess at. You need to be shown.'

Lyra looked up at Eve through the tangle of her hair and a warmth flooded through Eve's chest. She reached out and took both Lyra's hands in hers.

'And I do love you, my baby girl. I love you with all my heart.'

There was a moment before Lyra pulled away from her.

'God, Mum. Yes. Of course.' Lyra turned to Skye and nuzzled into her armpit which made Skye squeal.

'Mummy! You're tickling me!'

The pair of them fell into a heap of giggles on the carpet and Eve lifted Stanley out of the way so he didn't get damaged, or set fire to the rug, and then watched with a fond smile until they had laughed themselves out and lay back, exhausted.

50

Eve needed fresh air. The heady smell of the cigarette was making her feel a little woozy, so she left Lyra and Skye with Stanley and headed out through the back door and out into the garden. She took a welcome gulp of cold air, feeling it rushing down into her lungs. She hadn't realised that Lyra was as astute about Agatha as she appeared to be. It was comforting that someone on the outside could also see what kind of a mother Agatha had always been. And Lyra hadn't tarred her with the same brush. She had been doing something right.

Her gaze drifted over to the cottage. Perhaps she could go and see what was going on there, just out of curiosity, or neighbourly interest. Before she could talk herself out of it, she was wandering across the lawn.

As she approached, she heard the low hum of a power tool drifting from an upstairs window. The door to the cottage stood wide open despite the cold and Eve dithered on the threshold. The humming stopped, replaced by footsteps thundering down the stairs, and then there was Dylan. He was wearing workman's overalls and was covered in dust.

'Oh, hello,' he said as he saw her. His tone suggested mild surprise but no irritation.

He kept moving, searching in the boxes for whatever he'd come downstairs for. He didn't mind her being there but he wasn't about to stop for her.

'Hi,' she replied. And then she stopped, because she had nothing else to offer him. No invitation to supper, no question, nothing. She opened her mouth to add something, anything that might suggest the purpose of her visit, and then closed it again.

Dylan scratched at his dusty eyebrow, watching her, waiting, and then, when it became obvious that she wasn't going to speak, he came to her rescue.

'Have you met Cameron? My son. He was here a bit ago. He met Lyra and Skye. Skye was very taken with his cat. I'm not sure where he is now. Probably gone off to pick up supplies. He doesn't approve of the way I stock my fridge.' He rolled his eyes, parent to parent.

'I didn't know you had a son,' said Eve. 'Not that there's any reason why I should have done,' she added quickly. 'I know nothing about you really. Are you married?'

This possibility had never occurred to her. She'd assumed he was single, a lone wolf making his way through life unburdened by others. But a family? Eve hadn't even considered it.

What would his wife be like? she wondered. Maybe she'd be moving into the cottage as well? Could Eve and the wife be friends?

'Not any more,' replied Dylan. 'Caz and I split up years back.'

Disappointment washed through Eve.

'Do you have any other children?' she asked.

Suddenly she needed to know everything about him in case there was something that could fill in the gaps in her own memories.

'A girl,' he replied. 'Molly. I don't see much of her. She . . .' He paused, considering his words. 'Well, she chose her mum.'

'It wasn't a good break-up then?' asked Eve.

'Is there such a thing?' He located what he'd been looking for with a little triumphant sound and stood up. 'Although you seem to get along with your ex well enough.'

'We never really fell out,' Eve said. 'We just couldn't live together and both stay sane.'

'That's good,' he said, although his face was saying something else. 'Very adult. And nice for Lyra, I should think.'

Eve gave a tight little smile, unsure whether he was criticising her or how to respond if he was.

The silence stretched out. Eve shifted from one foot to another and wrapped her arms tightly around herself against the cold and his gaze.

'Erm . . .' he said eventually, one questioning eyebrow raised.

Eve didn't follow for a moment. And then she did. 'Sorry. I'm disturbing you. I don't know why I'm here really. I'll let you get on.' She turned to go.

'It's fine. I was due a tea break. I could make you a mug? Nothing fancy and I'm not sure there's any milk, but if you can drink it black . . .'

'Thanks,' she replied gratefully, although not entirely sure what she should be grateful for. 'And black would be fine.'

She followed him into the kitchen. He didn't seem to have started work in there and it still looked much the same as before.

'It's so strange to think we lived here, Justin and I,' said Eve. 'It all feels so very long ago.'

'When was it?' asked Dylan, opening the fridge and shaking the carton of milk. It sounded almost empty.

'The mid-nineties. And it wasn't for long. I got pregnant with Lyra and we moved into the centre of York to be closer to Justin's business. It's hard to imagine now,' she added wistfully. She tutted and shook her head. 'I don't know what's wrong with me today. I seem to be having an attack of nostalgia and it's not serving me well.'

Dylan didn't respond as he filled the kettle and found clean mugs, but Eve could tell he was listening.

'I think I must be having a mini mid-life crisis,' she continued, coughing out an unconvincing laugh. 'All of a sudden, I'm questioning things I thought I was perfectly happy with a fortnight ago. It's so silly.'

'That can happen,' he said, and she found herself willing him to ask her for details so she could unburden herself. When he didn't, she pressed on regardless, unable to rein herself back in.

'I mean, what am I doing living with my mother? I know why I came, but why am I still here? What exactly is preventing me from moving back to a flat of my own?'

'It's usually fear. The thing that stops us.' He said this without looking at her, without even turning round.

Fear. Was that it?

'Fear of what, exactly?'

Dylan shrugged. 'You tell me. Or don't. That's up to you.'

Eve pulled out a dusty chair and sat down. 'Agatha is an unusual woman,' she began.

Dylan poured what was left of the milk into one of the mugs and then offered her both for her to choose. She picked the black one.

'She's never been what you might call a conventional mother. She wouldn't let me call her Mum, for a start. Do you find that odd?'

Dylan shrugged again. 'It's just a name,' he said.

'I used to think it was cool when I was a teenager. But then I began to wonder whether she wasn't a little bit ashamed of me.'

Dylan made no comment, and Eve realised that unlike her female friends, who would have uttered comforting platitudes to make her feel better, he was only speaking when he had something to say. It was annoying that he wasn't offering her the solace she craved, but also it made her think for herself.

'I don't think that's it, though,' she added. 'I never did anything to make her ashamed, as far as I know.'

'Maybe she didn't feel like she'd earned the right,' said Dylan.

'What right? The right to call herself Mum?'

Was that the reason? This had never occurred to Eve before. Did Agatha not feel worthy of the title of mother? It seemed unlikely. Of all the shortcomings she could throw at Agatha, a lack of confidence in her own abilities definitely wasn't one of them.

'Do you know what is strange, though?' she asked him. 'I can't remember what I called her before my dad died. I have no memory of that at all.'

'Why would it be different?' asked Dylan. 'If she wanted you to call her Agatha then that must have always been the case.'

Eve considered this and then conceded that he was probably right.

'Do you know what else?' she mused. 'I'd never really considered any of this until you turned up. I think not remembering you when you clearly remember me has thrown me off balance. It's made me wonder what else I've forgotten.'

A flicker of something crossed his face and then was gone.

'And do you think you've forgotten other things?' he asked.

'I don't know,' said Eve, with a grin to try and lighten things. 'I can't remember.'

He grinned too and what had felt like it might be taking a turn for something dark came out into the light.

'I did remember something about us saving a baby blackbird,' Eve said. 'That gorgeous egg you carved reminded me.'

'Yeah. That'd be right. We were always up to something in that wood. It felt so huge back then. Funny really. It's barely more than a copse. And we liked being in here too, when we could get our hands on the key, which wasn't very often. Agatha used to hide it from us. I don't think she wanted us to come in. You were really good at finding it.'

'It sounds like we had fun,' said Eve. 'Tell me. What else do you remember?'

51

Dylan took a sip of his tea, put the mug back down on Justin's graffiti-scarred table and raised his eyes to the ceiling.

'Well,' he said. 'Let's see. I was nine when we moved away from here so you must have been, what, eight?'

'Depends on the time of year,' said Eve. 'When did you move?'

'1979. February.'

Eve did the maths in her head. 'I was born in May 1970 so I would have still been eight that February.'

'We went to the same school,' Dylan reminded her.

'Yes. The one in the village.' Eve did have some memories of school, she realised now. A few at least. A school hall, echoing with a cavernously high ceiling, a set of swings mounted in hard unforgiving concrete, warm milk in miniature glass bottles. 'Although Agatha sent me off to boarding school round about then. That's a whole other story.' She rolled her eyes as if boarding school had been a trial, although it hadn't been really. She had liked it there, with all the hustle and bustle. It wasn't quite Malory Towers but it hadn't been far off.

Dylan eyed her as if this was news, but he continued without mentioning it.

'But we didn't kick around together at school,' he continued. 'It was mainly here that we spent time. My parents used to bring me. They were friends, our parents.'

'Yes. Agatha told me that. Your dad was her friend Jack, right?' Dylan nodded.

'She told me they were close, her and your dad.' And then something struck Eve and it was so obvious that she couldn't believe she hadn't seen it before. 'Oh my God. Were they more than just friends? Is that it?'

That would make sense. What if Dylan was their secret love child, spirited away to live with Jack and his wife? Did that make Dylan her half-brother?

But just from looking at him she knew that wasn't right. They looked nothing alike. And he was laughing at her in a way that told her she was miles wide of the mark.

'No, Eve,' he said firmly. 'I can see what's going through your head but it's definitely not that.'

Eve suddenly felt very childish. As if this shared history would be something lifted straight from the pages of a trashy novel. It was ridiculous. She could feel her cheeks blush and she picked up her tea to try and disguise it.

'They were just good friends from when they were kids,' Dylan said. 'He was the farmworker's boy and she the lonely child in the big house.'

Eve forced her mind to reverse out of the cul de sac it had been heading down and focus on this new information. Dylan seemed to know more about Agatha's life than she did. She wasn't sure how she felt about that, but it wasn't a surprise. Agatha had shared so little with her over the years.

'Okay,' she said. 'Please don't take offence, but I'm glad we're not related.'

Dylan ignored this. 'And then,' he continued, 'when Agatha married your dad and my dad married my mum, they became friends as couples. I used to come over here at weekends sometimes and we hung out together. In the wood, mainly, and the cottage. We didn't go in the house much. And we fished in the pond.'

Eve remembered the photograph, the fishing net and bucket.

'Weren't we a bit young to be fishing unsupervised?' she couldn't help saying.

Dylan's look told her what he thought about that. 'It was the seventies,' he said. 'No one cared. And we survived.'

'Yes. I suppose so. And that's it? The mysterious part of my life that I can't remember?'

'Pretty much.'

Eve didn't know whether she felt elated or disappointed. There really didn't seem to be much that she couldn't account for, and now that she had the baby bird memory she had something to latch on to. Perhaps the fact that she didn't have any actual memories really wasn't that significant.

'Well, thanks,' she said. 'That's made me feel a bit better. It's been very discombobulating, not knowing.'

Dylan shrugged. 'Glad to be of service.'

They sat and drank their tea in silence but nothing about that felt awkward to Eve. This must be why she felt so calm in his presence, these shared experiences. Something in her subconscious must have been telling her that she was safe with him, had nothing to fear.

But she couldn't sit here all day.

'I should be getting on,' she said reluctantly. 'And I'm sure you have plenty to do.'

She wanted him to reassure her that he had all the time in the world for her and was happy to put the kettle on again, but instead he stood up, rinsed the mug out with cold water and put it in the sink.

'Yep. Me too. I don't want Cameron to come back and catch me skiving. That'll do nothing for my work ethic lectures.'

He threw her his small, contained smile and she worked to reconfigure him as a father in her head. It was going to take some time.

She too rinsed her mug.

'Thanks for the tea. And the chat,' she said, hoping that she sounded natural and not desperate to be liked.

In the cottage's tiny sitting room she picked her way around the sacks and boxes to the door. Just as she stepped outside a thought occurred to her.

'You said you left in February 1979,' she said.

Dylan nodded. 'That's right,' he confirmed.

'That's when my dad had his heart attack. How odd that your family should leave at the exact time my mum needed her friends around her.'

She sensed rather than saw Dylan tense up. It felt to her as if something closed in him, a door slamming shut. He offered no comment. In fact, his silence was so complete that she suddenly felt that despite the pleasant twenty minutes they had just spent together she was no longer welcome there.

'Well, thanks again for the tea,' she said awkwardly. 'I'll see you around, no doubt.'

But he had gone back up the dusty stairs and she wasn't sure he'd heard her.

52

December 1978

It was like something out of an old film. Henry sat at one end of the table and Agatha opposite him with five places between them on either side. Eve was occupying a setting halfway between them, looking lost in a sea of damask linen and shining silver cutlery.

Agatha had thought it would be funny when she set the table for their Christmas lunch in such a grand way. She had dug out her mother's Wedgwood crockery and the huge serving tureens that she remembered Mrs Banners filling with steaming vegetables. Crystal glasses twinkled in the light from the candelabras and she put two cheerful red and gold crackers in each place because they came in boxes of six and it seemed a shame to waste half of them.

Fully invested in her grand idea, she had declared that the three of them should dress for dinner. Henry had scoffed, but she had laid his dinner jacket out on the bed and, like Pavlov's dog, he had put it on without question.

Agatha had a few gowns that had belonged to her mother but none of them were quite right for the occasion. They were stiff and formal, difficult to wear, and she was always conscious of her mother's voice in her head telling her to be careful and not to spill anything down the front.

And so she had put on her favourite party dress, long and fitted close to her body, with a peacock feather design printed in emerald, sapphire and ruby on a black background. The dress swayed as she moved and always made her feel like a dancer and as if she should have feathers in her hair.

Everything was perfect, or at least as close as the three of them could come to it. 'I am a wonderful wife and mother,' Agatha told herself, 'and I can create a Christmas to stand up against the best of them.'

Agatha was no chef but she could pull together a passable Sunday roast, which was basically what Christmas dinner was. This year the dinner had been acceptable, she'd say, with all the component parts being ready at approximately the same time, although there had been a slight delay whilst they'd waited for the sprouts to soften.

There was no reason why it shouldn't be fine. It was dinner for three. She was hardly feeding the hordes with all that added pressure from judging mothers and mothers-in-law standing over and chipping in with suggestions, helpful or otherwise.

She let her mind skip to play its favourite game – what if. Not for the first time, she wondered how Christmas might have been if her brothers had survived the war. Would her table now be packed with all her nephews and nieces, sisters-in-law?

It was a nice idea, but she knew that if her brothers had survived there would have been no her, so the thought was pointless.

'Isn't this lovely?' she said, trying to reinforce the idea by voicing it out loud.

'It is indeed,' replied Henry. 'Nice touch, dressing up, too. Makes it feel like more of an occasion.'

Agatha smiled at him gratefully. He could do it if he had a mind to, behave as if he were normal, as if they were normal. He was just out of practice, that was all.

'Why don't you put a record on, Eve,' Henry suggested, and Agatha's heart rose still higher. He really was making an effort. Maybe this was to be her Christmas present. An engaged husband. 'What about that Carpenters one, or maybe Glen Campbell. What do you fancy, Agatha?'

Agatha fancied Abba or Elton John, something jolly that they could sing along to and maybe dance to after they'd eaten. But as nothing like that graced Henry's record collection she would have to make do. She made a note to buy some new records herself after the holidays, update their selection a little so that they were ready for any turn of mood.

Clearly proud to have been trusted with such a grown-up task, Eve got down from her chair, went over to the music centre and lifted the Perspex lid carefully. She wasn't usually allowed to touch it but Henry had shown her how to place a record on the turntable and select the right speed. She flicked the switch to turn it on and checked that the arm was in the correct position.

She turned to the record collection, running her finger along their spines and then selecting one. As she pulled it out, Agatha saw the familiar yellow sky, the palm trees, the outline of a tropical building. *Hotel California*.

The first track fascinated her and she had listened to it endlessly, trying to unpick its lyrics. She'd read somewhere that it was supposed to be a commentary on a hedonistic and greedy lifestyle in America but her interest had always settled on the final line, the one about not being able to get away. Its sentiment resonated too loudly with her.

'Oh, not that one please, Eve,' she said. 'It's Christmas. Can't we have something a little jollier?'

Eve slid the album back in between the others and continued her search, settling on one by Paul McCartney, which Agatha supposed would have to do.

As the opening chords of *Band on the Run* rang through Fox House Agatha relaxed, feeling pleased with herself. It might not be the Christmas of her dreams but it wasn't bad. There were many who were far worse off than she was. She must count her blessings. She had a beautiful daughter and a husband who, despite his faults, was loyal. And she had Fox House and enough money for their needs. There were people who would kill for half of what she had.

She took a sip of her wine and concentrated hard on making the warm flood of gratitude wash through her.

'Who's for Christmas pud?' she asked.

53

They had moved on to the Stilton when Agatha started to feel the day slipping from her grasp. Henry had worked his way steadily through two bottles of claret and was now demanding port.

'You can't have Stilton without a glass of port,' he pontificated, his words slurring together ominously. 'It's just not done. We do have some. I bought it myself.'

That was true. Agatha had noticed the port coming into Fox House and had promptly hidden it, hoping that Henry would forget or doubt his own memory. Port always made him morose and Agatha knew how matters usually ended after that.

'How about a nice glass of brandy,' she suggested. 'And then we can move through and see what films are on. I think it's *Diamonds are Forever*. You know how you like a good Bond film.' Agatha hated how she sounded, this wheedling, deferential tone that he made her adopt to try and maintain the knife-edge balance of the day.

'I don't want bloody brandy,' Henry shouted, pushing his chair back and stumbling to get up. 'I want port. And there is some. I bought it.'

He lumbered around the table, the damask cloth twisting itself around his leg and threatening to sweep everything from the table in a sad mockery of a magician's trick. Agatha leapt to secure the tablecloth at the other end.

'Shall I put another record on?' asked Eve. Her tone had an air of desperation, and hearing it, Agatha's chest tightened. The poor child was only eight and yet already she was aware of where the flashpoints were likely to be and how to avoid them.

'That's an excellent idea,' Agatha replied brightly. 'What was that you wanted before, Henry? The Carpenters, was it?'

'Forget the bloody music,' he snapped. 'I can't eat my Stilton without some port.'

They had reached the point of no return. Either Henry would get his port or he would ransack the entire house trying to find it. Agatha conceded defeat.

'I've had an idea where it might be,' she said, and then sped off to the pantry where she knew it lay hidden behind the pasta she had bought as an experiment and then abandoned when it turned out to be like eating slimy cardboard.

No one could accuse her of not trying, she thought as she retrieved the bottle. She had aimed for Christmas with the stars but had ended up a little shy of Fox House's roofline.

Maybe she could decant half the contents of the bottle into something else. Henry could easily have forgotten that he'd already opened the bottle. She decided against. It would be better to pretend it was all gone when he was drunker still.

She had only been gone for moments but when she got back to the dining room Henry was on his feet and had Eve in a kind of clinch as the two of them danced to 'Top of the World'. Eve looked tiny against Henry's bulk, barely reaching his waist. She had her arms around him, stretched as far as she could make them go. Her smile was fixed.

Henry was singing along, blithely unaware of how uncomfortable his daughter seemed to be. For a moment Agatha hoped that he would forget about the port and she could discreetly return it to its hiding place. But she knew this was a pipe dream.

'Ah, good,' he interrupted himself when he saw her. 'I knew I'd bought some. Can't have Stilton without port, now can you, Eve?'

'No, Daddy,' Eve replied.

She threw Agatha a look that said, help me, and Agatha joined them, loosening Henry's grip on Eve and putting his arm around her waist. The three of them circled like a tumble of wrestlers until Henry almost overbalanced and lost interest in dancing. He let Eve go and Eve, not anticipating the sudden change in balance, stumbled and careered into the music centre. As the record jumped the needle screeched across the vinyl.

There was nothing wrong with Henry's reactions, despite the alcohol. He grabbed Eve by the wrist and lifted her from the floor so she dangled by one arm.

'Be careful,' he snarled at her. 'That record will be ruined now.'

'We can replace it,' placated Agatha as Eve just kept repeating 'I'm sorry' over and over again.

Henry swayed slightly as he focused on his child hanging before him, then he flicked her across the room. Eve landed in a heap and immediately curled herself into a ball, protecting her head with her arms.

'You can bloody well replace it,' he slurred. 'Records don't just grow on trees, you know, my girl.'

He chuntered on under his breath, but Agatha wasn't listening. She rushed to Eve's side and cradled her in her arms.

'Are you all right?' she asked her, stroking her hair with one hand and her back with the other.

No one had asked Agatha this question when her own father had taken his belt to her. Her mother had bowed to him in every-thing, assuming that Agatha deserved whatever punishment had been meted out, but instinctively Agatha knew that her role was split between protecting her child and comforting her. And even in that moment she thought that she was determined to make a better job of being a mother than her own mother had managed.

Henry stumbled back to the table. He was talking to himself now.

'I need a glass. Where are the bloody port glasses? Can that bloody woman get nothing right? Never mind. This one will do. This will do very nicely.'

He slopped the port into the glass that had held the red wine, filling it almost to the top.

'Now. Did someone say something about James Bond?'

Carrying the over-filled glass in one hand and the bottle in the other he swayed out of the room, leaving little puddles of port in his wake.

Agatha felt Eve sobbing into her shoulder and she squeezed her more tightly.

'There, there,' she said awkwardly. 'You're all right now.'

She wouldn't be all right, though. Agatha understood very little about being a mother, but she understood this. Eve wouldn't forget her father's violence just as she herself had never forgotten the violence of hers. It was like a port stain on a white damask tablecloth. Even if the bulk of it could be shifted through careful laundry, the shadow would never come out. It would remain, a dark patch in the fabric forever.

54

NOW

It wasn't a date.

Lyra kept saying this to herself, but her stomach was still turning somersaults, which was irritating because Cameron wasn't that hot. She didn't bother getting changed, just to prove the point to herself, but she pulled her curls up into a bun and put enough make-up on to bring a dewy glow to her skin without looking as if she'd tried too hard.

Skye came in just as she was checking herself out in the age-spotted mirror of the wardrobe door.

'You look nice, Mummy,' she said approvingly.

'I'm going for a drink with Cameron,' she said. She made it a policy to always be straight with Skye, wherever possible at least.

Skye's face lit up and for a brief moment Lyra thought it was because of the date. Then she remembered that Skye was only five.

'Is Flea going?' she asked, which more than accounted for her enthusiasm. 'Can I come too?'

'I don't know about Flea,' Lyra replied, dropping down to her knees so that her face was level with her daughter's. 'But I'm afraid you can't come, baby, because they don't let five-year-olds into pubs. Will you be okay here with VeeVee and GeeGee?'

Skye nodded enthusiastically, this proposal apparently more appealing than time spent with the cat.

'GeeGee and me are playing this cool game with my horses. She knows lots about horses.'

'I didn't know that,' Lyra said. 'But she knows lots about all kinds of things. I won't be back late. I'll be here to read you your story.'

'Okay. But don't worry. GeeGee can read it if you're not here.'

Lyra remembered Agatha reading to her when she was small, too. It stuck in her mind because of the way she did it. Her mum had read to her quickly and efficiently. Her dad had used different voices which reduced her to fits of giggles, thus annoying her mother because she was supposed to be going to sleep and not getting all fired up. But her grandmother read as if she were discovering the stories for the first time, tentatively exploring each sentence. If Lyra hadn't known better she might have said that her grandmother had never read aloud before, or certainly not often.

'GeeGee is great at reading stories,' she said now.

Her mother was in the kitchen stirring something on the hob.

'I won't be in for tea,' Lyra said, wincing slightly at the lateness of this information. 'I'm going out for a quick drink with Cameron. Could you keep an eye on Skye, please?'

Her mother turned, brow furrowed as she tried to place the name. 'Cameron?'

'Dylan's son. He was here today helping out. We're just popping to The Green Man. I won't be late. I'll be back for bath time.'

Eve looked on the verge of saying something and then seemed to change her mind.

'I can plate some up for you,' she said. 'Just in case.'

Lyra smiled gratefully. She really didn't want to feel like she was being mothered, but then she had just given no notice of her intention to miss the meal.

'That'd be great,' she replied. 'Thanks, Mum.'

And then she left before her mother could give her the third degree.

The arrangement with Cameron was barely substantial enough to be called an arrangement. He might even have forgotten that he'd suggested it. Lyra dithered on the step, trying to decide what to do, and then set off in the direction of the cottage. If he'd forgotten she would know pretty quickly and would just style it out.

But he didn't appear to have forgotten. He was standing at the door chatting to Dylan, no longer wearing his overalls but jeans and a hoody. Flea was draped across his shoulders.

'Ready?' he asked her as she approached.

'Is Flea coming too?' Lyra asked. Were cats allowed in pubs? She had no idea.

'Flea can stay in the car,' he replied. 'He doesn't like it if there are too many people.'

They drove the five minutes or so down into the village. There wasn't much left of what had once been the hub of village life. The school had closed decades before, and the combined post office and general store had gone too. The pub would surely be next.

They parked on the road and Cameron led her inside, pushing open the heavy door and ducking so that he didn't hit his head on the beams. Inside the place was sparsely lit and warm, and it smelled of wood smoke.

He ordered their drinks and she chose a table not too close to the fire but away from the locals, so they had a bit of privacy. A couple of them nodded at her as she sat down, more out of polite-ness than because they knew who she was. Would they be interested to discover she and Cameron were the grandchildren of both the Fox House woman and her childhood friend? Lyra doubted it, but she still would rather they thought she was just someone passing through. And that was kind of true.

Cameron came back with the drinks and they started to pick their way through the conventional small talk, each asking questions about the other. Cameron hadn't been to university like she had. His parents had split up when he was fifteen. He and his sister Molly had lived with their mum and only seen Dylan intermittently to start with, and then Cameron had started to spend more time with him.

She told him about her design work and he told her he was an electrician.

'Hence helping your dad out with the cottage?' Lyra asked.

'I'd probably have been roped in anyway,' he said wryly, 'but I'd rather provide him with a skill than just labour. He can do his own heavy lifting!'

He took a mouthful of his pint and then asked, 'And Skye's dad isn't around?'

Lyra baulked at the leap to such a personal question but then she shook her head. 'He left me when Skye was little. Got a better offer.'

'I find that hard to believe,' said Cameron with a little smirk that suggested he was trying his luck but knew how corny he was being.

Lyra rolled her eyes and didn't bother to respond. Should she tell him about the Californian question? He would, at least, offer her an unbiased opinion. It might be worth hearing.

But whilst she was considering the idea, he changed tack.

'This cottage business is weird though, right?' he said.

'Totally. Me and Mum have no idea what's going on. Granny just announced that she owed your dad for something he once did for her and that she was giving him the cottage. We'd never heard of him until then. Well, Mum apparently knew him when they were kids but she says she doesn't remember. It was Granny and your grandad who were the real friends, I think.'

Cameron raised an eyebrow.

'Ah yes, Grandpa Jack. The family's black sheep.'

55

'What do you mean, the black sheep?' asked Lyra.

Cameron's expression suggested that he didn't really understand why Lyra was asking the question.

'You know,' he said. 'The family member that did something bad.'

'Yes,' tutted Lyra in exasperation. 'I know what a black sheep is. I meant, what did Jack do to claim the title?'

Cameron appeared to have a sudden attack of conscience. 'I assumed you'd know,' he said. 'I'm not sure I should . . .'

'If you don't tell me what he actually did after dropping it into the conversation like that, you can consider this embryonic friendship over,' she said, but with a grin so he'd know she was, in part at least, joking.

Cameron pulled a face as he considered his options and then he sighed.

'Okay. You win,' he said, and Lyra realised that he'd always intended to tell her.

'Jack went to prison,' he said, cocking an eyebrow for dramatic effect.

'Oh my God! No way.' She supposed she ought to be shocked or even horrified at this turn of events, but actually her curiosity outweighed all other emotions. 'What did he do?'

She was expecting the answer to be theft of some kind, maybe fraud or embezzlement, which she knew were crimes but always felt slightly half-baked when placed next to the nastier ones you saw on television dramas.

Cameron studied his pint glass for a moment before replying. This pause seemed to be genuine, Lyra thought, which made her all the more desperate to know.

Then he looked up and quite seriously and with no hint of a smile, met her eye.

'He killed someone.'

Hs spoke softly even though there was nobody close enough to overhear their conversation, and Lyra moved closer to catch his words. Even then, she wasn't sure she had.

'Killed someone,' she repeated.

Cameron nodded tightly, his eyes darting around as if checking that no one else was listening.

This time Lyra's shock was genuine. That Jack had been the kind of person to kill someone didn't fit at all with the story that Lyra and her mother had been trying to piece together. There'd been no suggestion that Jack was anything other than entirely ordinary, his role in the story thus far completely benign. So this new information took her a moment to process.

'What? Like murder?' she whispered back. 'Well, Granny kept that quiet!'

'No,' replied Cameron. 'I don't think so. Dad doesn't really talk about it so I don't know all the ins and outs. It was more a self-defence kind of thing. He didn't get life, anyway.'

Lyra sat back in her chair. 'Wow!' she said. 'I did not see that coming.'

Cameron shrugged. 'What can I tell you? Our black sheep.'

'Did you visit him? In prison, I mean. What was it like? I've never been in one. Not yet, at least.'

Her joke suddenly seemed to be in very poor taste and Lyra wished she could take the words back, but Cameron didn't seem upset. He shook his head.

'Nah. It all happened long before I was born. Dad was only a kid himself.'

'That must have been hard,' Lyra said. 'His dad having to leave him like that.'

'I suppose,' agreed Cameron. 'But then he left me when he split up with my mum.'

Lyra wrinkled her nose. 'It's not really the same, though, is it?'

'Suppose not.'

'Have you talked to your grandad about what it was like?' she asked, unable to let the idea of being in prison drop.

Cameron shook his head again. 'Never got the chance,' he said. 'He died in there.'

Lyra didn't follow him. 'But you said he didn't get life?' she clarified. 'So did he get ill?'

'No. He didn't die of natural causes. There was a fight, among the prisoners. Grandad got caught up in it. It was a case of wrong time, wrong place.'

Lyra's mouth fell open.

'God, that's awful,' she said.

Cameron lifted his pint glass to his lips and gave a tiny nod. 'Yep. Dad's always been resentful. Prison robbed him of his dad. The actual sentence wasn't that long because there were extenuating circumstances. A couple of years, I think. And with good behaviour he'd have been out in much less. But then he found himself in the middle of whatever was kicking off and that was it. He never came home.'

This new information floored Lyra. She didn't know what to make of it.

'That's so tragic,' was the best she could come up with.

They sat in silence for a moment or two then, as a mark of respect to a man that neither of them had known.

But, Lyra thought, Jack had killed someone. He had taken someone's life and been punished for it. They shouldn't forget that, even if he himself had then been killed.

Eventually Cameron grinned to lighten the mood and said, 'So come on, then. Who's the black sheep in your family?'

Lyra screwed up her nose as she thought about it, considering each person in turn before she reached a conclusion.

'Well, me, I suppose,' she said. 'My mum is as pure as the driven snow. Verging on the dull, if I'm honest. Grew up with just her and Granny because her dad had a heart attack when she was little. Married Dad. Had me. Divorced Dad. Went back to live with Granny. Her life is basically a circle.'

'Sounds pretty straightforward,' agreed Cameron.

'And Granny is a bit eccentric but I don't think she's ever done anything to put her in black sheep territory. So that leaves me!'

Cameron grinned. 'Go on then. Tell me why you're the best candidate.'

Lyra counted the items off on her fingers.

'Pregnant at nineteen thus screwing up a glowing academic career. My baby's father left me at twenty-one. Currently homeless with everything I own in various black plastic bags. Child has no school to go to because I dragged her away from the last one. About to be in a possible custody battle with father of said child.'

She sat back in her chair, hand open and fingers splayed indicating all her black sheep qualifications.

'Yep,' she added. 'That's pretty much it.'

Cameron curled his lip. 'Is that it?' he said, laughter in his voice. 'From where I'm sitting, that sounds like an adventure, not something to be ashamed of. And your little girl . . . Skye, is it?'

Lyra nodded.

'She's dead cute. And she says please and thank you without being told to. Not many kids do that.'

Lyra's cheeks flushed, both because this was true and because he had noticed.

'The other stuff. Well, that's just life, isn't it?' he added.

Lyra reframed her list in this more pragmatic light and had to agree that he was right.

'Maybe your family just doesn't have a black sheep. Or at least, not that you're aware of.'

'Maybe,' she agreed.

'Another drink?' Cameron waved his empty glass at her.

Lyra checked the time and concluded that she could still have one and get back for Skye's bedtime.

'Go on then,' she said. 'Why not? And then you can tell me why you have a cat that masquerades as a scarf!'

Cameron stood up and made his way to the bar, leaving Lyra to think about what it must have been like for Dylan to lose his dad like that. Cameron hadn't said exactly how young Dylan had been when it happened, but it didn't really matter. It was still awful. Maybe she could have a sneaking respect for him.

But only sneaking. He had basically stolen her cottage. And actually, when she thought about it, her mum had lost her dad as a child too, and she was perfectly all right, so maybe it wasn't such a big deal. And it certainly wasn't enough to have made Agatha give him the cottage.

Despite what she had learned, that decision still didn't make any sense.

56

Eve's phone buzzed and she dived on it, desperate for something to distract her from the tumult of her own thoughts. It was Justin, and a tiny part of her rejoiced that she had resisted the urge to message him earlier because now here he was, showing himself to be as keen on her company as she was on his.

She opened the message.

Fancy dinner tonight?

She smiled at the phone. Her ex-husband was an open book to her. His date must have let him down at the last minute and he couldn't be bothered to cook. She had agreed to look after Skye but Lyra had said she would be back to bath her and put her to bed so that should work out well.

Spending an evening with Justin would let her forget all about Dylan and her mother and the multifarious Fox House issues that currently loomed large around her. She could also chat through what she had pieced together about the Rafe situation with Justin. Lyra might be twenty-five years old but she was still their child.

Been stood up? she wrote and added a winking face emoji just because she knew it would wind him up. Justin hated emojis. Well, I can step into the breach. Where and when?

As she would have expected, Justin ignored her tease about his diary window and suggested a smart restaurant in town. He added My shout to the end of the message, which was his way of showing her that he hadn't taken offence.

Feeling happier now that the remainder of her day had structure to it, Eve went in search of Skye and found her in the sitting room curled up on the sofa next to Agatha. They were reading together and Eve felt an irrational stab of jealousy. She checked herself immediately. This was her granddaughter enjoying time with her mother, a lovely thing and not something that should prompt anything but joy. And she herself was fifty-two, far too old to be read to by Agatha.

But something about the scene stung. Eve had no memory of sharing similar moments with Agatha herself. She might have simply forgotten. It would have occurred almost five decades before and, as had been demonstrated so recently, her recollection of her childhood was not fully functional.

Of course, Agatha had read to her as a child. They had enjoyed many books, some of which were still on the shelves in her bedroom upstairs, their spines cracked and faded from overexposure to sunlight. Yet there was something about the tenderness of Skye and Agatha together, an intimacy that was unfamiliar to Eve. This was something she could be certain of: whatever her relationship with Agatha was based on, no part of it had ever been intimate. Or tender for that matter.

If a word could be chosen to describe her connection with her mother, it would be pragmatic. Commonsensical and unsentimental also came to mind. There had been relatively few heated arguments over the years but that, Eve suspected, was partly because she had been away at school for a lot of the time, but also because there had never been much to get heated about. Pretty much anything Eve had asked for she had got. This was not because she had been in any way spoilt. Her wants had been very modest. It was more that Agatha hadn't really shared the concerns that her friends' mothers seemed to get into such a spin about.

Once or twice Eve remembered trying to provoke a reaction out of Agatha. She knew that teenage girls were supposed to have troubled relationships with their mothers. She saw it all the time on the television and in magazines and could cite endless examples from her own friends' experiences. But Agatha had failed to take the bait. It wasn't as if she wasn't capable of having strong opinions; she had legions of them on politics, religion, women in the workplace. She could even get hot under the collar about which day the bin men came.

But when it came to anything to do with her daughter, Agatha was passive. Eve might almost have thought that she didn't care enough to bother with an argument. The two of them had trundled through life on an even keel until Eve had left to move into the cottage with Justin. Many might have thought the simplicity of it would make it a dream mother/daughter relationship, but Eve thought differently.

Where was the passion? Where was the fire? Eve had wanted her mother to behave as she saw all the other mothers doing, cursing their daughters to the high heavens but then prepared to defend them to the death should anyone else dare to criticise. Eve had longed for her mother to defend her too, a fearless lioness protecting her cub in the face of danger. She had always been desperate for some indication that Agatha loved her above all things.

But there'd been none of that, and all she'd got was tacit agreement to everything she asked for with no objections and rarely a cross word.

And definitely none of the tenderness she saw now between Agatha and Skye.

To disguise any emotion that might threaten to bubble up, she resorted to the jolliness that she always seemed to adopt when dealing with her granddaughter.

'Well, aren't you two having a lovely time,' she said brightly. 'What are you reading?'

'*The Tiger Who Came to Tea*,' replied Skye. 'I'm Sophie and GeeGee is the mummy.'

Eve knew the book, had read it herself to Lyra so often that there had been a time when she could recite it all by heart.

'How lovely,' she said. 'And who's the tiger?' She opened her eyes wide, a mischievous smile on her lips.

'The tiger is a tiger, silly. None of us can be him,' replied Skye, and Eve pulled her lips tight so Skye couldn't see her amusement.

'Did you know that this book is older than you, Eve?' said Agatha. 'It was first published in 1968. Can you believe that? And yet I've never come across it before.'

'How extraordinary,' quipped Eve wryly, resisting any comment as to why that might have been. 'Mummy will be back soon, Skye,' she added. 'And then it will be bath time.'

Skye tucked herself in closer to Agatha as if she needed protecting from the water.

'And Justin just texted. He's taking me out for dinner. You can fend for yourself tonight, can't you, Agatha? There's plenty in the fridge.'

Agatha waved a hand in the air without looking at her, as if to say that nothing would be less trouble. And then they continued with reading.

Eve turned to leave.

'You get off if you need to go,' Agatha added. 'I'm more than happy to hold the fort until Lyra gets home.'

Eve was surplus to requirements. Unloved and now, it appeared, redundant on top. Neither Agatha nor Skye looked up as she left the room, so neither saw the hurt on her face.

She texted Justin.

Let's meet for a drink first. I'll get a taxi back.

57

The pub that she suggested was busy, but Eve cut her way through the crowds to find the table that she and Justin preferred. It struck her as amusing that they still had favourite spots despite the divorce, but old habits die hard and twenty years of marriage was a long time to form them.

Justin was already there with a large glass of white wine poured and waiting for her.

'It sounded as if you might need this,' he said as she approached.

Eve rolled her eyes heavenwards and dropped into the chair.

'Thank you. You would not believe the day I've had,' she said, taking a large gulp and then sighing. 'That's better,' she added as the alcohol hit her system.

Justin's drink, a lurid orange Aperol spritz, was already half gone.

'You had a day of it as well?' she asked him, nodding at the glass.

Justin shrugged by way of reply. 'So, tell me,' he said, leaning back in his chair and putting his hands behind his head. 'What's up?'

Eve shook her head slowly as she tried to piece all the parts of the day together. 'I really don't know where to start. Rafe turned up with that new girlfriend of his, but I don't know what he wanted. They left in a hurry, though, so I don't think they got it.'

Justin sat forward in his seat. 'Curious. Did you ask Lyra?'

'I did, but she gave me some half-baked story about him calling in on his way home from somewhere. He's going to the States, apparently, with work. Won't be able to see Skye for a while.'

Justin pulled a face. 'And that was all?'

'Apparently.' Eve put her palm up to stop him questioning further. 'I know. It didn't make much sense to me either, but that's what she told me.'

'Has she said when she's going back to Manchester? I assume Skye must be due back at school next week.'

Eve shrugged and sighed loudly. 'Your guess is as good as mine. To be honest, I get the impression she has no idea what she's doing.'

'For a smart girl she can be remarkably dumb sometimes,' said Justin. 'Shall I talk to her?'

Eve pressed her lips together to stop herself from reminding him that she'd asked him to do just that when Lyra had first turned up at Fox House.

'You can try,' she said instead. 'She certainly doesn't want to talk to me and I can't force her to. Maybe she needs to work out what she wants for herself.'

'Like daughter like mother?' asked Justin.

Eve couldn't decide whether it was a help or a hindrance that Justin could read her so well. She decided to ignore the question.

'Anyway, she's gone out this evening, for a drink with Dylan's son.'

'What son?'

'Keep up!' said Eve with a grin, revelling in Justin's confusion. 'He's got a son. And a daughter too.'

'But no wife?'

'Divorced,' Eve confirmed.

Justin sniffed and Eve suppressed a smile. She enjoyed knowing that he was ever so slightly thrown by Dylan's presence. Even though she had no romantic interest in Dylan, it was fun to watch Justin assuming that she had.

'He filled in some of the gaps for me,' she continued. 'His parents were friends with Agatha and Dad and so we played together when we were little. Then they left around the time Dad died. He got a bit shirty when I mentioned that, actually. He's an odd bloke. I can't get the measure of him at all. One minute he's nice as pie and the next he's stopped talking and I don't know where I am.'

Justin snorted, as if she had thus confirmed everything he already thought about the man.

'And you're still no nearer working out why Agatha has given him the cottage?' he asked.

Eve shook her head. 'Haven't got a clue. He's started work on the place already, though. Isn't letting the grass grow.'

She took another mouthful of wine and realised, rather shamefacedly, that the glass was already empty.

Justin raised an eyebrow. 'That went down well. Another?'

Eve closed her eyes and nodded.

Justin trooped off to the bar and she realised just too late that she should probably have offered to get the round. Never mind. She could get the next one. There would be a next one, she felt sure. Suddenly all she wanted to do was get drunk and forget anything that came close to being a responsibility.

When Justin got back, they chatted about his business, what was going well and what less well. She told him about her far less interesting work and the suggestions Lyra had made about getting a decent chair.

'The thing is,' she said, 'getting a proper chair at Fox House smacks of permanence.'

Justin met her eye with a cool gaze. 'Remind me,' he said. 'How long have you been living with Agatha now?'

'Oh, shut up,' she replied. 'I know what you're saying and you're right. It's been over a year. But it is temporary.'

'If you say so.'

Eve put her head in her hands. 'God, what am I doing with my life?' she said, not really expecting an answer.

She didn't get one, either. When she looked up Justin was watching her, head tipped to one side with a hint of a smirk on his lips.

'If you're going to have an existential crisis, could you at least wait until we get to the restaurant?'

Eve was forced to laugh at herself. 'Sorry,' she said. 'Blame the wine. I shouldn't have drunk it so quickly. What time is the table booked for?'

A further drink later, they left the pub and wandered down the high street to the restaurant. Whereas the pub had been busy, the town was quiet with only a few people out and about, and Eve slipped her arm through Justin's and leant into him for warmth as he told her a terrible joke about a mermaid and a donkey which made her laugh more than it deserved to.

The meal passed pleasantly enough; the food was good and the wine continued to flow until Justin wound them back to where they had started.

'Why don't you just move out?' he said.

The question came out of the blue and it knocked Eve off guard.

'But I can't,' she said. 'Agatha needs me.'

Justin gave her a sceptical look. 'I'm not sure Agatha has ever needed anyone,' he said.

'Oh, that's not fair,' objected Eve. 'She's an old lady and she's not as able as she was.'

'She's plenty able,' said Justin. 'But for some reason that I truly can't fathom, you seem to feel that you have to be there at her beck and call. Her hip has been fixed for months. I swear she only walks with that cane because she thinks it gives her gravitas. And now she has the indomitable Dylan on her doorstep if she did need anything.'

His tone was scathing and even though Eve knew the barbs were aimed at Dylan and not her, she felt hot tears sting the back of her eyes.

'I see. So, what you are saying,' she said archly, 'is that I am entirely unneeded. Thanks for that.'

And then she stood and stalked to the cloakrooms, hoping that she could hold herself together for long enough to get there.

58

Mercifully there was no one else in the ladies. Eve went straight into a stall and locked the door behind her. It took three attempts to throw the bolt. Why had she drunk so much? It wasn't like her to throw caution away quite so wildly.

Of course, she knew why. Justin was such easy company and he allowed her to drop her guard in a way that no one else did. That was no reason to lose control, however.

She drew in a deep shuddering breath and squeezed her eyes tight. The room swam gently behind her eyelids. She would not cry. Crying achieved nothing. She had learned that lesson as a very young girl. If she'd become upset, Agatha had just stared at her until she stopped, apparently unsure what was expected of her.

She was probably just hormonal, she thought, and then immediately admonished herself. It was almost impossible to avoid mention of the menopause these days, and it appeared to be responsible for pretty much anything that happened to a woman after the age of forty-five. She knew that was just a cop-out though. This was just good old-fashioned self-pity and she wanted no part of it.

Someone else came into the cloakroom and prompted her to move. She flushed and then went to wash her hands, careful not to make eye contact with the woman who was touching up her make-up in the mirror.

'Don't you wish someone would invent mascara that stayed where you put it?' said the woman as she applied a clumpy blackened wand to her lower lashes. 'I swear I've tried them all, and they're not cheap some of them, and they all end up a good inch below where they start off.'

Eve smiled despite herself. Her own make-up was holding up relatively well in the circumstances.

'Yes. I don't know why we bother,' she said.

The woman stopped what she was doing, hand and wand hovering above her cheek, and met Eve's eye in the mirror's reflection.

'Now, you don't mean that,' she said sternly. 'We always have to keep trying to be our best self, whatever that looks like for us. Otherwise what's the point of it all?' She gave Eve what felt like a significant stare, and then switched her attention back to her own reflection. 'And for me, that's keeping my bloody mascara under control!'

'You're probably right,' conceded Eve with a weak smile. 'I'll keep trying.'

'That's the spirit,' said the woman. She spun round to check her rear in the mirror and then left the cloakroom, leaving Eve alone.

Was she right? Did Eve owe it to herself to try harder? On balance, Eve thought she probably did. There were bigger issues that couldn't be fixed overnight – predominantly her odd relationship with Agatha, which then made her question her own skills as a mother and now grandmother. But starting to paint again, committing to Fox House or leaving it, becoming less reliant on Justin – surely these were all things she could tackle now, and really the only thing getting in the way was her.

Feeling more in control than when she'd entered the cloakroom, she made her way back to their table. She was aware of Justin watching her closely as she picked her way across the room, and recognised the look of relief on his face when he realised that she appeared to be calm and not in the middle of some hideous emotional breakdown.

'Don't say anything,' she warned as she sat down. 'Not one word.'

He smirked and squeezed his lips tight.

'It is weird though,' she continued. 'This business with the cottage seems to have brought all kinds of things to the surface for me, things I can't really get a handle on. Take this evening. I saw Agatha reading with Skye. They looked so happy in each other's company and it made me feel jealous. Can you imagine that? Jealous of my five-year-old grandchild!'

Justin didn't comment, but clearly, he was listening.

'I read this article,' she continued. 'About generational trauma. Do you know what that is?'

'I can hazard a guess,' replied Justin.

'Of course. Anyway, I'd never thought in terms of a label like that before. Wounds that are passed down through a family without anyone realising. But it made me wonder. Agatha, well, she was always an unusual kind of mother. It was like she was never quite sure what she was supposed to do with me. Then Dylan said . . .'

Justin's expression altered subtly at the mention of Dylan, but Eve pressed on.

'He said that maybe the reason Agatha never wanted me to call her Mum was because she didn't feel she deserved the title. What do you think? Could he be right?'

Justin cocked his head to one side and looked up at the ceiling above her head.

'Well,' he said slowly. 'I suppose there might be something in that. Although what would have made her think that way in the first place?'

Eve shrugged. 'I don't know. She never talked much about her own parents but I don't think she was showered in love and affection. And it's weird that she never changed that bedroom, the one her brothers shared. I know we've never needed the space so there was no pressure to clear it all out, but it's still strange, don't you think? She never even knew them. They died before she was born.'

'Maybe she felt a sense of obligation to keep it the same,' Justin suggested.

'An obligation to whom?'

'Her own mother?'

Now it was Eve's turn to pause. Could he be right? Was Agatha harbouring some kind of unspoken duty to her own long-dead mother?

'You could always ask her,' said Justin, and Eve shuddered.

'Can you imagine?' she laughed, but Justin's face was serious.

'Why not? Maybe she has ghosts she needs to exorcise. You've always said she wasn't close to her mother. Maybe leaving the bedroom like some kind of shrine is her way of making amends. Maybe it's been long enough now and she just needs someone to give her permission to move on.'

Eve tried to think it through but her brain, muddled by the wine, was finding it hard to follow a thought through to its conclusion.

'I think that's part of what interested me about this generational trauma business. Agatha's mother was probably traumatised by the death of her sons in the war. So, she wasn't able to be a real mother to Agatha, who in turn wasn't sure how to be a mother to me?'

'Maybe,' said Justin, his face solemn. 'Although I think there's also a chance that you're overthinking it.'

Eve rolled her eyes good-humouredly. 'And then I'm next in line.' She pulled the corners of her mouth down in an exaggerated grimace. 'Do you think I've been a good mother? Be honest.'

Eve fixed her gaze deep into his familiar eyes, searching for answers. She wasn't fishing for a compliment on what a marvellous job she had done. She was looking for the truth, and in this moment she suddenly had a genuine curiosity about what he would say.

He focused on her eyes. 'That is a ridiculous question that I'm tempted not to dignify with a reply. Of course you've been a good mother, are a good mother. You're wonderful at it.'

She lowered her eyes so he wouldn't see the tears forming in the corners, and blinked hard.

'And Lyra. She's amazing with Skye,' she added.

'Well, there you go. Who do you think she learned that from?' he said. 'From her own mother. I mean, I know I'm a pretty fantastic father, but . . .' She looked up and he was grinning at her. She returned his smile gratefully.

She raised her glass to take a sip, discovered that it was empty and replaced it on the table.

'Thanks,' she said quietly.

He nodded, both acknowledging her thanks and conveying that it was spoken unnecessarily.

'I do need to move out of Fox House, though,' she added, the truth of this suddenly becoming apparent to her. 'And maybe start painting again.'

'Yes,' agreed Justin. 'You do.'

59

Lyra had enjoyed her evening. Cameron was a nice guy – of course, not in a 'watch this space – romance incoming' kind of way. She didn't have time for any of that kind of frippery in her life just now. But he was a good laugh and they'd had fun.

And that thing about Jack being in prison. That was gold dust, although she wasn't quite sure why. It just felt like a major part of the puzzle. As the taxi took her back to Fox House her stomach fizzed with anticipation. She couldn't wait to share her news. First, she would get Skye into bed and then she and her mother could have a proper deep dive into all the details over a glass of wine.

When she got back, however, her mother wasn't there. Skye, sitting at the kitchen table, was colouring in a beautiful, hand-drawn picture of a horse and carriage, her grandmother passing her the felt tips on demand.

'Wow! You two have been busy,' Lyra said, going straight over to the table and crouching over the drawing to fully admire Skye's penmanship. 'That's really good, Skye. I like how you're colouring in the wheels, with the yellow and green. Much nicer than plain brown.'

Skye looked up at her, beaming. 'GeeGee drew the picture,' she said. 'Isn't she good at drawing?'

'Very good,' agreed Lyra as she wondered why she didn't know that her grandmother was so artistic. But then her mother could draw, so she supposed it made sense. And anyway, weren't there so many things she didn't know about Agatha? Her skill with a pen could just join the list.

'Where's Mum?' she asked, as she looked around the room.

'Oh, she went out for dinner with your father. Not back yet.'

A dart of annoyance flashed through Lyra. Her mother had said she'd look after Skye and not go waltzing out for dinner. She checked herself. Skye was fine here with her great-grandmother.

'Well,' she said. 'It's bath time now, Skye, so do you just want to finish that wheel and then you can do the rest tomorrow.'

Skye gave a half-hearted little groan, but she put the pen she was using back into its place in the packet and got down from her chair.

'Night night, GeeGee,' she said, standing on her tiptoes so she could plant a kiss on Agatha's cheek.

'Goodnight, Skye,' replied Agatha as formally as if she were talking to an adult.

'Thanks, Granny,' said Lyra and put an arm across Skye's shoulder to encourage her to move in the right direction.

Bath time was fun, as it generally was. There weren't any bath toys at Fox House, but Lyra had improvised with a couple of yoghurt pots, a sieve and various spoons and ladles. Her own ingenuity pleased Lyra, and that took her mind to Rafe and his attempts to steal Skye away. She was a good mother, she told herself reassuringly, even if she wasn't bilingual. She was enough.

She was in bed when she heard the front door closing, somewhat more loudly than was ideal at eleven o'clock when there was a sleeping child in the house. Lyra went out on to the landing to investigate. She peered over the banister and saw her mother wrestling off her coat and muttering to herself, although Lyra couldn't catch what she was saying. There were little giggles too. It sounded as if Eve was remonstrating with herself over the coat. She was drunk, Lyra realised, which was a rare and somewhat surprising occurrence.

'Hi, Mum,' she whispered, sending Eve into apparent confusion, her head twisting this way and that as she tried to work out where the sound was coming from. 'I'm up here,' Lyra added. 'Did you have a good night?'

Eve finally looked up and Lyra saw her efforts to focus. 'Oh, hi, darling. Yes, thank you. I think I've had too much wine.'

'Come up here,' Lyra said. 'I've got something I have to tell you.'

'Ooh!' Eve seemed to have forgotten how to regulate her volume and Lyra shushed her. 'Sorry!' she added, and started to climb the stairs slowly and deliberately.

When she reached the landing Lyra ushered her into her room and closed the door gently behind them. She sat on her bed and Eve wobbled down too, giggling at herself again.

'Did you have a nice night with . . .' Eve struggled to remember the name.

'Cameron,' Lyra supplied. 'Yes. It was fun. He's a nice guy. But you will never guess what he told me.'

Eve opened her mouth as if she might be about to actually try and guess, but Lyra spoke over her.

'Jack went to prison for killing someone!'

She stared at her mother, eyes wide, and waited for the kind of reaction that her words merited. It took a while.

'Jack?' said Eve, her forehead creased as she tried to place the name.

'You know! Jack. Dylan's dad,' supplied Lyra impatiently.

'Oh, Jack!' Eve nodded, recognition flooding her face. 'Yes. And he what?'

Lyra sighed in exasperation. Maybe she would have been better waiting until the morning to impart her gossip, but she had started now. 'He went to prison. He killed someone. It was self-defence, apparently, but still! Granny didn't tell us that, did she?'

'No,' agreed Eve thoughtfully. 'She did not. Who did he kill?'

'God, I don't know,' said Lyra, frustrated that her mother didn't seem to be grasping the salient parts of the story. 'Some bloke. But then he died in prison. Never came out. Got caught up in some fight with another prisoner.'

Eve seemed to have sobered up. Lyra could see her mind piecing the story together, such as it was.

'So, when Dylan said that his dad had left them,' she said, 'that wasn't entirely true. He did leave them but that was because he went to prison.'

'Wild, isn't it?' said Lyra.

Eve nodded slowly. 'Not quite as whiter than snow as he makes out then.'

'Cameron said that Jack was the black sheep of the family, and we got talking and out it all came. Granny's never said a word. Do you think she knows? Maybe if we tell her, she might change her mind about giving Dylan the cottage. What do you reckon?'

Lyra was thinking as she spoke. She had resigned herself to letting the place go, but suddenly she could see this one last chance to get it back.

But Eve didn't reply. She had lain herself down and closed her eyes to think about it.

In seconds she was asleep.

60

Lyra slept fitfully. She'd been unable to shift the idea of getting the cottage back from Dylan. In her heart, she knew she was on a hiding to nothing, but she had at least to try. And she was running out of time. Skye was supposed to be back at school in five days and she was still no further forward in deciding what to do about America, or where to move to. This was the first time she faced a decision that would not just impact on her but would affect Skye's life too; where she decided to settle could have all manner of unforeseen consequences and it was up to her, as the adult, to try and anticipate as many of them as she could.

But before she could do that, she had to ask Skye the question that she was dreading. There was no getting around it. If she didn't ask her then Rafe would, and in her gut Lyra knew that letting him ask was definitely worse. Even though she couldn't bear to hear the answer, she had to ask the question.

And as a result, she couldn't sleep.

The birds started to sing long before the sky lightened. She'd heard tell of the dawn chorus but it wasn't something she could remember experiencing first hand, but now, as she lay in her bed, she couldn't believe how noisy it was. So many separate melodies all calling out into the semi-darkness. She let the music wash over her as she tossed her options back and forth in her head.

When Skye came into her room at seven, she was already up and dressed.

'Mummy! You're awake!' There was an edge of disbelief in her voice that Lyra didn't appreciate.

'You make it sound like I'm always asleep when you come in!' she replied, with a laugh in her voice.

Skye gave her a look that suggested this was true, and Lyra grinned. 'Listen, come and sit with me for a minute. I've got something I want to talk to you about.'

Nothing had happened in Skye's life thus far to make her even vaguely wary of this sentence and she clambered up on to the bed happily. They sat facing one another, legs crossed and knees touching.

'So,' began Lyra. 'You know we had to leave the flat . . .'

'Because silly Mummy flooded it by accident?' Skye gave a knowing blink (as she hadn't yet mastered winking), which made Lyra's insides cramp as she thought about how she had asked her daughter to lie for her.

'Yes. Well, I wanted to talk to you about where we should live next.'

A line appeared between Skye's eyebrows. 'I thought we lived here, with GeeGee and VeeVee.'

'Well, yes. We do right now but that can't be forever.'

Concern swept across Skye's little face as if she wasn't sure how she was supposed to respond. 'But I like it here. And now there's Dylan. And he made me my egg. And Flea.'

'Flea doesn't live here,' Lyra chipped in desperately, feeling that the conversation was already slipping from her grasp. 'But we can't stay here,' she said. 'There's no school for you. And you couldn't go to your old school because it's too far away.'

Skye's brow creased as she tried to follow the thread of what Lyra was saying. Lyra couldn't blame her. What *was* she saying?

'So, there are two choices,' she pressed on. 'Either we go back to Manchester and get a new flat near your old school. Or we decide to move somewhere new and start a new school with a new teacher and new friends.'

Skye cocked her head to one side whilst she considered the matter.

'It would be sad to leave my friends,' she said, although she didn't look upset by the prospect.

'Yes, it would be sad,' agreed Lyra, nodding and realising that she would be sad too. Skye didn't seem worried about not going back to Manchester, but Lyra found that she really was.

'But I can make new ones,' added Skye with a smile. 'I'm good at making friends, aren't I, Mummy? So I think we should go somewhere new.'

'You do?' asked Lyra with as much enthusiasm as her sinking heart could muster. She was tempted to mention her own friends, make a comment about how much harder it would be for her to find new ones, but she didn't want to guilt-trip her daughter into an answer. What kind of a mother would that make her?

'Is my new school near here?' asked Skye, and Lyra's guts twisted again as she saw the excitement in her face.

'I don't know,' she confessed. 'I haven't started to look yet.'

'But school starts again soon, Mummy, and so you need to find out the way there or we'll be late.'

Lyra swallowed hard. No part of her wanted to do what she had to do next, particularly in light of Skye's responses thus far, but it had to be done.

'There's another option,' she began. 'Daddy has the chance to go and live in America for a while and he wondered if you would like to go and live with him and Amina. Just for a bit.' Her voice wobbled, but she pressed her lips together and attempted a smile.

'In America?' asked Skye.

Lyra nodded, not quite trusting her voice.

'Would I go to school there too?' she asked.

The look she gave Lyra was so guileless, so trusting. Lyra bit hard on her knuckle and drew in a deep breath.

'Well, they don't start school until they're a bit older in America, but there is a lovely pre-school there. It's got a big wood in the playground.'

'Just like here,' chipped in Skye.

'Yes. Just like here. And they go on trips and you can learn to speak another language.'

Skye's mouth formed a little 'o'.

'Like French?'

'Yes, like French.'

'And would Daddy and Amina have a cat?'

The question surprised Lyra and the relief forced out a little laugh.

'I don't know,' she said. 'It's sunny, though, so you can play out all the time. And the sea isn't far away.'

'And would you be there too, Mummy?' she asked.

Lyra closed her eyes for a second.

'No,' she managed. 'I'd stay here, in England.'

Skye frowned as she thought about this.

'So just me and Daddy?' she said.

'And Amina.'

'And is it forever?'

Lyra threw her arms around Skye and squeezed her tight.

'No, my darling girl! It's not forever. Just for a few months. A year at the most.'

'Would I be there for my birthday?'

Lyra hadn't even considered all the occasions that she would miss if Skye were on the other side of the world. Consequences of the move started to form a disorderly, jostling line in her head.

'Maybe,' she said. 'Probably.'

'I'm going to talk to my egg about it,' said Skye. 'Can we have breakfast now? And then I need to finish my picture, the one GeeGee drew for me.'

She wriggled down from the bed and scampered away. Lyra heard her chasing down the staircase and into the kitchen.

Lyra stayed where she was a minute longer, feeling too bludgeoned to move. Had she really expected that Skye would just dismiss the idea of going to California out of hand? Of course she hadn't been going to do that. She was five. She couldn't see the complications of the plan and she was a positive child who was thrilled by the prospect of adventures, just as Lyra had brought her up to be. If Lyra suggested a trip to America with her daddy then she wasn't going to be fazed by that. There would be more questions, Lyra was sure, but Skye trusted her not to make her do anything bad.

So maybe, rather than looking at flats and schools, Lyra would have to start preparing herself for the inevitable.

61

Agatha was sitting at the table reading a book on libraries of the world when Lyra came into the kitchen, her heart in her boots.

'Good morning, Lyra,' Agatha said without looking up from her book.

Skye had got herself a bowl and was trying to pour breakfast cereal into it, her tongue just peeping out between her lips. The cereal refused to appear and then came out all in a rush. Skye jerked the box back up quickly and then looked in dismay at the huge mound of little wheat bricks in her bowl.

'Oops.'

'Just tip them back into the box,' said Agatha with a wink. 'No one will know.'

Skye threw a glance at Lyra for confirmation and Lyra nodded and grinned at her, putting her finger to her lips.

'I might be going to America with Daddy, GeeGee,' she said as she fed dry cereal into her mouth. 'Mightn't I, Mummy?'

Lyra looked over her head at Agatha, who raised an eyebrow.

'That's right, sweetie,' Lyra said, squeezing her eyes tightly shut against the threatening tears.

'That sounds interesting,' said Agatha. 'And what about Mummy? Is she going too?'

Lyra opened her eyes. Agatha was staring directly at her, the spoken question also written all over her face. Lyra blinked, her mouth fell open slackly, she blinked again. That was it. That was the solution.

'I don't know much about these things,' continued Agatha, 'But I believe you can stay in America for ninety days without a visa, longer if you have a visitor's one. And what's that expression you use, Lyra? Digital nomad.'

Agatha was smiling now, or the Mona Lisa-type expression of hers that passed for a smile.

'Yes,' replied Lyra, which was all she could manage as the answers to her problems fell neatly into place.

'Of course Mummy must come too,' said Skye. 'Otherwise she'll miss everything. Please can I have some milk?'

Dazed, Lyra walked to the fridge, got the milk and was going to pour it unthinkingly.

Skye objected. 'I can do that, Mummy. I'm big enough.'

Lyra dropped down to her level and planted a kiss on her cheek.

'You definitely are,' she said.

Once Skye was happily eating her cereal, Lyra sat down next to Agatha.

'Thank you,' she said.

'Simply applying logic to the problem,' said Agatha curtly. 'I'm surprised you didn't think of the solution yourself.' But there was that fleeting smile again.

Lyra needed some time to google US visas and think about where she would live, but first she had the mystery of Dylan to unravel. She compartmentalised the American issue for later and brought her mind back to Jack and prison.

'No sign of Mum yet?' she asked.

'No. I didn't hear her come in. Was she very late?'

'Not really,' said Lyra. Loyalty stopped her saying anything else, but she imagined that her mother might well be sleeping off a hangover, given how drunk she'd seemed.

Should she wait for Eve to appear before asking Agatha about Jack? Lyra thought about it for a second and then dismissed the idea. Cameron had told her about their black sheep. It was her news to explore.

But not in front of Skye. Her little ears would be flapping at the mention of dead people and prisons and she'd had enough excitement for one morning already. So instead, Lyra put the kettle on and made herself a piece of toast with all the things she wanted to say but couldn't almost bursting out of her.

She had made a cup of tea and was just sipping at it thoughtfully when a pale face loomed up from nowhere at the window, dark eyes staring at her. She leapt backwards, spilling hot tea over her hand and all over the stone floor.

'Shit!' she screeched automatically and then, 'Sorry, Skye,' who didn't approve of bad language. 'What the hell does he want?'

It was Dylan she could see now, dressed in navy overalls with a dark beanie pulled down over his hair. He was gesturing and mouthing something at her. There was no hint of an apology for having made her jump.

'Jesus. Why doesn't he knock at the door?' she muttered. 'He can't just keep creeping up on us like that. Has he never heard of privacy?'

Dylan was still standing there, waiting for someone to reply to him.

'Well, let him in then,' tutted Agatha.

Lyra was tempted to bolt the door and draw all the curtains until he went away.

'I will,' said Skye, slipping down from the table and rushing over to the back door where she had to stand on a crate left there for that very purpose so that she could reach the lock. She turned the key with some effort and then got down and moved the crate so the door could swing open.

'Morning, Dylan,' she said brightly. 'You made Mummy swear.'

'Did I indeed?'

'Yes. You made her jump and she said . . .' She covered her mouth and whispered the word 'shit'. 'And then she said "Jesus" too, but I don't think she realised.'

'That's not good, is it?' replied Dylan. 'Can I speak to Agatha, please?'

Agatha didn't get up. 'Come in, Dylan,' she called. 'Come in.'

Lyra's views about Dylan were still very confused, not least because her scalded hand was stinging. He had stolen her cottage, a cottage she realised now that she didn't really want anyway, and she didn't like the way he hung around Fox House and kept creeping up on them. Yet, he seemed like a decent bloke at heart, and she actually quite liked his son. And now there was this stuff about Jack to get to the bottom of. So she rearranged her face into a smile.

'Morning, Dylan. You made me jump, popping up at the window like that. We do have a door, you know.'

He ignored her. 'I need to turn the water off. Do you know, is it on a separate stopcock?'

Agatha got to her feet. 'I can't remember,' she replied, 'but we can turn off the water to the house and see what happens. It's out here.'

She led him back the way he'd come to the utility room and pointed at a cupboard with her cane.

'In there, I believe.'

'How long do you need the water off for?' asked Lyra. 'Do we need to fill kettles and stuff?'

'I'm fitting the central heating so it'll be for as long as that takes.' There was no suggestion that this might be inconvenient for everyone else and Lyra felt her tolerance slipping again, but resisted the urge to complain. 'I'm sure the cottage must have its own water supply, though. I just need to know where it is.'

He got down on his hands and knees and peered into the cupboard. Maybe it was because he was lower than her, on the floor as she stood above him, that for some reason a feeling of power washed over Lyra and before she'd stopped to consider the wisdom of her actions, she spoke.

'Cameron tells me your dad died in prison,' she said in as matter-of-fact a tone as she could manage.

Skye was suddenly alert, and Lyra remembered that she hadn't been going to say anything until her daughter was out of earshot. Well, it was too late now. She squared her shoulders and stood her ground, waiting for the response.

Dylan barely reacted, although as his head was buried deep in the cupboard it was hard to tell. There was a brief pause and then he said, 'That's right.'

'Cameron said he killed someone,' she continued brazenly.

'Cameron should learn to keep his mouth shut about what's private,' said Dylan, pulling himself out of the cupboard and standing up. He was very close to her. She could feel his breath on her cheek and her natural urge was to step away, but she stood her ground.

Nothing about his expression invited further comment, but Lyra was like a heat-seeking missile determined to hit her target.

'It's true, though?' she asked.

Dylan opened his mouth to reply but Agatha beat him to it. Her tone was sharper than Lyra had ever heard her use before.

'That, young lady, is none of your business,' she said.

Lyra spun round to object, but then she saw her grandmother. Their mutual conspiracy over America had disappeared. Anger had brought a high colour to her cheeks and pulled her face tight.

Lyra had seen Agatha cross before but it was usually with a waiter who had been surly or a reporter on the television who was delivering news she didn't like. It had never been directed at her before and she immediately felt like a child.

'Well, I wouldn't say that,' she replied defiantly. 'He's living here and you've given him the cottage for no reason that any of us can see. And now it turns out that his dad, your good friend, was a killer. So why would you do that? It didn't make much sense before and now it makes absolutely none. And as me and Skye and Mum are your only living relatives I'd say that it totally is our business.'

Lyra knew that she was overstepping the mark. She would never normally dream of speaking to her grandmother like this, but the tensions created by the previous two weeks were suddenly crashing down on her and making her reckless. She pressed on.

'It's obvious there's some massive secret here that you're not telling anyone. Well, keeping secrets about stuff that happened forever ago is stupid and me and Mum have had enough of it. And now there's this about Jack on top. We want to know what's going on and we deserve to be told.'

And then her mother appeared, in a dressing gown, her hair dishevelled and her face ghostly.

'Deserve to be told what?' she asked.

62

February 1979

It had been snowing for days. The garden at Fox House was buried in white, the leaves and branches of every plant and tree bowing under the strain of the extra weight. The temperature outside had barely risen above freezing all week and so, obviously, the ancient boiler had chosen this as the best time to finally give up the ghost.

Agatha had spent hours on the phone trying to find someone to come out and repair it. She tried to tempt plumbers in with the promise of the work of fitting a new boiler if they could just get the old one to stumble on until the end of this cold snap, but to no avail. The plumbers had plenty of easier jobs to deal with, burst pipes and the like, without having to tackle the prehistoric heating system of Fox House.

And so the family shivered under eiderdowns and extra jumpers. It made sense to stay together so that the warmth from the open fire could at least keep one room above freezing, but tempers were becoming frayed by their enforced proximity, and as soon as one of them moved elsewhere to lighten the atmosphere the Baltic air rushed in and the temperature dropped like a stone.

Little Eve was delighted by the weather. School was closed because even though the small contingent of pupils all lived locally, the teachers drove in and so were unable to get there. Agatha had been tempted to offer to teach them herself just to get out of the freezing house, but she knew that she really had nothing to contribute to their education and so had kept her idea to herself.

Henry couldn't get to work either and was spending most of the time – when she wasn't using the telephone trying to secure a plumber – speaking to his clients and colleagues. Agatha shuddered at the thought of the forthcoming bill. From the way he stomped around the house cursing and muttering under his breath, she was under the impression that things weren't going well, but she knew better than to ask.

Instead she was doing her best to keep warm, keep the house warm and to spin out what food they had left until they could dig the car out and get to the shops. It felt like she was mounting an Arctic expedition without actually leaving home.

By the third day, pickings were very thin indeed and when Henry stomped into the kitchen expecting lunch, all she had to offer were three tins of pilchards and a packet of Jacob's cream crackers.

Henry stared at the paltry offering of food and then up at her. She grinned back at him, hoping that some humour might dilute the argument that was bound to be coming.

'Well, doesn't this look delicious,' she said, whipping a tea towel up from the back of a chair and dropping it over her outstretched arm like a waiter in a smart restaurant. 'Please, if sir would like to take a seat.'

She gestured at a chair and Henry's lips twitched in what might be the start of a smile, although it had a long way to go before it was the complete article.

'Where's Eve?' he asked, shooting a glance at the empty place setting.

'Out making snowmen.'

'Again?'

'There's a lot of snow. And it's not like lunch is going to go cold.'

Henry sat down heavily and reached for a cracker.

'And still no sign of a plumber? It's ludicrous. They can't all be busy and this is an emergency.'

'Either busy or snowed in,' replied Eve. 'I wondered if I should ask Jack to have a look.'

Henry grunted. 'I don't know what you think he could do. He's a carpenter, for God's sake.'

The modicum of fun that she had generated with the tea towel was gone.

'Yes, I know that,' she said, 'but he's very handy and he might have some idea.' She was tempted to say that in any event he'd have more idea than Henry, but she resisted. Baiting Henry was not going to improve matters. 'I'll ring him. They're nearer the shops than us too. Mary might be able to pick us up some groceries. It's like being in a siege, living out here in the sticks.'

'What happened to that Merlot?' Henry asked, glancing around the kitchen, apparently uninterested in where his next meal might be coming from and only concerned about his next drink.

'You finished it last night,' said Agatha, who had tipped the last glass down the sink in peevish irritation after Henry had fallen into a noisy sleep in a blanket cocoon on the sofa.

Henry frowned. 'I'm quite sure I didn't. It must have been you. Get me another one, would you?'

'I thought you were working this afternoon,' Agatha tried. The last thing they needed now was Henry drunk and morose.

'And your point is . . . ?' said Henry. 'Don't bother. I'll get it myself.'

'No, no. I'll go,' she said, leaping up. She certainly didn't need Henry to see how little wine was left. She was delighted that their stocks had fallen so low, but it would send Henry into a spin.

She went into the pantry and then down into the cellar to retrieve a bottle. For once the temperature down there was much the same as it was in the rest of the house. Agatha shivered violently and buried her nose and mouth in the cowl of her sweater. In her parents' day, the wine cellar had been full. It wasn't all good stuff but there had been a few bottles that her father had told her to keep for very special occasions. She used to go down there as a child, hidden away from the emotional charge of the rest of the house, letting the cool darkness engulf her. For many years afterwards, the initials that her childish fingers had traced in the dust on the bottles were still there for all to see. She'd liked that, her younger self reaching out to her from the past.

The bottles and their dust were long gone now, replaced by the cheap supermarket plonk she bought to keep up with Henry's increasing consumption.

'What are you doing down there, Aggie? A man could die of thirst.'

'Coming,' she called back as she grabbed the nearest bottle and carried it up the stone steps to the kitchen. She handed it to Henry and he fell on it like a man starving, removing the cork slickly and pouring himself a generous glass.

'Want some?' he asked.

Agatha shook her head. Tempting though it was to drink her way through to the great melt, one of them had to be present for Eve.

She sat at the table and served herself with pilchards, which she balanced on a dry cracker.

'How's work going?' she asked.

Henry shook his head. 'They're all idiots,' he said. 'Wouldn't know a decent deal if it ran up their trouser leg and bit them on the cock.'

Agatha wasn't sure of the significance of this comment. Did it mean that Henry was doing well or badly? It was impossible to tell, and she certainly wasn't going to probe further.

Henry reached for another cracker but Agatha moved what was left of the pilchards.

'We must leave something for Eve,' she said.

'If she's not here at mealtimes . . .' Henry said, but he didn't object.

'There's some cheese if you're still hungry. And the end of the ham, although I was saving that for supper.'

Henry poured himself a second glass of wine and then seemed to have a change of heart.

'Don't worry about me,' he said. 'You make sure Eve has something.'

Agatha smiled to herself. He wasn't all bad. There were still glimpses of the man on whom she had pinned all her hopes and dreams, even if those glimpses were getting harder and harder to spot.

'I'll go and ring Jack,' she said.

'Good idea,' replied Henry, mellower now. 'Tell him to bring his best spanner!'

He was chuckling to himself as she headed for the telephone.

63

Jack arrived just as the sun was going down. The snow held the darkness off for longer than normal, the last rays of light bouncing around the garden making it feel fresh and bright like a new dawn rather than the dregs of what was left of the day.

He had trudged three miles through the snow to get to them, wearing a heavy woollen coat and a hand-knitted hat. He carried an ancient canvas knapsack on his back.

'Emergency services!' he said, stamping his boots on the doormat to dislodge the worst of the snow.

Agatha threw her arms around him, not easy given how many layers of clothing she was wearing, and then stepped to one side to let him in.

'Thank you so much,' she said as he went to take his coat off and then thought better of it given the ambient temperature of the house.

'Mary's sent what she could,' he said. 'I can bring more tomorrow after she's been to the shops.'

'You're a saint, a proper St Bernard,' said Agatha. 'You have no idea how dreadful it's been. We had pilchards on crackers for lunch.' She grinned at Jack and shook her head despairingly.

'That is bad.'

'Terrible! Henry would have gone himself, but he's been so busy with work . . .'

She trailed off. What was the point? Jack knew Henry and he had evidently made no effort to go and find food.

'How's he been?' Jack asked, dipping his voice so that they couldn't be overheard.

Agatha wrinkled her nose and Jack nodded, catching her drift at once. No other explanation was required.

'Any idea what's up with the boiler?' he asked.

'Haven't a clue,' she said. 'It just packed up and no amount of persuasion seems to get it going again.'

Jack shuddered. 'It's colder in here than it is outside. Make me a cup of tea and I'll see what I can do.'

They went through to the kitchen, which felt marginally warmer simply by virtue of the fact that the lights in there were all blazing. Jack opened the knapsack, pulling out his tools and then a bottle of milk, half a loaf of Homepride, some apples and various other items wrapped in silver foil. Agatha peeked inside each little parcel with as much delight as if they contained treasure and murmured yet more thanks. Then she showed Jack the offending boiler, cold and silent in the corner of the room, filled the kettle and flicked on the switch.

'At least we don't have a power cut on top,' she said and then grimaced and crossed her fingers. 'And having the immersion heater means that at least we have hot water, thank God. I couldn't cope without that.'

The boiler hung on the wall and required Jack to stand on a chair to see it properly. He dragged the nearest across the stone flags and then climbed up and stared at it for a moment, as if by communing with it, the boiler could tell him where it hurt. Then he began to take the front panel off calmly and competently.

Agatha watched. Here was Jack, her closest friend, who had traipsed through the snow to bring her help without having to be asked twice. Would Henry have done the same for him? Agatha knew the answer to that. Henry hadn't even made the effort for his own wife and child.

'Do you think you can fix it?' she asked.

'Give me a chance! Just let me work out what's stopped working and then I'll see how we can mend it.'

Agatha made the tea, making a cup for Henry as well, using up precious milk even though she knew he wouldn't want one, much less drink it.

She opened the kitchen door a crack to try and keep what warmth there was inside the room, and shouted out into the dark hallway.

'Henry, Jack's here and I've made you a cup of tea,' she called, closing the door again quickly.

She busied herself putting Mary's provisions into the fridge, a pointless exercise given the temperature of the room, and then sat down at the table. She picked up her mug and cradled it in her hands, letting its warmth seep through into her chilly fingers.

Noises in the hallway outside suggested that Henry was making his way towards them, and Agatha sat up a little straighter in her chair in preparation for his arrival. There was a kerfuffle and then a crash and the sound of breaking china. Her heart sank. That would be the vase on the hall table, empty at least, but still one of her favourites.

'Which bloody idiot put that table there? Bloody stupid place to put a table, right in the middle of a room.'

Agatha squeezed her eyes shut. They might be in for a rocky ride here, although it was difficult to predict how Henry might behave when they had company. Sometimes the presence of others gave just enough impetus to keep him civil, or even entertainingly amusing.

The door swung open and Henry appeared, glass in hand.

'I've always said that table was in a stupid place . . .' he began gruffly with no sign of apology for the broken vase.

Then he spotted Jack standing on the chair.

'Jack, my man. How the devil are you? Bloody nightmare with this boiler business. Agatha here has been freezing her pretty little backside off, haven't you? Done nothing but nag and complain about the cold for days but has she done a blessed thing to get it fixed until now . . . ?' He made a questioning face and then answered his own question. 'No. Just complained. Do you know what she gave me for lunch? Pilchards and crackers! I ask you. What kind of wife presents that to the table?'

His tone was almost jocular, but Agatha knew that he wasn't really joking. She bit her tongue. There was no point contradicting him when he was like this. Jack, apparently, had no such qualms.

'As I hear it, she's been on the phone day and night trying to find a plumber,' he said. His back was to Henry as he examined the boiler.

'Tell you that herself, did she?' scoffed Henry. 'Well, the proof of the pudding and all that. Where are all these plumbers?' He waved his arms expansively and wine sloshed out of his glass and on to the floor. 'Conspicuous by their absence. That's where.'

Agatha clamped her jaw together to stop herself responding, and in the absence of any response, Henry pressed on.

'I should have married your Mary. She's a sensible woman, knows how many beans make five. Always said so. Bet she's nice and warm in bed too. It's like sleeping with an ice maiden with this one. And that's when the heating is working.' He broke into a guffaw and Agatha felt heat rising up her face. 'All sharp elbows and bony shoulders. Not a bit of comfort to a man. Now your Mary. She's a very different measure of woman altogether.'

'For God's sake, Henry,' muttered Agatha under her breath, unconcerned about the slights to herself but not wanting his comments to upset Jack.

'We both have wonderful wives,' replied Jack calmly, without turning round. 'We're lucky men.'

'Some of us luckier than others, though, eh?'

'Your tea is over there by the kettle,' said Agatha.

'Tea? Tea?! It's too bloody cold for tea. Brandy. Now that's what we want. Where's the brandy?'

He started opening cupboards randomly and then slamming them closed. 'I know you've hidden it. She hides the bloody booze, Jack. Can you believe it? I bet the fragrant Mary doesn't do that.'

'There isn't any brandy,' said Eve flatly. 'You finished it. Remember?'

'Like hell I did. I know there was half a bottle left. And I swear when I find it there'll be some questions to answer.'

His searching became increasingly erratic as he opened doors he had already tried.

'For God's sake, Henry,' Agatha said. 'There is no brandy.'

And then there was the banging of boots against stone at the back door and Eve walked in.

64

Eve's cheeks and the tip of her nose were rosy red from cold and the straggles of hair that hung out from beneath her bobble hat were damp, but her eyes shone bright.

'I've made a whole family of snowmen,' she said breathlessly.

Her smile was enough to warm the whole house and immediately Agatha dropped her argument with Henry to focus on her daughter.

'Gosh. Isn't it a bit dark out there now?' she asked.

'No! It's ever so light with the moon on the snow, like daytime really.'

Agatha turned to look out of the window and saw that Eve was right. Even though the sun had set, the trees still cast sharp black shadows over the snow.

'And how many snowmen have you made?' she asked.

'Well, three of course. A daddy, a mummy and a little girl.' Eve beamed up at her, quite thrilled by her labours. Then she noticed Jack standing on the chair in the corner of the room. 'Oh hello, Uncle Jack. Have you come to fix the boiler? It's freezing in this house!' She turned back to Agatha. 'Please can I have some clothes for the snowmen. Hats and scarves. And coal and carrots for their eyes and noses.'

'If we had any bloody carrots we'd have eaten them,' muttered Henry. 'And we need all the coal so we don't actually freeze to death. And shut that bloody door!'

Eve's smile fell from her face at once and she bit her lip. Agatha's heart tightened. At just eight years old, her beautiful daughter was already adept at reading and judging the atmospheres in her own home, the home that was supposed to provide her with sanctuary. Eve could predict as well as Agatha when Henry was likely to explode and, within seconds of entering the room, had correctly interpreted the mood and was no doubt working out a strategy for diluting it.

How could that be right? What child should need to have those defences ready to employ at a second's notice? She should be happily playing in the snow, not dealing with her father's erratic temper.

'Let me find you some hats and scarves at least,' said Agatha, smiling broadly and leaping to her feet before Henry could say anything else. 'And why don't you borrow this?'

She rushed to the rack where they kept the umbrellas and fished out the fox head cane that Jack had made for her. Eve's eyes opened wide. Usually she wasn't allowed to touch the cane, let alone play with it.

'Are you sure?' she asked.

'Of course,' said Agatha, offering the cane to Eve. She met her gaze, trying to signal to her through that one look how sorry she was about Henry and how she promised that she would fix it.

Eve took the cane from her and Agatha turned to find suitable hats from amongst the coats. Her back was turned for only a second but she heard Henry's voice, sharper than it had been.

'For God's sake, shut that bloody door.'

Agatha spun round to remonstrate with him but her jaw fell open as her brain processed the scene. Henry had taken the few short strides to the door where Eve had been standing, her child filled with delight and excitement at the snow. Now she was crouching almost at his feet, her arms wrapped over her head creating a protective shell. Agatha could hear her whimpering.

'I'm sorry, Daddy. I'm sorry.'

Had he hit her? From the way Eve was cowering beneath Henry it certainly looked that way. Agatha strode across the room, knocking a chair over in her haste. Jack was also leaping down to get to Eve.

'Leave her, Henry,' he shouted.

Agatha saw Henry's arm rise in the air. Was he going to strike their daughter? Had he hurt her already? Eve was on the floor, shrinking away from him, trying to make herself as small as she could. Agatha's brain was in overdrive. Everything was happening so quickly.

'Get off her!' she screamed.

Henry didn't seem to be registering anything that was being said to him. He was entirely fixated on the open door.

'It's bloody freezing in this house and you . . . leave . . . the . . . door . . . open.'

With every word, he hit Eve across the side of her head with the flat of his hand. Eve flinched with every blow and repeated that she was sorry over and over again, her words so fast that they all ran into one another.

Agatha's fury drove her into him.

'Leave her alone,' she screamed in a voice she barely recognised as her own.

The fox head cane was on the floor next to Eve and Agatha swept it up and swung the handle at Henry. He turned his head to see what was coming towards him and the heavy bulk of the carved fox's head made contact with his temple. He let out a surprised little exclamation and then he dropped on to the stone tiles in front of the open door.

Agatha bent over Eve, throwing her arms around her.

'Are you all right?' she asked desperately. 'Did he hurt you?'

Eve trembled beneath her but she shook her head.

'Let's get you up,' said Agatha, helping the child to her feet. Eve stood, arms pinned to her sides and head bowed as if she were expecting to be in yet more trouble.

'Are you all right?' Agatha asked again, placing a finger beneath Eve's chin and lifting her head up so that she could look into her face.

Eve nodded. 'I'm sorry,' she said again. 'I didn't mean to make Daddy so angry.'

'It wasn't your fault,' said Agatha. 'You did nothing wrong.'

'Agatha.'

She had forgotten that Jack was there, forgotten everything except making sure that her baby was safe. But now she turned and saw that he was on his knees beside Henry. It might have been a reflection from the snow outside, but his face seemed unnaturally pale.

'Why don't you take Eve upstairs for a nice warm bath?' he said.

Agatha was confused. Why was Jack making suggestions like that? She was about to object, but then she registered his expression. There was desperation in it. He tipped his head frantically in the direction of the door until finally Agatha's mind caught up with him. He was trying to tell her to take Eve away.

Of course. Jack needed to talk to Henry, make him see that he couldn't let his temper get the better of him like that and she should get Eve upstairs and settled. The immersion heater was on. There should be enough water for a bath even if the boiler had failed.

Her head filled with the practicalities, Agatha ushered Eve from the room with promises of bubbles and a story.

It was only as she turned back that she saw the thin ribbon of blood trickling from Henry's ear.

65

Agatha ran Eve's bath, prattling about the snowmen and what they would do the next day. Eve asked about Henry and Agatha reassured her that he would be fine, but all her mind's eye could see was the trickle of blood. Bleeding from the ear was never good, was it? She must have hit him harder than she had realised. It had looked as if he was out cold. Maybe he'd hit his head on the stone flags and knocked himself out.

Either way, Jack would have brought him round by now. He'd probably have a hell of a headache but there would be no permanent harm done and anyway, it would serve him right if his head did hurt. He had hit Eve. He had to know that that would have consequences.

As Agatha supervised Eve's bath and bedtime and her anger subsided, half her mind was occupied in playing out a little fantasy. Was this the turning point she had been hoping for, the kink in the road that brought Henry to his senses and stopped him drinking so much? A wake-up call. Wasn't that what they called it? Maybe they had to reach this rock bottom point so that they could rebuild. Perhaps it wasn't too late. They might even have another baby. She was only in her mid-thirties. Her mother hadn't had her until she was forty-two. They might be able to have more than one, siblings for Eve who would bring the noise and fun to Fox House that Agatha had always longed for.

By the time Agatha said goodnight to Eve and went back downstairs, she had their entire future life mapped out and it was looking rosy.

But as she approached the kitchen, something struck her as odd. She couldn't hear any voices. She'd expected to find Jack and Henry sitting at the kitchen table laughing and joking about something trivial, the drama of the last half hour all but forgotten. Yet the house was silent.

Agatha pushed open the kitchen door and went in. Jack was indeed sitting at the kitchen table, but Henry was still where he'd fallen. Agatha didn't understand.

'What's going on?' she asked Jack, her head whipping from Jack at the table to Henry on the floor. 'Henry, why are you still down there? Have you broken something?' And then to Jack, 'Is he still out cold? Have you called an ambulance?'

She couldn't understand any of it. Then Jack stood up, taking her hand to lead her to the table and then gently encouraging her to sit. Then he sat too, turning to face her so that he could look directly into her eyes. He took both her hands in his. His hands felt very cold.

'He's dead, Agatha,' he said. 'Henry is dead.'

Agatha heard the words but they made no sense. 'No,' she said. 'No, he isn't. He just knocked himself out when he fell. He'll come round in a minute. My mother kept some smelling salts somewhere. Now, where would they be?'

She made to stand up and go in search of the salts but Jack put his hand over hers and forced her to look straight at him. She tried to read his expression but it wasn't anything she'd ever seen before.

'He's dead,' he repeated. 'I need to call the police. It'll take them a while to get here, what with the snow. But when they do, this is what we're going to tell them. We'll have to explain about hitting him with the stick. They will work out that that's what happened from the bruises or whatever so there's no point trying to pretend that it didn't. But we'll say it was self-defence. I'll tell them that I hit him because he was about to hit you.'

Agatha felt like she was trying to think through treacle. She shook her head as she worked out what he was saying.

'But you didn't hit him. I did,' she said. 'It's my fault. I killed him.'

'It's no one's fault,' said Jack quickly. 'It was an accident. No one meant to kill anyone. That makes it manslaughter, not murder. Self-defence is a defence to manslaughter and you will be able to back up my story.'

Agatha shook her head. 'No, no, no, no,' she said. 'We can't say that. You can't take the blame. It was me. I did it. He was hitting Eve and I hit him.'

Jack took both her hands in his and squeezed them tightly.

'Think about it, Aggie,' he said. 'You can't go to prison. If we say it was you and you get locked up, who will be there for Eve? She might end up in care. It makes much more sense for me to say it was me. I probably won't get a custodial sentence anyway, but even if I do it won't be for long and Dylan will have Mary. I've thought it all through. Trust me. It's much better this way.'

Agatha couldn't take it in.

'Prison?' she said. 'They'll put me in prison? But I didn't mean it. It was an accident.'

'No,' he said firmly. 'They'll put me in prison if we stick to the story. He's dead, Aggie. The police can't ignore that. They will be looking for answers so this is what we'll tell them. Then there'll be a trial and hopefully we can show what he was like, that he was becoming increasingly difficult with his drinking. Mary can testify to that too. She's seen it with her own eyes.'

'But what about Eve?' Agatha asked. The room was spinning around her with nothing solid to grasp on to. 'Will she have to give evidence too?'

'I think we need to keep Eve out of it,' said Jack. 'She didn't see what happened. She's only eight. She doesn't need to know. We can tell her that Henry had a heart attack and that's why he fell. We'll explain to her that it would be better if she didn't tell the police about Henry hitting her. We can say we don't want the police thinking badly of her daddy. She's a smart girl. She'll understand. And if I confess and you back me up then they're not going to look that hard for an alternative explanation.'

Agatha couldn't keep up, but she was starting to see that what Jack was saying made some kind of twisted sense.

'But . . .' she began, but Jack cut her off.

'I'm going to ring the police now. I'll tell them that Henry was about to hit you, that I lashed out with the cane and accidentally caught him on the side of his head and that he died. Then you will tell them that too. It's for the best, Aggie. It's the best way out of it.'

'No!' said Agatha as all the parts of what he was telling her dropped into place like the tumblers in a lock. 'I won't let you confess to something that I did. It's not right.'

'But think of Eve,' Jack replied. 'What will happen to her if you're not here? I've thought it all through, Aggie. We don't have a choice.'

66

NOW

'Deserve to be told what?' asked Eve as she walked into the kitchen.

Her head was banging and if she didn't get something in her stomach soon then she feared she might regret it, but she seemed to have inadvertently interrupted some kind of drama and that made her instantly forget her hangover.

They were all in there, even Dylan. He was in the pantry with Lyra standing far too close to him, encroaching on his personal space. Little Skye was in the centre of the room, her gaze darting from person to person as if she were trying to guess who would speak next.

'Skye, can you please go upstairs and play?' asked Lyra.

Skye looked as if she might kick up a fuss, but instead she sighed and scampered out of the room. Eve put her hand on her head as she passed, her hair soft and warm.

Agatha was sitting at the table. She looked very pale and even her lips, squeezed into a tight line, were bloodless.

'About Jack and who he killed,' said Lyra.

She stood, one hip and her chin jutting out defiantly, a stance Eve recognised from when Lyra had been a little girl. She'd always been a determined soul when she got the bit between her teeth, and it was apparent that she wasn't about to let whatever this was drop.

Then Eve registered what she had said.

What?

Jack had killed someone?

Her befuddled brain couldn't keep up. She opened her mouth to ask, and then the hazy fragments of a conversation began to dance in the corners of her memory. Hadn't Lyra told her this last night when she'd got in from her dinner with Justin? Yes. That was it. Dylan's son had told her. And now, in typical Lyra style, she had gone in, all guns blazing, demanding explanations.

'Lyra, I'm not sure . . .' she began, but Lyra spoke across her.

'I was just saying, Mum, that Granny has given the cottage to Dylan out of the blue and now it turns out that Dylan's dad went to prison for killing someone. How do we know Granny isn't being forced into doing things against her will?'

Lyra avoided looking directly at Dylan, but it was apparent, even in Eve's confused state, that she was accusing him of coercion. 'I think it's about time someone told us what's really going on here,' she added.

This was not at all how Eve would have gone about things, but Lyra wasn't her and Eve couldn't make her back down. She would just have to allow matters to take their own course.

Agatha's shoulders slumped and the fight that had been in her a moment before seemed to seep away. She opened her mouth to speak, closed it again, looked up at the ceiling and then back down at the floor; anywhere, Eve noticed, except at any of them.

Then Dylan took a couple of steps, which moved him away from Lyra.

'My dad went to prison for killing a man,' he said. 'The man concerned was threatening a child. He had to be stopped and my dad acted instinctively, but unfortunately the man never recovered

328

from the blow. Technically, that's manslaughter and someone had to be punished for it.'

He spoke so calmly, without any unnecessary emotion, and his words seemed to leach the tension from the room as if he were a healer.

Lyra lowered her chin and stopped looking like she was about to step into a boxing ring.

'That's all very noble,' she said. Her tone was still aggressive even if her body language was less so. 'But it doesn't explain why Granny has given you the cottage.'

Dylan turned towards Agatha and so Eve did too and saw something pass between them that she couldn't read. Her mother seemed to give Dylan a tiny and almost imperceptible nod, as if a tacit agreement had been reached.

And then Agatha spoke.

'The man who was killed was your father, Eve.'

Eve wasn't sure she had heard her mother correctly. Her eyes tracked round the room, searching for clues from the other faces, but it was clear from their expressions that she wasn't mistaken.

Yet it made no sense.

'But Dad died of a heart attack,' she said.

Agatha nodded and her gaze dropped to the floor in a way that was so out of character that Eve could immediately tell not only that she was speaking the truth but also that it was difficult for her.

'Yes. That's what we told you,' she said. 'It seemed the kindest thing.'

All the blood rushed from Eve's head and she lurched at a chair and sat down before she lost her balance.

'But actually,' Eve said slowly, pointing at Dylan, 'it was his dad, Jack? He killed him?'

Agatha opened her mouth as if to correct her, but Dylan spoke first.

'Yes,' he said, 'although the intention was to stop him, not to hurt him.'

'Stop him from hitting a child, you said,' continued Eve slowly as she tried to piece it together. 'Me?'

Dylan nodded.

Eve went very cold as if iced water were suddenly running through her veins.

'It was a single blow,' Dylan continued. 'But it hit him in a vulnerable spot. He died almost instantly. It was a tragic accident, but as I say, technically it was manslaughter and so my father was given a short custodial sentence.'

'But then he got caught in a fight and died in prison,' added Lyra, her tone altogether softer than it had been.

Dylan nodded again. There was a stillness about him, more than his usual remoteness, and Eve could tell this was difficult for him also.

'So we both lost our dads that night,' she said.

Dylan turned and their eyes met. His glistened in the light.

'We did,' he said.

A silence fell over the room, punctuated only by the insistent beat of the dripping tap.

It felt forever before anyone spoke.

Eve had understood the words but she couldn't seem to formulate them into something that made sense within the terms of how her life had been until that moment. Her father hadn't died, as she had always thought, of a tragic early heart attack. He had been killed by someone trying to prevent him from hurting her. Her own father had been trying to hurt her.

How?

Why?

Eve looked across at Agatha, searching for an answer, but Agatha's gaze was planted firmly on the stone tiles of the floor.

'But I still don't get it,' said Lyra. 'If both Mum and Dylan lost their dads why does Dylan get the cottage and Mum doesn't?'

Eve didn't have the strength to deal with her daughter's endless questioning. She was too busy trying to work out what all this meant. All of a sudden there were far more important things here that needed unpicking.

'Just let it go, Lyra,' she said. 'Just let it go.'

67

Eve was lost.

Nothing she knew about herself made any sense now.

Her life had been based on a lie. Randomly, her mind tried to estimate how many people she had told over the years that her father had died of a heart attack. Dozens. Hundreds maybe. A tragic heart attack when she eight, that was the line, an event that had turned her already small family into a pair of people, one of whom was carrying the lie. Carrying it every day.

'But when I got old enough to understand,' she said to Agatha, addressing her as if they were the only two in the room. 'Why didn't you tell me the truth then?'

'What good would it have done?' asked Agatha. 'You didn't need to know. You accepted what I told you as the truth from the start and then never mentioned that night again. It was as if you'd wiped the memory from your mind. I sent you away to boarding school after that so you wouldn't hear anything at school. I couldn't risk anyone being unkind to you about it when you were totally blameless.'

This was also new. Eve had always assumed Agatha had sent her to school because she hadn't wanted her around, had tired of being a mother to her or couldn't cope with being a single parent.

Yet now Agatha was saying she had done this to protect Eve, to keep her safe. Or to perpetuate her lie. Eve couldn't work out which.

Agatha was still talking, and Eve fought to bring her attention back and listen.

'And then after a while you stopped talking about your father,' Agatha continued. 'He just never came up. It was as if he'd never existed for you, just a name from the past. Why would I bring it back up years later? I couldn't think of a single reason. So, I just let you believe what we'd told you when you were a girl.'

'But you knew?' Eve was dumbfounded. 'You knew all this time. And you kept it secret.'

'I did,' Agatha said, her tone crisp. 'I thought it was best. I was protecting you. That's what a mother is supposed to do.'

Eve looked at her mother, trying to read her expression. Contrition, maybe, but Eve couldn't swear to it. There was certainly the determination that Agatha brought to everything. Determined that she was right or determined not to be challenged? It was impossible to say.

Was it right to let her think her father had had a heart attack? Eve had no idea. She couldn't in that moment work out how her life might have been different if she'd known that he had died a violent death at someone else's hand rather than one instigated by his own body.

That wasn't the only lie, though, and the second revelation was much, much bigger. Eve swallowed before asking her next question, wanting to know and yet not wanting to know at the same time.

'Had he hurt me before that night?'

Agatha folded her arms, neatly placing one over the other. There was a pause as she seemed to decide what to admit to.

'The situation was escalating,' she said eventually. 'He was drinking more than was good for him and his behaviour was becoming more erratic. It hadn't occurred to me that I should be keeping you safe from him. Matters weren't as bad as that. But then he hit you that night and something . . . Well, it was all instinctive, in the moment . . .' She stopped herself, appeared to regroup. 'That's all there was to it. It was an accident.'

Eve shook her head slowly, still struggling to absorb what she was hearing.

'I barely remember him,' she said. 'When I try to visualise him it's like he's in a photograph, static. I have no feel for what I thought of him. I've always assumed I must have loved him because he was my dad, but I have nothing to hang that on. It's just an assumption.'

'You did love him,' said Agatha quickly. 'And he wasn't a dangerous man generally. I wasn't fearful for our safety when he was there.'

'But there was an edge to him . . .' suggested Eve.

'Precisely that.'

Dylan cleared his throat. 'Look, I only came over here to turn the water off. Could I do that and then get back to work?' His tone was apologetic but he was sidestepping his way towards the door.

'The stopcock for the cottage is under the manhole cover on the drive,' said Eve mechanically.

'Great. Thanks, Eve,' he said. 'Look, I'll be . . . er . . . I'll catch you later.'

And then he fled.

'Like rats deserting a sinking ship,' said Lyra, rolling her eyes.

Eve wanted to tell Lyra to grow up and stop being so black and white, but she didn't have the energy.

'Can we run through it again?' she said instead, as if Lyra weren't there. 'Dad had been drinking. Is that right?'

Agatha nodded. 'We were snowed in,' she said. 'And the boiler had broken. Jack came round to try and fix it. The house was freezing. You were making snowmen. You came in to . . .' Her eyes dropped to the fox head cane. 'Anyway, you left the door open. Your father got angry. He hit you.'

'And that's when Jack hit him?' asked Eve. 'But why did Jack hit him? What was it to do with him?'

'It was just a spur of the moment thing. We needed to stop Henry from hurting you.'

Eve nodded slowly, but she was frowning. 'And Dad fell and hit his head?'

Agatha nodded slowly.

'And he died instantly?'

Another nod, less tentative this time.

'Oh my God,' said Lyra. 'Did he die in here? In this kitchen?'

Agatha seemed to regain her usual composure.

'For goodness' sake, child. Don't be so macabre.'

Lyra was clearly struggling to balance her excitement at the unravelling story with a sense of decorum, but she was right, though.

'Did he?' Eve asked, her voice low. 'Did he die in here?'

Agatha nodded again. Then she shook her head and shoulders and stood up, and the room seemed to breathe.

'That's quite enough of that for the time being. It was all a very long time ago and there's little to be gained by raking it all up again now.'

She picked up the cane and stalked out of the room. Normal service was to be resumed, it appeared. The door closed behind her with a click.

'Bloody hell, Mum,' said Lyra. 'I did not see that coming.'

Eve was still reeling.

'No,' she managed to say. 'Neither did I.'

68

Eve's head felt blank, like a clean slate. It was as if anything she had been thinking had been lost and replaced with a numb nothingness. She screwed her face up as she tried to piece together what she had just learned and sit it next to what she thought about it, but her thoughts couldn't seem to grip on to anything.

'But what we still don't know . . .' said Lyra.

Eve dragged her attention from her empty mind and tried to focus on her daughter.

'What we still don't know is what that has to do with giving Dylan the cottage,' Lyra finished. 'Are we to assume that she's done it because Jack killed your dad to stop him from hitting you? I suppose he did go to prison for it so—'

Something in Eve snapped and she screamed at Lyra. 'For God's sake, Lyra. Stop. I don't know, all right. I didn't know any of this. It's all new. So can you just stop going on about the bloody cottage and let me think.'

Lyra's face collapsed and Eve immediately felt terrible. None of this was Lyra's fault. She put her arms around her daughter and pulled her in tightly, something stable in a world that was tipping around her.

'I'm so sorry,' she breathed into Lyra's hair. 'I didn't mean to shout. I just don't know what to think or what any of it means. It's so much to take in.'

They stood there for a moment or two and then she let Lyra go.

'I think I just need . . .'

She didn't know what she needed but it certainly wasn't standing in this room where her father had been killed to prevent him from hurting her. Blindly, she pushed her way out of the house and out into the cold fresh air where she could at least breathe.

She needed to talk it through with someone. The obvious person was Agatha, but Eve knew that she had had everything she was going to get out of Agatha about this, for now at least. Those shutters had come down and they wouldn't come back up until Agatha was good and ready, which might be never.

Strangely she still felt drawn to Dylan, despite the revelations. But this was a feeling that she didn't understand and couldn't trust. And there was still something that wasn't being said. Eve had no idea why she thought that or what it could be, but the sense of it still being unfinished business was strong. She needed to figure that out before she talked to Dylan again.

That left Justin. Was it only a few short hours ago that they had gone out for dinner? Eve could barely credit it. She'd thought life had been difficult yesterday, but things seemed to have got a whole lot worse. She pulled out her phone and rang his number. It went to voicemail.

'Justin. Something's happened. Agatha. Well, I'm not sure where to start. She told me . . . It doesn't make any sense. No, it does make sense. It's just so hard to take in. I'm not sure what to do. But you're not there . . . It's fine. Don't worry.'

Eve stopped talking and killed the call. Her hand dropped to her side but the rest of her remained motionless. Birds sang all around her, so many birds, a veritable choir. She listened, wondering why the sound was suddenly so clear, why she didn't hear it like this every day.

69

Agatha clutched the fox head cane to her chest. She liked to keep it nearby, the weapon with which she had killed her husband, as if, if it somehow left Fox House, her secret would escape.

Was killed the right word, or should she say murdered?

She had always understood that legally whichever was correct rested on what her intention had been in that moment, which was where her thinking stalled. Could she swear she hadn't intended to kill Henry when she had seen him hurting Eve?

It was a question she had thought about so many times. Was she the kind of mother who would defend her child to the death?

Without a doubt. Which mother wouldn't do that?

Henry had been drunk and not in control of his senses. He had been battering their daughter in front of her eyes. Of course she had stopped him. But had she intended to kill him? No. She couldn't accept that. When she examined her conscience, for all that Henry had become difficult, dangerous even, she had never wished him ill. She had intended to make him stop. What happened next had been an accident.

And from that moment, everything had changed. She had never been a good mother. She had tried. Lord knows she had tried, given it all she had, but she just didn't have the tools for the job. Nothing about motherhood had come naturally. Nothing, it seemed, except defending her baby when she was in danger. That maternal instinct she did seem to possess.

She had tried to be a good mother, though. Inside, she had always loved Eve with all her heart and soul. It was demonstrating it that she had struggled with. It was ironic that the greatest validation of how much she loved her daughter was the one incident that she could never, ever talk about. The night Henry died was what had proved the strength of her love above all other things. When her child had been in danger Agatha had acted instinctively to save her. Could there be any greater display of a mother's love than that?

But it had come at what price?

Eve had been left without a father and whilst he had been lacking in so many ways, he had also been doing the best he could. Eve would always have been better off with Henry than without.

Agatha had stolen that relationship from her daughter. One impulsive reaction and Agatha had left Eve with only one parent, her totally unsatisfactory mother. A fissure had opened between them that night, a crack that Agatha had never managed to seal back up.

Was it guilt that spoiled their already precarious relationship? Or shame? Or perhaps it was a surging feeling of inadequacy that she was the only parent Eve had left and she wasn't fit for the position?

It was all of these combined.

She had wondered, over the years, whether she had distanced herself from Eve intentionally in an attempt to mitigate the damage done to Eve that night. She had certainly put a physical distance between them by sending Eve away to school. However, when she dug deep into her conscience, she had to conclude that the distance had always been there. It was true that she had closed a part of herself off that night, but all it had done was to confirm her already strongly held conviction that she was inadequate. Just like her mother before her, she had failed in the role. What had happened with Henry did nothing to make her think differently.

Her conscience was pricking her for another reason now. She had had the chance to come clean, to explain what had really happened that night, and she still hadn't taken it. She had let Dylan lie for her. The moment to tell the truth had been presented to her and she had kept quiet. Poor Dylan had simply picked up the lie that his father had told for her and kept on running with it. Admittedly, Agatha hadn't asked him to do that, but she had done nothing to set matters straight.

That wouldn't do. This had been going on for long enough. How could she let Dylan carry her lie forward into the next generation? It was so noble of him that he seemed prepared to do exactly that, but that didn't make it right.

But stacked against that was the risk that Eve might turn against her. Learning about Agatha's part in Henry's death, on top of the lie to cover it up, all the subsequent consequential lies and sending her away to school was a lot. If Agatha were to confess now, how might her daughter react? The fear that Eve would turn her back on her was real and very, very chilling.

The options chased each other around Agatha's head but she kept settling on one point. Now they had come this far, she owed it to Jack, her oldest and closest friend, to tell the whole truth. She owed it to Dylan too, and of course Eve had a right to know. If she ran the risk of losing Eve then that was no more than she deserved.

All this was out in the open partly because Lyra had kept pushing for answers. Despite everything, Agatha smiled at this thought. Her feisty granddaughter, now excelling at bringing up her own daughter, was the one who would finally bring all this darkness into the light.

Agatha saw something of herself in Lyra. Although Lyra was a far better mother than she had ever been, it was a comfort to see her own strength reflected back at her in her granddaughter. Agatha had steadfastly protected her secret with the same determination that Lyra had used to uncover it. They were so alike.

And with that she knew what she had to do next. She would go and find Eve and tell her everything. She would hold no detail back.

Clutching the stick, she set off to find her.

Eve was outside in the garden, standing against the fence and staring at Dylan's cottage. Seeing her there, Agatha's determination faltered. Was there really any need for her to confess? Dylan had provided her with a way forward. She could hide behind that until she died, surely not that far away now. She could continue to cover things up just as she always had.

But she had had enough. This lie had been with her for too long. Suddenly the burden of it was unbearable. It pressed down on her, making it harder and harder for her to take a single step. She had to put it down.

'Eve.'

Eve turned, saw her coming and Agatha tried to interpret the expression that crossed her face. Could she read anger there, or was it pain, confusion, disappointment, all of those?

Whatever it had been, it was fleeting. Eve's face closed down.

'What?' she said, inscrutable.

It threw Agatha. She had been so determined in her course of action just a moment ago, but now it came to the execution she was full of doubt.

'I just . . .' she began. 'I wanted . . .'

'What do you want, Agatha?' asked Eve coldly.

Instead of feeling like the strong, self-reliant woman she had always been, it was as if Agatha were a child again. She could under-stand why her daughter was so angry, but she wanted more than anything for Eve to comfort her, tell her that she was forgiven and that everything was going to be all right.

She didn't deserve that, however. In fact, she deserved everything that Eve wanted to throw at her. And the last thing she wanted was to hurt Eve more than she already had. She needed everything to be out in the open. Let the consequences come. She would deal with those. Eve had to know the truth.

'It was me,' Agatha blurted. 'I did it.'

Eve clearly didn't understand.

'Did what?'

'I was the one that hit Henry. I killed him. It wasn't Jack, it was me. Jack took the blame because otherwise you would have been left without anyone. He went to prison for me. And then he died there because of me.'

If she had expected to feel lighter as a result of her confession, she was disappointed. Instead her heart was consumed by a heavy sense of dread. How would Eve react? Would Agatha lose her there, a few short yards from the place where she had lost Henry?

Agatha focused on her daughter's face, searching for clues as to what was going through her mind, but found nothing. There was no anger or disbelief. Her face was blank.

'Did you hear what I said?' Agatha asked, anxious to know that Eve had understood. 'It was me. I killed Henry. With this stick!' She raised the cane above her head and shook it.

Eve's gaze followed the fox head as it flew through the air and then she looked back at Agatha. There was something in her eyes, though, and it certainly didn't look like anger. Agatha let herself hope.

'For me,' Eve said quietly.

Agatha nodded.

'Because you love me.'

Agatha nodded again.

Of all the things that Eve could have chosen to centre on, she had chosen this. A mother's love.

'Of course,' Agatha said. 'Always.'

Tears gathered in Eve's eyes and then, when they could no longer be contained, they ran silently down her cheeks.

'I never knew,' she said. 'I never knew. Not for sure.'

What was she saying? Agatha didn't know whether she was talking about Henry's death or the depth of her own love, but she feared it was the latter. Did her daughter really not know how deeply she was loved? Somehow, with all the guilt and the shame and her inability to demonstrate her feelings, had Agatha failed to get across this most basic of human emotions?

'You are my child,' she began, her throat starting to constrict as unfamiliar feelings rose in her chest. 'I have always loved you more than anything else in my world.'

'But I never knew,' repeated Eve.

70

Lyra wanted answers and no one was coming up with the goods. Yes, it was all very shocking, what had happened to her grandfather, but he had never been more than a concept to her. She knew she must have had a grandfather, but that was all. She had no other connection with the man, certainly no emotional tie.

His death, no matter how violent, did not seem to explain her grandmother's actions. Jack killed her grandfather. Jack went to prison. That was as it should be. Yes, she could see that he had done it to stop her grandad hitting her mother, but parents did hit their kids sometimes, especially back then. That didn't mean they deserved to be beaten to death for it. And it certainly didn't follow that Jack's son should come along now and claim the cottage as a reward. That made no sense. No, there was definitely more to this than she was being told. She was certain of it.

Yet what could she do? If her grandmother wasn't going to spill the beans then Lyra could hardly force her to, and it wasn't for lack of trying, but for whatever reason Agatha was remaining tight-lipped.

And so, with a show of self- control that was almost visceral, Lyra dragged herself away from her thought process. She had to let it go.

Anyway, she had other things to think about. America. Could she really just pick up her life and relocate it to America? Not forever, of course, but for the duration of Rafe's contract there. On the face of it, she couldn't think of a single reason why not. If her grandmother was right and she could get a short-term visitor's visa then it might work. Rafe could help her find somewhere to rent. In fact, he earned enough to pay for somewhere, and if making a contribution meant that Skye went with him to California then maybe he would at least go halves with her. It would be an adventure for all three of them. And Amina, she supposed grudgingly.

And just like that, what had seemed insurmountable a few days before was fixed. Or at least almost fixed. She pulled out her phone to ring Rafe, but how could he possibly object when her going too meant that he got exactly what he wanted?

A car was pulling up outside. It might be Cameron, she thought with a little buzz. He was here helping his dad yesterday so it made sense that he might be back. She went to a window at the front of the house and peeped round the curtain, keen not to be spotted.

It wasn't Cameron, however. It was her dad. What on earth was he doing here? Her mother must have summoned him. Again. They should just get back together, Lyra thought with an internal eye roll. It would make so much sense.

She made her way to the front door and got there just as her dad opened it to let himself in.

'What's going on?' he asked. 'I think I got a distress flare from your mother, but her message didn't actually make much sense.'

'It's all kicking off here,' Lyra said with a grin. 'You won't believe it. Apparently Grandad didn't die of a heart attack at all. Jack killed him by accident because he was about to hit Mum. And then went to prison for it.'

'Bloody hell.' Her dad ran his hands through his hair. 'Never a dull moment with Agatha around, is there? Where's your mum now? Is she okay?' He started looking around the hall as if Eve might be hiding in a cupboard.

Lyra shrugged. 'Dunno. She's outside somewhere. And I'm going to America with Skye for a few months.'

'What?' Justin jerked his head round to look at her. 'Stop. Wait. One major development at a time, please. America? Fantastic. But hold that thought until I've found your mother. Then I want to hear all about it.'

Lyra was tempted to say that her exciting news was current and so far more important than something that had happened almost fifty years ago, but when she did chat it all through with him she didn't want there to be any distractions so she let it go.

She followed him out into the garden. The day was dank with heavy grey clouds hanging ominously in the sky so that it had barely got light at all, rather matching the mood of the morning so far, Lyra thought.

She peered through the gloom. Her mother and grandmother were standing by the gate that led into the wood. They didn't seem to be speaking but their body language didn't suggest a stand-off either.

'Is everything okay?' her father asked as he strode towards them.

Dylan appeared then, emerging from the cottage, spanner in hand. He paused where he was, seemingly reluctant to cross to the fence.

When Lyra got close enough to see faces, her mother's expression was one she'd never seen before. Beatific. Was that the word? She looked serene, like a painting from an art gallery.

The same couldn't be said for Agatha. She was twisting that blessed cane round and round in her arthritic hands and staring at Eve. This was another new expression. Lyra had never seen her grandmother look anything other than one hundred per cent sure of herself, and yet she seemed to be imploring her mother to give her something. Lyra had no idea what.

'What's happened?' her dad tried again. 'Is something wrong? Eve? Are you okay?'

This seemed to break the spell and her mother looked up.

'Mum's just told me something that changes everything,' she said.

Mum? Lyra didn't think she had ever heard her mother call her grandmother anything but Agatha.

Dylan took a few steps closer to them, wanting to listen but evidently fearful of intruding.

'Oh yes?' her father said.

'And now things make a kind of sense to me,' Eve continued. 'Things that I've never really understood before.'

Lyra was almost bursting. 'What? Just tell us!'

Her grandmother opened her mouth to speak but Eve put her hand up.

'No,' she said sharply, and then in a softer voice, 'no. It's your grandmother's business. And now mine. But no one else's. I know you don't want to hear that, Lyra, but I'm afraid you're just going to have to accept it.'

Lyra stared from her mother to her grandmother and back again. 'For God's sake, you have to be joking. We all need to know what's going on here.'

Her mother shook her head and then she took Agatha's hand and squeezed it tightly.

'No,' she said simply. 'You do not.'

Then her mother looked over to Dylan and smiled at him. Something passed between them, too, but Lyra couldn't read that either. The whole situation was beyond frustrating.

Skye appeared on the lawn, skipping towards them, a huge smile on her face.

'Grandad!' she said. 'Look at my egg. Dylan made it for me. And I can do a cartwheel and it's really good but I'm not doing it now because the grass is all yucky. And me and Mummy are going to America so I can see Daddy and learn French, aren't we, Mummy?'

'We are, sweet pea.'

Eve's expression changed then. She threw a questioning glance at Lyra over Skye's head and Lyra nodded, grinning. Eve still looked confused but she beamed at Skye, opening her arms out to welcome her granddaughter into them.

'Well, isn't that exciting?' she said to Skye. 'I can't wait to hear all about it.'

Lyra knew that comment was aimed at her.

'I've only just decided,' she said a little sheepishly. 'I'll tell you at a better moment.'

Eve seemed to accept that and then turned her attention back to Skye, who had positioned herself between her grandmother and great-grandmother and was hugging them around their thighs.

Part of Lyra wanted to maintain her extreme irritation with her mum, her granny, that bloody man, but what was the point? Being annoyed wouldn't provide her with answers and if they weren't going to tell her then wild horses wouldn't drag it out of them.

She had to move beyond it. She didn't need the cottage. It would never have been the right place for her and Skye. She could see that now. She needed to be back in the thick of life, Manchester, California, anywhere other than this tiny little backwater. Dylan could keep the place, knock himself out.

'It's all a bit up in the air,' she said. 'We might have to stay with Heather for a bit until everything's sorted so that Skye can get back to school, but then we'll see about going with Rafe. In fact, we'll probably leave here tomorrow if that's okay with you, Granny.'

She hadn't realised that she wanted to go until that moment, but now she had purpose and a plan she suddenly knew it was time.

Her grandmother nodded slowly. Then she straightened her spine and pulled her shoulders back, raised her chin.

'You must do as you please,' she said. Her tone was characteristically sharp but her smile was broad. 'You must always do as you please, Lyra.'

And then she winked at her.

71

Eve was shivering, her teeth chattering together noisily, and she couldn't stop. She hadn't even been aware of being cold although her breath was making dragon plumes in the still grey air. It was probably the shock, she thought, as well as the chilly morning.

It felt like being on her own in a room where all the walls were glass. She was aware of everyone she loved being around her, but they weren't quite within her reach, there but not quite there. It was part of the process, she supposed, as she tried to make sense of the new realities of her life. As she pieced it all together doors would open up in the glass and let them all back inside, one by one.

She looked at them, the people that she loved, each in turn. Agatha, of course, and Lyra with Skye, but also Justin and now Dylan, too. No, she didn't love Dylan but there was that bond, the connection she had felt the first time they'd met. She hadn't understood it then, but now things were becoming clearer. She didn't know whether that was something that would grow with time. Maybe today was the pinnacle of that relationship, the summit to which they had been unconsciously moving all their lives. She hoped not though. She hoped there would be more for them to discover.

And what of all those childhood memories? Lost, erased. She had been searching so hard for them but now she realised that she didn't need them, was better without them even. That was certainly what her subconscious mind had thought, as if protecting her from the trauma of losing her father so suddenly.

Imagine what her subconscious might have done if she'd known the truth from the start.

Had Dylan known all along? She supposed he must have done. How else would Agatha have explained her need to give him the cottage? Of course, that all made sense now. Dylan had lost his father because of what Agatha had done. When you looked at it in those terms the cottage was the very least she could do for him. She and Lyra had thought it was a ridiculously grandiose gesture when in fact it was so meagre.

She felt an arm around her and the touch, interrupting her thoughts, made her start.

'Let's get you inside,' said Justin.

His voice was comforting by reason of its familiarity but Eve didn't want to go inside. And she didn't want Justin. She had to stand on her own two feet. She had leaned on him for too long. He had moved on from their marriage, retaining a healthy friendship with her but no longer reliant on her emotional support. She had to do the same.

'I'll come in a minute,' she replied, gently brushing his arm aside and purposefully not meeting his eye so she couldn't see his shocked expression. She didn't want to hurt him, but she needed to find a new place in her life for their relationship.

Instead, she turned to Dylan.

'Can we talk?' she said.

Dylan looked surprised and then bemused but he shrugged his agreement.

'If you want,' he said. 'Shall we . . . ?'

He gestured towards the cottage. Eve would have preferred to go into the house where it was warm and relatively clean, but she needed to be away from prying ears and eyes. She nodded and followed Dylan, leaving Justin to stare after her. As she moved, she was aware of Agatha walking away towards Fox House. She was barely leaning on the stick at all, Eve noticed. Something had shifted in her too.

Dylan led her into the chilly cottage with all its dust and the smell of plaster in the air. They picked their way through the boxes and building materials into the kitchen which was still relatively free of mess.

'Tea?' he asked her.

'Is everything better with a cup of tea?' she asked. She was only partly joking.

'Pretty much,' he replied. 'And if it isn't then at least we tried.'

Dylan set the kettle to boil and gave two mugs a cursory rinse under the tap. Eve watched him, trying to establish what she wanted to say. She could just let the truth that Agatha had shared rest, never to be mentioned again. But then the lie would always be there between them, each knowing but neither acknowledging it. That was no basis on which to start building a friendship. The secret belonged to the three of them on an equal footing.

'Agatha . . .' She paused and then began again. '*Mum* told me. What happened. What really happened, I mean.'

Dylan left what he was doing and sat down opposite her, clearly wanting to give whatever was coming next his full attention.

'Ah,' he said.

'Have you always known?'

He traced a trail of carved graffiti with his forefinger until it came to an end. Then he met her eyes.

'That it was Agatha that hit Henry and not Dad?' He shook his head. 'No.'

'When did you find out?'

'Mum told me before she died. She'd kept their secret right to the end, even though it destroyed her life. She wanted to keep you safe at the start, I suppose, so she went along with it. But then Dad died and she was angry, bitter. She was never the same after that. I thought it was because Dad had died, but it wasn't that, as it turns out. Or not only that.

'But she protected me from it. She never once shared her resentment with me. Mothers are truly amazing. What they go through for their kids. Incredible.'

He moved to the window and stared out at the wood beyond.

'We've both been loved like that, I suppose,' he mused. 'Spared the horrible truth of what happened to them all.'

The kettle boiled and then switched itself off. Neither of them moved.

'She told me she'd tried to talk Dad out of confessing,' he continued. 'But he was adamant that it was the best solution. And his prison sentence was short. He would have been out in a few months, with good behaviour.'

'But it didn't work out like that,' Eve said.

'No.'

'Do you hate me?' she asked.

Dylan's focus snapped back to her, confusion sketched across his face. 'Hate you? No. None of it was your fault.'

'Well, no,' agreed Eve. 'But you lost your dad because of me.'

'You lost yours too,' he said.

He made the tea and brought it back to the table. Eve cupped her hands around the mug and let the steam warm her face.

'I'm sorry I forgot you,' said Eve.

'You didn't mean to,' replied Dylan.

Eve shrugged. He was right. 'We were close, weren't we? Back then, I mean. I've always felt it, a connection, but I couldn't explain it until now. Some of the pieces were missing.'

Dylan nodded tightly. He looked up at the ceiling then down at the floor, anywhere, Eve thought, except at her. His breathing was ragged and it took a couple of goes to start his sentence.

'It was hard on me, when Mum took me away,' he said, dusty fingers picking at a loose thread on his overalls. 'I didn't just lose you. I lost all my friends and the only life I'd ever known, and I didn't understand why. And then Dad going to prison. They never told me where he'd gone. Working away, that's what Mum said. Until he died. She had to tell me that, but I only found out that he'd been in prison when Mum was dying herself.'

'But why didn't you tell us?' she asked. 'We've been so vile to you, especially Lyra.'

'It wasn't my secret to tell,' he said simply.

Eve eyed him over her mug. 'You're one of the good guys, aren't you?'

Dylan just shrugged.

The conversation dwindled again but Eve noticed how safe the silence felt.

'I think I'm going to stay,' she said.

Dylan gave her a questioning look and a wry smile crept over his face.

'I'm a way off finishing the renovations.'

Eve laughed. 'Not here! I mean at Fox House. I thought something was missing in my life. I thought I needed to leave to find it, that I was just passing through. But now it feels like I have things to do here.'

'With Agatha, you mean?'

Eve nodded. 'I don't know what my relationship with her might turn into, but I want to try and find out.'

'Are you sure?' he asked. 'You've never struck me as particularly happy here. It's felt like you were only staying under sufferance.'

Eve grimaced. 'I think I probably was. But now we have some things we need to get straight. I'm not calling her Agatha any more, for a start. I don't care what she says. She's my mother and I'm going to bloody well make her own it if it kills me.'

Dylan opened his mouth to speak, closed it again.

'I talked to her about that,' he said.

Eve stared at him in disbelief. 'What? Me having to call her Agatha? You never did! How did that come up?'

Dylan put down his mug. 'Just came out with it. I asked her if she wouldn't let you call her Mum because she didn't feel she had the right.'

Eve felt her eyes widen. 'God. That was brave of you,' she said. 'And what did she say?'

'I think you probably need to ask her,' he said.

Eve flopped back in her chair. 'Did anyone ever tell you that you're the most frustrating person on the entire planet?'

Dylan shrugged but then he grinned. 'No, but I'll take that,' he said.

◆ ◆ ◆

Justin was in the kitchen with Lyra when Eve wandered back to Fox House. They were poring over the US Citizenship and Immigration Services pages on the laptop, discussing the various requirements of each type of entry to the country. Justin looked up when she came in.

'All okay?' he asked.

Eve nodded. She walked over and wrapped her arms around Justin from behind.

'Thank you,' she said.

'What for?' he asked.

'Oh, you know.'

Justin put a hand on her arm and squeezed.

Lyra looked from one to the other. 'You two are bloody weird. You know that, right?'

'But in a good way, right?' replied Justin.

'In a very good way,' said Eve. 'Now. What's all this about America? Start at the beginning and tell me everything. Don't miss anything out. I want every single detail.'

72

SIX MONTHS LATER

'I'm not sure there's any reason to celebrate an eighty-first birthday,' said Agatha. 'Can you pass me a gold balloon, please, Eve?'

Eve smiled to herself. This was so like her mother, objecting to the party on the one hand and then wanting the most fuss possible on the other.

She had been blowing up a mixture of gold and silver balloons for what felt like forever and was starting to feel light-headed. She picked a gold one from the little pile at her feet and passed it to Agatha.

'Every birthday should be celebrated,' she said. 'And especially an eighty-first. Here!'

She cut a length of white curling ribbon and handed it over. She watched as her mother struggled to tie the ribbon around the neck of the balloon, the arthritis in her hands making it tricky, but she knew better than to offer to do it for her.

'Well, possibly,' replied Agatha as if it had never really been in doubt. 'I suppose when you get to my age you need to celebrate that you're still alive!'

Always so dramatic. It was tempting to point out that the way she was going, Agatha would see plenty more birthdays yet, but Eve knew that she was being fed a line, and after a lifetime of dancing to Agatha's tune knew how to avoid it.

'Of course I'm sure you must celebrate,' she said instead. 'And anyway, it's good to have an excuse to get everyone together.'

'Oh, I see. I'm just the excuse, am I?' replied Agatha in mock outrage. 'You don't actually want to celebrate my very great age. You just want to use me to pull the family in to you.'

'Don't be so difficult, Mum,' laughed Eve. 'You know what I mean.'

Agatha tutted.

'Pass me a silver one,' she said.

The party had been Eve's idea and whilst she didn't need an excuse to invite her daughter and granddaughter to Fox House for the weekend, making it the weekend of Agatha's birthday meant that the visit was more likely to happen, so about that Agatha had been right. There had been a degree of self-interest in the plan. Lyra and Skye would be leaving shortly for their three-month trip to California and Eve wanted to see them before they went. Also, she wanted to show Lyra her new office, as having a decent workstation at Fox House had been Lyra's idea in the first place. Lyra had been talking in terms of an ergonomic chair but Eve's idea was altogether grander.

She and Agatha had been taking tea on the terrace outside, their chairs turned so they could watch Dylan and Cameron going backwards and forwards with the wherewithal for the cottage's new kitchen, although it was harder to see them now that the trees were in full leaf.

'I was thinking, Mum,' Eve began.

It felt peculiar to address Agatha in this way after a lifetime of not doing, but Eve was determined, and the objections that Agatha had mounted at the outset had quickly fallen away so quickly that Eve was certain they weren't genuine.

'Hmm?' replied Agatha.

'How would you feel about clearing out the twins' bedroom?'

Eve held her breath. The bedroom had almost never come up in conversation and certainly not in her adult life. It was just there, a room behind a locked door. A room that simply reverberated with the past.

Agatha put down her teacup and stared out across the lawn. She didn't speak for so long that Eve wondered if her mother had heard her, but when she gave Agatha a sidelong glance she could tell she had.

'Look, it doesn't matter,' she said quickly. 'It was just an idea. We can leave it just as—'

'I made a promise, you know,' said Agatha, cutting across her. 'When your father and I got married and he moved in, your grand-mother asked me to keep the room as it was until it was required. And I agreed at the time, but I didn't mean it.'

'But then why . . . ?' asked Eve.

'Why didn't I clear it out years ago? Guilt, maybe. Ghosts. And then there was no need. We only had you and there was enough space without that room.'

Agatha's demeanour switched in a second and she put the tea-cup down forcefully, the chink of the china on the saucer making Eve flinch.

'I hated them,' she said, spitting the words out. 'My brothers. I never met them but I hated them with all my heart.'

Eve waited. She had never heard her mother talk with such vehemence about her family, but then again, she had barely heard her talk about them at all.

'My parents only had me to try and replace them,' Agatha continued. 'I imagine it was my father's idea. He was always pandering to my mother and she was so very feeble. It was a tragedy, their deaths, but women the land over lost their children in the war. They carried on, made the best of it. My mother seemed to disintegrate. You know, I have no memories of her smiling. None.'

Agatha had smiled. This was something Eve did recognise. Confidently, cockily, triumphantly, with joy, with irony, sometimes even through tears, Agatha had smiled throughout Eve's life.

'Of course, I didn't know that at the time,' she went on. 'You don't think like that when you're a child, that you might only have been born to fill an enormous gaping hole. I just knew that the twins had been there and then they were gone and my mother wanted them back. She used to cry constantly, you know, every day. Her grief consumed her entirely. There was simply no room for me.'

Eve held her breath, not wanting to make a single sound that might break Agatha's flow.

'She kept that room as a shrine. And I kept it because I didn't want to think about what it represented. A mother who didn't love me, who only wanted her dead children and not her live one.' Agatha lifted her chin defiantly. 'No one tells you how to be a mother. You're just expected to know. Did you find that?'

She turned to Eve now, genuine curiosity in her voice. Eve wasn't sure what she was expected to say. Was Agatha inviting criticism of her own parenting or maybe expecting Eve to say that she too felt like a poor mother?

But the question, it seemed, was rhetorical.

'Certainly, you did. All new mothers are lost to some extent or other. I'm sure that goes with the territory. You're doing a much better job than me, Eve. And I hope I did a better job than my mother.'

'You're a great mum,' said Eve.

Agatha turned to face her, an eyebrow raised. 'Hardly great. But not bad. A little unconventional perhaps. I do love you though, Eve.' She reached out her hand and placed it over Eve's. 'I'm not sure my own mother could have said the same.'

Eve thought she could count on her fingers the number of times she had heard this from her mother and yet she knew it to be true. Agatha had always shown her love, she knew now, even if she hadn't always felt able to express it.

Eve knew she could offer assurances about her grandmother's feelings for Agatha but they would be trite, glib and possibly Agatha was right. Maybe she hadn't been loved as a child. What did Eve know about their relationship? Next to nothing, and from what little she had deduced, this might be true. A mother's love was not guaranteed.

'So, yes,' Agatha said, her tone decisive. 'Let's clear it out. Get rid of the past. What did you want the room for, anyway? I thought you were happy in that bedroom.'

Eve swallowed, not entirely sure of her ground.

But then she said, 'I wondered if it could be a home office so I don't have to work at the kitchen table. And also somewhere to paint. The light is fabulous in there. I thought I could set my easel up, have another go at a bit of art.'

Agatha tipped her head to one side, a small smile on her lips.

'You're planning to stay a while longer then?' she asked.

'I thought I might,' replied Eve.

73

Lyra and Skye arrived at the appointed hour and Eve felt the frisson of pleasure that always passed through her when she saw them. They were one of her life's successes. She hadn't always believed that but she did now, and with all her heart.

'Hi, Mum,' called Lyra cheerily as she opened the front door. 'Happy birthday, Granny!'

She was carrying a bottle of Prosecco and Skye followed, proudly holding a bouquet of rich burgundy dahlias out in front of her like a bridal bouquet.

'We bought you some flowers, GeeGee,' she said.

Agatha beamed at them. 'Oh, you really shouldn't have done,' she said, stooping to accept the flowers from Skye.

'Don't be silly,' objected Lyra. 'It's your birthday.'

'I was only saying to your mother earlier, I'm far too old to be having a party.'

'Rubbish,' laughed Lyra.

Eve saw her glance towards the window that looked out on the cottage.

'I think he arrived half an hour ago,' she said with a wink.

Lyra screwed her nose up. 'Can I . . . ?'

Eve tutted at her and rolled her eyes, but she was teasing. 'Yes. Off you go,' she said with a smile. 'Now, Skye, come and see all the balloons we've blown up.'

Eve took Skye's hand and led her towards the sitting room as Lyra left to go and find Cameron.

'Tell me all about school,' said Eve. 'Have you got a new teacher this year?'

'Yes. Her name is Mrs Albrecht and she's very nice and she wears really cool earrings. And my new teacher in America is going to be Miss Walters. We spoke to her on Zoom. She's very smiley.'

◆ ◆ ◆

They ate in the dining room. Eve and Dylan had painted it over the summer and Agatha had been persuaded to exchange the threadbare rug for a new striped one that complemented the new powder-blue walls. Eve had handwritten place cards for everyone and had let Skye arrange them. Skye had placed herself between Agatha and Lyra and Eve between Justin and Dylan. Cameron she'd put on Dylan's other side, but Eve had seen Lyra switch his place card so he was next to her.

Justin poured the drinks, making a point of showing that he knew where everything was kept. Dylan, for whom this display had been intended, barely seemed to notice, although Eve was sure he feigned indifference just to wind Justin up.

When all the glasses were charged, Justin got to his feet.

'A toast is in order,' he said, raising his glass.

'Sit down, young man,' snapped Agatha. 'You may be my ex-son-in-law but that doesn't give you the right to make the speeches.'

Eve rolled her eyes at Justin, who shrugged and sat back down.

Agatha stood up, the fox head cane held loosely in her hand.

'If anyone is going to make a speech around here,' she said, 'it will be me. Now, as you know, I don't generally like a fuss.'

A snort of laughter erupted around the table.

'Now that's just not true, Granny,' objected Lyra, and Agatha raised a finger for silence.

'Be that as it may,' Agatha continued. 'Today, on the occasion of my eight-first birthday, I would like to . . .' She stopped mid-sentence and looked around the room, taking them all in one by one. Then she shook her head. 'Oh, you all know what I'm going to say so there's no need to gush.'

They raised their glasses and toasted her.

'To Granny,' said Lyra.

'To motherhood,' said Eve.

ACKNOWLEDGEMENTS

I love writing books about strong women, so this one has been a joy. I am, of course, surrounded by strong women. My own mother, of course, and my three daughters, but also my friends. I am so lucky to have them all with me.

When I began thinking about Agatha, Eve and Lyra, I was in Italy leading a Writers' Retreat. The writers had come from the four corners of the globe to attend and were all women. We had a wonderful week and all learned lots not only about how to write a book but also about each other and ourselves. There was much discussion about how trauma can inadvertently be passed down through the generations and these conversations helped me to solidify my ideas for the book. Thanks must go to all the attendees and also to Cally Albrecht who runs the retreats at her beautiful farmhouse home. What a fabulous bunch.

Talking about strong women, thanks as ever must go to my editor Victoria Pepe to whom I will be forever grateful both for finding me in the first place and then steering my career so wisely. Thanks also to everyone at Amazon Publishing who I always fight shy of naming individually in case I accidentally miss someone off the list. They are a fabulous team and I am delighted to have them in my corner.

Finally, thanks to you for reading this far. You will never know how grateful I am.

If you have enjoyed the book, then please consider leaving a review on Amazon or Goodreads. You might also be interested in my website https://imogenclark.com/ where you can read more about me and my writing, and also sign up for my monthly newsletter.

IN A SINGLE MOMENT

Why not read another book by Imogen Clark? Turn the page for an extract from *In a Single Moment* – out now.

1976

1

It was the heat. It bore down on her, forcing its way into her already burgeoning body. Sweat trickled from her hairline and across her face. She could feel it pooling in the hollows at her collarbones.

She longed to fill her lungs with cool, crisp air but there was only the stale sort that felt as if it had already been breathed in and out a hundred times. She tried to visualise a mountainside, fresh green grass sparkling with dew, a crystal-clear brook babbling its way down to a deep lake where the water was so icy cold it would take your breath away.

But then the image was snatched away from her, and the oppressive, heavy atmosphere filled her nostrils again. She could smell the sharp tang of antiseptic and beneath that hot bodies, no doubt washed less frequently than usual due to the effort of collecting water from the emergency standpipes along the street.

And then another wave crashed over her, and all thoughts were washed away as she focused entirely on the pain of the contraction.

'That's it, Michelle,' she heard the midwife say. The voice sounded distant, as if the woman was speaking to her from another room. 'Try to keep your breathing nice and steady. It won't be long now.'

Michelle wanted to scream at her that she was doing her best but this was as steady as she could manage. It was her fourth baby and she'd got the measure of her labours, so she knew the midwife was right. It would be over soon, but the awful, overwhelming heat was shifting all the goalposts. She really wasn't sure she had the strength to keep going. One minute she felt as insubstantial and limp as a damp rag and the next a rigid poker of pain seared through her, making every muscle in her body as solid as steel. The rhythm of it was relentless.

The pain subsided again, and Michelle felt her aching muscles sag. Dean would be in the pub now, celebrating the birth of his child before he even knew it had happened. She pictured him, pint in hand, laughing with his mates without a care in the world whilst she . . .

The thought of the pub made her realise just how thirsty she was. Her tongue was sticking to the roof of her mouth and her lips felt as if they might crack if she smiled, not that there was any danger of that.

'Water,' she croaked.

It came out more dramatically than she'd intended, like something from *Lawrence of Arabia*. The midwife passed her a half-filled tumbler and Michelle craned her head up and took a gulp. The water was tepid and unsatisfying but it would have to do.

And then the pains were at her again and this time she knew it was nearly all over. She gritted her teeth and pressed on.

Michelle and Dean had first got together at school where neither of them had been convinced about the importance of a solid education. They had married in haste to avoid scandal, Michelle's bouquet hiding what it could, and Carl had come along four months later. After that Tina and Damien had followed in quick succession and then there had been a merciful hiatus before Michelle unexpectedly found herself once again pregnant at twenty-five.

She had been horrified at first. What would they do with another child? Where would it sleep, for a start? The house was already rammed full. And then there were food, clothes, all the other stuff kids needed. Dean brought in a decent wage from the garage, but without what she earned at the engineering works she knew they'd struggle to make ends meet. But how could she hold down a job and bring up four kids? It was impossible.

But as the baby began to grow inside her, Michelle had known that they would muddle through somehow. Even though they might never have got married but for the accidental first child, she and Dean made a strong team. He wouldn't let her down. And he hadn't. When she'd told him that five were soon to become six, the fear on his face had been fleeting, and swiftly replaced by a not-unconvincing grin.

'Well, there you go,' he'd said, with a lascivious raise of an eyebrow. 'There's plenty of lead left in my pencil!'

She'd swung her handbag at him, bashing him gently on the side of his head and he'd swept her off her feet and squeezed her tightly. She'd known then that she truly loved him and always would.

But right now, she could cheerfully saw off his head with a plastic knife and feed it to the seagulls on the Brayford. And why was it so hot? Did they not have fans in these places? How could she possibly be expected to give birth when she couldn't actually breathe? The window was open but its pale green curtain dangled limply with no hint of a breeze to move it. The air felt stifling, cloying, sticky on her already sticky skin. She needed to get this baby out just so that she could have a shower. They had water in hospitals, she assumed. No standpipes here.

And then the pain changed again and the primal need to push overtook her.

ABOUT THE AUTHOR

Imogen Clark writes contemporary fiction about families and secrets. She has sold over a million copies of her books and has topped the Amazon Kindle chart eight times. *Where the Story Starts* was shortlisted in the UK for Contemporary Romantic Novel of the Year 2020.

After initially qualifying and working as a lawyer, Imogen left her legal career behind to care for her four children and then returned to her first love – books. She went back to university, studying English Literature part-time whilst the children were at school. It was a short step from there to writing novels.

Imogen's great love is travel and she is always planning her next adventure. She lives in Yorkshire. You can find out more about her by visiting her website https://imogenclark.com. She also writes as Izzy Bromley. Visit https://izzybromley.com/ to discover more.

Follow the Author on Amazon

If you enjoyed this book, follow Imogen Clark on Amazon to be notified when the author releases a new book!

To do this, please follow these instructions:

Desktop:

1) Search for the author's name on Amazon or in the Amazon App.
2) Click on the author's name to arrive on their Amazon page.
3) Click the 'Follow' button.

Mobile and Tablet:

1) Search for the author's name on Amazon or in the Amazon App.
2) Click on one of the author's books.
3) Click on the author's name to arrive on their Amazon page.
4) Click the 'Follow' button.

Kindle eReader and Kindle App:

If you enjoyed this book on a Kindle eReader or in the Kindle App, you will find the author 'Follow' button after the last page.